the Award-winning Series
'The Gauntlet Runner'

"Those who enjoy serious yet entertaining historical fiction with epic conflicts that reflect the times would do well to read this..."
Judge, Writer's Digest 21st Annual Self-Published Book Awards

"S. Thomas Bailey gives an unflinching look at the hardships of frontier living. His books are hard hitting and adventure-packed and leave the reader gasping for more."
William P. Robertson, Author of *Attack on the Alleghenies*

"Mr. Bailey does a remarkable job with his descriptive depth of historical detail along the Eastern Frontier."
Tim L. Jarvis, Author of *Shadows In The Forest,*
Woodland Warriors of the Mississippi Valley

"This was the way of life on the early eastern frontier and Mr. Bailey has made it all come to life."
Dave Hasler, Artist of 18th Century Life

"...Anyone who loves history and the American frontier will be truly mesmerized by Mr. Bailey's books."
Mr. Bill Miller, Amazon Review

"S. Thomas Bailey brings history to life..."
Brenda Castro, for Readers Favorite

"This is a gripping tale...S. Thomas Bailey masterfully weaves the history of the era in the pages of this book..."
Deb Fowler for Feather Quill Book Review

Books by S. Thomas Bailey

The Gauntlet Runner Series

The Gauntlet Runner-A Tale from the French and Indian War
ISBN 978-1-4620-5123-6

Shades of Death-The Gauntlet Runner Book II
ISBN 978-1-4602-1879-2

Awards for
The Gauntlet Runner Series

The Gauntlet Runner–A Tale from the French and Indian War

2012 NABE Pinnacle Achievement Book Award
Best in Historical Fiction

2012 Reader's Favorite International Book Award
Honorable Mention in Action Fiction

Shades of Death–The Gauntlet Runner Book II

2013 NABE Pinnacle Achievement Book Award
Best in Historical Fiction

2013 Reader's Favorite International Book Award
Gold Medal in Adventure Fiction

Produced by:

FriesenPress
Suite 300 – 852 Fort Street
Victoria, BC, Canada V8W 1H8

www.friesenpress.com

Distributed to the trade by The Ingram Book Company

Forest
Sentinels

The Gauntlet Runner Book III

S. Thomas Bailey

Dedication

To Maria, Madison, and Kennedy, who continue with me on our new path, meeting great friends and exploring all the great colonial sites across North America.

Also, to Mr. George Lower and the wonderful folks at Lord Nelson's Gallery in Gettysburg, PA, who continue to support my books. They are truly part of our family, and we are blessed to be able to call them friends. Thank you!

Author's | **Notes**

My first award-winning novel in the series, *The Gauntlet Runner*, was an adventure. I realized it would be a lesson in learning not just about writing, but in a medium that would explain, entertain and educate the reader. At the same time, I was conscious of the fact that I didn't want to bog down the story with too many facts just to prove that I knew the time period. Opinions vary and critics are everywhere, but the bottom line is that I did this out of my passion for this amazing time period and out of respect for the actual settlers who forged a path for me to do so.

My fascination and appreciation for the French and Indian War period has grown even more since spending time with many fellow authors, re-enactors, living historians and artisans through a great year promoting my two novels in the series.

This is the third book in the ongoing series surrounding the Murray family. Please enjoy Jacob and Maggie's struggles and hardships as they continue to fight to reunite and survive.

Watch for future novels in *The Gauntlet Runner* series and most importantly, explore, visit and read more about this great time in history.

A special thanks to Todd Price (www.nightowlstudio.net) for providing the amazing cover art for 'Forest Sentinel'. Much like 'Shades of Death', I liked the piece so much I purchased the original art work and it is displayed proudly in our home. Thanks to the people at Friesen Press who had a big hand in producing this novel.

Another thank you to Catriona Todd, my editor and friend who is invaluable in making my manuscript and book the best it can be!

Special thanks to Dave and Judi, they have been great friends, advisors and promoters of my books. Thanks!

"…hardly able to conceive of a woods without end."
~William Smith, 1765

"…why do not you and the French fight on the sea? You come here only to cheat the poor Indians and take their land from them."
~Shamokin Daniel, a Delaware, to Missionary
Christian Fredrick Post, August 28, 1758

"I have succeeded in ruining the three adjacent provinces, Pennsylvania, Maryland, and Virginia, driving off the inhabitants, and totally destroying their settlements…."
~Captain Jean-Daniel Dumas, 1756

"We know our lands have now become more valuable. The white people think we do not know their value; but we know that the land is everlasting, and the few goods we receive for it are soon worn out and gone."
~Canassatego, Mingo

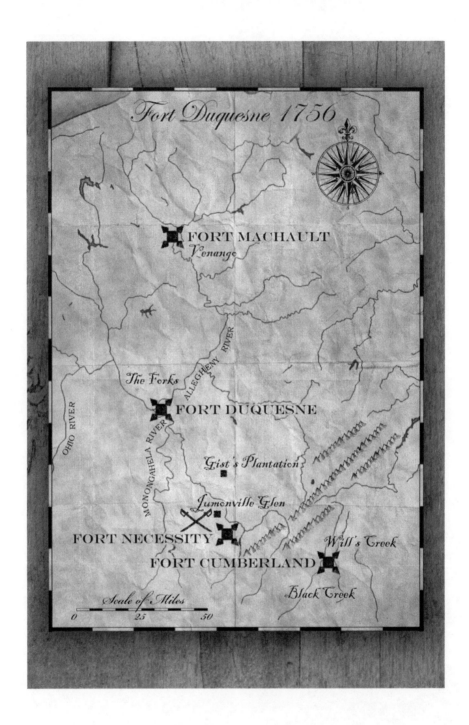

Chapter | **One**

Instinctively, Jacob pressed his hand against his pocket to make sure Jack's watch was still there. The little bob of silver was a life preserver, the only tangible evidence Jacob had to turn the tables on Taylor...if the bugger lived to tell anyone about Braddock's death.

He had been so wrapped up in his thoughts, vacillating between anxiety and relief that he jumped when Joshua's voice came from a few paces behind him.

"Sir, wait up!" the young man called.

"There you are, lad," Jacob said with a small smile. "I was just coming back to look for you."

"Are you sure?" Joshua smirked. "It looks like you were just standing there daydreaming!"

"Aye, perhaps I was. How are you feeling? Is the shoulder holding up?"

"It is still sore, but I daresay I'm better off than many others in this line today."

"That's true," Jacob said, glancing at Joshua out of the corner of his eye. "I just saw Private Taylor; he's not looking too well at the moment."

Joshua nodded but remained silent.

"Braddock died a few hours ago," Jacob said softly.

"There was a rumor to that effect back when we stopped to rest," Joshua replied. "It is for the best. I know you already realize what a mistake it was, but I just can't help thinking about what would have happened if you had been caught."

"I know, lad. My temper got the best of me. It is something I will always regret. In the meantime, it looks as though Taylor was the only one with any knowledge of what happened."

"You are well liked by the ranging company, and Colonel Washington seems to respect you well enough," Joshua said. "I cannot see them taking that drunken Taylor at his word about such a seemingly preposterous claim."

"I pray that you are right, but in the meantime, I have laid hold of some evidence that will likely seal Taylor's fate."

Joshua looked intrigued and Jacob realized that he knew nothing of what had happened to young Jack Nettle. Over the next several miles, Jacob related all the particulars and the two men began to feel some of their tension slip away.

Amid the confusion and melancholy of retreat, Jacob Murray had found a ray of hope. For the first time in several days, he felt that he might soon be clear to move forward in his personal mission to find Maggie and reunite his family.

After their disastrous defeat and the death of Braddock, the remnants of the once glorious British army staggered back to Fort Cumberland. The remaining officers wasted little time in reorganizing their men and continuing their retreat towards Philadelphia. They left a token garrison, comprised mainly of local militia under the command of Lieutenant Colonel Washington, to man the fort and aid the wounded.

The British regulars who remained behind were a mixture of injured, sick and trouble-makers. It had been several weeks since the majority of the army had moved out. As soon as Washington raised additional militia-men from the Virginia territory, any British soldiers who were well enough would be sent to join their compatriots.

Washington was careful not to let his men intermix with the British soldiers, and made sure they were kept occupied with drills and patrols.

Desertion was always a concern, especially since many of the units that had experienced Braddock's disaster had already departed for home. He was careful to make sure the men were well fed and rested; though he knew it would be a miracle if he could keep even a small garrison at the fort once winter hit.

Jacob and Joshua, still posing as father and son, made a concerted effort to stay away from the others and volunteered to keep scouting along the river or take out hunting parties. The Virginia Ranging Company had not been immune from desertions after returning to the fort, but the two men had too much respect for their captain to consider leaving without permission.

One evening as they returned from a short expedition, they found Captain Stevens standing near the fort's main gate watching the men go about their duties.

"Sir," Jacob politely approached, "It appears that many of our men have left for their homes. Will you be returning to Virginia as well?"

"It seems I am to stay until the first snow, so now I'm praying for an early winter," Stevens responded with a smirk. "What are your plans, gentlemen?"

"We look forward to heading home so we can prepare for the winter months," Jacob replied, "but in the meantime, Washington has asked us to do a bit of scouting to the north. We will leave at first light."

The men remained silent for a moment as they observed the activity going on around the fort.

"Well then, Sims," Stevens broke the silence, offering his hand to each man, "I wish you Godspeed on your mission. When you return, I will say goodbye before sending you home."

Jacob and Joshua stood motionless and watched as Stevens slowly disappeared back inside the fort.

"Well, sir, what are our plans for now?" Joshua asked after a moment.

"If things were different, we would move north to try to find any signs of Maggie or One-Ear. Unfortunately, with the British gone, the bloody territory is abuzz with French and savages. The only way to move north would be to head east to the Susquehanna first."

"The poor settlers who live in these parts will be left to fight off the Delaware, Seneca and Shawnee by themselves," Joshua murmured with an air of foreboding. "I think there will not be any white people left on this side of the mountains in just a few short months."

Jacob patted Joshua on the back and the two moved to pack up their belongings to depart first thing the next morning.

Washington had asked the two men to scout north of the fort to check for any signs of a potential French-led counter-attack on the sadly under-manned Fort Cumberland. Jacob knew that the Lieutenant Colonel would cherish the opportunity to fight the French in the forests, using tactics that were much more suitable than the Braddock strategy had been. He personally doubted that the French would spread themselves so thinly between here and Fort Duquesne.

Amid a pouring rain, Jacob and his trusted companion left the fort as soon as it became bright enough to see the trail. They had packed lightly and planned to push themselves hard to cover as many miles as they could. Neither man felt very fatigued by midday, so they continued their trek and ate as they walked.

When night began to fall, Jacob found a small clearing off the main trail where they could rest and still be aware of any movement around them. They hadn't seen any evidence of Indians or the French, but they knew better than to let their guard down. They did not allow themselves the comfort of a fire and, without much conversation at all, they both rested.

Jacob and Joshua had made several short scouting trips north of the fort over the past weeks and were prepared to see the debris left along the trail by the army's hasty retreat. They pushed forward through a steady rain and treaded carefully to avoid discarded packs, weapons, red coats and other small items. As they grew closer to the site of Colonel Dunbar's camp, they were met with the gruesome sight of over a hundred stripped, mutilated and scalped soldiers spread over several miles of the cut trail. Some of the poor souls had been too injured to make the long trek to the fort, while most of them had been the stragglers, unable to keep up with the main army. They had most likely been picked off one by one by eager savages searching for mementoes of their great victory.

"I honestly thought I had seen hell after what happened at Fort Necessity," Jacob said quietly, "but this disaster makes that engagement like a minor skirmish."

"The flies and wild beasts have certainly had their work cut out for them," Joshua managed to reply before he gagged. The putrid smell of the decomposing remains engulfed the surrounding woods and made it hard to breathe.

Despite the constant rain that alternated between light, refreshing showers and blinding downpours, they arrived at the remnants of Dunbar's encampment by the early evening.

Equipment had been strewn across the area as the army beat its hasty retreat, unable or unwilling to move all of the heavy weapons with them. The area had certainly been picked over by the French and Indians after they had finished with the stragglers.

Joshua had walked over to check out the numerous spiked cannon that had been left behind when he saw Jacob signal him to take cover.

He moved quickly to Joshua's side and pulled him towards the woods whispering, "Stay down, boy, I think I saw something moving just over to your right."

"I can't see anything, sir," Joshua whispered as he strained to see what Jacob thought he'd seen. "Do you think it was an animal?"

Jacob said nothing and kept his eyes peeled for any sign of movement. They both understood there was a chance they could encounter some roaming bands of Indians on this mission, but the last thing they wanted was to battle a small war party or worse, be captured.

They knelt as low as they could while still able to scan the area. It took only a brief moment for the culprits to reappear. Coming within a few paces of where they were hiding, several French regulars were rummaging through the leftover stacks of equipment and refuse that hadn't already been pilfered.

The Frenchmen spoke freely, caring little that their voices could echo through the woods. They had no reason to fear an ambush or attack from the long-departed English. Jacob sensed that the men felt at ease and had no reason to think that they were in danger.

Joshua leaned closer to Jacob and whispered, "Do you think there might be more of them around or just a lone party out scouting the area?"

"Just to be safe, let's not make the first move and we should be fine. It appears they only want a few trinkets. Honestly, I would love to talk to one of them, but we need to be sure that they didn't bring any savages with them. We are not in a good spot if more of them arrive."

Jacob and Joshua remained still for over a half hour and simply watched the Frenchmen toss pieces of muskets, uniforms and other gear around, hoping to find something of value to take home with them. Eventually there was a conversation about heading back towards Fort Duquesne. Most of the men were satisfied with what they had foraged, but a couple of the men decided they wanted to stay longer and sift through more of the camp. After a brief argument, the other soldiers left the two men behind and headed north.

Watching as the larger group of men departed, Jacob said, "This might be our best chance to get some valuable information from these two greedy buggers."

He moved slowly to get a better view of the two men and Joshua followed quietly. They crouched behind a couple of dismantled cannon, only a few paces from the Frenchmen as they continued to dig through the debris, occasionally depositing small items in their pouches.

Jacob was disgusted by the display and whispered, "These miserable bastards are too busy looking for meager scraps of junk to realize they have left their muskets out of their reach. We might just be able to take them alive."

Before Joshua could manage to offer his ideas, Jacob stepped out of hiding and casually approached the two shocked men. Without missing a beat, Joshua swiftly ran directly towards the muskets the men had abandoned near an empty powder cart and held them up so Jacob could see that he had them secured.

"Excuse me, messieurs," Jacob called out as he approached with his rifle cocked and pointed directly at them.

Stunned and clearly frightened by the sudden appearance of this unexpected Englishman, the two immediately attempted to retrieve their weapons, which they thought sat only a few paces behind them.

It was at that moment, they saw the second Englishman standing with their muskets in his possession, grinning ear to ear. They attempted to scream and alert their recently departed mates, but Jacob rammed his rifle into one man's back, driving him to the ground. At the same time, Joshua closed the distance between himself and the other man, kneeing him in the midsection and shoving him onto his back. Jacob and Joshua quickly covered the mouths of their two French captives, ensuring they could not yell for help.

Jacob had hoped that the men preferred to live and would accept their capture like gentlemen, but the man he had subdued began to kick wildly at him. Unable to safely restrain the foolish man, Jacob had no other option but to drive his scalping knife under the man's ribs with a twist. The Frenchman scratched out one last breath before a small bubble gurgled from his wound and he went stiff.

With all the confusion, Joshua's prisoner attempted to make an escape, but Joshua simply held him down and wrapped his arm around the man's neck. His grip convinced the man to stop his struggle in time to watch his friend take his last breath.

Jacob stood up and coldly wiped off his bloodied knife on the dead man's coat. He then walked towards their other prisoner, removing his neck cloth as he did so. With Joshua's assistance, he secured it around the man's mouth before pulling him up sharply by his arm. Joshua pulled off his own neck cloth as well and tied the man's hands behind his back.

By this time, the prisoner had stopped jerking around and appeared to have accepted his fate. Jacob looked the man in the eyes and said, "If you want to live, monsieur, then you would be smart to behave and not fight us. I would just as soon kill you but my superiors might want to speak with you. If you decide not to cause us any trouble, then you just might survive the trip back."

Pushing the man ahead of them, Jacob said to Joshua, "Let's get him back to the fort before his friends decide to return and look for them. You take him ahead and I will catch up with you momentarily."

Jacob waited until Joshua had pulled the man up the side trail and was out of sight. Expecting that the other Frenchmen might decide to come back looking for the two stragglers, Jacob dragged the dead man behind the mass of damaged cannon and made it look like the two were ambushed by some Indian hunting party. He scalped the man, throwing the bloody piece of hair deep into the woods, and then sliced the man up a bit, to make it appear he was mutilated by a Shawnee hunting party.

Finished with his work and finding a thick length of rope that was once used to move one of the destroyed cannon, Jacob sprinted to catch up with Joshua and their captive. They said little and kept moving quickly along the well-traveled side trail, pushing the Frenchman every so often to encourage him to keep pace. Jacob had threatened the captive with the rope, motioning he would secure it around his neck and pull him the entire walk back.

They covered as much ground as they could, using all the remaining daylight and a few hours of bright light from the waxing moon overhead to move deeper into the once held British territory. The Frenchman had decided not to fight his predicament and did his best to keep up with the two fast-moving Englishmen.

Once it became too difficult to maneuver safely in the dark forest, they took a break to rest and eat some dried meat and hard bread, feeding a few pieces to their captive. As the night gave way to the first rays of sunlight, the three men were back on the trail.

When Jacob felt they had moved far enough to the south and were approaching the heavy mountain region, they untied the prisoner's hands. There was little reason to fear an escape attempt; Jacob knew that if the man made a run for it, he would not make it far. Having no weapon or idea exactly where he was, he would most likely be captured by the ever-present savages or killed by a number of the wild beasts that inhabited the deep forests in the area.

The daylight began to fade just as they reached the base of the Chestnut Ridge area. They were less than half a day's brisk march to Fort Cumberland. With the Frenchman keeping the pace, they decided to press on through the night. Jacob knew the trail was relatively flat and much easier to traverse than the trail they had managed to cover the previous night.

The three tired men stepped out of the dense forest onto the path to the fort's main gate just as the bright morning sun broke over the surrounding mountains. The prisoner garnered a lot of attention from the men milling about the fort. Jacob looked at Joshua and said, "Get yourself some food and I'll take the Frenchman to Washington."

Joshua happily obliged and went directly to a small row of tents that housed what passed for a kitchen for the undermanned fort.

Jacob passed by two guards at the main gate and immediately noticed Washington speaking with the fort's doctor. The poor man seemed overwhelmed by the quantity of the remaining wounded who lined the edges of the parade grounds.

Standing back to not interrupt the two men, Jacob could hear the Lieutenant Colonel voicing concerns over the threat of disease that might strike the wounded and spread to the healthy men. He waited patiently with his captive until Washington dismissed the doctor.

The commanding officer immediately turned his attention to Jacob and his French prisoner. Looking over the disheveled and dirty Frenchman, Washington seemed pleased with the results of the scouting trip.

"So, scout, who do we have here?"

"We found him at Dunbar's old encampment," Jacob explained. "He was with a larger French patrol, but was too greedy to return with them."

"What do you say, sir?" Washington asked, turning to the Frenchman who remained silent with his head down.

"I suggest you say something, monsieur," Jacob growled, jabbing the man in the ribs. "The officer asked you a question."

Recovering from Jacob's well placed poke, the man whispered, "Water, monsieur."

Jacob could see that Washington was quickly losing patience in this man as he called to one of his aids to bring a canteen of fresh water for the prisoner.

"We English treat our prisoners with dignity," Washington barked as the canteen was produced, "nothing like your damn officers who conveniently turn a blind eye towards the actions of your savages and the bloody Canadians."

Watching the man gulp down most of the contents as if he had never tasted water before, Washington turned to Jacob and asked, "Did you manage to get a word out of him, or was he this tongue-tied for you as well?"

Frustrated by the prisoner's lack of cooperation, Jacob pulled the prisoner to face him and said, "Maybe we should just let him climb the 'King's Rope and leave it at that."

"Forget it, Sims," Washington said, clearly tired of this pointless interrogation, "just take him down by the river and shoot him. You can let his body float back to his French friends at Fort Duquesne."

As Jacob grabbed the man's arm to pull him away, the captive stopped him and said, "Sir, all I know is the savages are excited to kill as many of the white settlers as they can, now that they have no fear of the English. They feel they can take back their land from your people."

Though it was obvious to everyone that the British departure from the frontier left the settlers to defend themselves, having this French prisoner say it out loud made Washington bristle with anger.

Unable to intercede before Washington's infamous temper burst out, Jacob took a step back as his commander screamed so loudly the entire fort stopped, "Scout, please do as I ordered. Take this miserable soul down to the river, bind him up and put some lead in his head. Send the bloody fool back to his mates." Washington ordered, then turned abruptly and walked away.

Jacob pulled the man's arm and directed him towards the fort's entrance and down to the riverbank. Joshua caught up with them and, after Jacob quickly explained what had happened, the two did as they were so bluntly instructed.

They could see a small crowd starting to gather near the shore, as well as, the soldiers on guard duty watching from the top of the palisade. Jacob and Joshua tightly bound up the Frenchman's hands and legs. Neither was comfortable with how this situation had played out, but they understood that they were under orders. To cross Washington would not bode well for them.

Not wishing to linger any longer, Jacob wrapped a cloth around the man's head to cover his face.

Even though Joshua had come over to help him with this task, Jacob felt he should be the one to carry out the command. When he had the man in position, Jacob stepped five paces back, took aim and discharged his musket directly into the man's skull. The impact drove the Frenchman backward into the shallow water, where his blood spilled out to form a dark cloud around his submerged head.

Jacob stepped into the shallows by the slowly twitching body and unceremoniously kicked it into the deeper waters.

The surrounding crowd, including a handful of the more mobile injured, cheered wildly as the dead man's body floated into the deeper water and slowly drifted them north.

Most of the men knew the body would never make it anywhere close to Fort Duquesne. It would most likely be dragged out of the water by one of many bears or wildcats, but it was still a moment of victory for the defeated men…no matter how small.

Jacob looked around and caught a glimpse of Washington standing with the other soldiers near the main gates. Once his order was fulfilled, he simply turned and walked out of sight.

Joshua left the scene with Jacob and ignored the accolades of their fellow mates. Neither man said anything, both feeling that this was a part of war that made them question why they had ever become involved.

Chapter | **Two**

Maggie was once again a captive.

Pontiac didn't speak to her as they moved down the trail. He led his small band of warriors west towards the fort at Niagara to secure canoes for a trip to Fort Duquesne, where he had heard there was to be a battle against the British. She could not believe she was being forced to return to the place she had so desperately fought to avoid.

The Ottawa were far different from most of the Eastern Woodland tribes that lived in the Ohio Valley. They were true warriors and spent most of their time fighting the British or other tribes. Pontiac was a staunch supporter of the French and fought with them to keep the English from moving into Ottawa territory to the west.

The French used them as 'shock troops' to strike fear into the enemy ranks. Unable to control them, the French usually left them alone to fight as one unit. The surrounding tribes in the Pennsylvania territory may have feared the Huron, but they were terrified of the Ottawa.

Pontiac was a ferocious leader and he pushed his men through the woods, moving from trail to trail, many of which were very seldom traveled on. Maggie did her best to keep up even though she had only rested briefly since they left the village.

She received no special treatment because she was a female. They ate on the run, never stopping for water as they moved through the deep, dense forest like wild cats.

The men remained silent as they moved.

Pontiac positioned himself in front to lead the way. He did not send out advanced scouts since they had no reason to fear an ambush from the Delaware or Seneca, and they knew the English had not yet moved into the northern territory.

Maggie was positioned behind Pontiac and his lead warriors. She was struck by how gracefully he worked his way along the trails. He moved at top speed, never missing a step as he pushed branches out of his way and dodged the ever-present tree roots.

As dusk fell over the forest and Maggie could barely see the warrior running only a few paces in front of her, the leaders slowed to a comfortable trot. She slowed as well and was surprised when several warriors from the rear suddenly sprinted past her.

They spoke very briefly with Pontiac before sprinting out of sight down the trail. She assumed they had been sent to set up camp for the night, but she was wrong.

Pontiac and the remaining warriors stopped suddenly and everyone remained silent. Maggie had no idea what was happening, so she boldly approached Pontiac and asked quietly for an explanation.

He didn't bother to look at her, but responded with a cold, harsh tone, "I sent my warriors ahead to a small Delaware village that sits a short walk over that hill. You will need to listen; do what I say and you might live through the night."

Maggie didn't know how to react to such a statement and stepped back slowly. She had once thought he was an impressive, confident leader, but now she knew him to be nothing more than an unlikeable bully.

She could just imagine how the poor village must have been panicking to ready themselves for the Ottawa leader's arrival. They soon continued up the trail and Maggie got her first look at the village. It was not a large place, nothing like the place she had just visited, but it sat nicely near a river. It was a mixture of permanent wooden structures and several smaller wigwam-style homes that she assumed were used by French traders or visiting hunters.

The Ottawa warriors were pleasantly greeted by a pair of elders, while most of the women and children ran about preparing for their unexpected guests. They rushed around gathering wood for the main fire and preparing food for an impromptu feast.

Maggie could see that Pontiac was clearly upset that he was not greeted by a larger delegation of villagers. The two elders were quick to explain that all the men and young boys were away at Fort Duquesne to fight alongside the French. It appeared Pontiac was satisfied by this explanation and Maggie marveled as he was treated like some kind of monarch, being presented a large bear skin and several other trinkets as a tribute to his visit.

She was tersely directed by one of Pontiac's warriors to assist the women with the preparation of the meal. The villagers ignored her for the most part, only occasionally acknowledging her when they pointed to bring over some water or a handful of corn meal.

Maggie wondered to herself why the village didn't set up the traditional gauntlet for her to run. She suspected that Pontiac sent word ahead that she was to be treated like an Ottawa woman and therefore she was to be respected.

She watched as Pontiac walked around the village, looking unimpressed by the elders' attempts to please him. The bear skin they had presented him was thrown on the ground near the now raging fire, and the trinkets were left for his men to fight over. The insult did not go unnoticed by the villagers, but they were not in a position to express their displeasure.

Maggie guessed that the elders were just trying to appease the Ottawa in hopes that they might leave quickly after a meal and a brief rest. Without the benefit of having their own warriors on hand to even the numbers, the elders were at the mercy of the visitors and needed to keep them as happy as possible.

As she let her eyes finish scanning the village, she eventually noticed that not all of the village's men had gone off to fight. There was a small contingent of men who were clearly too old, young or injured to join the warriors. During the meal, they were pushed to the back of the line and were only offered food after the Ottawa had taken their own portions.

The village women busily served the food, carrying large wooden planks full of fruits, vegetables and dried meats. Maggie kept her head down throughout the meal and was surprised when a young native woman abruptly sat down beside her and said softly, "Hello, my name is Anne. You are English?"

Maggie was naturally apprehensive about speaking with the woman, but it did appear that she only wanted to strike up a conversation. She responded quietly, saying, "Hi, Anne. I am Maggie Murray, and I am Scottish. I used to live in the western Pennsylvania territory with my husband and children."

The two women were careful not to draw attention to themselves or be caught speaking together. They kept their heads down and cleaned some of the wooden plates used by the men.

"How is it a Delaware woman can speak English so well?" Maggie asked, glancing towards Pontiac, who was contentedly eating some fresh berries. She saw him refuse an offering of rum from one of the elders, waving it away to ensure that none of his men indulged in the drink. The Delaware saw his displeasure and immediately had the rum taken away and put in one of the storage sheds.

"I am a Delaware," Anne responded, "but I was once an English settler. I think it has been three summers since I was taken by the Shawnee and then traded to this village. They had raided our little settlement and killed my parents and took my brother away. I have no idea where he might be, but I pray every day he is alive and well."

The women paused in their conversation as several other women approached and took several baskets of hard bread back to the men. When they were out of earshot, Maggie whispered, "How old are you?"

"I suppose around eighteen or so," Anne said.

Maggie assumed the villagers must have seen Anne as more Delaware than white, so they didn't seem concerned that the two white women might be plotting something. She attempted to get more information out of Anne before they might be called away from what they were doing. "Where are all the men?" she asked.

"They left a couple of weeks or so ago. They were heading to join up with the French at the fort near the three rivers. I heard rumors of a great force of English soldiers planning an attack on the fort."

"We can only pray that the English win and run the French and all these savages all the way to Canada," Maggie replied bluntly.

Just as the rest of the women approached their position, Anne whispered, "They treat me well and I have no reason to want them harmed. I feel more Delaware than white and to be honest, far better off."

Maggie did not know how to respond to this pronouncement and remained silent as the village women sat down with them to eat what remained of the meal. A few pieces of cornmeal bread and a small slice of dried meat passed to her satisfied her appetite. The rest of the meal was spent staring at Anne, wondering how she could simply forget her English roots and so easily adapt to this life.

She wondered if her own children had forgotten her and Jacob. The thought nearly brought tears to her eyes, but she was quick to catch herself, unwilling to show any weakness to the others.

When everyone had finished eating, Maggie was quickly ordered to her feet. The men began clapping as she was pulled over to a small clearing, and Pontiac directed the women to line themselves up in two parallel lines. As they organized themselves, several picked up branches, sticks and whatever else they could find.

It was clear what they were doing…Maggie had seen this all before.

Her assumption that that they had been ordered not to perform this ceremonial practice or had forgotten about it proved to be foolish. Maggie watched the women lining themselves up and was shocked to see Anne join the line, holding a sharpened tree branch in her left hand.

Maggie took a deep breath and heard Pontiac start clapping once again. She saw the warriors move closer to get a better look and cheer on the villagers.

They began to shriek and howl as Pontiac waved his hand, directing Maggie to move forward.

Having run the gauntlet several times, Maggie knew what to do to increase her chances of success and lessen the pain. She put her hands in front of her face and ran as fast as she could toward the waiting women who were now screaming and shouting.

As the branches and sticks lashed at her exposed arms and legs, a few well-directed blows struck her cheek and ripped into her hands. Maggie valiantly pushed forward, dodging some of the strikes and even managing to knock down several of the women. She noticed through a gap between her fingers that Anne had positioned herself near the middle of the pack and was particularly cruel as Maggie rushed past.

Maggie could feel the skin on the back of her legs tear with every whip of the branches. The sticks were far easier to block than the thinner switches, which tended to blur with the speed the women put into them. Her hands hurt and her left arm was bleeding heavily under the constant strikes from the visibly excited women.

The villagers did their best to put on a good show for their Ottawa guests. Despite the women's feverish strikes and aggressive actions, Pontiac and his warriors displayed little emotions that indicated their approval.

It was over in less than a minute, yet the damage done to her, left her in severe pain. Maggie made sure the Delaware were given no satisfaction that they had hurt her. When she reached the designated pole at the end, she spun around and glared towards the women. She noticed she had bloodied some of them with her retaliatory strikes. Bloodied and beaten herself, she unleashed a shriek that echoed through the village and made even Pontiac look.

The Ottawa laughed and cheered at Maggie's display of courage, and Pontiac himself slightly smiled, but not directly at her. The warriors quickly dispersed and returned to the remains of their meal as if nothing had happened.

The women also returned to their duties quickly and Maggie was left alone, standing with one hand on the pole. She swiped at some of the blood on her forearms and saw Anne meekly approach.

Anne said nothing, offering no explanation for her actions and used a piece of cloth to clean Maggie's wounds. She also applied some bear fat to some of the deeper wounds to soothe the pain that would haunt Maggie for several hours.

Despite this act of kindness, Maggie barked, "You looked like you enjoyed that."

Anne still said nothing. When she was finished cleaning the many small cuts on Maggie's arms and legs, she simply walked away.

Alone again, Maggie was unsure what she should do next.

Anne returned a few minutes later with some water and a piece of bread and said, "Eat this; it will help."

Maggie took the bread and snapped, "I hope my own children never act like you just did towards one of their own."

Careful not to draw attention to them, Anne calmly replied, "I couldn't show you any mercy. I had to prove to the others that I am part of their village. If I took it easy on you, they would judge me as being weak. Soon you might be put in a similar position and you would be wise to do the same. I have been welcomed into the tribe, but it took a very long time for them to finally trust me. They were hesitant when I first came here and treated me more like a slave than a woman. If your children want to survive, they will be forced to participate in similar situations to prove their loyalty. If they do not, they will be severely punished or possibly killed."

Her chilling words hit Maggie harder than running the gauntlet ever could have done. The thought of her children being subjected to such horrors made her pray that she would soon be able to hold them all and put this nightmare behind them.

Before they could say another word, Pontiac paused in his own conversation with the elders and called out to Maggie to pick-up a nearby deer skin sack and brings it to him. It was filled with water and was extremely heavy. After her ordeal, she noticeably struggled with this task, but she managed to carry the sack and dropped it at the feet of the Ottawa leader. She stood nearby awaiting further instructions as he continued his conversation.

When he had finished with the elders, Pontiac said to Maggie, "The Delaware have told me more of the French and the great battle being fought near the fort at the Forks. You will be staying with these villagers while I take my warriors to fight alongside our French fathers. I have told my warriors that after we rest, we are to go fight the English and help drive them from this land. After we kill many English, I will return for you and take you back to my village. Do not try to escape or cause problems for these people; I have told them to punish you if you do so."

That was it. Maggie stood rooted to the spot. She was shocked and unsure how to respond. Pontiac returned to his conversation with the elders, but soon ordered with a harsh tone, "Woman, go back with the other women."

Summarily dismissed, Maggie slowly walked back to where the other women were still busy cleaning up after the meal. Strangely, she was greeted with a couple of smiles and nods, but nothing was said and she refused to return their attempts to ease the tension.

Maggie sat back and observed as the number of villagers began to dwindle, most of them deciding to leave the post-feast celebration for the Ottawa. Even Anne left early, offering only a brief smile before she departed with a couple of Delaware villagers.

When only a few warriors remained dancing and howling around the nearly extinguished fire pit, Pontiac retired to one of the elder's homes without a word to Maggie. Eventually, the remaining celebrants left the fire and bedded down wherever they wanted, including in some of the homes of the reluctant villagers.

Maggie finally found herself alone and she grabbed some cut tree branches and threw them on the embers of the dying fire as she contemplated her situation. She considered making a run for it once the Ottawa left the immediate area, but decided that such a plan would either be fatal or result in her recapture and further punishment.

At any rate, if the rumors of the great battle were true, the surrounding area would be teeming with French and Canadian militia and their Indian allies moving south from the fort at Niagara. A lone English woman traveling at night in these woods would certainly make a rather nice prize for some French officer.

As tempting as the thought of escape was, making a mad dash into the pitch black forest without the guidance of One-Ear was not an option. The thought of One-Ear and how she was forced to leave him behind brought tears to her eyes. She prayed he was still alive and they might somehow be reunited. The memory of his lifeless body lying in the short grass brought more tears. She quickly rubbed them away, not wanting anyone to see her crying.

Maggie quickly decided it would be smarter to remain at the village and bide her time. She knew if Pontiac was truly going to leave her here and head south, she could face a few uncomfortable weeks to plan out her escape before he returned.

Suddenly, Maggie could think of nothing beyond resting her weary body. She rubbed her face with dirt to keep the hordes of biting bugs off of her and applied some more soothing bear fat to her numerous small cuts and scratches.

Dawn broke and the bright morning sun blanketed the entire village in the warm, early summer rays. Maggie sat up and noticed that many villagers were already awake and performing their chores, including drawing water from the small stream that meandered along the eastern boundary of the village. She spotted Anne well before the younger woman noticed she was up.

Once Anne saw Maggie sitting up by the fire pit, she walked over and asked politely, "Did you get much rest?"

"It was fine," Maggie replied coolly, still unsure where Anne's loyalty lay. "Honestly, over the past few months, I have slept in far worse places."

"Some of the women have been talking about the fact that the Ottawa would be leaving today," Anne continued despite Maggie's inhospitable reply. "Will you be going with them?"

Maggie had no interest in giving her too much gossip for the others, but answered, "I was told that I would be remaining behind to wait for their return."

They kept busy piling up some of the firewood around the pit as they spoke. Anne walked towards the outer woods to gather some more fallen branches and Maggie decided to walk along with her. She was fully aware that the villagers were watching their every move, as were a number of Ottawa warriors who had just gotten up.

Well out of listening range of the villagers, Maggie decided to press Anne for some more information. "Have you ever tried to escape?" Maggie asked, grabbing a handful of twigs and keeping her eye on the villagers.

"I thought of it constantly, especially in the beginning," Anne replied. "Early on, the villagers were especially brutal towards me. They beat me, refused to share their food and made me sleep outside, no matter the weather. I honestly had a number of opportunities to escape, but I had no place to go. Once they finally accepted me, my standing improved and they now treat me as their equal."

Maggie remained silent for a moment and watched Anne collect an armful of good-sized tree branches before placing them in a pile in the grass. She hadn't gotten a good look at the girl the night before, but the new morning sun gave her a much clearer view of this 'white' Indian. Maggie noted her skin was darkened from a couple seasons' exposure and toughened by the hard work she did around the village. She could see why she had mistaken Anne for a Delaware woman when they had initially met. Her face still held onto her youthful years and her long black hair was braided into a long strip that reached her lower back. She wore a comfortable-looking deer hide dress, decorated with beads and a well-worn pair of center-seam moccasins.

Grabbing another armful of branches, Maggie turned her attention back to finding out as much as she could about Anne's experiences with the villagers. She was unsure if they would have another opportunity to talk like this, so she pressed her for additional details. "How many white people have you seen over the past two years?"

"Besides the regular French traders and hunters, I have only seen two maybe three, now that I think about it," Anne replied, nervously glancing toward the village. "One very young girl and two boys that I was told were brothers were brought here separately by some Huron who just stopped in the village very briefly before continuing north. I had no opportunity to speak with or even see much of them. They did appear to be in relatively good spirits and the Huron were treating them well."

Before they could say anything else, Anne was summoned by one of the village women to assist in preparing corn meal. Maggie continued to add more wood to the pile, until Pontiac finally made an appearance.

She moved closer to the center of the village in case he wanted to take leave of her.

He called together his warriors and spent a few minutes in discussion with them. They decided not to take the time to sit and eat the meal that the women were so busily preparing. Instead, they paid their respects to the village elders, giving them a few token hides and knives for their hospitality. The rest of the women frantically packed reed baskets of leftover meat, corn bread and berries from the previous night's feast.

By late morning, the Ottawa were gone. Pontiac had not spoken to Maggie, and she was still unsure of what she was to do in this village in his absence. She decided to stay busy and finished moving the wood she and Anne had collected, closer to the fire pit.

The change that came over the village once the Ottawa departed was immediate. The elders and other villagers were much more relaxed and were noticeably friendlier with Maggie. They made it clear that she was permitted to walk about the village freely and without an escort.

They presented her with a brain-tanned deer skin dress and, although the clothes she had arrived in were not very worn, she quickly exchanged them for the new dress. It was nice to have a clean change of clothes and it was very comfortable. Anne gave her a newly-made pair of moccasins that were far better than the old pair she had worn for several months.

Enjoying this rare moment of peace, Maggie sat near a group of women who were doing some bead work. Anne sat amongst them and, for the most part, they were all welcoming. One of the older women sat behind Maggie and slowly combed out her hair before braiding it much like Anne's style. The woman garnished her completed braid with a small band of beads to keep it in place.

Nodding her appreciation to the woman, Maggie sat and watched the other women work with a number of colorful glass beads and several piles of porcupine quills. One of the women put a couple of the quills in her mouth and softened them up by soaking them with her saliva. Anne and some of the other women took the soaked quills and began to weave them through a piece of brain-tanned deer skin. Maggie was impressed with their work and the beautiful pieces they produced.

The village turned out to be a fairly nice and peaceful place. It had only been a few days since the Ottawa warriors had departed and Maggie, who had been given the Indian name 'Wild Flower', had already been taken in by a family consisting of a young mother, her grandmother and three children. She really enjoyed having the young ones around and it brought back some wonderful memories of what she once had. She was glad to help around their small dwelling and more than content to watch over the children to give their mother a break.

Since the village was off the main trails, they were virtually left to themselves. Only the odd French trader and Delaware hunting parties from nearby villages were ever likely to visit. Maggie found out that the only reason Pontiac knew of this place was because one of the former elders had been married to one of his relatives.

After a few weeks of peace, Maggie woke up one morning to an empty home. Before she could leave to find the others, Anne entered and told her to remain inside until she was summoned.

In answer to a puzzled look from Maggie, Anne said, "Early this morning, several French traders entered the village and I think it would be better if you stay out of their sight. Most don't stay long, but if they see you, they might want to purchase you. They just might tempt the elders with enough goods that they could be swayed to let them take you. The elders fear the Ottawa, but some traders have been known to be rather persuasive in getting what they want."

It wasn't long before the mother returned with her children, and Maggie remained indoors feeding them and cleaning the small house. Anne helped her with some of the chores, leaving periodically to check if the traders had yet departed.

When Anna returned from one such investigation, Maggie asked, "What about you? You're a white woman too. Don't the French value you just as much as me?"

"My husband is a powerful warrior and holds great standing amongst the Delaware. The French would never dare to even suggest a trade or to purchase me. It would be an insult to our village and would mean their certain deaths."

Maggie was initially stunned by the news Anne was married to one of these savages. The thought made her cringe so much that she knew Anne must have noticed it.

"How did a proper English girl become the wife of one of these Delaware?" she asked, finding it difficult to hide her disapproval.

"It was by choice," Anne responded stiffly. "He has been a kind husband and provides me with whatever I need or ask for. The Delaware treat their women with the utmost respect, far more than any Englishman would bother to offer me." She raised her chin in defiance, waiting for Maggie to rebut her suggestion.

"Anne, it is not my place to judge you, and God knows that if it meant surviving versus death…I just hope you are happy with…" Maggie couldn't finish her thought and could barely manage to hide her utter disdain for the situation.

"What of you?" Anne said defensively. "Once Pontiac returns for you and he takes you back to the Ottawa territory, what do you think he will do with you?"

The question hit Maggie hard. Was this going to be her life? Was she destined to be some Ottawa leader's wife and be forced to live the rest of her days as an Indian? She couldn't fathom the thought and knew that escape was her only option. She wanted to find Jacob and her children even more than ever and she briefly considered making a run outside the house to find the French traders. She suddenly felt it would be better to be a French slave than a savage's wife.

Maggie remained silent and took a moment to pray. At this point, she had to hold onto the hope Jacob was still alive and was searching the endless wilderness to find her. She knew that it would be next to impossible, but her heart still held out hope that he would find her. Being stuck in an isolated Delaware village, despite how well she was treated, made her virtually impossible to find.

She knew what she had to do.

Chapter | **Three**

After the morning's debacle, Jacob and Joshua retired to the tent they shared. They remembered what Captain Stevens had said about saying goodbye to them the next time he saw them, but they had been on the trail for days and were exhausted. As excited as they were to return to Jacob's homestead, they were even more excited to see their bedrolls.

The sun was high in the sky when they finally emerged, refreshed and ready to start packing up their belongings. Captain Stevens took them by surprise; he was leaning against a nearby stump and it appeared that he had been waiting for them to wake up.

"Captain?" Jacob nodded by way of greeting, but left a question hanging in the air.

"Well, lads," Stevens began and looked briefly at his boots, "I know I said that we'd be parting ways when you got back from your scouting trip, but in the meantime, Washington has requested I keep as much of my old company intact as possible. He has been promoted to Colonel and is now in charge of the Virginia Regiment and left in charge of the Pennsylvania frontier. He's already expecting some new recruits from the Virginia militia. He also informed me that I have been promoted to the rank of Major, so guess it is Major Stevens now."

"Congratulations, sir, I mean Major Stevens!" Jacob offered his hand, then continued, "Back to the matter at hand, how will a few of rangers and raw, inexperienced volunteers protect the endless miles of wilderness, not to mention the hundreds of families left behind to fend for themselves by the bloody British?"

"It is Washington's plan that a chain of forts and blockhouses be built across the open frontier covering Pennsylvania to Virginia. They are meant to provide protection and a sense of security for the settler families. To that end, he has requested funds from your tight-fisted Pennsylvania provincial leaders to aid in our efforts. If they come through with what is needed, we will certainly fair better off in the region, but this is a scheme approved by the British leaders, regardless if the individual provinces refuse to commit."

Jacob's thoughts had drifted to Maggie as soon as he detected where this conversation was heading, but he was quick to give Stevens his attention and responded, "If this plan relies at all on the damn Quakers giving up funds to assist in building defensive fortifications, then I will be sure to send up extra prayers for anyone living west of Philadelphia."

"Should I then assume that you would not be willing to help?" Stevens asked with a note of disappointment exhibited clearly in his voice.

Jacob remained silent for a few long moments before answering, "I don't want to speak for Joshua, but while it would be an honor to lend you a hand, I need to head north."

Joshua immediately piped in, "Sir, I too would be honored, but I go where my father goes."

"Well, maybe we can still help each other," the major insisted. "Depending how far north you plan to go, would you consider taking a company with you to build one of the fortifications? More than anything, they are a show of strength and solidarity to let the frontier families know they are not alone."

Jacob glanced at Joshua before offering Stevens a smile and saying cautiously, "I'll need a day to think about this. Do you know when Washington was expecting a reply from the government?"

"You have a day, Sims," Stevens replied, ignoring the question. "Please consider all your options; I would truly appreciate your expertise in this matter." Stevens offered his hand to both men before dismissing himself to attend to some other business.

Jacob watched Stevens depart, waiting for him to get out of earshot. "What do you think, boy?" he asked, turning to Joshua.

"Moving through a territory infested with renegade savages would be difficult at the best of times. We would obviously cover far more territory by ourselves, but having a company of men with us would give us so much more firepower, increasing our chances of finding out something about Miss Maggie and One-Ear."

Jacob patted Joshua on the back and said, "You are certainly far more intelligent than me, lad, and you are right about the additional numbers. Even though we will lose time building the fort, what could be better for us than having a permanent base sitting in the wilderness while we look for my Maggie and your friend?"

Major Stevens had inadvertently offered the two men the opportunity and increased security to search for their loved ones. The decision to accept the position was far easier than Jacob could have ever anticipated and he sought out the Major right away to tell him.

The morning sun broke over the mountains and signaled the men to be up and about with their daily chores. Jacob had risen well before the rest and immediately noticed that a small company of Virginia militia, mixed with a unit of rangers, had arrived. They were busy staking out where they were to sleep, while their officers were inside the fort looking for their orders.

With the additional men, Jacob began to feel much better about the prospects of what Washington had planned. He had seen firsthand that an experienced unit of backwoodsmen were far more effective than an entire company of European-trained, British regulars who had never set foot in this country.

Now, if they could add a few thousand or more men, it might be possible to defend such a wide-ranging frontier. He was still skeptical about building a series of defensive fortifications and whether they would prove to be effective enough to guard the majority of the wilderness. If he was an Indian or, God forbid, a French Canadian, he would just avoid the forts and work his way around them. It was impossible to build enough forts or stockades to cover every corner of the vast Ohio Valley territory.

Stevens was not in the immediate area and Jacob assumed he was with Washington, discussing their plans. He didn't care to interrupt the men, but he felt the need to stay active. He decided to take Joshua out on one last scout along the main trail north.

He found the young man down by the river splashing some of the cold water on his face, and said, "Lad, what do you think about taking a little walk?"

The unexpected voice caught Joshua off-guard and he narrowly avoided falling into the shallow water when he jumped up in surprise. "Bloody hell, sir!" he yelped, taking Jacob's outstretched hand. "Were you trying to scare me to death?"

"Sorry, lad," Jacob laughed, pulling him away from the sandy riverbank to steady him, "but I assumed the Huron taught you to keep your wits about you, particularly in such a defenseless position!"

After he calmed himself down, Joshua walked back up the river trail with Jacob. "Did you speak with the Major yet?" he asked just as they stepped past the outer tents of the camp.

"No, I think he is busy with Washington. That is why I thought we might want to do a short scouting trek. You know I hate sitting around the camp doing nothing."

Before they left, Jacob spoke briefly to the two guards at the main gate, asking the visibly disinterested soldiers to pass on to Major Stevens that they were heading out to do some scouting.

Soon they were far into the deep woods, a good distance from the various smells waffling from the fort. They were able to cover a lot of ground by using the old Delaware hunting side paths that traversed most of the territory.

Taking a brief rest by a small ridge, Jacob made himself comfortable on a fallen tree that was coated in thick, green moss. Joshua sat against an old rock wall and rested his musket on a nearby boulder.

"I can't believe the Shawnee or Seneca didn't continue forward and attack our column as we retreated," Jacob said, keeping his voice low in case there were any unseen enemies in the area, "We were so shattered and disorganized; they could have taken more than just stragglers. Now it seems like all the savages have just disappeared into the shadows."

"The Indians in these parts are far more defensive fighters then the Mohawk or Abnaki to the east," Joshua replied, keeping his eyes closed as he listened to the sounds of the forest around them. "They fear that if they were to launch a full-scale war on the English, the sheer numbers of the British army would result in too great a loss to their people. The Indians just don't have the warriors to lose, and if they expose themselves to the firepower of the English, it would be devastating."

A sound coming from the boulder where his musket rested startled Joshua and just as he started to rise to investigate, Jacob put his finger to his lips and motioned him to move slowly. From Jacob's vantage point, he could see what had caused the sound and he cautiously rose and unsheathed the long knife that hung from his belt.

As he inched his way in front of the boulder, the noise came again, louder and longer. When it stopped again, an echoing rattle hung in the air. Jacob never took his eyes from a twitching pile of leaves under the boulder. He mouthed, "Rattler," to Joshua, who had already drawn his own knife.

The two men stood a few paces from the boulder and through a gap in the leaves could see the snake's rattle, as thick as Jacob's thumb, moving quickly side to side. Jacob signaled Joshua to move to his left to try to draw the snake's attention. If it could be distracted, Jacob could possibly pounce on it and use his knife to kill it.

Unfortunately, if the snake managed to strike either of them, it could mean a painful, drawn out death. They were knowledgeable about snakes and knew that rattlers normally gave a warning bite before releasing venom in a second bite if they felt a continued threat.

Jacob wished he could just use his musket to blow the damned snake to pieces, but he wouldn't risk drawing the attention of any savages that might be within the radius of a few miles. As Joshua attempted to keep the large snake's attention on his left hand, Jacob took a deep breath and leaped, slicing as hard as he could at the still partially obscured rattler.

Before Joshua could offer his help, Jacob stood proudly with the head-less snake in his right hand.

The creature was five feet long and as thick as a man's forearm in girth.

He swung it quickly around his head to show Joshua its massive size. "This damn thing is one of the biggest snakes I have ever seen; the bloody thing could swallow a brush wolf!" Jacob laughed as he threw it to the ground and watched the headless, now harmless, body continue to slither.

"Nice work, sir; that monster could have certainly killed either one of us," Joshua said as he grabbed his musket and kept it closer by his side.

"How do you feel about roasted rattler?" Jacob asked cheerfully as he ran his knife along the underside of the snake and easily removed the skin. "We can have a good meal tonight!"

"I think it's delicious. If you cut it up, you can throw it in my pack." Joshua was quick to suggest.

Once the task was completed, the two men got back on the trail and continued to move northward. They could feel the trail beginning to get steeper as they reached the base of the mountains. It was only about midday and time to decide whether to push forward or head back to the fort to discuss their next mission with Major Stevens.

It was agreed that they should proceed over the mountains and stop for the night before returning to the fort.

They moved quickly, albeit cautiously, along the open mountain path. When they reached the peak, they spent a number of minutes taking in the panoramic view of the valley below.

During their descent, the trail continued to present them with good vantage points of the valley. Just as they had worked their way half-way down the ridge, Jacob moved to the edge of a lookout and noticed a plume of smoke billowing from the far eastern skyline.

Calling Joshua over to the lookout atop a dramatic cliff face, Jacob pointed, "That is more than smoke from a couple of log cabins. I fear we finally found some signs of the damn savages that have eluded us for so long."

"It certainly looks bad," Joshua replied and the pair instantly picked up their pace down the steep pathway to the base of the mountain.

Jacob estimated that the smoke was less than five miles away and as the two men quickly made their way down to the level ground of a small meadow, they were hit with the bitter stench of burning wood. Jacob also recognized a grossly familiar odor that was intermixed with that of the scorched logs. He had smelled it at the remains of Fort Necessity and it was seared into his memory ever since.

Continuing on, Jacob decided to use the much more traveled main trail, despite the risk that they might run into the party responsible for this attack. Both men instinctively held their muskets at the ready and tossed their packs behind a clump of small boulders to lighten their load. If they did run into the attackers, it was of the utmost importance that they could move swiftly and unabated without any unnecessary weight.

Intently watching ahead for any obvious signs of a war party or the persons involved in the matter, Jacob led the way and was careful not to walk into an ambush. They soon reached a shallow river crossing and, after working their way over the slippery rocks, they noticed the fresh tracks of over fifty men pocked into the soft sand of the bank before them.

Jacob took a moment to get a better look at the prints while Joshua dutifully remained upright, watching the woods for any movement. The burning smell was noticeably stronger and they saw that an ominous, smoky cloud had settled eerily just above the forest canopy.

"These tracks are pretty fresh," Jacob said softly as he stood upright. "By the prints, it looks like a large Delaware raiding party moving to the east. There seems to be a number of similar moccasin tracks, plus a few that must be either French or possibly some Seneca. There are way too many for us to fight, so we will have to watch out and not walk ourselves into a trap. Let's keep moving and pray we don't run into these bloody heathens."

They walked into the woods with their muskets cocked and slowly moved towards the source of the smoke. Every slight noise or movement in the dense brush made them react and tighten the grips on their weapons.

They continued on for another mile or so, slowing to a near stop when they came to a sharp curve. Carefully, Jacob led the way and waved Joshua on once he saw all was clear.

The curve led them to a large, open field. It was a little over an acre in size and newly cleared of trees. There were still several tree stumps that had yet to be removed and the ground had never been tilled or planted.

They took their time scanning the area from the safety of the forest. It would be foolish to rush headlong into the open where they could be vulnerable to a counterattack. From their position, they could see the smoldering remains of what had been a small family cabin that sat on a small rise to one side of the field. An outer building, just to the right of the main cabin, now lay in a pile of ashes and rubble.

The cabin still had a few hotspots that flamed out of control and spewed more black smoke into the open sky. The only remaining piece standing was a nicely constructed fireplace that would have been the focal point of the room. It sat proudly upright and almost completely intact, a sad reminder of far happier occasions.

After their initial observation, they began to move through the woods along the border of the field. Their greatest concern was the gap in the trees on the far side of the field. It likely indicated another trail to a neighboring homestead, and with it the increased danger that the perpetrators were lurking nearby.

The forest was an unforgiving tangle of trees and brush and it slowed them to a near crawl. "We need to get to the cabin to see if there are any survivors, but it will take us an hour to weave through this mess at this pace," Jacob whispered.

"Let's just make a run for it," Joshua blurted impatiently, still managing to keep his voice low. "If the damn war party is still around, they must know we are here by now."

Jacob stood for a moment, thinking back to when he first discovered his own homestead in a similar condition. He prayed silently that this family had been taken captive, versus being slaughtered and left for the animals to feed on. Life, even as a captive, must be preferable to murder at the hands of savages.

Jacob knew Joshua was right and was just readying himself to make a wild dash towards the cabin when a large crash echoed through the clearing.

Both men pulled farther back into the woods and listened for any other sounds. All was quiet and they crept back to the edge of the field to see that the massive stone chimney had collapsed. Sparks and ashes now filled the air and shot smoke well over a hundred feet into the blackened sky.

Jacob said, "I'm going."

Before Joshua could offer a reply, Jacob was running straight towards the destroyed cabin.

Joshua stood with his musket to his shoulder, ready to provide cover if there was an attack. Jacob ran as fast as his weary legs could move, and was only slowed by the maze of tree stumps that jutted from all around the newly cleared field. Weaving his way through, he stopped about halfway and turned to wave Joshua on to do the same. Both men were now running at full speed to reach some cover before they could be spotted by any straggling unseen members of the raiding party.

Jacob jumped the remains of a fence that had enclosed the cabin, out building and a small garden patch before it had been broken down and trampled. He felt the ground slope upward slightly and when he was soon only a few paces from the smoking ash heap, he stopped as though he had run directly into a wall.

Now that he had reached the source, Jacob knew for certain that these settlers had not been captured; they had perished with the rest of their pioneer dreams.

He had no idea who had lived here or if there were children amongst the rubble, but he knew they deserved a better fate. All they had sought was a little piece of land to call their own and an opportunity to hack out a meager life. They meant no one any harm, just as he and Maggie had desired.

Joshua was again at his side and the two men surveyed the damage, their breathing labored from the hard run and the heavy smoke that hung over them. Their eyes burned as did their throats and they grabbed their canteens, choking down the contents quickly to provide them some relief.

"Bloody hell," Joshua managed before he broke into a fit of coughing.

Jacob grabbed his hatchet and cut down a small lonely tree that sat oddly out of place amongst all the ruins. He hacked off all the limbs and used the pole to push around the ashes. He moved carefully, not wanting to disturb any bodies if they were to be found here. The embers and smoke that kicked up from his ministrations made him step back to clear his eyes once more.

"Let's take a better look around the back field and especially behind the outer building over there," Jacob suggested, needing to get away from the smoldering ruins of the main cabin.

It wasn't long before they faced a terrible scene that made them stop in their tracks.

At the base of the small slope behind the cabin and out building were two piles of bodies, left mutilated and unburied in the open sun. When they could move again, Jacob and Joshua approached slowly, weighed down by their own dread and sadness.

The first pile consisted of the mother and two young daughters, their colorful day dresses incongruously cheerful amidst the devastation. The second had two older boys, scalped, shot and mangled together in a grotesque heap.

It took Jacob a few more steps to locate the father.

He was tied to a nearby tree and had been mercilessly tortured to death.

"The poor man probably fought back, maybe managed to kill a couple of the bastards," Jacob whispered, wiping tears from his eyes.

Joshua could see that Jacob was getting emotional and suggested that they bury the family.

"There's no time for that, lad," he said, composing himself. "I fear this is only the beginning of what we might find along this trail. If we are to give a full report to Stevens and Washington, we need to act quickly."

Joshua nodded and the two men turned to the gap in the trees where the trail continued to the next homestead. It was a painful decision to leave the unfortunate, nameless family exposed to be ravaged by wild animals and the hordes of bugs, but they had wasted enough time already in trailing this murderous raiding party.

Jacob realized that this was a scene that could have greeted him when he returned to his little piece of land. He felt lucky that the raiders had decided to spare his family. Being a captive certainly wasn't the ideal situation for any person, but it was far better than being tortured and left for dead in this lonely wilderness.

Once they made their way back into the dense forest, Jacob noticed that Joshua seemed particularly affected by what they had seen. The horrors they had just witnessed brought back terrible memories for both of them.

"Everything alright, lad?" Jacob asked as they struggled to move single-file along the narrow, rough-cut trail.

He looked back in time to see Joshua nod his head that he was fine, but Jacob understood what images he had in his mind. Even Jacob had shed tears back at the site they had just left, but Joshua held the pain within.

While the sight of that poor family made Jacob think of his own family and the terror they had faced, Joshua had experienced the same tragedy first-hand. He had witnessed the deaths of his family at the hands of the Huron.

Jacob didn't know what to say to the young man, especially in light of what they were likely to come across next.

He simply said, "Sorry we both had to see that."

The next few miles followed another old Indian trail interspersed with clearings just like the first. At each clearing, they were greeted with the same horrific scene: burnt-out cabins, dead and mutilated families and scorched land. At the few homesteads that had livestock, Jacob and Joshua found the animals slaughtered but left otherwise untouched for the wild scavengers to consume.

They seemed to be a few minutes behind the destruction at every turn. This was not just a group of raiders; this was a fast-moving war party with eradication of the settlers as its primary focus.

The entire wilderness was now congested with a thick cloud of smoke held down by the forest canopy.

The smell of death was everywhere.

Frustrated that they could not catch up to the coldblooded war party, Jacob knew that they could do little to help the remaining settlers left in the path of these killers. He was struck by their speed. They left behind enough crops and slaughtered livestock to feed a dozen villages. It was clear, they were not interested in acquiring food or belongings; they were determined to destroy every innocent settler in their wake.

"We can't keep up with them," Jacob finally said as they came upon yet another burned out homestead. "Even if we did, I am not sure how we could stop them. Our time and the settlers' interests would be better served if we returned to Fort Cumberland to speak with Major Stevens."

"It is rare that such a raiding party cared more about killing than reaping in the value of the food, personal belongings or livestock," Joshua replied. "The sheer speed of their attacks and the inability of the settlers to put up more of a fight are surprising. You would think that the settlers would have some type of warning system so the next farm would be able to at least run to a trading post or the next farm. We need more men to help these people. Do you know of the nearest English settlement or trading post in these parts so we can at least warn them of the attacks?"

Jacob tried to consider all their options. He stood for a moment, staring off towards the trail and wondering how many other families would be murdered before nightfall.

Tormented by the guilt of not being able to do more, he finally answered Joshua, "Our best bet would be to get back to the fort as fast as we can. The only trading post I know of is miles east of here. There was an old abandoned Ohio Trading Company encampment, but it would provide little protection from such a large war party. I have also seen a couple of small German settlements near the Susquehanna, but they are also miles to the east. Most of the homesteads around here are new and have probably had no time to organize themselves."

They turned back to the south and began to move as fast as they could. It was almost twilight, and it would take nearly a full day to get back to the fort. The moon would be full and, if it could break through some of the lingering smoke, would light their path quite well. They agreed to push on for as long as they could. There was only a slim chance of meeting any Indians in the direction they had just come, but they never let their guard down as they moved swiftly.

Speaking very little as they progressed, each man fought down his own guilt over leaving the settlers to the roving war party. They had come to the realization that it would be a few weeks before they could return with a substantial force to help the other defenseless families.

They were driven to get back to the fort as quickly as possible and pressed on to the point of exhaustion. When they finally crested the mountain from which they had first seen the smoke, they collapsed against two trees and slept a couple of hours, sitting upright with their muskets across their laps.

In an impressive display of stamina, Jacob and Joshua managed to arrive at the fort just after midday.

It was a bustling camp once more. Another company of Virginia militia and volunteers had arrived in their absence, and the two men's spirits lifted with the hope that it might not take as long as they thought to get started on their next mission.

They found Major Stevens standing amid the organized chaos of camp-building and he looked on them with a relieved smile. "You two are a sight for sore eyes! I thought you changed your minds and headed home after all."

Jacob chuckled and said, "Well, we did leave word with the guards that we were going out scouting."

"Those 'guards' apparently couldn't care less about passing on messages to higher-ranking officers or doing their duty," Stevens said with a scowl. "Well, do you have anything to report? Any signs of the Indians or French nearby?"

"I'm afraid the news isn't good, sir," Jacob sighed. He looked at Joshua, who dropped his head. "Is Colonel Washington available? He'll want to hear this as well."

"Washington just left for Philadelphia yesterday in order to secure more funds for the new fortifications. I wish him luck dealing with the Quakers! Enough of his troubles, now what is this all about?"

"We were on the trail of a war party. If I were made to guess I would say it was Delaware, maybe Shawnee. They are moving very fast, torching homes and killing entire families. They do not appear to be concerned with anything of value; they have not taken any captives, crops or livestock. They only seem interested in killing as many settlers as possible."

"This is very grave news indeed," Stevens said as his face hardened. "As you have probably already noticed, two companies of men from Virginia have already arrived. Among them are a number of carpenters and other tradesmen.

"I understand that there are several forts being planned in Pennsylvania and Virginia and another here in Maryland. I myself have been ordered to the east a ways to oversee the construction of a stone fort. It was Washington's hope that you would move to the north since you are so familiar with the countryside.

"While it is hoped that many additional forts will be able to be constructed across the territory, winter is not very far off. Therefore, you have been ordered to prepare a fortification at a location of your discretion in preparation for the winter. You will reach out to the settlers surrounding your fort and offer them what protection you can. You will report directly to me, and I in turn, will report directly to Colonel Washington."

Jacob was taken aback slightly at the speed with which everything was apparently happening and at the trust placed in him by Washington.

"I understand, sir," he said. "How many men will I have, and when can we depart?"

"You will be taking two hundred men, including an engineer, carpenters and a blacksmith, when he decides to arrive. They are all encamped together over there," he said, pointing. "While your ultimate objective is to complete a fort by winter, it would be prudent to use the men to build up and strengthen any existing trading posts or well-situated plantations and settlements you come across. That will offer some additional protection, even without fortification." Stevens went over his orders with Jacob as Joshua made his way towards the camp.

"It is also advisable that you do as much recruiting among the settlers as you can. Greater numbers will help, of course. Depending on how Washington does in recruiting additional Virginians, I may be able to send more men to you in the coming months." Stevens added.

Jacob scanned the encampment quickly to see what kind of men he would be expected to lead into the wilderness. He saw Joshua doing the same, but neither revealed their thoughts.

"I leave it to you, Sims, to decide when to leave," Stevens continued. "You both must be exhausted after your travels, but I know you're eager to get moving.

Both men nodded and moved to make their salutes when Stevens interrupted them.

"Oh, one last thing," he said, "I've promoted you to the rank of Sergeant. It gives you a bit more authority over the men. Unfortunately, it won't guarantee you their respect, but I'm sure you will be able to earn that in no time." Stevens smiled and shook Jacob's hand. "Godspeed, gentlemen, I pray we will see each other again soon."

Jacob offered a slight salute and watched him walk away to see to the preparations for his own departure to the east. Joshua returned from reviewing the men but neither man spoke.

It appeared to be a ragtag group of volunteers, derelicts and displaced settlers. Jacob guessed there were likely a few criminals among them, but felt better not knowing too much about them.

Some of the faces were familiar, though. Privates White and Sinclair had remained and had volunteered to be a part of Jacob's company.

"Corporal, we're honored to be under your command again," Private White said as he and Sinclair shook Jacob's hand and offered Joshua the same.

"Thank you very much, gentlemen," Jacob said before humbly informing them about his new rank.

Having Joshua, White and Sinclair with him gave Jacob greater confidence about their mission. He and Joshua quickly filled the other two men in on their latest scouting trip. When asked when they would be expected to leave, Jacob glanced at Joshua's weary face and decided that as much as he'd like to leave at first light, they should be given the opportunity to rest before meeting and preparing the men to leave.

He decided that they would leave at daybreak the day after the next. While he and Joshua rested, he asked that White and Sinclair take some time to talk with the men and determine who might have experience or show promise at scouting. He knew he could depend on these men, and their information would help him better organize his column when it was time to depart.

Joshua and Jacob quickly ate some bread and meat and retired to their tent to collapse in exhaustion.

"What do you think about all of this, Joshua?" Jacob finally asked.

The young man examined the canvas ceiling for a moment before answering. "Don't you think that the Delaware, Shawnee or Seneca will just work their way around any fortification we build and attack the more isolated farms and settlements? That is, of course, assuming they don't just attack our fort instead. With the Quakers running this territory, I fear little will be done to help us once we're out in the wilderness on our own."

Jacob considered what Joshua said. The British had pulled back to Philadelphia and he expected Washington would pull back to fortify Virginia. It seemed like everyone who could actively help had sacrificed the Pennsylvania frontier for their own interests.

"Aye, lad," Jacob finally replied before sleep claimed him. "I understand exactly how you feel. With the British cowards behind us and the French bastards ahead of us stirring up the savages, we certainly seem to be on our own."

In addition to investigating the men's scouting abilities, White and Sinclair had carried out the important task of informing the men about the raids on the frontier settlements. Once the news of the raids spread through the camp, there was very little need for any additional motivation from Jacob's quarter.

The British abandonment of the frontier was old news, but with this new knowledge, the men understood that their role was now one of real importance. They were the only line of defense, and some of the men began calling themselves the Forest Sentinels. Jacob approved of the moniker and was proud of the men for taking such a view of their mission.

When he had risen that morning, he found Joshua speaking with White and Sinclair. Most of the men were already awake and bustling about the busy camp. Jacob was surprised to find that he had slept past his usual hour, but was glad to see that his men were ready to move out.

"Gentlemen," Jacob shouted over the activity, "could I have your attention please? Gentlemen…"

A few men glanced up from what they were doing, but most simply ignored him. Jacob wasn't surprised or offended. He figured he would have reacted the same way.

Would he have paid much attention to a fellow enlisted man who appeared more like a backwoods trapper than a commanding officer? He had become so used to his ragged appearance that he had forgotten how he must have looked to these new recruits.

Before he could shout again, Private White stepped forward and screamed, "Get up, you sorry blokes and give the sergeant your attention, or maybe a few lashes might change your minds?"

White's threatening tone made every man in the camp look up and immediately give Jacob their undivided attention.

"Thank you, Private White," he said. "Some of you men know me, but for the others, my name is Sergeant Sims. I have been ordered by Major Stevens to take you men out into the wilderness to help our fellow settlers fight off the savages. With the British licking their wounds for God knows how long, we are now the self-appointed sentinels of the Pennsylvania territory."

Most of the men erupted in cheers of, "Huzzah! Huzzah!" until White once again stepped forward to quiet them down.

Jacob was happy to see the men's enthusiasm and continued, "I understand there are a fair number of Virginians with us. You may be wondering why you should risk your lives for settlers in Pennsylvania. If the French and their Indian allies manage to take over the rest of our frontier, then you can bet that Virginia and Maryland will soon face the same fate.

"It is our mission to move northward to build a fortification and reach out to as many settlers as we can before winter comes upon us. Are there any questions?"

He waited a brief moment and was greeted by silence. He smiled and continued, "Very good, men. We will leave at first light tomorrow. Please pack lightly and make sure your weapons are in good working order."

The men immediately dispersed and went about their duties. Jacob took the opportunity to walk through the camp and observe his men personally. Their excitement and anticipation was tangible. He stopped when he came to two large wagons being packed by the tradesmen that had been assigned to him.

He was glad to have wagons to carry the supplies, but he knew that they would restrict his use of the side paths he so preferred. At least he would benefit from the wide road Braddock had insisted on having cut through the wilderness. Besides, he could always send scouts along the side paths to keep an eye on the advancing column.

Jacob had already determined the path he wished to follow and as he looked at the wagons again, he thought that they might run into some issues once they had to turn off of the road Braddock had forged. If they had to abandon the wagons, at least they would have the horses to help carry supplies.

As he continued walking among the men, checking their packs and observing their various interactions, he found White and Sinclair busily packing their own gear. He approached them and said, "Thank you, gentlemen, for your support. I hope you will let me lean on you both for some assistance with this bunch?"

"Yes, sir; it would be an honor to help in any way," White quickly replied.

"Looks like we are in for some more fun, sir," Sinclair added. "No need to ask sir, you know I too will help you in any way I can."

Jacob nodded his head at Sinclair's comment. "I asked you yesterday to look the men over to determine who would be good scouts. I would like each of you to be in charge of a scouting party, so you can help train the men. You both know the area well, and the damn savages most likely already know we are coming. I honestly don't know how many of these men have ever experienced a battle or an Indian attack, so it will be most interesting."

"I'd like you each to pick thirty men for your scouting parties. White, you will take the lead; Sinclair, you will take the rear guard. I think if you are finished packing your own belongings, now would be a good time to speak with your men and give them a few pointers before we hit the trail. Just leave me a couple of good men, if you please." Jacob added and smiled.

The men saluted and immediately went to work building up their scouting parties. As they departed, Joshua approached.

"Sir," he said when Jacob nodded in greeting, "I've just checked on the laborers and they have finished loading their wagons. They said they can move out as soon as the rest of the column is ready in the morning."

"Thank you, Joshua; that is good news. I would like you to stay with the wagons to make sure they keep moving. I am determined to maintain a quick pace, and the wagons and horses will have to keep up or be left behind. I'm not sure what we will do with them once we are forced to leave the main trail, but we will deal with that when the time comes."

Joshua nodded and left to see to his own preparations. Jacob watched as White and Sinclair herded their selections a short distance away from the rest of the men. They had decided to conduct a joint training session and Jacob was relieved to see that each new scout listened with rapt attention to the lesson.

Everything seemed to be going smoothly and Jacob returned to his tent to make sure that his own weapons and pack were in order. The bustle of the camp continued for a few more hours, but fell silent well before the sky grew completely dark. They had a long day ahead of them and an early start. The men knew it might be the only good night's rest they would have for a while.

Before he fell asleep that night, Jacob said a short prayer of thanks. The men that had been assigned to him had already exceeded his expectations and he felt that they might be able to do some good on the frontier after all.

"Private, I don't intend to cover more than twenty-five or -six miles a day, so there is no need to get too far ahead of us," Jacob said as he briefed Private White early the next morning. "You are our eyes and ears and I expect you to send regular updates via messenger."

"Yes, sir," White responded.

"We will see you at Little Crossings then, private. If you and your men have an opportunity, please send out a hunting party before the main column's arrival."

"You can count on us, sir. I was very impressed by the scouts Sinclair and I chose yesterday. We will see you this evening." White saluted.

"I wish you Godspeed then, private," Jacob said, returning the salute. "Keep your wits about you, for heaven's sake."

White smiled at that and motioned for his men to follow him into the woods just as the first ray of light shot over the horizon.

Jacob looked to the rest of men standing at the edge of the forest. They were organized into several groups. As he ordered them to move onto the trail, he stood to the side and reminded them to keep their talking to a minimum and their voices low. Otherwise, they could be heard for miles.

Jacob was forced to leave five of his men behind to wait for the blacksmith. The man had been expected two days earlier, but had not arrived as of yet. Jacob didn't like the idea of traveling on this mission without a blacksmith, but also did not want to get too far ahead of the men he was leaving behind. He told them to wait one full day before departing to meet up with them, whether the blacksmith was with them or not.

The first group was a single file line of ten young rangers under the authority of a Private Scott. They were followed by a unit of forty men split into two lines. They marched shoulder-to-shoulder, but once the entire company was on the trail, Jacob would have them spread out single file to lessen the chances that one shot would hit two men if they were ambushed.

Next was Joshua. There were fifty laborers walking behind each of the heavily-laden wagons. Jacob smiled his approval as the young man walked confidently past amid a cloud of dust.

The thunderous creaking from the massive wheels as they passed by him gave Jacob some concern. After telling his men to remain quiet, the noise and cloud of dust kicked up by the wagons would forewarn any possible enemy for miles. Jacob prayed that their journey would be uneventful but knew he would probably have no such luck.

Following up the wagons was another unit of forty men. When they had moved onto the trail, Jacob nodded to Sinclair, whose thirty scouts awaited their turn to begin their trek.

"Private," Jacob said, "Keep a few paces to the rear and your eyes open. You may also want to have a couple men spread out along the side trails to monitor our flanks from above."

Sinclair saluted, saying, "Yes, sir; we will make sure the column keeps moving. None of the damn Frenchies or their savage friends will be able to sneak up on us."

Jacob returned the salute and moved onto the trail at a quick pace to return to the front of the column. He was excited at the sight of the men moving out on the trail. Far from the regal British columns that had departed a few months earlier, his men had no uniformity and each carried their weapon of choice. Despite some of the men being experienced woodsmen, once they finally entered the dark veil of the forest, all the men walked cautiously.

They flinched with each noise or chirp that echoed along the trail. Jacob was experienced with the strange noises the wilderness exuded, yet he also found himself reacting to many of the continuous sounds.

Jacob caught up to Joshua and walked alongside him for the first few miles. Neither said much and Jacob moved ahead to see how the forward unit was doing.

As he moved up the relatively flat path, Jacob couldn't believe he was once again on the same trail that had only recently caused him so much pain. He was not sure of the exact location where he would build the fortification, but he knew he wanted to be out of the reach of Fort Duquesne's hunting and scouting patrols. There had been a heavily-used Indian trail that moved to the northeast from the site where they had crossed the

Youghiogheny River with Braddock. He hoped that as it passed across the mountainous ridge, it would provide the perfect location for his men to set up a permanent structure before the cold weather gripped the area.

Thankfully, the first couple days' march was uneventful. Except for a minor scare from an erroneously reported Indian attack on the advanced scouting party, the men appeared to be in good shape. The wagons kept pace and the horses showed no signs of tiring.

Jacob took advantage of having a company of laborers and carpenters at his disposal and used them to repair some of the work that had been done by the work crews on Braddock's march. Most of the temporary bridges that traversed the miles of swamps and bogs were now strengthened and repaired. If they met a similar fate to Braddock's men and required a hasty retreat, he wanted them to have reliable bridges and roads to use.

The men took the long marches each day in stride. The only problem they encountered came in the form of relentless, ever-present hordes of mosquitoes. The weather was warm and the breeze was non-existent. The blood-suckers mercilessly attacked any exposed skin and irritated both the men and the horses. The men quickly resorted to spreading mud on their faces and hands to try to deter the menacing buggers.

Jacob was impressed by the skills of the men; they certainly did not match the original image he had of them as being raw and inexperienced. The majority of the men kept the hectic pace he had set, pushing through the wilderness without complaint.

As one would expect, a handful of individuals who couldn't handle the march either straggled behind the column or simply deserted. Private Sinclair did his best to keep the stragglers in tow, but after a while, he was tired of threatening them. Those who simply refused to keep up would have to face the possibility of falling into the hands of a Delaware raiding party or a French patrol from Fort Duquesne.

On the fifth day of the march, a messenger ran back from White's forward guard. Jacob was at the head of the column with Private Scott's men when the man arrived. Alarmed at first, Jacob smiled when he read White's scribbled words.

At camp on one of the previous evenings, Jacob had explained to White exactly what he was looking for in a location for the fortification. He wanted a place that would offer some natural defenses in addition to what they would build. A water source was also a priority, and he had ordered White to ensure that there was a good source within walking distance of any location to be considered. In addition to drinking water, a stream or small river would be a reliable source for river fish like trout and a good spot to find beaver, minks and other small game.

About thirty minutes after receiving White's message, Jacob arrived at a nice sized, level meadow situated just at the western base of the Allegheny Mountains. White's men had set up a perimeter guard and ensured there were no signs of the French or Indians nearby.

The meadow had a fresh, mountain stream running along its southern edge. There appeared to be good natural drainage as the meadow itself sat a little higher than the banks of the stream. Even though winter hadn't arrived yet, they had to give thought to spring thaw; they would not want to put an effort into a fort just to have it flood when the snow melted.

Jacob found it difficult to contain his excitement and he took several deep breaths of the intoxicating mountain air. He immediately approached Private White and said, "I must congratulate you and your men on your fine work preparing such a place for our arrival."

"Thank you, sir," White replied with a smile. "The men have done a wonderful job securing the area and organizing a picket."

"If you've not done so already, please send out a hunting party or two to check the area for game. It looks like white-tail and wild cats should be abundant here."

White nodded and advised Jacob that he had already seen to the hunting parties. Jacob continued, "I am going to examine the perimeters of the meadow. Please have your pickets keep an eye out for the rest of the column. Have Joshua report to me when the laborers arrive."

With a salute, White left Jacob alone. Walking along the edges of the forest that bordered the meadow on three sides, Jacob tried to imagine what a small fortification would look like and how it should be armed to defend this particular position.

He liked the fact the mountains were to his back and the closest trail through the main gap was narrow enough his men could put up a good defense, if needed. The gap basically acted like a funnel and it would force any raiding party or small army unit to rush forward into the open field to fight.

Within the hour, Joshua approached Jacob along with one of the men from the group of laborers. "Sir," the young man said, "It is a pleasure to be here at last. This place looks promising and I am sure the rest of the men will feel the same.

"Before I forget, this is our lead engineer, Mr. John Tate. With your approval, he will be the one setting up the layout of the fortification."

Tate was a small, round man and Jacob was mildly surprised that he had made the march without collapsing. He assumed the man had never been this far into the wilderness and prayed he was not one of those pompous, arrogant engineers that so often plagued the colonies with their ideas of grandeur and useless structures.

"Mr. Tate, I assume your trip was satisfactory?" Jacob asked politely, waiting for the man to complain or demand special privileges.

"Please call me John, sir. We are thankfully far enough away from the rules of the civilized territory."

If first impressions were anything to go on, Jacob already liked this man. He smiled and asked, "May I be so forward as to ask if your accent brings you here from the area around Boston?"

"Actually closer to New Hampshire, I was raised in a land similar to this place, save for the presence of the ocean."

"I know you have only just arrived, but would you be willing to take a walk with me around the perimeter to get your bearings?"

When Tate nodded, Jacob turned to Joshua and said, "Lad, please assist the rest of the laborers and make sure that the horses are being seen to. We will join you shortly."

Joshua left immediately to see to his duties and the two men walked in silence until they were out of earshot of the troops who were still steadily arriving.

"Please, John," Jacob finally said, "what is your initial opinion of this place? Will it provide us with a good base for our operations?"

"Right off, I like the fact that most of the useable land is already cleared. That will save us some time and wear on the men's backs...for the time being, anyway. The forests are thick with an endless supply of hardwood and the soil appears to be loose enough to let us build up some earthen work. What do you want me to work on first, sir, a blockhouse, the outer walls or your quarters?"

Jacob's first impression was holding true; he liked this man very much. If Tate proved trustworthy enough to take on this venture with little to no supervision, Jacob could concentrate his efforts on getting his men out scouting and locating the nearby families.

"I like this place too. I think we should be able to build a fortification solid enough for the men and settlers to fight off these bloody raiding parties. I appreciate your enthusiasm, but as for my quarters, that can wait until we have the outer walls secured and the blockhouse built. I will sleep in a tent like my men."

They paused to watch the growing number of men pour into the meadow and get organized. Jacob could see Joshua moving the laborers and the wagons into the center of the field so the soldiers could set up camp around them.

Jacob looked at the engineer and said, "I have great faith in your planning abilities, John. The only things I would specifically request are high walls and bastions tall enough for the men to shoot from without being too exposed. The Indians will fight from the woods; without a cannon, we will have to make every shot count."

Tate looked uncomfortable for the first time and said, "Yes, the savages. They might be the only unknown in all of this. Do you think they know we are here, sir?"

"Call me Jacob, please. I assume the savages began watching us the moment we left Fort Cumberland. I expect they will make themselves known to us sooner rather than later."

"I see," Tate displaying his nervous for the first time. "With your permission, I will see to my men. I would like to get them started first thing tomorrow morning. We need to get the structure put up before the ground freezes and the snow starts to accumulate."

"Go see to your men, John. Let us plan to meet again over dinner this evening. I am glad to see that you grasp the speed with which we need to complete this project."

Tate nodded and walked back towards the wagons. Jacob glanced around at the bustling camp and was pleased to see Sinclair appear from the gap in the woods. The entire company had finally arrived.

Tate was true to his word and the men were put to work early next morning. Already, the surrounding forests echoed with the sound of falling trees and scent of burning wood.

Jacob was very happy with the location. It was out of the reach of all but the most die-hard French patrols, leaving the Indians as the sole threat. The physical position of the fort itself was a matter of some consideration. Jacob had consulted with Tate and requested that it be far enough away from the forest line so an attacking force would need to move out into the open field for their shots to count. Jacob had seen the effects on an army when their enemy was able to remain concealed in the woods, peppering them from the safety of the trees. He was satisfied with the work of the axe men who had cleared several yards of the surrounding forest, providing the carpenters with lumber and expanding the openness of the outer field.

During their discussion over dinner that first night, Jacob and Tate had decided to build a larger fort than they had originally planned. It would include a stockade and a more predominant blockhouse. They even planned a larger storage building and the possibility of including a small trading post just outside the main gates. Jacob's foremost consideration was to have a place that would make the surrounding settlers feel secure and part of a larger community.

Tate had proposed a traditional-style fort that was common on the frontier. Within days, he and his men had built up a rough outline of the earthen work that would provide the first line of defense. During the same time, the fort's exterior wall was outlined and it gave Jacob's men a glimpse of what the fully-built fort would look like.

Over the next several weeks, Jacob sent out regular scouting parties to reach out to the settlers. It was reported that the Indian raids appeared to be subsiding for the moment. Daily hunting parties saw to the health and well-being of the men at the camp. The morale of the men was very high and they viewed their activities as an Indian deterrent.

Jacob was pleased with how things were going and late one afternoon called together a council of his most trusted men to get a full update. Joshua had gone out with a hunting party that morning, but was expected back soon. John Tate and Privates White, Sinclair and Scott approached Jacob and said, "Gentlemen, I would like to thank you all for your hard work. It has been just a few weeks since we arrived here, but we have made great strides in both construction and our main objective of reaching out to the settlers.

"I have only two concerns as we move forward. The first is the approach of winter. It is already mid-September and the leaves are starting to change color. Snow will not be very far behind. The other is about the lack of Indian sightings. While I'm glad they have not attempted to disrupt our progress, it is still a matter of concern."

"I agree, sir," Sinclair said. "The number of times the men have been out scouting without an encounter is very strange."

"Do you think they are just keeping closer to their French allies?" White asked.

Jacob paused to watch as a large tree was felled, kicking up a massive cloud of dirt. The loud crack echoed all around the meadow and must have been heard for miles.

"The savages know we are here," Jacob said thoughtfully. "Yet, I fear they are just sitting back and waiting us out for some reason. At least the attacks on the settlers have subsided momentarily; that makes everything well worth it. I will remind you, though, that we must remain resolved to keep the men on high alert."

Jacob was about to continue when he spotted Joshua entering the camp, leading a group of hunters. They carried three large bucks, a fully-grown black bear and a wild turkey tied to the end of each man's musket.

Joshua smiled proudly and Jacob beckoned to him, saying, "Well done, lad! It appears you had some good luck out there."

The other men murmured their appreciation and Jacob dismissed them back to their duties, thanking them again for their hard work. He turned his attention back to Joshua who could barely cover up his own excitement.

"This place is amazing!" he exclaimed. "I have never seen such plentiful game."

"I am certainly glad to hear it!" Jacob said as he began to walk the perimeter of the camp.

"We visited a couple of families while we were out. They had heard about the same raids you and I had witnessed and had considered fleeing back to the east, but expressed relief in knowing that there is a small army nearby."

"That is good news," Jacob said. "I want word to get around that we are here. While I'm still concerned by the lack of Indian activity, perhaps we really can deter them from resuming raids in this area."

"My first reaction when I returned from the hunting trip was how much work had already been completed in my absence. I was only gone for twelve hours! The men are working so quickly that the fort transforms each day. It is amazing to think of what it will look like in just a few more weeks."

"I have honestly never seen a fort being built from the ground up," Jacob replied, "but I must agree it is rather impressive. Mr. Tate has done a great job organizing the laborers and work crews. The last time we spoke about his progress, he was optimistic that the fort would be completed well before the first heavy snow."

Joshua nodded and Jacob saw him stifle a yawn. With a chuckle he said, "You should go get some rest. We will be able to enjoy a great feast tonight thanks to you. It will be a great reward for the men's hard work and keep their spirits raised."

Without any further prodding, except a pat on the back from Jacob, Joshua walked back to his tent. Jacob stopped walking and observed the activity before him. Tate had organized the men into several work crews with his skilled laborers scattered across each group for guidance.

One group was busy building up the earthen works along Tate's outline to a height of six feet. Others used hatchets to sharpen the ends of several thick logs to be placed along the earthen works to slow an enemy's advance.

While one group worked to raise the log walls of the large blockhouse, another worked on framing the outer wall of the fort. It had smaller bastions than most forts, basically because they did not possess any cannons. Jacob had initially requested cannons, but not a single one was available. He had hoped a gunsmith would number among the company to help him construct wall guns in lieu of cannons, but there was not and the project would have to wait until one could be sent from the south.

As he admired the work, Jacob could feel his confidence rising. He wanted to scream at the forest, daring any unseen foe to approach them. He squelched the feeling immediately. Such confidence should be approached with caution. He remembered how invincible he and the other men had felt, marching with Braddock's army just after they forded the Monongahela River.

Jacob consistently reminded his men to remain on high alert at all times against the possibility of an attack from the French or Indians, especially with the fortification not yet completed. He had ordered White and Sinclair to rotate pickets every four hours to keep them fresh. All the men, even those off duty, were under strict orders to keep their weapons at the ready and close at hand at all times. They were all glad to be free of Indian sightings, but Jacob worried that they were just waiting for the right time to strike.

One well organized attack could set them back weeks and basically waste all the work they had done to this point. Jacob's greatest fear was that the Delaware were sitting back and would attack one morning to burn down all that had been done to this point. Jacob had ordered the morning pickets increased and had patrols out much earlier than they had in the previous few weeks.

The food Joshua's hunting party had retrieved supplied a wonderful feast and leftovers were housed in the temporary smoke house to be dried for the winter. They deserved the meal and their spirits remained high. As the sun began to sink lower in the sky, they lit fires to provide additional light and continued to work well into the night. At a late hour, Jacob managed to get a few, uncomfortable hours of much needed sleep, but he was shaken awake by Joshua who said urgently, "Get up, sir! We need you at the western side of the meadow."

"What the hell?" Jacob mumbled and momentarily staggered as he struggled to get his bearings straight.

"What is it, lad?" he asked when his head had cleared somewhat.

"Please, sir, please come with me," Joshua said urgently and stepped out into the early morning fog that engulfed the meadow.

Jacob quickly scooped up his hat and rifled musket and matched Joshua stride for stride.

The camp was a flurry of activity and Jacob could sense panic in the air. Joshua increased his pace to a run, pointing ahead of him to the west.

Jacob guessed that the pickets must have been attacked or killed. He saw a number of men, including Tate and several of his laborers, standing atop earthen work, staring off into the far woods. He scrambled to the top of what was completed of the outer wall and gripped one of the posts that held it in place.

Unfazed by what he saw before him, Jacob ordered the ever-present White and Sinclair to get a line of men in place. He calmly asked Tate and his men to step aside to make room for the militia.

At the edge of the tree line a mere hundred yards away, a mixture of Delaware, Seneca and a handful of Canadian militia stood facing the unfinished fort. There were over a hundred of the painted, well-armed warriors standing calmly in a long line just one or two paces in front of the tree line. They held their muskets by their sides and, despite their menacing appearance, did nothing to outwardly threaten Jacob's men.

Jacob asked for a scope and Joshua immediately handed one up to him. At such a short distance, the long scope allowed him to see a small group of Delaware talking and pointing towards him. He did not recognize any of them, but assumed they were the leaders of the war party.

"What do you think they want, sir?" Joshua asked.

"I fear they are playing mind games with the men. Maybe they think if they can intimidate and scare us enough, we will just run back home. It appears there is a small group of chiefs contemplating their next move. I suspect this will only be the start of things.

White approached Jacob and said, "The men are ready, sir. If the bloody savages want a fight, the boys are more than ready and willing to oblige them."

"Thank you, private just keep the men back and under control. We do not want to fire the first shot here. Also, please reinforce the pickets on the outer boundaries. We don't want to be ambushed from behind. Were any of the men on the western picket injured?"

"All the men are safe and accounted for; they warned us of the savages before any of us spotted them," White said before rushing off to carry out his orders.

The soldiers and the warriors faced off for several more minutes, neither side making a move or a sound. Jacob grew weary of the games and suddenly jumped down from the wall.

Leaving a surprised Joshua in his wake, he called out, "Watch my back, lad," and climbed over the earthen work into the open meadow.

Joshua stayed behind and lifted his musket to his shoulder; some of the other men followed his lead and set their sights on the small group of leaders.

Jacob casually walked alone into the center of the open field and waited for a reaction from the war party. He was just short of their range of weapons and simply leaned on his musket and stared towards the chiefs.

He remained silent and just looked at them, scanning the line of warriors.

After what felt like a lifetime, sudden deafening screams broke the tense silence that had gripped the meadow. In unison, the warriors yelled and barked the familiar war cry that would frighten most men into dropping their weapons and running.

Jacob had expected this reaction. He never flinched and his chest swelled with pride when he heard his men reply to the Delaware with their own calls and roars.

This defiant reaction puzzled the Delaware and they stopped immediately.

Jacob grinned at the leaders who appeared to be arguing amongst each other about what to do next.

The stillness was shattered when Jacob spotted a burst of movement from the far left of the long line of warriors. A lone, heavily-painted warrior broke free of the line, heading directly towards Jacob. His war club was raised and he swiftly dodged the numerous tree stumps that covered the first twenty yards of the field. Once he cleared the obstacles, he broke out in a sprint and unleashed a hellish war cry.

Jacob stood still, letting him get closer. He knew the warrior was trying to prove his own courage to the other savages. With less than a hundred feet separating them, Jacob calmly raised his rifled musket and took aim. The bone-chilling cry hung in the air for a few seconds after Jacob's well-placed shot cut down his attacker. The savage convulsed violently and then went still.

The entire dramatic scene had played out in just under a minute.

There was a brief pause on both sides as they took in what had happened. Then Jacob's men delivered a cheer en masse while the war party remained shocked by the actions of this lone gunman.

Keeping his wits about him, Jacob quickly reloaded his weapon and stood ready to offer another shot at any of the stunned warriors foolish enough to try another charge.

The leaders waved their hands and the whole line of warriors disappeared back into the forest. Two warriors ran out to retrieve their dead mate and disappeared into the darkness. Jacob remained rooted to the spot watching them, but neither savage so much as glanced at him. Well aware that a mass of bullets could easily be unleashed from the cover of the woods, Jacob remained at the ready and waited a few long minutes before he decided it was safe to move.

He prayed it was over for now, and slowly stepped backwards, careful not to take his eye off the dark woods. He saw a large pile of chopped wood out of the corner of his eye and knew he had already reached the earthen work. He turned around and was greeted by a hand.

Joshua pulled him up to the top so he wouldn't need to scramble. Jacob jumped down the other side amid deafening cheers and many admiring pats on the back.

"Great show, sir, but you sure the heck had us on pins and needles," Joshua laughed, shaking his head. "You know next time they will not let you insult them like that."

"HUZZAH! HUZZAH!" the men continued to cheer.

"Bloody good show, sir," Private White smiled, extending his hand. "The damn savages had no idea what to think of you!"

Jacob was embarrassed by all the attention and attempted to get the men re-focused on the task at hand.

"Now, let's get back to work, gentlemen," he said when he had signaled them to quiet down so he could speak. "Double the pickets on all sides and we must all be on high alert at all times. Mr. Tate, I suggest we put every available man to work on the wall so that it is completed when the savages decide to visit us again."

With his admirable display of defiance, Jacob could feel the spirits soar within the camp. The scouting and hunting parties were quick to spread the word about Jacob's exploits, and over the next several days, settlers from the surrounding area arrived to re-enforce the militia.

All appeared to going well…for now.

Chapter | **Four**

Soon Maggie noticed an increased number of French traders seemed to be stopping at the Delaware village. They carried news from Fort Duquesne along with their usual wares. Maggie heard snippets of news, but nothing very detailed. There had been a battle several weeks earlier, but news was very slow to reach the small, isolated village.

One morning the elders held a village meeting and Maggie stayed with the children she cared for. She could sense excitement in the air as the villagers walked home from the meeting. She saw Anne passing nearby and called out to her. Both women still remained rather guarded in their conversations with each other. Maggie did not trust Anne's loyalties and Anne always seemed very vague in her address to Maggie.

Maggie was anxious to hear about the battle and hoped that this meeting had presented some details. She hoped that the French had exaggerated their accounts of the encounter or lied outright. She longed for news about Pontiac and his men, to know what their plans were for her.

Anne's response was far from satisfying, "What I know is the French, with a large force of our people, defeated the great English army on the outskirts of Fort Duquesne several weeks back. Many English soldiers were killed or taken prisoner. The elders are very excited and happy their French fathers have finally driven the English out of our territory."

Attempting to get Anne to drop her cautious demeanor, Maggie asked, "Have you heard word about your husband?"

"I have received no word, but hopefully the gods have kept him well. We were told that the warriors have been celebrating for the past few weeks and should be leaving for home over the next couple of days. We have much to do to prepare for their welcome."

Anne abruptly left and Maggie remained still, her head ringing with thoughts of escape. If the battle had taken place several weeks ago, then the Ottawa had been too late. She imagined that they would not be happy about this. If the other warriors were returning, she assumed Pontiac would arrive soon and take her to Fort Detroit.

The sun was already beginning to set earlier each day and leaves on the surrounding trees were beginning to give up their vivid green hue. Winter was approaching quickly and Maggie considered her options. Even if she escaped, she was in a territory that would be filled with French regulars and traders trying to make it to Quebec before cold temperatures and snow would trap them into over-wintering at one of the wilderness outposts.

She certainly did not relish the thought of remaining in the village once the warriors came back. Apart from her fear of Pontiac's return, she knew that the Delaware warriors would most likely have captive English soldiers with them. The defeated and frightened men would inevitably be made to run the gauntlet before becoming victims of ceremonial torture.

The women, including Maggie, had been working long hours to prepare for winter. They collected and cut cords of wood, hunted and trapped for food and hides, and spent an endless amount of time smoking the meat to dry it out for the winter food supply.

With the imminent arrival of the men, the work load increased with the preparations for the celebration and feasting that was sure to last many days. Maggie carried wood for the fires, swept away the ever-present dirt around the village and pounded an enormous amount of corn into fine meal for bread and soup. She slept soundly after the long days of work, but every waking thought worked toward a plan to escape.

Over the next couple of days, warriors began to trickle into the village. They were sent ahead by the larger parties to let the village know they were close. Maggie could feel the atmosphere around the village intensify as the anticipation increased.

The first of two larger groups of warriors arrived to a hero's welcome from the excited women. They returned with a couple of horses, a number of British muskets, a few heavily decorated grenadiers' mitre caps, a dozen or so red coats and an endless number of stretched and dried out scalps that were presented to the elders.

The second group reached the village just after dawn the next day and included Anne's husband. Maggie was up early gathering fire wood and immediately noticed that this group had several captives with them. A single glance showed that most of the poor prisoners were in bad shape, either from already having been tortured or from the long trek to the village.

Maggie was horrified by the sight of them and remained apart from the celebrating villagers, trying her hardest not to reveal her emotions. The half-naked English prisoners were dragged to the edge of the village, where most visitors were graciously greeted by the elders. None of the men raised their heads and their sobs and heart-wrenching pleas for mercy were ignored. Maggie could tell that some of them were mere boys, only a few years older than her eldest son.

Her heart wrenched when she saw the warriors begin to line up in two rows. She was appalled by the number of women who joined the line, including Anne. Maggie was disgusted by the villagers' actions and, though she knew she could do nothing to help the unfortunate captives escape their fate, she refused all attempts by the elders to persuade her to join the line.

Screeches and cries resonated through the small village as the men and women in the lines began to urge the first soldier to run the gauntlet. The noise drowned out the pitiful cries of the captives. Most could barely stand without assistance from their fellow mates, and most of their exposed skin was pitted with cuts and bruises already.

The first of the unfortunate young soldiers was obviously confused and frightened. The warriors in charge of the captives were furiously pointing at a far pole that sat several yards on the other side of the screaming villagers. It was clear the young man still had no idea what they wanted him to do, as tears streamed down his bruised face.

The ferocity of the villagers and their obvious hatred for these poor soldiers shocked Maggie. They were indeed savages. How could they find honor in beating captives that had already suffered unspeakable torture? The last few weeks of peace she had enjoyed were all but erased from her mind as she saw what these Delaware were really about.

The young man was violently pushed from behind by one of the warriors and directed towards the mouth of the awaiting gauntlet. Utter fear was etched in his face as he was shoved closer to the screaming villagers. Maggie wondered if the village had lost any men in the battle because the viciousness of this gauntlet stunned even her.

An impatient warrior shoved the young man forward again, forcing him to start his run wildly off balance. He did his best to deflect the relentless attacks, but the sheer volume of the well-directed strokes drove him to his knees. The unyielding beating from the heavy war clubs, upturned tomahawks and sharpened tree branches used as switches, bloodied him even more. Somehow the soldier managed to get back on his feet and stagger blindly to the pole. Beaten to a bloody pulp, he pulled himself to it and hugged it like it was his own mother. He soon collapsed in a heap of blood and sweat, barely keeping his hand on its base.

Maggie instinctively moved to assist him, but caught herself before making such a fatal error. To show them mercy would surrender the acceptance she had garnered to this point in the village and risk insulting the warriors. She could do nothing for the men but pray they would survive the first leg of their ordeal.

She looked at the three remaining soldiers who now knew what was in store for them. Their fear was visible as they stood defeated, awaiting their own turn at the gauntlet.

The next man up was a grenadier. His uniform was in tatters, but Maggie recognized it and imagined how impressive he must have looked before the battle. As he approached the starting point, an unexpected wave of determination crossed his face and Maggie found herself anticipating his run.

He was much taller than the others; in fact, he stood a good foot above the two warriors that tried to push him forward. The soldier reminded Maggie of her murdered friend, Daniel, who had inflicted more damage on the gauntlet participants than they had done to him.

This man had an injured thigh, which would possibly hinder his speed. Despite that, he confidently took in the scene before him. The same warrior who had unceremoniously shoved the first runner now grabbed the grenadier's arm to do the same thing. The defiant soldier wheeled around and pulled the stunned warrior's war club from his sash. Before the startled warrior could retrieve his club, the soldier brought it down with all his strength on the warrior's head. The force of the strike drove the club deep into the savage's skull and he fell instantly to the ground. The blood splashed on the grenadier's shoes and pooled on the surrounding ground.

Wrenching the club from the dead warrior's head, the grenadier turned his attention to the awaiting gauntlet. The villagers erupted in renewed shrieks and pounded their sticks and clubs furiously on the ground. The soldier rushed towards them, wielding the war club to fend off his attackers. The lines quickly engulfed him and Maggie could see him thrashing, hitting anything he could reach with the club.

It was a fruitless fight; he could not fend off the mass of tomahawks, clubs and sticks that drove him to the ground. Maggie knew the man had no interest in surviving this encounter just to endure further unknown tortures that he knew faced him.

The assault took less than a minute and resulted in several bloodied warriors, two seriously injured and one dead. The valiant grenadier had been scalped, mutilated and deposited at the feet of the two horrified remaining captives.

The villagers were clearly angered by the defiant actions of the grenadier and their rage was taken out on the remaining, defenseless prisoners. When it was all over, the three battered and bloody men, one of them still unconscious, laid collapsed in the dirt by the pole. They were surrounded, stripped of their remaining clothes and the conscious ones were paraded through the village. Spoiled food was thrown at them, dirt was rubbed in their wounds and boiling water was splashed on their exposed backs.

Finally, they were kicked into a small pen normally reserved for the livestock. The men collapsed into the mud and openly wept. They cried out for mercy from the villagers who ignored them and left to prepare for the feast. They cried and prayed as one lone guard stood by the pen to dissuade them from any attempts at escape.

Repulsed by the inhumane treatment of the prisoners, Maggie could barely watch as a few warriors dragged the unconscious soldier by one leg through the village and into the pen. When all their energy had been spent in their misery, the men huddled together in the filth to await a certain death.

Maggie did not know how she would ever be able to live out the rest of her life among people who could treat other human beings so callously while exhibiting so little remorse. She was sickened by Anne's participation in the degradation of her fellow English and her lack of repentance. It was true that women in Indian society were given a better social standing than in the English society, but at what cost?

The remainder of the day would be devoted to preparations for that evening's feast. The celebration itself would likely last for several days, as would the torture of the prisoners. With all the villagers preoccupied, it seemed the time to escape was at hand.

Apart from staying off the main trails in an effort to avoid the French or Canadians, Maggie didn't really have a plan. She figured that heading east would be a plausible idea. The thought of traveling through this vast wilderness without One-Ear was daunting and she thought about trying to head back to the village where she had last seen him. Her heart ached when she thought of him, unsure if he had died from his wounds or if he had recovered and searching for her this very moment.

Realistically, if One-Ear was out looking for her, he would most likely have headed west towards Ottawa territory, taking him hundreds of miles in the opposite direction from where she was.

She thought of Jacob, whose last knowledge of her whereabouts had her moving towards Quebec with a French merchant. Who knew where he was by now? If he had followed her to Canada, he too would be hundreds of miles from her. If he had signed on with the British, now routed by the French, he could even be dead.

Maggie swallowed the lump in her throat and avoided thinking about such things. She prayed for Jacob and her children and for both One-Ear and Joshua. She prayed for a miracle, that she might be rescued. Despite her faith in prayer, she decided that she could not wait much longer to act.

Taking herself out of the way of the busy villagers, Maggie made it appear that she was studiously collecting wood. She was actually scanning the woods for the best place to make a run for it. There was a short trail nearby that led to a small river, but it would certainly be more prudent to stay off a well-used trail like that. Deep in thought, she was caught off guard when Anne approached her.

"I have heard word about Pontiac and his Ottawa warriors. My husband, Running Cat, told me he had seen Pontiac and several French officers arguing over how to split up the goods taken from the English dead. Running Cat said that the Ottawa arrived after the battle was done, but they still expected to benefit from the great victory. He said Pontiac and his warriors left several days before the Delaware and were visibly upset. The rumor is that they were going straight back to Fort Detroit."

Maggie was very uncomfortable being anywhere near Anne after the scene at the gauntlet. Maggie responded cautiously, "That certainly leaves me in a rather vulnerable position. What will the Delaware do with me now?"

Anne was quick to respond, "You have nothing to be worried about. The Delaware are honorable people and they will most likely take you in as one of their own."

Maggie had nothing to say and just looked off into the center of the village as some of the returning warriors were preparing three large wooden stakes, with piles of freshly cut wood. They stacked up the wood almost four feet from the base and she had to look away, knowing what was going to happen a few hours from now.

Unable to hold her tongue, Maggie snapped, "Where is the honor in degrading these poor defenseless English boys?"

Anne immediately shot back to defend her adopted people, "The Delaware see the torturing of these soldiers as a way to honor them. It is the same treatment they would hope for if they were captured by the English. It appears awful to an Englishwoman who knows nothing of their society and simply looks at them as savages." She turned and walked away before Maggie could respond.

Maggie swallowed her pride and ran after the young woman. "Anne," she said, "I am sorry for my outburst. I do know that your life is good here and I am glad that you have been treated so well and accepted by these people."

Anne appeared to appreciate the apology, saying, "Maggie, I will never forget my past, but these people have been kind to me and I want to be part of their village. My life has been so much better than I could have expected, probably even better than if I was still in your world."

Maggie's disgust had still not ebbed, but she had something much more important on her mind and tried not to be confrontational, "Anne, how would it be viewed if I took food and water to the prisoners?"

"Let me speak with one of the elders and they will decide if you can."

Anne walked away and, to Maggie's surprise, returned a few minutes later with a plate of meat and a small deer-skin sack full of water. Maggie guessed that the meat was from a deer, but it had spoiled. She accepted the food and thanked Anne for her kindness.

"Would you like to accompany me and help see how the men are?" she asked the young woman.

Almost before she could finish, Anne replied, "I couldn't, even if I wanted to. My husband would never approve to such an act and I am not willing to take such a chance for them. They will be dead by…" Anne stopped herself before she finished her thought.

Maggie held her tongue and once again thanked her for her help.

While Anne returned to her duties, Maggie walked over to the muddy, reeking livestock pen and past the guard who seemed less concerned about the captives than about missing out on the feast that was being prepared. She held the plate in one hand and some old rags and the sack of water in the other.

The men were huddled together, covered in mud, excrement and refuse. As Maggie approached them, she said softly, "Gentlemen, I have brought you some food and water."

One of the pitiable men finally dragged himself towards Maggie. In a dry, crackled voice he said, "Ma'am, why are you here?"

Without answering, she smiled and handed a rag to the man before offering him the plate. He smiled slightly as he accepted both items. The other men immediately joined him and devoured the spoiled meat. All three of them appeared to be struggling to chew and swallow, but their ravenous hunger overcame their pain. She handed the first man the sack of water, which he took gratefully. She felt such sadness in her heart as she watched them consume what was probably their last meal.

"I wish it was more," she said softly.

"Thank you, ma'am; you are too kind," the soldier replied, as he struggled to swallow a mouthful of water.

After a horrible defeat in battle, forced to march through the wilderness and then run through the gauntlet, Maggie was impressed that they had any life left in them at all. She let them finish eating and handed rags to the other men.

Their spirits seemed to rise a bit after they finished eating and leaned against the fence. They were still in horrible condition, but her kindness had given them some comfort.

"How does a white Englishwoman, dressed like a savage, find herself here in this wilderness?" one of the men asked politely. He had cleaned off his face with the cloth and Maggie could finally see how young he was. She guessed he was no more than eighteen; without the bruises and cuts, she imagined he would be a very handsome young man.

"I was brought here as a captive of the Ottawa," Maggie replied and leaned down to help one of the men wipe off his face and neck.

She sat down by the fence next to the men and glanced towards the warrior guard before she continued. "Please tell me about what happened in the battle, this whole village has been talking about it for the past weeks."

The young man's face clouded with sadness as he took a deep breath and replied, "If you can imagine hell, it would not even be close to what happened. Sadly, even this place was so much better than what we faced. At least we know what we're up against here and what our fate will be. We were trapped like animals, taking fire from all sides; we could not even see the bloody enemy. Please excuse my language, ma'am, but it was pure hell. We had no place to go; all we could do was blindly fire into the wilderness, reload and fire again. It was something I would never wish on my worst of enemies."

Maggie said nothing. She could see the pain on his face and the others' as they slumped down and nodded their heads in agreement.

"They were faceless savages," he continued, "with their dreadful war cries echoing over the sounds of all the musket fire. You could hear them over all the confusion and the death; it was like fighting ghosts."

There was a long moment of silence as the men relived their excruciating memories. Finally, one of the other men mumbled just loudly enough for Maggie to hear, "They told us we couldn't lose."

"I'm sorry, gentlemen," Maggie said with tears in her eyes. "My intention was not to upset you."

Just then, the warrior guard approached Maggie and said, "You must leave now, woman."

"Give me one more minute," she said defiantly.

The warrior said nothing, but turned his back and moved back to his post.

"Unfortunately, I must leave you to your prayers," Maggie said as she rose and gathered the plate and water sack. She tried her hardest to fight off her tears, not wanting to upset the men further. There was nothing more she could do to ease their pain or their fear of what was to happen next. "God bless you all," she murmured.

The soldier who had done most of the talking looked up and said, "Thank you for your kindness, ma'am. If I may be so bold, what is your name?"

"My name is Maggie, Maggie Murray."

"Thank you, Maggie," He whispered and the other men nodded.

She walked away slowly, passing by the guard who watched her without speaking. She could not force herself to look back at the poor soldiers who deserved a much better fate.

The tears that filled her eyes spilled onto her cheeks and she quickly wiped them away with the remaining rags she carried. She was glad that none of the villagers were nearby to witness her deep despair. Most of them, she could see, had gathered at the center of the village to await the impending festivities.

When she had sufficiently pulled herself together, Maggie looked over the village. Many were already seated awaiting the feast. Others were milling about, listening to the warriors tell stories of the battle. With all the activity in the village and her own preoccupation with the captives, Maggie had missed the arrival of a contingent of French officers. They were accompanied by a handful of marines and were being treated like heroes by the village elders.

Maggie's eyes moved to a large fire pit where three wild beasts were roasting over the flames. The aroma from the burning coals and cooking meat was wonderful, despite the reason for their preparation. Maggie imagined that the breeze must have carried the aroma for miles through the woods.

The entire scenario made her relive the night that her friends were so viciously murdered by the Huron villagers. Even though she hadn't witnessed their torture and burning, she could never forget the aftermath. Burnt-out posts and the stench of burning flesh and hair were etched in her memory. A new wave of helplessness and fear for the young men held captive in the nearby livestock pen washed over her.

Maggie quickly returned to the spot where she and Anne had last spoken. It would soon be dusk and the feast would begin. Once darkness fell, she knew the first of the captives would be tortured. She couldn't remain here. She looked at the woods and took a deep breath. Before she could lift a foot to run, a voice startled her from behind.

"Madame, this is no place for a proper English woman."

Maggie spun to see the speaker and gasped in surprise, "Fredrick!"

"It has been some time since our last meeting, Madame," he said politely. "How have you been?"

It was Fredrick, the kind but dutiful French officer she had left bloodied and unconscious before escaping with One-Ear. Maggie was in such utter shock at seeing him right in front of her that she couldn't form any audible words.

As proper as ever, Fredrick bowed and tipped his hat to the stunned and silent Maggie. A wry smile that played over his lips betrayed his amusement at her reaction. Her brain struggled to find something to say that would sound neither too contrite nor too repentant for what she had done the last time they'd seen each other. She decided to ignore it and act nonchalant. "How have you been, Fredrick?"

"Just fine, Maggie," he said brusquely. "After I recovered from your surprise attack, I moved to the Fort at Niagara before leading a small company back to fortify Fort Duquesne. I was lucky enough to participate in our victory over the much larger English force just south of the fort. It appears we have been successful in driving the last of the British occupiers from our land, and I am here to congratulate our Delaware brothers."

"I am sorry for your injuries," Maggie said, matching his tone, "but I had made it abundantly clear that I had no intentions of going with you to Fort Niagara."

"Enough about the past," Fredrick said in a more cordial voice. "I must say you look very different from the last time we saw each other."

"I would rather dress as an English woman, yet, truth be told, it is rather comfortable," Maggie said with a smile, as she dusted off her dress to make herself somewhat more presentable.

"We must take more time to speak of your adventures another time, but now I think my men and I should depart. I fear my Delaware hosts have plans for their prisoners that we would rather not be party to. The warriors have already been at their captured English rum and I sense this will be a rather horrible night for the unfortunate prisoners."

Maggie looked to the villagers and saw that Fredrick was right. The feast had begun and the rum was flowing freely. It would only serve to extend the festivities and add to the frenzy. After their last encounter, Maggie was not in a position to ask for Fredrick's protection, nor was she certain she would accept it if it were offered.

This was not a scenario she had imagined when she thought about her options for the future. She had weighed the risks of remaining with the Delaware and of navigating the forest trails alone, but she had never thought of what would happen if she had been picked up by contingent of French soldiers.

"I agree with you," Maggie responded after a moment. "My plan is to return to my host's home and remain there until morning. It will be over by then, and things will return to normal." She spoke with an authority she did not possess. She knew that if she did remain, she would never be able to block out the sounds of the cheers and the screams.

"Madame, I would feel much better if you were to come with me," Fredrick said. "This village may not be safe for an unprotected English woman tonight; indeed, the festivities may last several days. You must leave this place immediately. My encampment is not very far from here and is just up the river a little way."

Maggie felt that this was an answer to her prayers, but she was still concerned by what would happen to her if she was once more in the hands of the French. "What are your plans once you leave here?" she asked. "I actually had no plan of staying here with these savages and was about to escape on my own before you arrived."

Fredrick seemed slightly entertained by her defiance and glanced towards the villagers to make sure their prolonged conversation had not garnered any unwanted attention. "I am heading north once again. First to the Fort at Niagara, then I will be leaving with a company of French Marines for Fort Carillon. The fort sits on the southern end of Lake Champlain in the province you English call New York."

Maggie's options were limited and common sense dictated that the most prudent course would be to accept Fredrick's generous offer. However, she remained cautious. The last time she had moved north to Niagara with this man, it had not ended well for him. She was concerned that his motives might not be entirely honorable. Wouldn't she be his prisoner once more?

"What are your plans for me once we reach Niagara?" she demanded.

"You have my word, Madame; you will be free to decide your own fate once we arrive."

"You have no intentions of completing your original mission to deliver me to the merchant?" Maggie immediately shot back.

He let out a quick laugh, but caught himself before the noise drew looks from the villagers. When he caught Maggie's look of puzzlement, he realized she had no idea of what had taken place.

"Madame, your merchant is dead. His luck ran out at the hands of some escaped English prisoner back at Fort Duquesne. You are property of no one unless the Ottawa chief decides you are too valuable to leave behind."

She was thrilled and relieved, but kept her happiness to herself. She realized that the English prisoner must have been her Jacob and was about to ask Fredrick for more details about the merchant's demise when an ear-shattering shriek caught them both off guard.

During the short time they had stood conversing, the Delaware warriors had opened another cask of rum. They had also prematurely begun the night's main attraction by dragging one of the young prisoners from their pen. The young man pleaded for mercy as he was dragged by the hair to the center of the village. The villagers kicked, punched and spat at the other men as they too were led to the posts to be secured.

"Madame," Fredrick said urgently, "I am ready to depart for our encampment immediately, with or without you." He motioned to his men who had moved away from the feast and stood near the trailhead, clearly ready to be on their way.

"I accept your offer of protection and pray that your word stands for something," she replied.

Fredrick appeared to be pleased by her decision and bowed his head, "Very well, Madame, please gather what you can carry and meet me back here as soon as possible. Would you like one of my men to accompany you?"

"I have very little, so I will only need a few short minutes," Maggie said and walked quickly to the home where she had lived since her arrival.

Before she made it to the doorstep, Anne approached her, calling, "Maggie, are you coming to the festival?"

Maggie jumped like an errant child caught misbehaving and scolded Anne to keep her voice down. She was close enough that Maggie grabbed her by the arm and pulled her behind a good-sized tool shed that stood next to her temporary home.

Frightened by Maggie's forceful reaction, Anne attempted to speak again, but her mouth was immediately covered up by Maggie's strong right hand before she could utter another word.

She leaned into the younger girl and whispered, "Please, Anne, let me explain. I am leaving, and if you were smart, you would come with me. I cannot believe that you would take any joy in watching these poor soldiers be tortured and murdered right before your eyes."

She relaxed her hand over the girl's mouth to let her reply and heard fury in Anne's voice as she said, "Let me go, or I will call for my husband and you will be punished for dishonoring my village…"

Maggie stopped her words once more with her hand. She didn't appreciate being threatened by this tiny, frail girl who had turned her back on her English roots.

Anne feebly attempted to free herself from Maggie's grip, but to no avail. Maggie knew that if she let Anne go now, her plans to leave with Fredrick would be thwarted.

Left with no choice, Maggie waited for another wave of cheers and screams to come from the crowd of villagers. When it came, she grabbed a fistful of Anne's blonde hair and drove her head into the shed's heavy wooden door.

Anne's body slumped to the ground, blood oozing from a large gash on her forehead. Maggie quickly deposited her on the cold, dirt floor of the shed. She took a cloth she wore around her neck and tore it in two pieces. She shoved one in Anne's mouth and used the other to secure her hands.

Satisfied that Anne would not be soon discovered or able to escape, Maggie slipped out of the shed and jammed one of the crude tools into the latch. She made a mad dash into the empty house and grabbed a small sack that held a few personal items. She also took a small knife that hung by the door and grabbed a musket that leaned against the fireplace.

Moving as hastily as she could without drawing attention from the villagers, she approached Fredrick and his men waiting at the head of the trail. She was relieved to see them, but didn't say a word as she passed them and headed up the trail. Fredrick shook his head and motioned his men forward.

Catching up to her in only a few long strides, Fredrick grabbed Maggie's arm and managed to slow her hectic pace. "What was that all about, Madame? One moment you were unsure you wanted to come with us and now suddenly you appear overly eager to depart. I must also mention that I noticed you have found a musket that I am certain you did not possess when you arrived at this village."

Maggie did not respond and Fredrick dropped her arm and his questioning.

Without looking back, Maggie mouthed a silent prayer for the unfortunate soldiers she was forced to leave behind. It was her most ardent hope that their ordeal would not last long, but she knew that the warriors would test their prisoners' strength and courage late into the night.

Chapter | **Five**

Jacob couldn't have been happier with the progress of the fort. The men were putting all their energy into completing as much as possible before winter descended and the snow forced them to wait until the spring thaw. Their spirits remained high and they basked in the accolades that poured in from the settlers.

The outer wall was now complete and secured, giving the men protection while they worked on the inner buildings. The carpenters had completed the frameworks for three of the inner buildings. The two larger structures would be the barracks and Tate had designed them to utilize the outer walls on the eastern and western sides as one of the four walls for each of the buildings. He did this to save time and resources, but utilized the positions by adding musket loopholes so the men could defend the eastern and western sides from the safety of the barracks.

The third building was smaller and would house the officers and a doctor. Jacob had kept Major Stevens informed of all that had taken place and requested that a doctor be dispatched to attend the fort during the winter. He also mentioned there was still no sign of the blacksmith. Luckily one of the men had apprenticed as a blacksmith a few years earlier; despite not having the proper tools, he managed to produce nails, hinges and other crude materials for the carpenters.

The men were content for the most part and put in long days of work without complaint. They ate heartily and were treated well and fairly by their commanding officer. Jacob had to smile the day a small relief force sent by Major Stevens arrived to replace those who were ill or injured. They came bearing much needed supplies like wool blankets and several huge cooking pots to help them get through the winter. Most of the men who were scheduled to depart were visibly upset at being forced to leave and take up winter quarters in possibly a much worse place. After great debate, Jacob decided that any of the sick or injured could stay if they so desired. To a man, none wanted to leave.

Joshua was also enjoying life at the fort. His wounded shoulder appeared to have healed completely, and he even spent a few days working with the carpenters lifting heavy timbers to support the main walls and massive main gates. Private White commented to Jacob that Joshua was a natural builder and very gifted with his hands. Jacob was very proud of the young man and relied on him often to lead hunting and scouting parties.

The days began to grow shorter, affording them less sunlight to work with. The air grew cooler and the winds coming down off the mountains began to pick up intensity and frequency. While their plans were right on schedule, the pressure was on to make sure they had all the major buildings built and food stores complete before the first snow arrived.

To stay warm, the men cut some of the blankets up to make coats. A number of the female settlers did a good job sewing them to make them much more functional and comfortable. Joshua and his scouts had provided enough pelts from the animals they had hunted that the men made fur hats and heavy blankets to keep them warm at night, or when they were on picket duty.

It was the third week in October and the Indian attacks on the nearby settlements had not plagued the area since the fort was started. The fort itself had become a focal point for the settlers and they appreciated that Jacob and his men were there to defend their land.

After Jacob's brief encounter with the large Delaware war party, most of the expanded pickets reported no signs of the same group. Every few days, large hunting parties were sent out to build up the winter stores. Several of these groups saw signs of small Indian scouting parties. One sentry reported seeing a good-sized war party lurking in the deep woods behind the eastern wall, but a patrol that was sent out found no sign of it.

With this fort nearly completed, the men were excited by the prospect of expanding their defenses against the French and building another in the spring. Jacob decided that instead of beginning a new fort, they would head east to assist in building the line of forts being built just to the west of the Susquehanna. There were a couple of small settlements along the way whose defenses could be built up with simple stockades to provide some defense for the more isolated settlers.

Jacob sent patrols deeper into the wilderness and it was reported back to him that there was a large Delaware village called Kittanning within a few days' hike. He was told that the village chief, nicknamed Captain Jacobs, was out to burn as many English settlements as possible before the snow got too deep. While it appeared that this war-minded savage had either not yet reached the area surrounding the fort, or was intentionally avoiding it, reports from his patrols contained details of burned homesteads and murdered families.

Jacob ordered more men to be added to each patrol and hunting party for additional security. He also sent additional patrols to alert the nearby settlers of the attacks. He wasn't certain if he had ever seen Kittanning in his own travels, but now that he knew it was where the main body of Delaware lived, he decided it would be important to find out more about it.

The first snow arrived one morning and blanketed the ground with a foot of heavy, wet snow. While the men cleared as much of it from the interior of the fort as they could, a surprise visitor arrived.

Private White had noticed the approach of several horsemen and a small wagon, and moved to meet them at the gate. They made surprisingly quick progress through the fresh snow, owing to a skilled driver and a large pack horse that seemed to pull his load with ease. When they dismounted, White handed the reins to some of the waiting militiamen and escorted a cold Major Stevens directly to Jacob.

When Jacob saw Stevens, he excused himself from a conversation with some of the engineers. He saluted then smiled and extended his hand, saying, "Sir, it is good to see you in this part of the territory. What do you think of our little piece of paradise?"

The answer was already clear from the look on Stevens' face. "I must say, I am impressed at what you have been able to accomplish in such a short time, especially without a blacksmith."

"Thank you, sir. We did have one man covering as much of the blacksmithing duties as he could manage. All of the men have worked long days and done a first rate job. The engineers and their crew certainly deserve much of the praise for where we stand today."

Jacob asked Private White to take the other horsemen to get some food and a fire, and then guided the major indoors where he could warm himself by the fire in the officers' quarters. When they were settled, Stevens said, "Well, I'm glad to hear that you've managed without a proper blacksmith until now, but I happen to have one with me. He should have arrived a while ago, but he was caught up with other business. We brought all of his supplies by wagon."

"That is certainly good news, sir," Jacob said excitedly. "We still have plenty to keep him busy, and I'm sure the settlers will enjoy having him here. Now, how have you been keeping? I thought you were still in Maryland."

"Frankly, the work there is not going as well as yours is here, Sims," Stevens responded. "Work on the stone fort has been quite a chore, to say the least. The quality of the men I have been able to recruit is certainly not anywhere near what you have in your ranks."

After a brief silence, Stevens continued, "Have you encountered the French or any of their savage allies? I have heard rumors about a Delaware chief called Captain Jacobs, plaguing the poor settlers in these parts. What do you know about this character?"

"We have seen the Delaware around," Jacob replied. "They did show themselves a few weeks back, but they appear to be more curious than anything. I have sent out regular scouting parties and increased our pickets. Except for the odd sighting, they have left us to continue our work here. The Delaware you asked about lives in a settlement called Kittanning and he is the main leader of the Delaware here in the Pennsylvania territory."

"Do you have anything planned for the northern region?" Stevens asked.

"What do you want me to do, sir?" Jacob asked, wondering why Stevens would feel there was a need to push deeper into French-held territory and stretch out an already thinned out defenses.

"You have this place in good order, and I feel that you would be best to judge what you should do next in this territory," was the major's candid reply. "With winter on our doorstep, I imagine you would do best to keep building up this place and venture out once spring hits."

"Well, we have worked very hard to contact as many of the settlers in the region as possible," Jacob explained. "Most wish to remain on their homesteads over the winter, and I have asked several with larger homes to allow some of the men to quarter with them to offer them more protection. There is a German settlement nearby where the farms are situated very close together. I have dispatched fifty of the men, including a dozen laborers, to build a blockhouse where the settlers can go in case of an attack."

After a slight nod from Stevens, Jacob continued, "In the spring, I thought about sending men to see if the forts being built near the Susquehanna need some extra hands. In the meantime, though, I was considering leading a scouting party to see for myself what this Delaware settlement at Kittanning is all about, and find this Captain Jacobs fellow. It sits about forty miles northeast of Fort Duquesne; I might consider a winter attack, just to let these savages know we are here."

"Sounds like a well thought out plan," Stevens said. "You obviously have everything in order. I forgot to mention that another company of men will be arriving in a few days. They are at your disposal. I think most of them are the recovered ill and injured from Fort Cumberland."

"Good sir," Jacob said, with pleasure in his voice. "The more hands the better. Winter will be here in full force sooner rather than later, and the extra help will be welcomed by the others."

Stevens smiled as he stood and said, "I knew you'd be happy. If you'll forgive me, I must be going now. The men will also be transporting some additional supplies for the winter. If I were you, I would send out an escort to make sure the men arrive safely. Wilderness like this has been known to devour an entire army."

Jacob was surprised that Stevens was not going to stay longer, but he appeared to be eager to keep moving, despite the snow. "Sir," Jacob said, "I had hoped you would stay a few days and let your men rest. Isn't the snow tough on your horses?"

"Funny thing, Sims, the only snow we encountered was here. We have not seen a snow flake in Maryland or most of southern Pennsylvania. As for the horses, they are good animals and are treated well by the men. To be honest, I am afraid if we don't leave soon I might be trapped here until the snow stops. No offense, but I would much rather be in Maryland." Stevens smiled and put on his hat and coat.

"There's just one more thing, Sims. Your old friend Private Taylor is amongst the company set to arrive. Do your best to be kind to him, unless circumstances warrant otherwise."

If Stevens was looking for a reaction from Jacob in regards to Taylor, he was disappointed. Jacob politely saluted his major and said, "Godspeed, sir."

Stevens returned the salute and departed towards the south alongside his horsemen.

Jacob stood alone and watched the men ride away, struggling through the calf-high snow as their horses forced their way along the trail.

"Damn," he murmured under his breath.

He summoned White, Sinclair and Joshua to meet with him in the officers' quarters to give them an update. While he waited for them to arrive, he stared at the fire and did his best to hide his emotions regarding Taylor's arrival.

Jacob was in no mood to talk, but needed to prepare the men for the potential problems Taylor could create. The three men arrived at once and politely greeted Jacob, who continued to stare at the fire.

"Gentlemen," he began, "I just had an interesting conversation with our Major Stevens. The first piece of good news is that our blacksmith has finally arrived."

The men were clearly excited and after a moment or two, Jacob raised a hand to silence them.

"I was also told to expect another company of men and supplies for the winter," Jacob said. He paused to choose his next words carefully.

"What is it, sir?" White piped up. "If there is good news, there must be bad as well, right?"

"Aye, Private Taylor is numbered among the new men," Jacob blurted out.

The three men sat in silence, but Jacob saw his own feelings reflected in their faces.

"We can't do much now," Jacob continued, "although we will all have to control his influence over the others. I would assume that Taylor has already infected this new company of men with his own brand of lies and rotten ways. We should keep the new men separated from our current men until we are certain who the trouble makers will be."

He had little appetite to talk further about Taylor and dismissed the men. He knew they felt the same and was encouraged that whatever influence the bugger had over the men would be extinguished quickly. Jacob had noticed Joshua's face after he heard the news and being the only other soul that knew of Jacob's actions against Braddock, he prayed the lad wouldn't do anything foolish to silence Taylor.

The blacksmith hailed from one of the Dutch settlements in the southeast and was instantly popular with the men and settlers alike. A forge was quickly set up for him and he was kept very busy filling the needs of the fort and frontier families.

When word soon got out that he was a gunsmith as well, the fire in his forge stayed lit long into each night. The men liked having the smithy around, especially to work on their muskets and to keep them well supplied with lead bullets and smaller grapeshot. He also rifled several muskets to be used by the more experienced men. He told them he had done it on a few occasions for some of the German settlers who were happy with the results.

The work was tough and involved dismantling the barrel from the existing musket and putting small ridges inside the barrel to force the lead ball to rotate. The rotation increased the distance and accuracy of the weapon. Some of the men found it harder and longer to load but Jacob knew with the added distance of around two hundred paces, a man could reload and get another shot off well before the enemy could get close enough to use their short ranged muskets. The accuracy of a rifled musket made hunting much easier as well, particularly against a moving target. Jacob usually preferred a long rifle, but he felt safer amid an unseen enemy with a weapon that allowed such range.

Jacob also asked the blacksmith if he could construct wall guns to be placed in the bastions. Neither he nor the blacksmith had ever actually seen or fired a wall gun, but two of Jacob's men had served at English-held forts in the Carolinas. They did their best to draw some rough pictures to give the smithy a basic idea of what Jacob was requesting. The best way they could describe one was to compare it to a regular musket, only several times larger. It was fired by two men and could be fitted on one of the high walls with the addition of a few braces. The ball they shot was as big as a man's closed fist. The way the men described their effectiveness gave Jacob some hope that the fort could hold off an attack from a large French force or Delaware war party.

It had been several days since Stevens' visit and Jacob had waited to organize a full escort for the new company of men until they were closer to the fort. Light snow continued to fall intermittently, and he sent out regular scouting parties to cover the trail to report the first sign of them.

The expected arrival date of the reinforcements came and went. One of the scouting parties reported that there was no trace of the men, but got word a Delaware raiding party had attacked a small farm only a few miles south of the trail.

The continued presence of the Delaware in the area was strange. Jacob had expected them to leave for their winter hunting grounds in the south before the snow started. Their decision to remain in the north to raid and fight kept Jacob's men on edge.

Jacob was concerned, not only for the fate of the men who were missing, but for the men at the fort who were surrounded by an unseen foe. He called together White, Sinclair, Tate and a man named Weathers, who was Tate's right-hand. They met to discuss their options.

"Gentlemen," Jacob began, "We need to send out a small party of soldiers to look for the company of men that should have arrived already. I assume you are all aware of the news of continuing Delaware raids in the region? It does appear that the winter will not stop their attacks; therefore, we must be diligent in our scouting and defense of this area."

Private White, as usual, was the first to comment, "I do not doubt the need for an organized search party; I am just concerned by the weather. Except for the storm a while back, the snow has not been very heavy or very deep, but that could change quickly. Losing one company of men is bad enough, but for another to be stranded while searching for them worries me. Whatever we decide, our actions must be carried out immediately."

All the men seemed to be in favor of some action and Tate politely added, "Sir, my concern lies in weakening our numbers. We have already sent fifty men, plus a dozen of my laborers to build a blockhouse in that German settlement, they will most likely not return until spring. We have large hunting parties going out regularly, in addition to scouts. I cannot help worrying that we might just be inviting an attack from the bloody savages. Maybe they are using our missing company just to draw most of the garrison out into the open. These devils will do just about anything to weaken our garrison at the fort."

Jacob respected Tate and his opinions. For a non–military man, he certainly ran a tight ship and his men were extremely disciplined. Nodding his head, Jacob said, "Good point, Mr. Tate. We must consider all scenarios and it is a definite possibility that the Delaware are purposely drawing out as many men as they can from the fort's defenses. If they strike when it is undermanned, all this hard work will have been for not."

Usually not a very vocal contributor in these group settings, Private Sinclair piped up, "I know we all have concerns about sending out a search party, but I don't really see that we have a choice. Something may have befallen them, but they may also simply be lost in this overgrown and unfamiliar wilderness. Whatever has happened, I'm sure we are in agreement that if we were in need we would all hope for and expect the same consideration from those who were in a position to offer help."

Jacob stood back and rubbed his eyes. Faced with the dangers they had spoken of at this meeting, he would rather be dealing with Private Taylor's bad behavior in the safety of the fort right now. Realistically, though, what options did he really have? Sinclair was correct in pointing out that they would all expect the same help and consideration from any nearby English settlement.

"Thank you, gentlemen," Jacob said after a moment. "It is clear we need to send out a search party immediately. I will take twenty-five men down the southern trail just short of the Fort Duquesne area. White, Sinclair, you will remain behind and keep the men ready for a possible attack. Tighten up the pickets and extend the patrols within five miles of the camp. We will also move all the men inside the walls; no more tents out in the field. It will mean tight quarters, but at the moment, we must be prudent in our resolve."

Jacob could see that Private White was about to object, so he added, "Please respect my decision. I know this country like the back of my hand, and you men are far more valuable here."

It took Jacob less than an hour to get his hand-picked patrol ready. They were to bring the bare minimum of equipment, only carrying what Jacob deemed necessary. That meant no packs, blankets and only a days' worth of provisions. He wanted to move very quickly and not to be weighed down. Jacob picked the more experienced woodsmen and most of the best shots in the company.

Both White and Sinclair stood waiting at the gate as Jacob arrived carrying only his newly rifled musket, a powder horn and a small shot pouch. Joshua had just returned with a hunting party and Jacob spoke briefly with the three of them, "I would prefer if you did not send out any more hunters at this time. I think our stores are plentiful enough to skip a couple of days' hunt. I expect to arrive back here by nightfall tomorrow. If for whatever reason we do not return, do not send out any more men after us. Secure the fort and prepare for the possibility of a Delaware attack. Tate may be right; they may just be trying to empty the fort to weaken us for an attack."

The men saluted Jacob who saluted in return and thanked them. His patrol had arrived at the gate and he led them into the darkness of the nearby woods. He sent three scouts ahead to alert them if they spotted the enemy.

Less than a mile from the fortification, signs of the Delaware were all around them. Symbols carved into a number of tree trunks and obviously well-used side paths that were flattened by a large number of moccasins.

Despite so many warnings of their presence, they had yet to see any of the Delaware themselves. At every blind curve in the trail, the men slowed down and advanced in small groups of four to five to secure the trail a step at a time.

They saw no signs of the missing company of men, and Jacob wondered at what point on the trail they had gone missing. He had an odd feeling in the pit of his stomach that said they were walking themselves into an ambush. He felt they had been observed from the moment they left the security of the fort.

After several hours' advance, Jacob stopped the men and recalled the scouts. A large swampy area that had yet to freeze stood to their left and a rocky hill inclined sharply to the right. Jacob decided that this might be a good time to stop for a while and re-evaluate the situation. The men took up a defensive position and tried to get some rest.

The scouts had reported continued evidence of the Delaware, but no sightings of the savages. Jacob was sure they were nearby, but obviously remained well-hidden. He had to decide whether to return to the relative safety of the fortification or continue their course and move deeper into Delaware territory. The chances of running into a war party increased the farther they moved away from the fort. He was also wary of the thought that the Delaware might just be drawing them further into the wilderness to either ambush his party or launch an attack on the undermanned fort.

After allowing the men to rest for a couple hours, Jacob divided them into two smaller groups of thirteen men. The smaller groups would be able to move more swiftly, particularly around tight curves that required so much caution.

His group would continue west while the other would take an old Seneca trading path back towards the fort. His hope was that in using the other trail, the second unit might manage to flush some of the Delaware out into the open where they could be dealt with.

Jacob asked Private James, an experienced ranger and someone Jacob trusted, to lead the second unit. He was a Pennsylvanian and knew this area better than even Jacob. He ordered James to inform White and Sinclair of Jacob's plan and keep the fort on high alert.

Without waiting for discussion, Jacob moved his unit to the west and watched the rest of the men turn east. He sent two of his men to scout ahead of them on the trail and report back.

The men moved cautiously, and their hesitation was clearly visible to Jacob. He did not want to push them faster than they were comfortable, but at every turn, they slowed to a crawl. He grew concerned by their pace and felt they would never cover enough ground to find any sign of the missing company before they had to return to the fort. Despite his forward scouts, Jacob felt blind.

Even though there had already been some snowfall, it was still only late autumn and the thousands of leaves that continued to fall in a storm of yellow, red, and orange, made footing treacherous and aided in covering any tracks left by the Delaware.

Frustrated and tired, Jacob decided to stop and make camp for the night. Their mission seemed fruitless. He feared all it would accomplish would be the death of more of his men. He decided that they would head back as soon the sun broke through the canopy the next morning. The return trek would be just as difficult and he wanted the men to be well-rested. They were also on the last of their rations and all of the men, including Jacob, wanted to get back and have a proper meal.

He stopped the men and quietly informed them of the new plan. "We will be stopping soon for the night, but I need a volunteer to move forward with me to find a suitable place for camp and alert the forward scouts that we will be stopping."

A ranger named Collins stepped forward and Jacob told the men that he would return soon. He ordered them to continue moving forward until they reunited and reminded them to move in a single file.

"The Delaware are out there," Jacob said over his shoulder, "so don't give them any reason to ambush you or make it easy for them."

Jacob ran quickly with Collins on his heels. They dodged exposed roots as best they could, despite the slippery carpet of leaves. It was almost as difficult as maintaining footing on an icy lake in the middle of winter. They soon slowed as Jacob pointed towards higher ground to their right flank.

"I think we should work our way towards the high ridge," Jacob said. "Setting up camp on elevated terrain will permit us to keep an eye on the trail overnight."

Collins nodded and said, "Lead the way, sir."

Using the barrel of his musket to push limbs away from his face, Jacob led Collins up a steep slope, which leveled at the top to form a nice, flat ridge. The summit offered an unobstructed view of the surrounding mountains.

"If it wasn't so bloody dangerous, a person could learn to love this place," Jacob quipped.

No sooner had the words left his mouth when his sentiment was abruptly confirmed. Musket fire shattered the stillness and Jacob feared for his men. Collins was still by his side and Jacob quietly pointed along the ridge and said, "Follow me; we'll keep above the trail to find out what is going on. I pray the lads haven't been ambushed."

As they scrambled over a number of boulders and half-buried rocks, the echoes of more musket fire reverberated up from the lower trail. Jacob could see a white cloud of smoke rising above the canopy and the acrid smell of burnt gunpowder warned them they were close to the fighting.

Their view was obstructed by a clump of trees that still maintained a great deal of foliage. "We need to get down there and see what the hell is going on," Jacob said quietly.

They slid part way down the steep embankment, using the trees to brace them. As they grew closer to the action, they could hear shouts and yelps from both sides amid the wild exchange of musket fire. The two men reached flatter ground near a cluster of small trees, just to the side of the trail.

From this vantage point, Jacob could see his men positioned ahead of him on the trail, facing northward. They had found cover and split themselves into two groups, one on either side of the trail. Jacob could not see who was firing at them and realized that his men were simply firing blindly ahead of them in hopes of holding back their still unseen enemy.

The screams and deafening war cries exposed the enemy as the Delaware, who had finally decided to make their presence known.

Jacob whispered to Collins, "I fear if we attempt to join the men, we most likely will be cut down before we reach them. The trail is fairly open, and we would have to run without cover to get to them."

Collins hesitated then suggested, "What if we crossed the trail here and moved through the woods to try to get behind the Delaware? The ground is flatter over there and we could cover more territory."

Jacob nodded, took a deep breath and sprinted across the open trail. Collins was right behind him, and the two men kept running straight into the woods until they reached a line of thick brush that ran parallel to the trail. They crouched behind it to catch their breath and get their bearings. They quickly realized that there was a convenient, natural cut pathway behind the brush that allowed them a smooth surface to run while the thick growth screened their movements.

They used the sound of the musket fire to gauge their location and were able to tell when they had drawn up even with the trapped men. Jacob and Collins slowed their pace, but continued forward to try to come up behind the Delaware. As they grew closer to the attackers' gunfire, they were able to estimate that there were only about fifteen savages firing shots. Jacob thought it might have been a hunting party that had run into his men by accident. He and Collins were outnumbered, but Jacob hoped that if they could surprise the Delaware, they might be able to force them to retreat.

When he was confident they had passed the line of Delaware and might be able to turn onto the trail behind them, Jacob approached the trail to assess their situation. He stood behind a thick tree and scanned the opposite side of the trail. He thought he had seen some movement, but was not sure.

He saw no signs of Delaware beyond those that were firing on his men. Just as he was about to give the signal to Collins to open fire on the rear of the hunting party, Jacob saw a flash of color nearby and said, "Damn, we're all dead."

In the very same moment, Jacob and Collins were set upon by several hideously painted warriors. They had no time to so much as raise their weapons and decided to keep their scalps over risking their lives.

Jacob put his head down and dropped his weapon in hopes that the warriors would not kill him immediately. Two of the savages pushed him to the ground and kicked him in the ribs.

Collins had also dropped his weapon, but fared far worse than Jacob. Two other Delaware warriors grabbed him by the arms while a third drove a spiked club into his temple. Without a sound, the young ranger slumped to the ground near Jacob who instinctively reached out to him. The club-wielding savage stomped on his hand just before Jacob instinctively pulled it back.

The warriors laughed and Jacob saw a pool of blood seep from Collins' head as he went stiff. The young man was quickly scalped while Jacob was held down by two of the warriors as the rest moved in on his men to complete their attack.

Jacob's face was flattened into the dirt and he was unable to call out a warning to his men. One of the Delaware stood over him with a foot pushed into his lower back. The ground vibrated and he could hear an explosive volley of shots from the warriors. Unable to move, Jacob was forced to listen to the sounds of the short-lived battle. The chilling screams of his men and savage war cries of the Delaware punctuated the crescendo of gunfire for a few minutes before the forest was plunged into an ungodly silence.

Unable to process what had just taken place, Jacob was pulled up by his arms and a thick leather line was immediately secured around his hands and neck. One of the warriors tugged hard on the line to make sure it was tight then pulled Jacob towards the scene of the attack. The savages had made quick work of his men. They had already been scalped and stripped of their belongings.

Jacob now had a much better view of the impressive number of Delaware involved in the attack. He was pulled towards a small group of warriors who stood observing the effects of their attack. The obvious leader of the group dismissed the others when he saw Jacob approach.

Jacob attempted to put up a fight as he was pulled along by the tight line. The two warriors who escorted him soon pinned his already secured arms behind him and he prayed that he could just loosen them enough to fight on more equal terms. As he continued to squirm, one of his escorts tripped him and he landed at the feet of the leader.

He remained still and refused to give the Delaware any satisfaction that he was injured from their mistreatment. His face was callously pressed into the dirt by one of his captor's feet. He was then pulled to his knees and the handle of a tomahawk was shoved under his chin to force him to lift his eyes towards the Delaware leader.

The chief was very short. Even on his knees, Jacob was almost face to face with him. The savage stood proudly with several fresh scalps in his hand, blood dripping on the ground in front of Jacob.

Jacob showed no emotions, just staring into the Delaware leader's soot-blackened face. He had silver piercings in both ears and his head was shaved in the front. He looked familiar and Jacob struggled to recall where he had seen him before. The man was clad in a green coat that had been stripped off of one of the unfortunate rangers. It was obviously too large for such a diminutive man, and the sleeves hung well over his hands. Under different circumstances, Jacob would have laughed at his absurd appearance.

"This is what is left of your men," the savage boasted, holding up the bloody scalps. "The same can be said of the other men you sent back to the tiny walled village you have been so busy building to keep us out."

The rest of the warriors stood around watching the exchange between their leader and the white prisoner. They laughed at the description of the fort.

"Do you like my new coat?" the leader taunted Jacob, who continued to resist the bait. The chief's tone grew hard and he threw the scalps to the ground, grinding them into the dirt with his foot as he said, "I care little that my French fathers will pay me with furs or rum. I kill you English to rid you from our lands and I need no promise of trinkets or drink to tempt me."

Jacob still remained silent and his defiance earned him a well-placed punch to the ribs from the warrior firmly holding the leather lead.

The leader laughed and continued his one-sided conversation, "I am Chief Tewea of the Lenape people. I hear I am known to you English as Captain Jacobs."

Jacob still refused to answer the man, but instantly realized where he had seen him before. Captain Jacobs had been one of the leaders of the war party that had approached the fort a while back when Jacob had stood alone in the meadow and shot one of their warriors.

His defiance infuriated the chief and made him explode into a verbal rampage. "Did you locate the large group of soldiers sent to you from the south? No, of course you did not. We harvested bushels of English scalps and captured many prisoners. Some were lucky enough to be given away as slaves to Delaware warriors across our lands."

Captain Jacobs had finally struck a nerve, but before Jacob could respond, the chief waved the two warriors to take Jacob away. Just before he was out of reach, though, the chief grabbed Jacob's right arm and jerked him forward so they were face to face.

With an ugly grin, the little man said, "I will enjoy watching you die, but first you will be a witness to all that I do to your English settlers. I have made a promise to my people that I will burn every English settlement built on our lands. You will have the opportunity to see your men die at my hand."

As Jacob was once again pulled away, he thought of Joshua back at the fort. The image of a burning fort and his men dying at the hands of these savages ate at his very core.

It seemed like a lifetime since the last time he had been dragged along wooded trails by savage warriors. He remembered the trip to Fort Duquesne at the hands of the Huron. This time, it was different; Joshua was not with him and the warriors in charge of him certainly did not have his best interest in mind. He was pulled so violently that the leather ties began to cut deeply into his skin and after a few miles his shirt sleeves were stained to the elbow with his own blood.

They followed the same trail Jacob's men had traveled earlier in the day. The sky grew darker, but the warriors simply lit torches to light their path. They had no reason to fear an attack and didn't care that the lights made them visible for miles.

Jacob had been under the impression that Captain Jacobs intended to attack the fort immediately, so he had been surprised and confused when they turned off the main trail and began moving slightly northwest away from the fort. He assumed that it must have been the lateness of the season and the promise of snow that convinced the chief to return to the safety of his village and wait for a more opportune time to attack the fort.

Jacob was fatigued and cramps in his legs shot violent streaks of pain down to his feet making every step excruciating. The few times they stopped, he could barely manage to stand on his own. Sadly, if it had not been for the warriors holding onto the line, he would have collapsed.

The number of warriors seemed to increase at every turn, and Jacob watched the oddly impressive Captain Jacobs divide them into four separate, far more manageable units to cover more ground. Despite the fact that they had little reason to fear an attack, the chief employed a defensive formation. Two units had been sent well ahead to scout and finally prepare camp for the night. The main body fanned out into a half-moon formation, ensuring that they would not be ambushed or overtaken by the enemy. He also kept another unit behind him so nothing could flank him or surprise them from the rear.

As the war party continued its trek to the north, Jacob lost all track of time. He was not certain if he had been on the march for one or two whole days already. His exhaustion was both physical and mental. His concern for the men at the fort consumed his mind. His body was weary from remaining on his feet. With the exception of the moments he had spent pinned to the ground or kneeling at eye level with Captain Jacobs, Jacob had been forced to stay on his feet. He had been dragged across miles of wilderness, swamps and rocky terrain and whenever they did stop to rest or make camp, he was forced to remain upright to sleep.

When they stopped, the escorts would tie him to a tree about the width of his back. They positioned him with his back against the tree and his arms and legs wrapped backward around the trunk. This pushed his chest and stomach forward and put a great deal of pressure on his hips and shoulders. Every tiny movement he made shot streaks of pain throughout his body. They even placed a much thicker piece of hard leather around his neck to keep his head up. He was always positioned facing away from the rest of the men, so he could only hear them eat and celebrate.

He would have preferred death alongside his men to this inhumane treatment. Left alive, he was ironically the most unfortunate of them all. His stomach ached from the pain of being empty. He had not had anything to eat or drink since he had left the fort. His captors' cruelty reached new heights when at camp the second night, they killed an adult buck and roasted it over an open fire a few steps from where he had been positioned. As great as his hunger was, he'd have traded the entire deer for a tiny sip of water. His lips were parched and the smoke pouring off of the fire pit blew all around him, dehydrating him even more.

His shoulders ached, his legs had lost nearly all feeling, and he could not move his neck enough to relieve any pain that crept down his spine. Stomach spasms from intense hunger led to dry heaves, which resulted in more pain as his body jerked uncontrollably.

Jacob was already in a great deal of agony, but the night was only getting started. He could hear the warriors celebrating their victory by sharing a cask of rum. The putrid scent of the liquor wafted amid the aroma of the deer. Left in such a vulnerable position, Jacob prayed fervently that the men would be content with the deer and rum and not choose to make their lone prisoner a part of the celebration.

He was not so fortunate, though; his luck had run out the moment he left the fort. Just as his weary body was about to lose consciousness, his two escorts staggered over to check on his straps. Tugging hard on his already cut and pounding wrists, they appeared to be satisfied Jacob would not be going anywhere. He prayed that they were done, but they decided that they wanted to have some fun with their vulnerable captive.

Jacob could not see exactly what they were up to, yet he heard both men pull their knives from their sheaths. One warrior walked away while the other stood directly in front of him. With one quick move, the warrior ripped Jacob's shirt down the middle and exposed his chest. The other warrior soon returned with two red hot scalping knives in his hand and Jacob understood what they had planned for him.

They tauntingly waved the knives in front of Jacob's face and began to slowly run them over Jacob's skin, slicing thin lines across his chest and stomach. The scalding heat coupled with the cuts to his skin made him naturally flinch, yet he refused to scream out.

A number of the other warriors gathered around, curious to see what they were doing with the prisoner. Jacob smirked weakly, knowing that the men would be embarrassed by his defiance in front of their fellow warriors. It was not perhaps the best idea to provoke them in this manner, but Jacob refused to let them be victorious as long as he could help it.

Fueled by rum and the laughter of their fellow warriors, the two men ran to reheat their knives. While they were busy with their weapons, a couple of the onlookers decided it would be amusing to rub Jacob's chest with dirt, just to open up the small cuts a bit more. Another clearly drunk savage splashed a cup of rum at him, but most of it just spilled onto the ground. This infuriated several of the others and they began pummeling the warrior for wasting their prized drink.

As the two frustrated warriors returned with their newly heated knives, they were abruptly stopped by their chief. Jacob could see that he appeared to be upset at the men and the now dispersed group of onlookers. Jacob was wavering on the edge of unconsciousness from the pain, but was alert enough to hear Captain Jacobs push several of the warriors out of his way and take up a position in front of his prisoner.

"Get back to your food and drink," he screamed. "This man will be saved until we reach our village. No Lenape will touch him unless they want to challenge my authority."

The anger in the chief's voice was clear and all the warriors departed quickly, not wanting to risk insulting their leader. The two warriors who had initiated the scene simply followed the others and stuck their hot knives into the ground beside where they sat.

Captain Jacobs moved his head close to Jacob's ear and said, "Don't die on me, Englishman. You will be my prized guest when we reach my village. I had planned to burn your fort, but winter grows near and we must return home. You will face a most honorable death that will match your bravery."

Jacob made no response and the chief walked away.

One good thing had come from this episode, and that was the confirmation that they were indeed going to bypass the fort and head north. It gave Jacob some solace that his suffering was worth it. If he could keep the Delaware busy and they didn't venture out on their raids until next spring, the men at the fort would have the time to complete their work and build up the defenses.

The night grew colder and the bloodied, starving Jacob fell in and out of consciousness. Most of the warriors had fallen asleep and, though he was facing away from the camp, Jacob could hear a few men moving around to keep the fire going and patrol the edges of the camp.

Jacob was alert before most of the camp arose the next morning. He wondered where exactly they were and where they were headed. He figured they were either going to Logg's Town or the main Delaware village at Kittanning.

Several warriors left immediately at sunrise to scout well ahead of the main party. Jacob was finally cut down from the tree, but his legs were unable to support him and he fell to his knees. His two escorts laughed as he struggled to get to his feet. Uninterested in his comfort, they jerked him up by his armpits and supported him until he could barely walk. Before he was completely steady, they bound his hands once again. They didn't bother to tie a line to his neck and he could only figure that they didn't feel they were in any danger of having him escape.

The three men quickly fell in line with the main column, despite Jacob's clear struggle to take more than a few steps in a row. Only after they covered a good half mile did the full feeling return to both legs and Jacob was able to keep pace with his escorts.

After an hour or two on the trail, one of the warriors mercifully handed the severely weakened prisoner a few rotting chestnuts and a handful of mushy, over-ripened wild raspberries. Starving as he was, Jacob would have eaten dirt; he quickly swallowed the whole soggy mess. The food burned the entire way down his parched throat and instead of easing the pain in his stomach, he felt instantly queasy. Just as he thought the sensation had passed, his stomach lurched and heaved the food back up with a vengeance.

The two warriors by his side were taken by surprise as Jacob spit the acidic contents of his stomach all over their leggings and moccasins. They shrieked in disgust and despite his discomfort and continued dry heaves, Jacob found amusement in the sight of the warriors frantically rubbing leaves on their leggings to wipe off the harsh smelling liquid.

Out of the corner of his eye, he saw that the men had drawn their war clubs. They wildly rushed at Jacob as he drew himself upright. Just as the first warrior was about to bring his club down on Jacob's head, he ducked down and swiped one of his feet out. The quick move caught the first attacker around the ankle, driving him off balance and directly into the other warrior's path. The two savages were left entangled together, withering in pain and trying to get themselves free.

Jacob immediately stood back upright and could hear several of the on-looking Delaware warriors laughing at the sight of their fallen mates. Humiliated once again by the troublesome Englishman, the two warriors reorganized and were ready to launch their second attack. Before they could strike again, their chief yelled out, "Stop before the Englishman kills you both."

Shamed once again by Jacob and garnering further wrath from their chief, the two warriors meekly stopped and returned their war clubs to their sashes.

"Let's keep moving with no more interruptions," Captain Jacobs screamed out again, looking directly at the two warriors.

Jacob was still trying to fight off the sick feeling in his stomach, but felt he had won some respect from the others and especially from their leader.

His two escorts were clearly upset with him and he fully expected that they would try in some way to reclaim their lost pride.

Thankfully, the rest of the trip went relatively smoothly for Jacob. His hands remained bound and he was still very hungry, thirsty and fatigued, but he was left to himself most of the time. When they stopped to rest he was still tethered to a tree, but not nearly as tightly as he had been. He was even able to sit down from time to time.

He spent most of his time during the march observing the actions of Captain Jacobs. The Delaware chief appeared to be well-trained in the French way to fight; positioning vanguards, sending out advanced guards and scouting parties. He was surprised by the lack of French accompaniment. It was Jacob's experience that most of the larger war parties included some French or Canadian militia. He could only figure that the French had moved to winter quarters, or had encouraged the savages to raid the frontier at their own discretion.

As they continued on their journey, Jacob began to notice that the large war party had dwindled down to around twenty warriors led by Captain Jacobs. The smell of wood smoke reached him from time to time, and he assumed that the rest of the column had broken off to complete short raids whenever they came near a frontier homestead.

Evidence that his speculation was correct came in the form of fresh scalps, some with long, feminine braids, and English or German weaponry that were brought to the chief for his approval. Jacob was disgusted, but not surprised.

They maintained the same quick pace they had since the beginning, but when they came within sight of a large river, their speed became nearly frenzied. He remembered hearing that Kittanning was located on the banks of the Allegheny and assumed they were nearly there.

Jacob knew what awaited him as a prisoner being brought to this village. He had heard all about the tortures that male captives were forced to endure. In the effort to test an individual's courage, warriors could sometimes drag out the punishment over many days. He had resigned himself to his fate, but that didn't mean he wished to rush towards it. His pace slowed, but he was forced to keep up with the main body of the warriors.

He could tell that they were very close to the village when he began to smell the aromas of cooking meat and herbs. Rich hickory smoke wafted through the air and taunted his stomach with the thought of smoked meats.

His stomach growled loudly and he prayed that he might be able to partake in some of the food. He knew it was a waste of prayer, however; he would only be able to feast on the aromas as the warriors gorged themselves in celebration of their victory.

The trail carried the men up a steep grade and when they crested a hill, Jacob caught his first glimpse of the village. It was rather impressive and reminded him more of an English-style town than any Indian village he had ever seen before. It was much larger than he had expected, with many well-built, wooden log houses and large tracts of cleared land. It was packed with women, children and what appeared to be the rest of the large raiding party.

The town was bustling with activity as everyone prepared for the arrival of Captain Jacobs and his men. Jacob immediately noticed that there were several white captives lending a hand with all the preparation. The chief had paused at the top of the hill to allow two scouts to reach the village and announce him so they could be greeted triumphantly.

Jacob was so engrossed by the sight of the screaming and cheering villagers organizing themselves in two long lines along the path at the bottom of the hill that he hadn't noticed Captain Jacobs step up beside him.

"What is your name, Englishman?" the chief asked.

Jacob responded respectfully, "My name is Jacob. Jacob Mur…Sims."

"Do you see all of this below us? That is for me and my warriors. My village has heard the news of the many scalps we have taken and how we killed many of your fellow English soldiers. They are happy, and I want them to be able to celebrate our great victories. That is why you will be tortured tonight…so they can partake in our victory."

With those ominous words, Captain Jacobs walked like a king down into the village, followed by his proud warriors. The cheers and screams reached a fevered pitch as their leader walked amongst the villagers.

As Jacob drew near the village, he was held back by the two escorts.

His turn to enter the village was fast-approaching, and he could see that several of the young warriors who had marched here with him had joined the line of cheering villagers. Dozens of people held their weapons of choice, from thin switches and hemp ropes to thick branches and heavy war clubs.

The two warriors cut Jacob's hands free and cut away what was left of his clothing, leaving him naked. He prepared himself for what was about to happen. Despite being severely weakened from having no food or drink for several days, he knew what he had to do.

"Stay on your feet...Just stay on your feet..." he began to chant to himself.

Without warning, one of the warriors shoved him forward and Jacob was forced into the mouth of the gauntlet.

Chapter | **Six**

Thankfully, Fredrick was right when he said that the French encampment was a short distance from the village. Maggie found the meandering river trail relatively easy, considering the hellish trails she had been forced to negotiate over the past year and a half.

The temporary camp was nothing elaborate, but Maggie immediately felt much more secure. She noticed over a dozen canoes of varied sizes pulled up and secured on the sandy shore, along with twenty or so canvas tents placed in a circular formation. A large tent sat in the center, and she guessed it was reserved for the officers.

"I'm afraid it is not much, Madame, but the alternative was far worse," Fredrick offered with a smile.

He escorted Maggie to the campfire near the large tent and suggested that she warm herself by the fire while he spoke with his men. The men had cut down two massive trees and laid them down as benches near the fire pit. They had notched several comfortable seats in the hard wood, making it a comfortable place to relax and stare into the flames.

"Please make yourself at home, and I will get one of the men to prepare you some tea and smoked meat," Fredrick said before he disappeared into the officer's tent.

Maggie was still unsure whether she trusted Fredrick completely, but her actions towards Anne had made this the only option. If she had learned one thing over the past year or so, it was that in order to survive, she needed to live in the moment. She could only do so much to decide her own fate before just allowing the rest to play out as it was intended.

Her life was in a constant state of change now. She desperately longed for Jacob and her children, but if she dwelled too long on the past, she left herself vulnerable. Maggie had promised herself that she would never do that to herself again.

She picked the most comfortable notched seat and let herself relax. A few moments later, a soldier brought her a steaming cup of herb tea and several generous slices of salted pork. Maggie offered the kind soldier an appreciative smile. She was just about to bite into a piece of pork when another soldier dropped off a large plank of wood that held a small loaf of bread and a block of hard cheese. There was also a small knife to cut the food into slices.

She wasn't sure if Fredrick planned to join her, but her hunger got the best of her and she began eating the small feast immediately. The bread was hard-crusted yet soft inside; mixed with the salty meat and the strong cheese, it made a wonderfully simple meal.

"You must be starved, Madame," Fredrick's voice startled her from behind.

"I am not certain if it is my sudden freedom or what, but this is much too kind considering what happened…"

"That is in the past, Madame," he said, cutting her off. "All is forgotten and forgiven. We have turned to another chapter. I just hope it might end a bit less painfully." He smiled and rubbed his head in jest.

They sat in companionable silence and Maggie made a sandwich for him from the board she held in her lap. When she had eaten her share, she placed the tray on the log next to her and stretched her feet towards the fire.

Fredrick was called away to deal with some issues with the canoes, and Maggie began to fret that the Delaware might come looking for her once they found Anne. She argued with herself that she ought to mention the situation to Fredrick. She eventually decided that if they were going to leave the next morning, the news of her assault might not reach the French camp; she would not need to tell him after all.

Fredrick soon rejoined her, obviously pleased at the progress his men had made to this point.

"What are your plans?" Maggie blurted as he sat down beside her.

"Straight to the point as ever, Madame," he laughed. "You are still nervous I have some deceitful plan waiting for you at Niagara?"

Maggie squirmed at his use of the word deceitful. She remained silent and turned her attention to a small piece of cheese she had picked up off the tray. She decided to wait for him to provide a real answer.

Fredrick appeared confused by Maggie's behavior and said, "To ease your mind, Madame, I will go over my plans in detail. They are much like what I described before, with the exception that I forgot to mention we must make a stop to deliver some trade goods to a large Delaware village called Kittanning. It sits right on the Allegheny River, a mere half day's paddle north of here.

"We will not stay long at the village as I am determined to reach Niagara by early November. That leaves us just over two weeks to reach the fort, which I think will be plenty of time. Even if it snows, the river should not freeze over yet."

Maggie was happy to hear the details of their trip, but still wondered if Fredrick had any specific plans for her. "That sounds simple enough," she said, "but how will you explain to the commander at Niagara why you have an English woman accompanying you?"

Another amused smile crossed his face as he tried again to reassure her. "Maggie, it is frankly no concern of the commander or anyone else. As I said, you are free to leave whenever the time suits you, no questions asked."

Despite his assurances, Maggie remained guarded. Unfortunately, the only person she had been able to fully trust over the last year was One-Ear and he was no longer with her. She was safer with Fredrick than she would have been at the village, but she would have to wait until they arrived at Fort Niagara to see if he was really true to his word.

Fredrick was called away once more and Maggie remained by the fire, feeding it logs from time to time. The men busily packed the canoes and saw to other preparations until the only remaining light was from Maggie's fire.

As the rest of the camp began to turn in, Fredrick approached Maggie and led her to a small tent next to the officers' quarters. She knew that under normal circumstances a tent like this would house three or four soldiers lying feet to face. She couldn't image how unpleasant that would be and was thankful she had the tent all to herself. Of course, after spending the day with these men and watching how hard they worked, she decided they probably relished the opportunity to sleep, no matter how close the quarters.

A couple of the men had given her a heavy woolen blanket and some animal pelts that added to her comfort. Despite the cold night air, she remained wonderfully warm. She enjoyed a deeper, more restful sleep than she had in weeks.

The first rays of sunlight that seeped in her tent did not fool her. There was no way the early morning sun was as warm as it let on and she wished she never had to leave the warmth of her bed. Soon a loud commotion outside convinced her to rise and she discreetly peeked through the small slit between the tent flaps.

Fredrick was speaking with an unseen party and Maggie could see that several of his men had their muskets at the ready. The two men were conversing in French and Maggie was only able to translate the odd word. The conversation was heated, but Fredrick appeared to be standing his ground on the dispute.

Curious to identify the other individual, she shifted around slowly to get a glimpse of the person with whom Fredrick argued so intensely. When she realized who it was, a bolt of fear swept over her.

It was Anne's husband, with five or six warriors standing behind him.

Understanding how well the French valued their relationship with the tribes in this area, she fully expected that Fredrick would have no other choice but to hand her over to these savages. She honestly wouldn't blame him if he considered it. She had deceived him once again. Maggie wouldn't be able to fault him for wanting to rid himself of this problematic English woman once and for all.

Unexpectedly, the heated discussion ended faster than it had started. Fredrick presented the warriors with several prime beaver pelts and a small cask of rum and they left the camp peacefully.

Maggie decided she'd better wait for a few minutes before leaving her tent. She expected Fredrick to pull open the flaps and demand an explanation of what happened back at the village, but he appeared to return to the preparations for their planned departure.

Maggie adjusted her clothes and tied up her hair before meticulously folding the blanket and pelts. When she couldn't put it off any longer, she took a deep breath and stepped into the morning sun. She looked around nervously then quickly walked over to the fire pit and took a seat on the tree trunk.

To her surprise, she was greeted by several smiles and nods from the men. It was only a moment before one of them handed her a steaming cup of tea followed by a thick slice of bacon that had been grilled over the fire.

Her soft, "Merci," was met with a kind nod.

She didn't see Fredrick anywhere and watched the men pack up their tents as she sipped her tea. The tents were loaded onto the canoes, which were then lashed together with thick hemp ropes and floated into the deeper water to keep them from getting grounded in the shallows. The canoes were very full and Maggie wondered to herself how many of the men would fit into them and how well they would stay above the water surface with so much weight packed into them.

Lost in her thoughts, Maggie didn't notice that Fredrick had emerged from the officer's tent until he called out to her, "Madame, I see you are up now. I hope you had a good night."

Surprised by the sudden interruption, Maggie hesitated, waiting for him to mention something of his earlier confrontation. He walked over to the fire and poured himself a cup of the tea. He stood silently, flexing his cold limbs over the flames and sipping his tea.

"As well as could be expected, I guess," Maggie finally replied, refusing to make eye contact with him.

Fredrick sat next to her for a moment then said, "We need to leave promptly, so when your tea is finished, please gather what you need and be prepared to depart."

Maggie didn't understand why he was being so coy and hesitated to say anything more.

Fredrick just slowly drank his tea and looked around the camp at his men rushing around to finish packing the rest of the supplies. Soon the only traces of the encampment that remained were a few flattened grassy spots and the fire pit where they sat.

Realizing they would be leaving soon and would have no time to speak openly, Maggie blurted out, "What was all the commotion about outside my tent earlier?"

Fredrick remained nonchalant, taking another sip of his tea before pouring the rest over the fire to extinguish the remaining embers. He kicked some sand onto the pit and said, "Strange thing, Madame, the Delaware were searching for some escaped English woman. I was told that the warrior's wife was attacked and left in a shed. He was under the impression that the escapee was with us, but I assured him there was no such person here. He appeared to be satisfied by my explanation and left to continue on with his search. Strange things seem to happen in this wilderness, don't you think, Madame?"

The sarcasm in Fredrick's voice annoyed her and instead of confessing everything in detail, she calmly asked, "Did the Delaware say how his wife was?"

Fredrick looked her straight in the eye for a moment before looking away. "Not really. He only mentioned she wasn't dead. He was careful not to press his accusations too far, fearing he might insult me and my men. I am familiar enough with these people to know that a few trinkets and some rum would convince him to continue his search elsewhere. I will consider the matter closed, Madame, but we must be moving out."

Maggie was confused by Fredrick's refusal to come out and directly question her about the incident, but she was grateful that he had let the matter go. She got up and, like Fredrick, poured what was left of her cup over the fire pit. She politely excused herself to collect her few belongings.

Her tent, as well as the heavy animal skins, had been packed into the canoes already. Maggie picked up her blanket and the little sack of personal items she had brought with her. The knife she had taken from the Delaware family's home where she had been living hung around her neck, but her musket was missing.

Fredrick still stood by the fire pit, watching his men work. She approached and said, "My musket was left by my tent; did you see if one of the men picked it up by mistake?"

"Your musket," he said coldly. "Yes, one of my men did in fact retrieve your musket. I will keep it for now. I fear you are far more dangerous than I suspected, and for my safety I would feel better if it is in my possession. You may have it back when you decide leave our company."

Maggie was naturally upset at having her weapon confiscated, but she could not begrudge Fredrick such a decision. She had attacked him in the past and recently lied to him. He had chosen to protect his men and her only hope was he would keep his word and return it when she left.

The men had completed their packing and had begun climbing into the canoes to depart. Without another word, Maggie and Fredrick climbed into the lead canoe. Maggie sat in the front and grabbed a paddle, while Fredrick positioned himself in the back to steer and keep an eye on the river ahead.

Their little flotilla stretched nearly a half mile and made good time. The river was easily navigated. It was not very shallow in the middle, so they did not have to worry about becoming grounded on the rocks below. The water was calm and the paddlers were able to move against the slight current quite briskly.

After several hours of bright sunshine in the morning, the clear blue sky became overcast with dark, ominous clouds. As they grew more threatening, Fredrick called out to the other men, "Pull to shore; we're in for some bad weather."

Just as the last of the canoes slid into the sandy bank, the skies unleashed a pounding bout of hail. The men had taken cover in the nearby tree line and watched helplessly as the ice stones, some as large as lead shot, bounced off the boats and their contents. The largest stones tore straight through the covers that had been stretched over the supplies to protect them.

The surface of the river churned as it was pelted mercilessly. The noise from the hail as it struck the water and solid objects around them caused the men to cover their ears. Maggie's thoughts flashed back to her near deadly canoe trip on the lake the previous year. She caught Fredrick's eye and could see that his thoughts mirrored hers.

The hail lasted about ten minutes before giving way to an intense downpour. The ice had covered all exposed surfaces around them like a blanket of chunky snow. The air temperature had dropped considerably, and the rain froze immediately as it hit the icy ground.

The foliage on the trees had naturally begun to thin from the lateness of the season, but the hail had definitely taken its toll as well. While Fredrick's men and Maggie were much dryer than if they had been completely uncovered, they were far from unscathed by the ice and rain.

The storm continued to rage for another half hour, and Maggie could tell Fredrick was becoming frustrated. They were losing valuable time and the trade goods sat exposed to the elements.

When the storm finally slowed a bit, Fredrick and his men carefully moved towards their boats. The ice had encased each of the vessels and accumulated on the ground to such a thickness that the canoes were actually frozen solid to the ground.

"It will take hours to chip all this ice off the canoes," Fredrick muttered to no one in particular.

Maggie remained where she was and waited for the French to decide what to do next. She watched Fredrick speak with one of his junior officers before approaching her.

"Madame, it looks like we will have to walk the rest of the way," he said. "My guide said that we are only a good day's march from the village, as long as the weather does not worsen again."

Maggie nodded and simply responded, "I would feel much safer in this wilderness if I had my musket to defend myself."

Fredrick offered no response and moved away to organize his men. Six were left behind to guard the boats and do what they could to chip away the ice. When the boats were freed, they would lash several of them together and paddle them upriver to catch up to the rest of the men.

The remaining soldiers and Maggie departed with Fredrick in the lead. Once they gained the main trail, three men were sent ahead as scouts and Fredrick fell back to have a quick word with Maggie.

"Madame, I need you to be less of a problem during this march. I am not sure how far we actually are from the Delaware village. I have honestly never used this section of the trail." Fredrick handed her the musket he had confiscated and added, "This is for you to use only if we are attacked, I assume you know how to use it?"

Maggie happily accepted it, ignoring his impertinent question. Fredrick simply shrugged and moved back to the front of the column of soldiers.

They made good progress along the flat trail, and Fredrick seemed to be satisfied with their movement. Periodically, he sent a few of his men to the river to check for any signs of the boats, but they were not realistically expected to catch up until the following day.

The light rain continued relentlessly, filtering down on them through the thinning foliage. Often, they hit pockets of cold air where snow replaced the rain and even began to accumulate on the trail.

Eventually, Fredrick called them to a halt to take a much needed rest. Maggie was grateful. Her legs had begun to feel the toil of the long march and the weight of the musket she carried on her shoulder. She had found a dry spot to sit under a tree and had just closed her eyes to rest for a few moments when Fredrick approached.

He sat next to her and said, "My apologies, Madame. I am beginning to think staying with the damned Delaware might have been your better option."

"No apologies necessary, Fredrick. I much prefer being cold and wet here than dry and comfortable among the savages."

There was an awkward silence between them as Fredrick looked around at his tired, drenched men. Keeping his voice low, he continued, "I have never marched the trails to Kittanning, having always used the river. Moving through the wilderness is difficult anyway, but when poor weather is added to it…"

Maggie did her best to reassure him, knowing that her own well-being depended on him for the moment. "Well, weather this time of year is unpredictable. It could end right now or never stop until spring. What other choice do we have besides pushing on to Kittanning?"

Fredrick rose and brushed off his clothing. "You are right, of course, Madame," he said with a slight smile. He asked four scouts to run ahead to find out how far they were from Kittanning and to select a suitable place to camp for the night.

Maggie and the rest of the refreshed men joined Fredrick on the trail and they set off at a brisk pace. After about an hour, the clouds finally gave way to some cool sunshine and their spirits became refreshed as well.

The scouts eventually returned to report to Fredrick who appeared relieved at their news. He made his way to Maggie and said, "Good news, Madame. The men found a good place to make camp that is not far from here, and they met some trappers who just left Kittanning. We will leave camp at dawn tomorrow and should be there by midday."

The rest of the day's trek was relatively relaxed and Maggie was pleased with the site the men had chosen to make camp. It was off the trail and in a well-protected outcropping of boulders. Being French regulars in this territory offered them the benefit of not having to fear an attack, but Fredrick still stationed pickets around the camp. To Maggie's utter delight, they would be able to have a fire overnight to warm them.

Maggie found a nice flat spot under a large pine tree that would protect her from the wind and shelter her from the rain if it returned. She scooped together dried pine needles and large clumps of moss then spread a blanket over them. Only her hunger kept her from retiring right away.

Fredrick had sent out a couple of men to hunt for dinner. Maggie noticed some early winter berries growing nearby that had not been decimated by the earlier hail and collected enough to give everyone a small handful. She received grateful smiles from each of the men.

After only about a half-hour, the two hunters returned with a raccoon, three black squirrels and a good-sized wild turkey. The meat was soon roasting over the fire and one of the men gathered some acorns and chestnuts to brew some hot tea. The resulting tea was very bitter, but Maggie enjoyed the warmth it gave her chilled body.

They ate well and when it was time to sleep, the camp grew silent almost immediately. Clearly, the men were as exhausted as Maggie. The crackling of the dying fire was the only sound heard over the snoring of some of the men.

Fredrick had planned to leave at dawn, which meant the camp arose slightly before the sun. Despite being sheltered by the large rocks and trees, the ground and most of the blankets wore a thin layer of powdery snow. Maggie had a difficult time shaking the morning chill from her body. She longed for something hot to drink, but the fire had all but extinguished during the night.

They only had a few hours left to travel, but Maggie understood Fredrick's hurry to be off. He did not want to chance the canoes and goods getting ahead of his main force.

Maggie found some leftover pieces of turkey from the previous night and grabbed a handful of wild berries as she scaled down the rocks to the trail. As the sun broke over the horizon and provided some better light, she saw that they were greeted by a couple more inches of snow that had accumulated on the trail.

The Frenchmen seemed well-rested and excited to be so near their destination. Even Fredrick appeared more at ease this morning. He had not set up a rear guard and only sent two scouts ahead of the main body. He did not push the men very hard once they were on the trail, and they moved forward at a casually brisk pace.

Despite her escorts' nonchalance, Maggie remained on her guard. Jacob had always warned her that it was when everything in the wilderness was quiet and peaceful that you needed to be the most guarded. As such, she kept her musket at the ready and was careful to keep scanning ahead and around the area.

The snow began to get slushier as the sun rose higher, and the trail became a bit more treacherous. The mixture of slop and wet leaves sent many of the men slipping and sliding along the trail. Several of them strapped small metal spikes to their shoes and Maggie envied them. Her soaked leather moccasins provided very little traction and she took shorter steps to prevent herself from being caught off balance.

The trail was well cut but had a series of blind curves. Most of the time it followed the river, but often it turned back towards the darker parts of the forest. After a few hours on the move, Fredrick ordered the men to take a brief break. They dropped their packs and sought dry patches of ground to sit. Maggie found a comfortable spot to lean against a tree trunk and kept her musket ready at her side.

As she looked around at the men, she noticed that many left their guns leaning unattended against the trees or lying several feet away from them. She marveled at how relaxed they seemed and what a change it was from all the intense travels she had undertaken over the last year.

Before she got too comfortable, the echoes of musket shots suddenly rang out nearby.

Their peaceful, easy march was shattered.

The men instinctively jumped, but Fredrick remained calm, ordering five men forward to check on the situation. Maggie assumed that the two advance scouts had probably spotted some brush wolves or a bear, although she primed her musket just in case it was something more serious.

The men waited tensely for the scouts to report back, but soon several more shots rang out. Fredrick immediately ordered his men to take cover.

Maggie followed the order as well and positioned herself just south of the rest of the men. She had lost sight of Fredrick and moved back a few more paces off the trail to try to get a better view of the situation around the trees.

There was still no sign of the advance scouts or the men who'd been sent to find them. She prayed they had just moved farther up the trail, and still hoped the gunfire had been directed at some animal. There had been no further shots and the forest was once again silent.

Oddly, there were no bird calls, no squirrels rustling in the underbrush; everything was perfectly still. Then a large, greasy hand clamped over Maggie's mouth from behind and pulled her backward into the next line of brush.

Her unknown captor was very strong and she was unable to escape as he dragged her up a small embankment where she was sat against a tree. The hand left her mouth, but before she could react, a piece of cloth gagged her into silence. She got her first glimpse of her abductor as he pried her musket from her hands and put it over his shoulder. He was very tall and signaled her to be quiet. Then he spoke into her ear, "Stay down and wait here, ma'am."

She realized he was English.

Maggie sat up taller and could see the forest was packed with about twenty other men clothed in various uniforms and civilian wear. She could hear them conversing in English and noticed that among them, one man towered over the others. He had his back to her and she could not see his face, but he was about her Jacob's height. He wore an old green coat with a silk scarf tied under a dirty, misshapen tricorn hat. His clothes were covered in dirt, making him blend into the surrounding forest.

From her perch above the trail, she was close enough to see the Frenchmen, fully exposed to the men in the trees. They had their backs to her position, foolishly waiting for an attack from the front.

The tall man signaled to some men hidden on the other side of the trail, and Maggie could see that the French had walked themselves into a clever ambush. They had no way to escape. Their forward scouts had run into trouble and, unbeknownst to them, any attempt to retreat would be blocked.

The trap was set and the strange English attackers were ready to spring it. The Frenchmen were doomed, and she could only watch. She attempted to spot Fredrick, but he must have been farther up the trail.

With a horrifying, grizzly shriek from the tall English leader, the forest trembled with the thunder of musket fire. The tree line sprang to life as the Englishmen swarmed over the frightened French soldiers with an unrelenting ferocity. The French could do nothing to defend their position, and most were soon overrun and butchered where they stood.

Maggie's heart had leapt with joy when she realized that the latest in her long series of captors were actually English, but she could not help but feel sympathy for the poor souls who had treated her so kindly over the past two days. She finally spotted Fredrick as he valiantly struggled to get his last few remaining men into a defensive position to hold off the attacks.

He was surrounded on all sides with no place to retreat. The tall Englishman that had reminded Maggie of Jacob motioned to his men to stop shooting and held a piece of cloth up to signal Fredrick that he wished to speak with him.

With the ambush ceased for the moment and the two leaders speaking under the flag of truce, one of the young Englishmen ran back to retrieve Maggie. He immediately removed the cloth from her mouth, pulled her to her feet and apologized. "I'm sorry, ma'am, but we couldn't have you warning the Frenchies and ruining the surprise we had for them. It was Captain Murray's orders."

Maggie's knees buckled and she grabbed the young man's arm. "It can't be…" she whispered, tears filling her eyes.

"Ma'am?" the young man asked, concerned.

"Who are you people?" she managed to gasp, watching the tall man speak with Fredrick.

"We are English militia, roughly speaking," he replied.

"What do you mean?"

"Well, we are made up of misfits, stragglers, deserters and men whose land's been taken by the French and savages."

Maggie's thoughts were a jumble. Hadn't Fredrick mentioned that the French merchant who'd purchased her had been killed by an escaped prisoner? Was it possible that her Jacob had found her at last?

"What are they talking about?" she asked the young man, signaling towards Captain Murray and Fredrick.

He didn't respond right away, caught up in the scene before him. "The captain is offering him the opportunity to live," he replied bluntly.

After a few minutes of heated debate, the tall Englishman turned from Fredrick and started to walk towards Maggie. The sun was to his back and she could not see his face.

"Jacob?" she whispered hesitantly as he grew closer.

The man did not appear to hear her and when he had drawn near, shifted to one side so she could see him in the light. Maggie gasped as she caught her first glimpse of his face. It was in fact not a face, but instead the horribly disfigured remains of a man. His skin was scorched into a terrible combination of blue, black and pink hues. His eyes were so deeply set back in his head that she could barely see them. His lips were basically nonexistent, and the green scarf he had worn tied around his skull had been to cover the fact that both ears were gone.

She looked away from his face and noticed that at the ends of his arms, where his hands should have been, were two nubby stumps where pink, scalded skin was stretched taut. She tried not to show her shock, but the man clearly noticed it.

"Please don't feel badly, ma'am," he rasped. His voice was deep, but it sounded like every word forced from his burnt mouth was painful. "I am used to the stares and horrified glances of others."

As he drew nearer, Maggie struggled to look directly at him and asked, "What are your plans with me, sir?"

"I assumed you were an Englishwoman," the man rasped again, swallowing forcefully before continuing. "We thought we might liberate you from your French captors."

"What of my remaining captors; what will your men do with them?" she asked, hoping Fredrick and his remaining brave soldiers would possibly be set free.

"Sadly, ma'am, the French officer did not want to surrender according to my terms." With that, the captain ordered his men to complete their attack before she could plead for the Frenchmen's lives.

Maggie was once again taken into the cover of the forest, but could not look away as Fredrick and his men were set upon by the much larger force. The assault did not last long. Fredrick was struck in the face by a well-placed shot from a man positioned in a tree. Once he was killed, the remaining men attempted to surrender but were afforded no quarter. The horde of Englishmen charged into the men, sparing none. Any who had survived the first onslaught with mere injuries were callously shot where they lay.

Maggie had seen such atrocities before, but not at the hands of Englishmen. She feared what might be in store for her.

Watching Fredrick die was a terrible thing to behold, but she did not feel anything other than sympathy for his untimely death. He had always been a gentleman and a dutiful officer. The winter they had spent in that little cabin with One-Ear had brought them closer than mere acquaintances, but there had never been a strong emotional bond between them. In the end, he was French and an enemy. She thought of the day the French-backed Huron raided her homestead and refocused on her own survival.

The bodies of the dead Frenchmen were combed over for useful items and soon the men involved in the attack moved into the woods near Maggie and began to climb the same embankment that had allowed them to remain so well hidden. The young man at Maggie's side led her up the steep hill after the other Englishmen.

"My name is Kennedy," he said as he held out a hand to Maggie to help her over a small boulder, "Caleb Kennedy."

"Mr. Kennedy, you may call me Maggie," she said as she followed the men and marveled at how skillfully they maneuvered across the heavily congested forest.

Nothing more was said as the two did their best to keep pace with the others. Soon they were following a roughly cut path in the side of a steep mountain. Maggie had no idea how long they had been on the trail or how far they had traveled, but none of the men complained.

Eventually, Maggie's legs grew weary from the rough terrain and she wondered how much longer she could last. As though he could read her thoughts, Caleb spoke quietly, "We will be stopping soon, ma'am. One of our fortifications is just over the next small ridge."

Maggie nodded and continued to keep her eyes on the path in front of her. The line of men stretched at least twenty yards ahead of her, and she became excited and perplexed when she saw several of the lead men suddenly disappear into a large overhanging rock that lay to one side of the trail.

As she approached, Caleb guided her up to the rock and she understood what it was. What looked like a solid rock face were actually two boulders. One stood slightly in front of the other and concealed an entryway. She stepped past the rocks to a large flat space filled by tents and men as far as she could see. The overhanging rock that she had seen from the trail was actually much larger and jutted out from the side of the mountain, acting as a protective cover against the elements. Small caves were visible in the mountainside and appeared to be used for additional sleeping space. This entire bustling camp had been completely undetectable from the trail and Maggie was instantly impressed.

She remained back a little and let Caleb approach a small group of his mates. She took the opportunity to absorb her new surroundings. It was an unbiased mixture of old and young; there were a couple dark-skinned men and several Indians dressed in English-style civilian clothes.

Before Caleb returned to Maggie, the captain climbed on a waist-high rock to address the men. He attempted to shout as loudly as his scarred throat would allow and the men fell completely silent in order to hear their leader.

"Gentlemen," he began in a painfully scratchy voice, "you fought hard today. I am pleased that none of you were killed. I would be remiss if I didn't mention our new guest. Ma'am, please be kind enough to introduce yourself."

Maggie reluctantly did as she was asked. "My name is Maggie Murray. Over the past year or so, I have been a captive of the Huron, French, Ottawa, and Delaware, and I am grateful that you and your captain freed me." She paused to see if she was expected to say anything else.

The men politely clapped and several let out a quick cheer. The captain remained silent and his eyes remained fixed on Maggie. She couldn't tell what he was thinking, but before she could say anything else, he seemed to pull himself together.

"I should not have to remind any of you to treat our guest with the respect she has truly earned and deserves." He turned to Maggie and struggled to smile with his scorched lips.

She gave a little wave to the men and the captain climbed down from the rock with some assistance. He soon moved away to organize the encampment.

Caleb returned to Maggie and said, "Ma'am, you must be cold. Let me help you find a place by the fire." He led her to one of the many fires that had been lit to keep the camp well-heated. The rock suspended above their heads did a fine job of reflecting the heat down towards the ground.

"Thank you, Caleb," she said as she sat down near the flames.

"Keep yourself warm and I will get you some hot tea," he said kindly.

For the first time in over a year, she didn't feel like a prisoner or a captive. It was a wonderful feeling, and she almost didn't want to enjoy it in case she had somehow misunderstood. As she rested her feet by the fire, she saw the captain approaching and immediately felt on edge again. He remained standing and she tried not to look away from his face as she did her best to greet him politely, saying, "Captain, thank you for your kindness; Caleb has taken good care of me."

He hesitated slightly and she could see that it was with great personal effort that he forced himself to speak, "Maggie Murray…Maggie, you have no idea who I am, do you? God knows you really shouldn't, considering my alarming appearance."

"Do we know each other?" Maggie forced herself to take a detailed look at the man.

"In fairness, you knew me before my face and body were disfigured," he said in his gravelly voice. "Those circumstances were far better than what we have both encountered over the past year."

Maggie struggled to identify this poor man, but she could not. She felt terrible and offered a heartfelt apology, "Sir, I am sorry, but I truly do not know who you are. When did we meet?"

"No need to feel bad, Maggie. I would probably not recognize myself either. Thankfully, I have not seen a reflection of myself since my disfigurement, but I can tell by people's reactions and how they avert their eyes when I am around. I must be a frightening sight."

He paused for a moment and Maggie continued to search his face for any clues that he was someone she knew.

"I am Israel, your husband's brother." A small tear rolled down his scarred face and dripped onto his muddy boot.

Leaping to her feet with a gasp, Maggie threw her arms gently around her brother-in-law's shoulders as she burst into tears. He gladly accepted her hug and wiped at his own wet eyes with the sleeve of his coat.

"Israel, I didn't know!" Maggie cried as she clung to him. It had been so long since she had seen any members of her family.

Caleb returned with Maggie's tea and was not sure what to do when he saw them still embraced. He placed the tea on a flat rock by the fire and started to back away.

Noticing his return, Israel called out to him, "Mr. Kennedy, thank you for taking good care of my sister-in-law."

Caleb stuttered a brief reply, "I–I didn't know, sir…"

"I didn't know myself, Caleb!" Maggie smiled, letting go of Israel, but remaining close to his side.

Caleb offered a very informal salute and left the two alone to catch up.

Maggie sat down by the fire and hoped Israel would as well. Thankfully, he obliged her and sat across from her. She could see that he struggled to lower himself to the low log bench. Once he landed safely he let out a deep sigh.

"So, Maggie, it feels like a lifetime, since we last talked," Israel said as Caleb approached with another cup for his captain and immediately stepped away again.

She looked at him inquisitively and Israel said, "I would love to join you in a nice cup of tea, but it would cause me great pain. My throat is tender. If it wasn't for this cold, terribly bitter drink, I would not be able to have much at all. The doctor told me to stay away from water unless it had been boiled, but that is bloody inconvenient even at the best of times."

They sat quietly, sipping their drinks and enjoying each other's company.

"Would you like help with your drink?" Maggie politely asked, trying not to insult him.

"No, thank you. Having no useful hands complicates my life, but it is far better than being dead. One of the men in the ranks was informally trained as a doctor's assistant. He is pretty efficient with a knife and needle. He did some wonderful work on my arms. He carved a couple of notches near my wrists to give me some mobility, to hold a cup or wield a sword." He held out his arms for her to see.

Maggie looked at him, but wasn't sure how to respond.

Seeing her reaction, Israel changed the subject, "Maggie, I must say, I'm happy to see you, but how did you get yourself this far north? I want to know about my Abby as well, but I fear that with you here alone news of her must not be good." Israel's voice cracked noticeably at the mention of his wife.

Maggie wasn't sure what she should tell him. He had already suffered enough and must have already resigned himself to the fact that he would never want Abby or the kids to see him this way. Her heart went out to him. Despite surrounding himself with loyal men, he would always be alone.

"Over a year ago, not long after you left with Jacob, our homes were raided by the Huron. They took all of us captive, dragged us through this godless wilderness, split us all up and I have been trying to survive since. You are the first family member I have seen since that time." She tried not to cry but failed. The pain in Israel's eyes deepened with every word she spoke.

"I am sorry, Maggie," he said quietly, struggling to his feet so he could move next to her. "I should have waited to talk about all of this."

"My tears aren't just for me; they are for you too. Some of them are from happiness as well. You can't believe how wonderful I feel, knowing I still have some family left."

"Have you gotten any word of Jacob?" he asked.

"A few months back, I learned he was near Fort Machault during my imprisonment there. As fate would have it, we were separated again. I heard he went towards Fort Duquesne while I was being taken towards the fort at Niagara." Maggie's tears were falling uncontrollably as she spoke.

"You need to get some rest," Israel said. "We can talk later. I have to send out more men to scout the area for any more French or their damn savage allies." His demeanor changed at the mention of their enemies.

"Before you go," she said, sniffing as she wiped her tears away, "what is this place and who are these men?"

Israel looked around proudly at the odd assembly of men. "We are settlers who have lost our families. We are former slaves and a few deserters. Some of us were abandoned by our own, and some just foolishly volunteered. We have been called raiders, pirates and thieves, but we are here to fight the French and kill as many savages as we can. I have heard that the savages call me 'la fantome' or 'the ghost', and I wear that name with pride."

Israel got back on his feet and greeted a small group of men who had just returned to the camp. "Excuse me, Maggie," he said. "I have to speak with these men. Please rest and save me a place beside you at tonight's meal."

Maggie smiled and watched Israel talk with his men. There was so much she wanted to discuss with him. For the first time since her capture, she felt safe and her heart felt a little less empty. She once again stretched her feet towards the fire and gave thanks for this latest development.

Chapter | **Seven**

Jacob recovered from the shove quickly and regained his balance. He kept his head low and held his arms protectively at the sides of his face. He soon began swinging his fists towards his attackers and connected with several of the shorter Delaware.

The two lines of villagers struck him hard, deliberately trying to weaken his legs. If they could bring the much taller man to his knees, they could inflict much more pain.

Bloodied from the constant, well-directed strikes, Jacob imagined his body looked far worse than it actually felt. He did his best to fight back and did manage to knock down several of the villagers as he ran. More than a few were left with bruised and bloodied faces.

Nearing the end of the line, struggling to maintain his balance in the midst of the constant attempts to trip him up, Jacob put his shoulder forward and surged through the remaining warriors. He knocked several of them down, stepping on their limbs and faces to finally reach the designated post that would end this torment.

Some of the village's other white captives clapped and cheered for him, despite glares from the on-looking villagers.

Bloody and naked, Jacob stood with one hand on the post and let out a thunderous scream that echoed throughout the entire village. He then looked defiantly towards Captain Jacobs, who was standing with some of the elders. Surprisingly, he was greeted by a smile from the 'captain', who looked more like a proud father than the threatening Delaware chief who had just forced him to run the gauntlet.

Captain Jacobs clapped his hands and, as quickly as the villagers had lined up, they dispersed to continue preparing the night's feast. Jacob kept his hand on the pole, unsure of what he was expected to do next.

Minutes later, two warriors approached him and pointed him towards an old wooden hut. It certainly didn't look like much and he guessed it was probably used to store their tools and field implements. Despite its decrepit condition, Jacob was in no position to argue and followed them to the building.

He noticed a number of white captives working around the large village and assumed that they had been adopted into the various families. Some of them smiled at him as he passed, while others just kept their heads down and continued about their work. He saw young white and Delaware children running around together playing stick ball in the far field.

The warriors opened the door, tossed the remains of his clothing inside and directed him to enter the hut. A heavy stench forced him back, but he was nudged forward again. His brief hesitation allowed a small shaft of light to pour in; at that moment, Jacob could see a straw-covered floor and several bodies huddled together in the far corner.

As soon as Jacob entered the room, the door slammed behind him.

Indescribable odors overwhelmed him and he strained in the darkness to distinguish the outlines of the people he had seen. There were cracks and knot holes in the wooden boards that made up the wall and tiny slivers of light were all that kept the room from sitting in utter darkness.

Jacob stepped carefully around the dank floor and looked for a place to sit. He had managed to get most of his old clothes back on and sat in silence while he waited for his eyes to adjust.

Eventually, he was able to see that there were about twenty other men crammed in with him. Jacob looked up at the sparsely thatched roof and imagined it did little to keep the cold air out. He didn't even want to think of the rain or snow.

"I assume you take issue with our accommodations?" an all too familiar, grizzled voice broke the silence.

"To whom do I have the pleasure of speaking?" Jacob asked. "Are there any soldiers among you men?"

"Most of us are from a militia company sent from Fort Cumberland," a different voice responded. "We were ambushed by these heathens just southeast of Fort Duquesne. This is what is left of a hundred of us."

"The bloody savages ambushed and killed our mates before most of us could ready our muskets," the first man added.

His voice stirred something in Jacob's memory and he suddenly recognized its owner "Private Taylor?" he asked, praying he was wrong.

"Aye, that's me, but who might you be, lad, and how do you know my name?" Taylor spat back as he got himself to his feet. He stepped forward and was now close enough that Jacob could smell the stench from his eye-watering breath.

"Speak up, lad," Taylor continued, struggling to locate the new man in the dark. "Give us your name now. Ain't no reason to fear us."

"Sergeant Jacob Mur...I mean Sims, commander of the new fort you were all assigned to," Jacob growled. "Now sit your backside down, Taylor, and keep your questions to yourself."

Taylor instantly backed off and remained quiet. The rest of the men who were well enough, propped themselves up to listen to the newest prisoner.

"How long have you men been here?" Jacob asked once he knew he had most of the men's attention.

"God only knows, sir," one of the men responded. "I think a week or so, but it's easy to lose track of time in this shack. There were more of us at first, but ten of the lads were badly injured and they didn't make it all the way."

The man's voice had started to waver and he paused to compose himself before continuing, "A couple more never made it to the other side of the bloody gauntlet. Two of them made it with the rest of us, but died from their wounds soon after running it."

The small room went deathly silent and Jacob assumed most of them were either reliving their experience, or praying for the dead and for themselves. He offered up his own prayer and asked God to guide them through this horror.

Jacob strained his eyes to try to identify any of the other men, but the sparse light and their slumped postures made it next to impossible.

"Are you part of Stevens Ranging Company?" another man broke the silence.

"I am still under Stevens' command," Jacob said respectfully.

"So you were also with Braddock?" the man continued.

Jacob was growing uncomfortable with the man's line of questioning, especially since Private Taylor was present. He tried not to jump to any conclusions, but he couldn't be sure what Taylor might have told the others.

"Bloody fool, that Braddock!" the man said angrily. "He did his best to get us all killed!"

Excited cries and shouts from the villagers resonated through the confined shelter and cut off their conversation. Jacob stood up and pressed his face against a gap in the wall to try to see what was happening outside. He could see the women quickly going about their preparations for the feast, but he saw no sign of the warriors. The other men in the tiny shack seemed to have no interest in what was happening outside of their own misery, so Jacob quietly remained at his post.

After a few hours of standing and peering out into the main square, Jacob saw several painted warriors arrive with a group of captured settlers. They appeared to be a young family, possibly from one of the German settlements on the other side of the ridge to the east. Terror was written on the faces of three young boys who clung to their parents in a tearful attempt to keep close and avoid looking at their wildly painted captors. They were all ragged in appearance, particularly the father, whose clothes were little more than shreds of cloths and were stained with his own blood. The mother still wore her nightgown and the three children were covered in dirt.

They looked completely spent and Jacob figured that they had likely been marched at least fifty miles over treacherous mountain terrain. He felt so helpless just watching them without being able to assist them.

Soon, the children were forcefully wrenched from their parents' arms and wailed so loudly that even Jacob's fellow prisoners rose out of their complacence to see what was happening.

The hysterical children were taken towards some houses but Jacob soon lost sight of them.

The poor mother wept hysterically until two elderly women took her to the far side of the square. The father was now all alone, silent with his head down. He was powerless and grossly outnumbered against his captors and they decided to make a spectacle of him.

It was difficult for Jacob to just stand back watching as these events unfolded. He couldn't shake the image of his own children and his Maggie being subjected to a similar fate. His gut tried to release the little food he had in his stomach, but he fought back the feeling. He didn't want to show any weakness to the men who had joined him at the wall, watching through whatever gaps they could find.

Jacob marveled at the man they watched in the square. He was a muscular giant with chiseled forearms that reminded him of a blacksmith or the Welsh axe men who had masterfully completed the backbreaking work of widening the road that led to Braddock's defeat. The man's body showed signs of terrible beatings and he visibly wavered on his feet, but he emanated an inner strength that had not seemed to wither.

A couple of warriors lashed the poor man's hands together and tore the remains of his shirt from his back. Two of the biggest savages held his body upright and his already heavily scarred torso was sliced further as each of the warriors danced passed him, running their tomahawks over his exposed skin. Some of the particularly over-eager warriors held their hawks over an open fire to add to the man's discomfort.

Jacob cringed at every strike and did everything in his power to stop himself from breaking down the door to offer aid to the poor man. It would be an impulsive and foolish act on his part; he would not only be unable to help the captive, but would bring about his own demise much sooner.

By now, Jacob's fellow prisoners had begun screaming insults at the warriors, but regrettably it just seemed to goad the savages into punishing the man even more.

Jacob and the others cheered loudly for the man as he impressively managed to stay on his feet. The savages continued their strikes until his entire chest and stomach were stained with blood. The warriors were clearly becoming frustrated with this strange white captive who refused to show them any signs of fear or pain.

He remained stoic and simply mouthed a silent prayer throughout the attack. His quiet defiance inspired the other captives to intensify their supportive cheers and screams. The noise drew a crowd of villagers who gathered to watch this preamble to the night's festivities. Jacob noticed that even Captain Jacobs stood among them and seemed to be interested in the man's display of raw courage.

The warriors became increasingly frustrated and embarrassed by the man's indifference to their attack. They were spurred on by the growing chants from the crowd and the once small slices became much harder blows that sadly started to wilt the man to his knees.

In spite of his own encouraging shouts to him, Jacob prayed that the warriors would just kill the poor man and save him from further punishment. He knew the frenzied warriors would never let the captive live at the risk of being shamed and laughed at by their comrades.

They pressed on with their now out-of-control torture. The villagers had begun to cheer more for the courageous settler than for their own men, driving the warriors to more intense blows.

After a few more minutes of chaos, three of the larger warriors rushed towards the man, simultaneously driving their weapons into his body. One aimed for his inner thighs, another for his calves and the third for his neck. Their precise blows drove the man's face down in the dirt. They stood triumphantly over the quivering body and let out horrendous cries that the rest of the captives would not soon forget.

Jacob willed the man back to life, but one of the warriors stepped over his dying body, pulled his head up by the hair and, with one quick movement, sliced off a large clump of dirty blonde hair. He waved the bloody scalp proudly and displayed it to the villagers to await their approval.

The majority of the villagers remained silent and simply stared at the brave captive's scalped and mutilated body. After a few tense moments, the villagers turned away to return to their work.

Such bravery as the captive had shown during his torturous death made him an instant hero and the prisoners in the shack let out a yell to honor his death. Jacob remained at his peep hole as the rest of the prisoners returned to their spots against the opposite wall.

He could tell that the warriors had not been expecting such a poor response from their own people. They too slowly dispersed, leaving the bloody corpse to be dragged away by a pack of wild dogs that roamed freely around the village.

Jacob was furious and watched as the villagers continued on with their work as if nothing had happened. He wanted absolutely nothing to do with the evening's celebration and refused to become mere entertainment for these savages.

He cared little for the other prisoners' attempts to keep to themselves. Jacob said in a low but forceful tone, "Gentlemen, I for one cannot just sit idly by and wait for the same bloody thing to happen to me. If any of you wish that upon yourselves, then so be it. Personally, I am not going to stand by and await my turn to be paraded around like some animal."

Not surprisingly, Private Taylor was the first to speak up. "What's your plan? We are certainly not in a great position to do much of anything."

Jacob was quick to respond, "I expected as much from you, Taylor, you coward, but what of the rest of you? I for one would sooner die trying to escape than let these savages have their way with me."

No one else responded and Jacob had no other choice but to let it be. He knew what he wanted to do, and if these sorry excuses for fighting men didn't care, then why should he give a damn about them?

He continued to stare out the small gap in the wall, scanning what he could see of the village in search of a weak point. A group of adopted white captives were hard at work splitting an endless pile of thick logs into smaller pieces. Some of the wood would be used in the fires to roast the game for the feast, but Jacob knew that most of it would be piled up around several posts he had seen near the center of the village on his way to the shack.

Jacob had never witnessed it firsthand, yet he had heard the horrid details about the gruesome ritual torturing of captives from Joshua and some of the other men.

He imagined that he and the other captive soldiers would be dragged out past the celebrating villagers, kicked and spat upon and strapped to the poles. The wood piled to their knees would be set ablaze and the drunken warriors would spend a long time slashing and poking at the defenseless men.

Jacob was told that the tribes in this area performed these ritual tortures out of respect for their captives. It would begin as some misguided ceremony to capture the dying men's honor, but in the end, it would become a drunken mess of savages using it as an excuse to kill more white people.

Jacob spent the next half hour or so memorizing the basic layout of the portion of the village he could see. Beyond the nearest buildings, he could see a field where a late crop of corn had recently been harvested. On the far side of the field, a thick forest beckoned to Jacob. It was about two hundred paces, if not more, from the shack where Jacob was held, but it looked like it could hide a man for a lifetime.

He struggled with the realization that he would need to coax some of the men to come with him. The distance was too great to cover without a diversion. A few men were all he needed. A lone man sprinting across an open field, no matter the distance, would present a pretty easy target, but five or six men would give Jacob a fighting chance to make it to the woods.

Alternately, the river lay just to the west of the shed. As he looked toward the broad Allegheny, he registered what he had only glimpsed during the march down the hill to the village. On the far shore of the river sat another, smaller village. Escaping by the river might have been a possible option, but he knew that even if he made it through the village to reach the mass of canoes that sat bouncing in the chilly water, he would never manage to get past two villages undetected.

He had just returned his vigilant gaze to the forest when movement at the riverbank caught his eye. Straining to get a better angle to view what was happening down by the water, he finally saw the arrival of two large bateaux, packed with a number of French marines.

Captain Jacobs and some of the elders had made their way down to the river to greet the contingent of French soldiers, but Jacob was too far away to hear what they were talking about. He watched as several warriors presented the French officers with a number of fresh scalp locks that were passed on to a couple of marines. The men were welcomed cheerfully by the villagers and slowly walked towards the village square.

While they were speaking, the French commander sent one of his aids to retrieve a small sack from one the boats. The aid quickly returned and handed it to the officer, who in turn gave it to Captain Jacobs. He gladly accepted it and put it in an inner pocket of the prized red British officer's coat he had put on for the night's feast.

Jacob knew the sack was full of silver coins, the bounty payment for English scalps. The Delaware were only too glad to take the payment, but

Jacob suspected they would have been just as eager to kill settlers without being paid.

Most of the British and colonial troops were aware of the bounty for scalps and that the French were 'encouraging' their Delaware and Shawnee allies to take up the hatchet against the English settlers. The situation on the frontier was made worse by such rewards and left the poor settlers an easy target for profiteering savages.

The British were certainly not innocent of such bounty payments, although most formally-trained officers tended to discourage such actions. The colonial militia, on the other hand, had maintained bounty offers on Indian and Canadian militia scalps for some time.

Jacob had been so busy watching the French officers that he never heard the approach of a party of warriors who pushed opened the door of the decrepit shed, flashing a blinding ray of light into the faces of the huddled prisoners. The sudden blast of sunlight forced all the men except Jacob to cover their eyes. Jacob had been looking out into the light for several hours and was able to look directly at the warriors when they entered. Inexplicably, he assumed they were coming for him.

He was right.

Two of the warriors stepped into the cramped quarters and pointed directly at Jacob. He hesitated but knew he had to go with them. He stepped over a couple of the men and was slightly annoyed that none of the men reacted or said anything in his defense.

His escorts didn't bother to secure his hands as they pushed him towards the French commander and Captain Jacobs who stood talking together. Jacob was placed directly in front of the two men. Off to his left, he noticed a large hemp sack of dried scalps.

"Do you see any of your men's scalps?" Captain Jacobs laughed.

Jacob said nothing to either man.

The French commander ignored Captain Jacobs' taunts and politely asked Jacob in English, "Who might you be, monsieur? For an Englishman, you are far north of where your fellow British army has retreated to."

Once again Jacob said nothing.

Without waiting for his reply, the French commander introduced himself, "My name is Captain Lapointe. I am stationed at Fort Machault, just north of where we are standing."

The officer was nearly as tall as Jacob, but seemed somewhat out of place in this wilderness. His polished boots and nicely tailored outer coat made him look far more ready for a posting behind the walls of Quebec City than a small trading post fort on the edge of civilization.

Jacob had a sense that this officer didn't particularly enjoy dealing with or being amongst the Delaware, although he appeared to understand the French would be nowhere without their Indian allies. Jacob would have loved to ask him what he thought of the bag of scalps now in his possession, but that would have to wait for another time.

Looking past the two men, Jacob finally caught a good look at the two large bateaux. Each carried over thirty men and was equipped with two small swivel cannon that were similar to the ones he'd seen back at Fort Necessity. Just over a half-dozen Huron scouts milled by the boats, refusing to intermingle with the Delaware villagers.

The officer did not seem tough, but he did command respect and Jacob replied politely, "My name, monsieur, is Sergeant Jacob Sims. I am under the command of Major Stevens' Ranging Company."

The two men exchanged salutes as Captain Jacobs stood by and offered his own mocking salute.

Neither man acknowledged him, but just as the Delaware leader was about to speak, Captain Lapointe bluntly continued, "How have you and your men been treated?"

Jacob was quick to answer, "Sir, you obviously are new to these parts if you expect me to answer such a question."

Removing his gold-trimmed tricorn hat, Lapointe ran his hands through his nicely groomed hair and replied, "I have heard of the way they honor their prisoners, but thankfully I have never seen it for myself. As much as I do understand that they just want to protect their land, I must admit I see no value in what they do."

A nerve had been struck and Jacob boldly shot back, "Yet they do the dirty work for your king and you openly pay them for the scalps of innocent English men, women and children?"

Captain Jacobs motioned to Jacob's two escorts to keep him quiet and they both drove their fists into his midsection. This drew the ire of the French officer who protested, "Keep your warriors under control;

there is no need for such actions. The Englishman is certainly entitled to his opinion."

Jacob barely moved, taking the punches without giving either warrior any satisfaction in knowing they'd hurt him.

Attempting to calm the situation, Lapointe looked at Captain Jacobs and said, "I would like to continue my conversation with the prisoner after I have met with your elders."

Captain Jacobs reluctantly obliged the request and motioned to the two warriors to return Jacob to the shed.

Before they could, Lapointe ordered them to stay and wait for him to return. The men just stopped and looked to their chief for direction. A simple nod from him made them let go of Jacob's arms. Two French marines were left beside Jacob just to ensure nothing would happen to him.

Jacob was left standing with the two confused Delaware guards and watched the small contingent walk towards the preparations taking place in and around the village square.

After a few minutes, the Delaware warriors left him unguarded, as did the two French marines who noticed a group of young Delaware woman doing some quill work nearby. He would never have a better opportunity to investigate the layout of the village and plan an escape.

He slowly stepped forward a few feet, waiting for someone to order him to stop, but no such command was issued. Not wanting to draw too much attention to himself, he took some time to count the number of houses that sat between the shed and the first cut of the field. He boldly continued to walk around, fully expecting to be stopped at any moment. He stood by the outer most house on the border of the large open field, looking towards the thick tree line.

Being this close gave him a far better view of the daunting task it would take to make such a run across this open field. Even if he could convince a handful of the men to come with him, they would easily be shot or run down. The distance across the field was too great to make such an attempt. With most of the men starved and weak, Jacob knew that it would be suicide to use this route as an escape.

He decided to rethink the river option. If he could reach a canoe, he might be able to make it. He took in the details of the small village across the water. It was impossible to guess how many settlers lived in either village.

Jacob continued looking around him and soon spotted the young mother whose husband had been killed so savagely a couple of hours earlier. She sat with a group of elderly Delaware women, who were busily combing out her blonde hair and braiding it Indian style. She had already been stripped of her old nightgown and was dressed in a beautiful brain-tanned leather dress, adorned with beads and quills. If not for the color of her hair, she would have been easily mistaken for a native Delaware villager.

Nearby, he caught a quick glimpse of the woman's three young boys, happily playing with several other Delaware boys. They were completely unaware of what had happened to their father and how their lives had been irreversibly altered.

Jacob walked slightly closer to the river and found that he had a difficult time navigating the village's oddly organized layout. In some areas, it looked like some of the families just put up a structure wherever they liked. It was a far cry from the English and German settlements that were so meticulously laid out and organized into streets and rows. This was more maze-like and would make an attack or escape very difficult to execute.

Jacob continued to move as close to the river as he dared. He was busy counting the paces from the shed to the shoreline until he was called back by one of his escorts. Satisfied that he had gotten a good look at all the possibilities, he returned to where he originally spoke with the French officer.

Just as he walked back, he noticed Lapointe returning with a group of village elders.

"Sergeant Sims, I have some good news for you and some of your men," he said rather happily. "I have negotiated the possibility for you and six of your men to return with me to Fort Machault for the winter. What are your thoughts about that?"

Captain Jacobs was clearly not in favor of such a parole and remained behind the elders, waiting to see how things would play out.

Jacob was not sure of what he should think, especially since he was unsure of the exact terms of this exchange. He thought over this unexpected proposal as quickly as he could.

Not wishing to squelch this rare opportunity to escape the coming tortuous celebration, Jacob politely asked what was forefront on his mind,

"May I ask, captain, why just six men? Also, will I be the one to decide who is to come and who must suffer certain death?"

Lapointe first looked at the elders before he answered quietly, "Well, Sergeant, the best I could do was six, and that was far more than my Delaware hosts wanted to give me. I was careful not to press too hard, and I recommend that you tread lightly as well. I will let them celebrate their small victory with a few men that were already set to die."

"There is little I can say in response to such a gracious offer. If I am to make the final decision about which men to bring, how much time do I have?" Jacob asked, not looking forward to such a decision.

"The Delaware want to begin their celebration very soon. I honestly have no desire to watch or participate, even if they see it as an insult. With nightfall fast approaching, I must request you decide now so we can leave and set up camp as far away as we can." Lapointe kept his voice low, being careful not to offend any elders within earshot.

Jacob felt an odd combination of happiness at escaping the evening's festivities and sadness at having to select who would live and who would be left behind and face the Delaware's torture. He bowed politely to the French officer who had so graciously extended the offer of amnesty and caught the eye of the glaring Captain Jacobs. Standing back up straight, Jacob offered the Delaware leader a smirk of defiance and turned away.

With all the formalities completed, Jacob's warrior escorts reappeared and took him back to the shack. Jacob took a deep breath of fresh air before he entered the dark and decrepit structure. The two guards left the door open, but remained outside waiting for Jacob to decide the fate of the men.

Even with the door ajar, his eyes took a moment to adjust to the dim light as the men more or less ignored his return.

He wanted to get this horrible task over with and decided not to beat around the bush. Jacob cleared his throat and said, "Gentlemen, I need six of you to come with me. Which of you men are married?"

He had not had much time to think of how to choose which men to take with him, but he thought to first narrow down the group into married and single men. Next, he would pick the men who appeared to be the healthiest, or the most likely to have enough strength to survive the winter in such a remote outpost. Jacob feared that the men would most likely be no better than slaves to the garrison, so he wanted to ensure that the six men could handle such duties.

Jacob waited for the men to point themselves out and only eight of the men claimed to be married. His heart went out to the unmarried men. It was hard to decide against men based on whether they were married or not, especially since many of them were too young to have had the chance to wed yet.

Choosing six men from his eight married men was made easier by the fact that two of them were far too injured to make the trip. Unfortunately, one of the remaining six was Private Taylor.

Jacob swore to himself when he realized that Taylor was among them and said, "How can I trust that you are really married, Taylor? I truly pity the poor lass who might be married to you."

Taylor calmly reassured Jacob of his status, saying, "You have my word, sir. I have a good wife and four young lads back on my farm. God can strike me down if I am telling a lie."

Jacob waited for a brief moment, hoping that a bolt from the heavens would make his life that much easier. Sadly, Taylor was left untouched and Jacob said, "Get up, private, and go with the others."

Once the six men were outside, Jacob felt he should address the remaining men, "God bless you, lads. I am not sure when I might return. As long as I am still alive though, I promise you I will…" He could go no further and simply offered the men a salute before stepping back outside. He wiped tears from his eyes before any of the men would have the chance to notice and directed the six towards the French boats.

They were dirty and ragged, wearing clothes even a London beggar would be ashamed to wear, and Jacob offered the sad looking lot a smile, saying, "Now, please follow me and do not speak until we are away from this godforsaken place." He looked directly towards Taylor, waiting for him to say something, but alas the private proved to be far smarter than Jacob gave him credit for.

Jacob stayed in the rear, watching the reaction from some of the villagers as the seven captives walked towards the French boats. Most of the men found it difficult to walk and Jacob couldn't imagine what the French thought of them. All the men except Jacob had been cramped up in their makeshift jail for at least a week and had become so severely weakened that they had to stop several times to rest during the short distance they were forced to walk.

Captain Lapointe noticed the men struggling to make it to the boats and sent a few of his men to offer some assistance.

As Jacob walked past a few of the warriors, they could barely hide their anger at having their prisoners taken by the French. Captain Jacobs was waiting just a few paces from the French and made it a point to speak with Jacob. "Englishman," he said in a voice just over a whisper, "this is not over. Once we rid our land of your English brothers, I will do the same to the French. They have a weak spot for their fellow white men and that will be their undoing."

Jacob said nothing, but just smiled at the visibly angered chief. He had a feeling that they would meet again soon enough.

Lapointe greeted the men as they finally reached the boats and politely pulled Jacob aside for a quick word. "Sergeant, these are the men you have decided on? I must say they are in far worse condition then I imagined. Our bateaux are full, but there is space enough for you. I have arranged for a small scouting party to escort your men to our temporary camp. It is thankfully only a few miles to the north and the trail is easy."

"The men," Jacob said stiffly, "have been beaten and starved by your allies and they are sadly the healthiest of the lot. As for your offer of a ride, I must respectfully decline so I can walk with my men."

"Well then, we will see you at the encampment," Lapointe replied.

"Monsieur, some food for my men would be helpful for their trip," Jacob requested respectfully. "They have not seen food for over a week."

"In time, Sims. I must be careful not to insult my Delaware allies and make them think I am displaying weakness towards my prisoners."

Jacob said nothing more and ordered his men to follow him. The only thing he could think of now was the captain's use of the word 'prisoners'.

He knew he was in a far better position to escape now, but he had no idea what the French had planned for him and his men. Only time would tell if their current position was better than the one they were leaving behind.

Chapter | **Eight**

Maggie was glad to have a moment alone to recover from the shock of reuniting with Israel. The chill in the air provided little opposition for the roaring campfire and, as heat drifted towards her face, she felt calm and relaxed. She sat and watched the odd assortment of men as they completed various tasks within the well-protected encampment.

She observed Israel as he spoke with several of his men and, despite his outer appearance, Maggie recognized the same kind man she had always enjoyed spending time with. Some of his gestures reminded her so much of Jacob that she found herself studying him intently, hoping for more glimpses of her beloved husband.

She smiled as she recalled the days of her courtship with Jacob. It had been difficult to tell the twin brothers apart at first, but their individual characteristics became distinguishable to her. Jacob was had a much better posture, which made him seem slightly taller. He was also far more confident and outgoing, while Israel liked to stay in the background and enjoyed quietly working his land. It was that same modesty and preference for the land that made Maggie question the odd courtship between Israel and his then-fiancée Abby. She remembered telling Jacob that the two of them seemed like such a terrible match. A city-raised girl and a backwoodsman certainly made for an interesting pairing, but the four of them quickly became close friends.

"Are you well, Maggie?" Israel asked as he suddenly appeared at her side.

Maggie jumped as her thoughts scattered. "Oh! Israel! Yes, I was just looking back on better days."

"I understand, I find myself lost in my thoughts all the time," Israel said with a slight sigh.

Maggie noticed several of the men preparing their muskets and packing up some of their gear and asked, "Are we heading out?"

"No, not right away, Maggie," Israel replied as he held a long stick between his wrists and used it to stir the logs in the fire. "I just received word that there is a small French scouting party just north of us. I want a few of the men to check them out and see what they are up to."

A young man approached and said, "Sir, we are ready to head out."

"Remember to keep yourselves safe and please don't do anything foolish," Israel said in a stern voice. "If you need help, contact Mr. Richardson at his home near the gap we use to pass through the mountains. Godspeed, lad."

Maggie smiled at the young man and moved closer to the fire as the dozen or so scouts disappeared through the cleft in the rocks. She marveled at the confidence exhibited by her brother-in-law and wondered how he had come by it.

When Israel turned his attention back to her, Maggie said, "I hope I am not keeping you from your duties, Israel."

"Do not worry about that. I have some good men to help me. They are more than capable of making some decisions in my absence."

Maggie still found it difficult to look at him directly, especially when he sat so close. She could see every detail of the damage the fire had done to his once handsome face.

"Tell me what happened to you, Israel?" Maggie asked bluntly.

"I forgot how straight to the point you are Maggie," Israel said with a short, screechy laugh. "I must say, it brings back some good memories."

Maggie felt her face redden and hoped she hadn't insulted him.

Seeing that she felt badly, Israel continued quickly, "I have truly missed you and Jacob so much. Our lives were so good, and the children...Oh, the children have, I fear, suffered the greatest loss."

He took a moment to compose his thoughts and continued, "As for my story, Jacob and I were together during the mess at Fort Necessity. I remember that I was shot and carried inside the poor excuse for a fort. Jacob stayed by my side as long as he could. The rest is mostly a blur to be honest."

Struggling to speak, Israel took a deep breath and forced out the rest of his story, "Once the militia left the fort, all the injured and undefended men were attacked by the bloody savages and most were killed and scalped. They let me be for some reason, but before they departed, they set the place on fire. My injuries prevented me from freeing myself and attempting to escape the flames."

Maggie stopped him before he could continue, "Please, Israel, I don't want you to rehash all these bad memories. We can speak of this at a better time."

He shook his head and said, "It is good to finally speak about this. I have kept everything buried for far too long.

Keeping his head down and pushing around the embers with the stick, he went on, "Ironically, the terrible rain that aided in our defeat also saved my life. Most of my body was submerged in water and the fire only managed to burn my face, hands and parts of my legs. The rest of my body was left scarred by the intense heat, but nothing like my face and hands. I managed to survive, despite the French and Huron bastards leaving me for dead."

"Thankfully, a small band of Mingo men and women came by to scavenge through the leftovers of the battle. They found me buried in the debris and took me back to their camp. They spent months covering my body in bear fat and cold cloths. God knows, if they hadn't come by and taken such care of me, I would have made an easy meal for a wildcat or bear." Israel explained, not once looking up.

Maggie was captivated by the story, but she could see that Israel was greatly affected by the memories it conjured up. She tried to give him a break in his narrative by asking, "When was the last time you saw or heard about Jacob?"

"Well, I heard that he did everything in his power to save me, but had no support from his fellow mates. One of my men told me that Jacob even deserted to go back and search for me. It was bloody stupid of him, but I value his bravery and loyalty."

Maggie instinctively reached out to hold his hand, forgetting it was now only a useless piece of disfigured flesh and bone. Her hand struck him lightly on the leg and he winced. "Sorry…I hope…" Maggie stuttered as she pulled her hand back quickly, trying to hide her uncomfortable reaction.

Israel looked away and said, "Please don't feel bad, Maggie. I have seen how people, even my own men, react when they meet me. Honestly, I don't know how I would respond to such a sight. I must look like something you would see in a bad dream."

Maggie didn't know what to say. She reached out again and this time, her well-directed hand landed on his forearm. He still flinched from her touch but he instantly relaxed once she left it resting on his arm.

"The Mingo called me 'Skin Like Birch'," he continued, "because when they found me, my skin was peeling and hanging from my body. They thought it looked like the bark of the white birch tree in the winter."

"Does it still hurt?" Maggie asked, as she gently rubbed his arm.

"It was really sensitive to light, or even to touch, but it is far better now. I have to watch what I wear; anything rough would rub my skin raw. My men made me a beautiful bear-skin cloak that protects me from the sun and the hordes of insects. I enjoy a brisk jump in the river now and again, especially in the winter. God knows what the beavers and otters must think when they see me swim past them, but the ice-cold water soothes the skin and it really gets my blood circulating." Israel stopped to take a painful breath and forced himself to continue, "The only unfortunate part was the loss of my hands. The Mingo did their best to save them. After all my skin died and blackened, though, they feared it might infect the rest of my body. My hands were heavily bandaged together to save my life and I will always be in their debt for making such a hard decision."

Once again taking a brief break, he swallowed and did his best to clear his raspy throat, "I have adapted to it, as you have seen. The men strap knives to them and one of the lads made a leather sheath that attaches to my sword and then to my wrists. It is awkward, but it works well enough."

"So, when did you get involved with these men?" Maggie asked, careful not to put too much strain on his damaged throat.

"It was more a matter of survival. The Mingo moved on and I wanted to stay near my home. I met up with several men who had deserted or were left behind by the British. More than a few of them lost their families and land to the raids and had no other place to go. We are a band of misfits and I am proud to lead them. We never judge anyone; you could be an escaped slave or an Indian and no one would say a word. I only ask that they fight with us against the French and savages." His voice noticeably cracked as he struggled to continue.

"Is there anything I can do to help?" Maggie asked. "I feel guilty taking up space in the camp without contributing anything."

Israel thought for a moment as he carefully rose to his feet. "We have some root vegetables and a few dried pieces of deer shank left," he said finally. "I think the men would die for one of your famous stews. I for one would love a cup."

"It would be an honor!" she said with a smile. "Just let me get my things ready. Would you be kind enough to have one of the men fetch me some water?"

"I will have it brought to you right away," he said as he turned to go. "Thank you, Maggie. It is so good to see you alive and safe."

Maggie gave him another big smile as she brushed off her clothes and started collecting her supplies. She worked quickly and had most of the roots and meat sliced up when one of the men brought her two large gourds full of cold, clean water.

Two other men had already positioned a large black pot on a rack over the fire. Several others happily assisted Maggie by scavenging around the camp to find more ingredients to add to the stew. They did not disappoint and soon ground onions, fall corn and a couple of other wild vegetables joined the thickening stew. Israel walked past at one point and looked in the pot. He refused the offer of a spoonful from Maggie, saying "If the wonderful smell matches the taste, Maggie, then I will wait with the men to enjoy it. Be sure to set some aside and let mine cool down."

She watched as one of the men ground some hard corn on a rock. He added a mixture of fresh water and sugary maple water, making a thick paste. A handful of wild berries had been gathered by one of the other men, and he blended them into the pasty mixture with his knife. He then spread his concoction on the flat rocks by the fire. Soon, the hand-sized pieces were cooked into lovely cornmeal patties to be shared by the men.

By the time the patrol Israel had sent out returned, the meal was ready and the men started to line up with their wooden bowls and cups. Maggie stood behind the pot, ready to spoon out the stew, but one of the men handed her a bowl and directed her to take the first taste. She filled her bowl with the hot stew and sat by the other fire.

"I have not seen the men so happy or looking so forward to eating in ages," Israel said proudly as he took a seat next to her. "We are always thankful to have a steady source of food, but the same roasted and dried meats day after day can get a bit tedious."

Maggie offered him a spoonful from her bowl but he respectfully declined saying, "Another damn problem with having no hands is you always need some poor person to feed you."

The two shared an uncomfortable laugh and Maggie was quick to change the subject, "You said that you heard Jacob had deserted after Fort Necessity. How is it that you have not managed to meet up with him again if many of your men are deserters?"

"We try to get information from trappers, hunters and traders, but most in these parts are French or Canadian and they give us very little. Most of the time, it is inaccurate or outdated.

"Of course I send my men out scouting, but sadly we have not received any reliable news of Jacob. There are always rumors about, and we have heard about a young ranger commanding the building a fortification near the mountains. Building a fort right in the middle of French territory seems like the type of bold behavior one would expect of Jacob. I have heard, though, that the ranger is part of the Virginia militia, so it seems unlikely that it would be him if the news of his desertion is true."

Maggie took several more sips of the steamy stew. She looked around the camp and watched the men devour their supper. The camp had fallen silent with only the dragging and scraping of spoons over wooden bowls breaking the peace.

"The men surely needed this change in their diet," Israel said. "I know I was getting tired of the same old smoked deer meat or squirrel soup, so I can imagine these lads felt the same way. They probably feel like we've stumbled into a fancy Philadelphia City eatery!"

Maggie laughed and said, "I am so glad that I can contribute something to make their lives a bit more enjoyable."

When Israel had finished eating his cooled down stew, he said, "We will be heading out in the morning and traveling north, towards Fort Machault. My apologies, Maggie, but our lifestyle is far more nomadic than what you and I were accustomed to back on our farms."

Maggie waved away his apology and said, "I have done a fair amount of moving myself over the past year, even as far north as Niagara. You do not have to worry about me."

Israel nodded and excused himself. He walked away, and Maggie saw him speaking with the scouts he had sent out on the northern trail.

Maggie was impressed by Israel's men. Most of them made it a point to come up to her and thank her for the meal; the rest nodded their appreciation, and she assumed they were shy. It felt so peaceful here in this secluded camp that she found herself wishing they could stay instead of getting back on the trail.

The stew pot was empty, much to Maggie's satisfaction, and she was able to wipe it clean. Then she rinsed the men's bowls in some fresh water and laid them out to dry. When she was satisfied her work area was cleaned up, she walked over to the fire to prepare her bed for the night. The men had given her a nice wool blanket and a heavy winter coyote pelt to keep her warm.

Israel returned from speaking with the men and said, "We will leave at first light. Is there anything you need, Maggie?"

"The men have made sure I will be warm through the night. Thank you for checking on me, Israel."

"Before I finish my nightly walk-around, there is something I want to ask. How did you find yourself traveling with a group of French marines?"

Maggie had been expecting this question, but she only gave him the barest account of her dealings with Fredrick. "I was at a small Delaware village, being held captive until some Ottawa chief was to return from Fort Duquesne. He was going to take me back west, but thank God he never returned. I knew the French commander killed during your ambush; he found me at the village and helped me escape."

Israel said nothing more, except to wish her a good night.

She watched him walk to the first picket and talk briefly with the man. Israel then disappeared down the entrance trail. Maggie fell into a deep sleep and had no idea how long he was gone.

The morning came far too soon, once again. Maggie arose and rolled up her bedding. The night had been cold, and the boulders and trees that surrounded the camp had a thin layer of fresh snow.

All the fires had burned out overnight, so a hot breakfast was out of the question. One of the men handed Maggie some salted meat and a canteen of water. She pulled off a small piece of meat and put the rest in the small sack she carried with her.

Maggie could tell that these men had a routine for packing up their camp. They moved efficiently and had their belongings packed and traces of the camp scattered before Israel even arrived to lead them. They stood in a line waiting to depart, and Maggie could see they were getting a bit restless. She asked the man next to her if he had seen Israel.

"No, ma'am," he responded, "the captain never sleeps, and he sometimes roams the wilderness until day break."

Just then, Israel walked into the camp and announced in the highest pitch his ragged voice could manage, "Gentlemen and Maggie, we are heading north today. We are to meet up with Mr. Tanner and his men around the usual spot. We will then continue north. We have reports of some new raids and a group of French soldiers trekking near Kittanning. I have been told they have some colonial militia captives with them. I think we need to liberate the lads."

The camp echoed with cheers from the men. They were clearly excited about the prospect of fighting the well-trained French marines.

"Mr. Kennedy," Israel struggled to continue, "Please take ten men and lead the way. Mr. Richards will take the rear guard for now. Once we find Mr. Tanner, we will split our forces and have some of you canoe up the Allegheny. Now, keep your eyes open and the noise down."

When he finished speaking, Israel moved to allow the advanced scouts to head up the trail. The rest of the party waited several minutes to let the scouts get well ahead. Soon they were all on the trail, and Israel walked next to Maggie when the narrow path permitted.

Israel was adamant that the men remain silent, keeping conversations to a minimum while they were on the trails. Most of the men were experienced in wilderness trekking and they certainly did not want to draw unwanted attention to themselves.

The terrain was certainly to their advantage. The snaking trails and paths were dotted with hundreds of places to set up and launch an ambush if required. Despite the thinning foliage, the trees were plentiful and helped to screen their movements from any prying eyes.

These men had traveled these trails and little-used side paths for months, and Maggie suspected they could traverse them blindfolded. Israel remained as cautious as if it was their first time on an unknown trail. Maggie respected his vigilance; just the day before, she had witnessed how easily a well-manned unit could be destroyed if its guard was down for even a moment.

Despite Israel's caution, Maggie was impressed by how quickly they moved. It was barely midday when they caught up to Kennedy's men, who waited at a large fallen tree.

"Gentlemen, what took you so long?" Caleb called out with a huge grin.

"How did you find the trails?" Israel called back.

Maggie was glad to hear that the mandatory silence was over. She was glad to see the rest of the men and hoped this reunion meant they would be able to rest for a bit.

Israel and Caleb walked to the far side of the downed tree and up a sharp incline until they were out of sight. Maggie waited with the rest of the men; they rested up against the broad tree trunk, but remained on their guard.

Israel returned part way down the path and called the rest of them to join him. He waited for Maggie and assisted her up the steep, leaf-covered trail. At the top, Maggie was surprised to find a rocky ledge similar to the one where they had camped the previous night.

The entrance was once again hidden by a large boulder. As she walked around the moss-covered giant rock and through a maze of downed trees and limbs, she was greeted by a man's voice saying, "You must be Mrs. Murray; I am Jonathon Tanner of Virginia."

Maggie looked up when her feet were no longer in danger of tripping and stifled a laugh at her first glimpse of the man. He wore an old pair of leather breeches, which probably fit him at one time in his life. They looked uncomfortably tight, and she immediately wondered how he could breathe in them. She guessed that he weighed no more than Israel, but he was jammed into a much smaller frame. His perfectly round head dwarfed the rest of him; the hair that remained on the top of his scalp was pulled over to one side before it met the long stringy pony tail that hung down his back. On the top of his awkward frame, he wore a poorly made hunting jacket that he seemed to be particularly proud of. His voice was unnaturally loud, as if he was totally unaware that he was shouting, but it had a friendly tone.

Tanner grabbed Maggie's hand and kissed it before turning to Israel with a glint in his eye. "Damn savages are attacking with a vengeance all up and down the Allegheny region," he said. "If we don't strike them soon, we will have to wait until the spring to do anything."

"I understand your frustration, Tanner, but if we permit the men to run all over the territory looking for fights, we will never be able to stop the bloody savages from murdering all our people," Israel responded, his voice straining to explain.

Maggie remained silent and watched the two men verbally spar. She realized it was all in good humor when the two men put their arms across each other's shoulders and walked into the camp.

She followed them and as they reached the center of the camp site, Israel said, "Maggie, I have a few more issues to discuss with Mr. Tanner. Please find a comfortable place to rest; I will return shortly."

Even though they had only stopped here to rest and plan their next move, the men built a small fire to keep away the late-October chill. Maggie found a small boulder nearby and made a cushion for herself out of thick piece of moss. She perched atop the rock and allowed the heat to permeate her skin.

The men busied themselves cleaning and inspecting their muskets. Soon young Caleb brought Maggie a steaming cup of coffee made from hickory nuts, a few chestnuts and water from his canteen. It was almost too bitter to swallow, but she appreciated the added warmth it provided. "Thank you, Caleb," she said, trying not to show her reaction to the bitterness. "This is very kind of you."

"My pleasure, Maggie," he said with a smile as he hopped up on another boulder nearby. "You don't mind if I join you for a spell, do you?"

"Please do; I welcome the company."

The two fell silent for a moment, unsure what to say next.

"My apologies for the coffee," he said. "It is certainly an acquired taste. I have been with these men for almost two winters, and I honestly still find it difficult to drink."

"It feels wonderful to drink a hot beverage, but it certainly is a unique taste," she smiled. "May I ask how such a young boy got himself into all of this?"

Caleb's cheeks turned pink and he replied, "I am eighteen, ma'am; I am no boy, I assure you."

Maggie was quick to ease her unintended insult, "I'm sorry, Caleb; I meant nothing by it. You just look so much younger than most of the others."

Caleb shook his head and laughed. "No, I'm sorry for overreacting. If you look over there, that is Nathan Gates; he is all of fifteen, but he is so tall that most folks think he is in his twenties. Those two Mingo boys by the fire are somewhere around fourteen or so. Hicks, over there by the big oak, is only sixteen. I am by no means the youngest here."

Maggie had no idea that any of the men were as young as fourteen.

"As for how I got here," Caleb continued, "like most of the younger lads, my family was taken by the Shawnee and I was the only one who survived. After they traded me to the Delaware, some of these men thankfully raided the village and took me with them. Since I have nowhere else to go, I asked to join with them.

"What about you? You said last night that you had been a captive of multiple tribes. What is your story?"

Maggie watched Israel talking with Tanner on the other side of the camp, and replied, "My story is very similar. My children and I were taken by the Huron. They split us up, but I managed to escape. The French found me and sold me to a Quebec merchant. On the way north, I escaped the French, only to be taken captive by the Ottawa. They left me with the Delaware and I was rescued from them by a French patrol."

She fell silent for a moment then said with sad smile, "I guess my story isn't really all that similar to yours after all!"

"What of your husband?" Caleb asked boldly.

"My husband is the twin brother of Israel. They left over a year ago to fight with the militia and I hadn't seen either one until yesterday when

Israel freed me from the French." She struggled against the tears welling up in her eyes.

"Sorry, Maggie, I didn't mean to upset you. I guess we have all been through hell and back."

They sat silently, sipping their coffee until Israel returned.

"Mr. Kennedy, thank you for keeping my sister-in-law company," Israel said and waited for a moment. He had hoped Caleb would realize that he wished to speak with Maggie privately, but he finally said, "You may go now, lad. Please check your weapon and be ready to leave shortly."

Caleb's cheeks flushed once more as he stepped down from the boulder. He politely touched his hat to Maggie and walked past Israel, who choked back a laugh.

"Israel, he is only a boy, you didn't need to embarrass him so," Maggie said as Israel sat on Caleb's rock.

"No harm, Maggie. He is one of the good lads and he knows that I see him as a son."

Israel stopped abruptly, and Maggie could see that he was thinking of his own little ones. The pain in his eyes reflected what she felt whenever she thought of her own children.

"I miss them so…" he said, "and Abby. I think of her every moment."

Maggie wasn't sure how to respond. She desperately wanted to tell him what she knew of Abby, but she wasn't sure what to say. Her information was at least a year old. Even if Maggie could tell Israel exactly where the Huron village was located, who knew if she was still there. For that matter, only God knew if she was still alive.

Israel recovered and said, "I'm sorry, but having you here has brought back a flood of emotions that I have managed to hide for a long time."

Maggie laid a hand on his arm and said, "I completely understand. You have done the same for me."

With a nod, he changed the subject, "Winter is fast approaching and I had planned to move south. However, the British retreat means the frontier is undefended. Tanner and I were discussing what we might do next. He is for immediately setting up a winter camp in an old Seneca village a few miles east of here. I, on the other hand, want to pursue a couple of raids before we hunker down for the winter." Israel was struggling to keep his voice from cracking.

He valiantly pushed himself to continue, "I just got word that there is another party of French marines near the Allegheny, heading north towards Venango. I assume they are carrying winter supplies to Fort Machault. If we can capture their supplies, it will weaken their fort and supply us with provisions for the winter. You have been in that fort, what is your opinion?"

Maggie could not get over how much Israel had changed. Being around the much more confident Jacob most of his life always kept him in the background, but now his self-assurance and leadership had flourished.

"The fort is very remote. Once the heavy snows settle in, the fort will be unreachable. I think confiscating their supplies would do more than weaken them; it would kill the entire garrison over the cold months. That would certainly send a message to the French that this territory wasn't going to be given up easily. It would also make the frontier settlers feel a bit safer through the long winter."

"I have to agree with you. There is also a large Delaware raiding party lurking about these parts. I would love to cause them some trouble before they move to their southern winter villages, but first thing's first."

Israel excused himself to talk over Maggie's thoughts with Tanner. Before he was out of earshot, he called back, "Maggie, can you still handle a musket like you once could?"

Maggie smiled and nodded.

"Then grab one of the extra muskets from the supply and get it ready; I want you to come with us."

Israel's men moved swiftly through the dense wilderness. They dodged the many fallen trees and never seemed to lose their footing on the slick leaves that smothered the forest floor. Maggie did her best to keep up.

After a while, Israel stopped the men to allow Maggie to rest. They had found another secluded outcropping of rocks and took the opportunity to eat and reorganize.

Israel walked up to Maggie and said, "We are only a few miles from catching the French unit we are targeting. My scouts have been monitoring them for several miles, and we have already decided on the best place to ambush them. I will leave half the men here with you and take the fastest men with me. It is to be a quick hit-and-run attack; we will be back before dinner."

Maggie had objections, but kept them to herself. Instead she smiled and said, "Please take care. I refuse to lose you after finally finding you again!"

Israel simply nodded and went off to prepare his men to leave. Just before they departed, Maggie saw one of the men produce a large black bear hide from his pack. It was complete with fangs and claws and the men helped Israel put it on. She was in awe of how menacing he looked with the head of the bear positioned over his own head. She could hardly imagine what the French would do once they encountered the sight of Israel.

He turned to give a slight wave towards Maggie and disappeared a moment later. Even though she knew it was Israel, seeing him in the beast's skin made her shiver. She was glad he was on her side.

To Maggie's delight, Caleb was one of the men left behind at the camp with her. He approached and said, "Captain Murray ordered camp to be set up here for the night. I heard you are a good shot; would you like to accompany the hunting party?"

She was surprised that any of the men would want a woman to go out hunting with them, especially one that might have a chance at showing them up. She smiled and said eagerly, "When do we leave?"

Caleb returned her smile and replied, "We will head out immediately if that suits you."

Maggie had a hard time hiding her pleasure at being allowed to go on the hunt. It had been years since she had hunted with Jacob. He would sometimes take her out, usually when he was hunting the forest immediately around their cabin. She checked her musket, grabbed a few lead balls and some powder and joined the five men waiting for her by the entrance.

Two of the men were sent out to guard the hunters and scout the area for any signs of savages or game. The frontier was always full of good, quality game, and it wasn't long before the hunters found fresh evidence of white tail deer. Maggie was excited and she already had her musket loaded and primed.

Caleb stayed by her side and soon they saw a deer herd grazing on some high winter grass that had sprouted in a small opening in the trees. Maggie and Caleb managed to approach within fifty paces of the two largest creatures. Caleb pointed to the buck he would take, and Maggie nodded. They would have to shoot simultaneously to keep the deer from being spooked. With slow movements, they shouldered their muskets and steadied their aim.

Their shots were almost perfectly timed. Once the heavy white smoke cleared, they saw the herd dash into the cover of the woods. It was difficult to see if either buck had fallen in the high grass, so Caleb and Maggie began to approach cautiously where they last saw the targets.

"Keep your eyes peeled," Caleb said quietly. "Our shots may have attracted some unwanted attention."

As they approached the area where the deer had stood, Maggie was excited to find the crumpled body of her buck. Caleb gave her a congratulatory smile and continued a few paces farther in search of his own buck.

Maggie stayed by her deer and watched Caleb walk almost the length of the entire clearing as he searched for some sign of his kill.

He looked at Maggie and shrugged his shoulders before working his way back to her. He looked at her deer and said, "I would have bet my boots that I had hit mine as well."

"At least we got one of them," she said. "It is better than returning empty handed."

She hoped Caleb was not too upset that his escaped, apparently unharmed.

"I just can't believe there is no blood trail or anything. I know I had him in my sights." Caleb continued to look around the immediate area.

"Maybe I got my shot off too soon and scared your buck." Maggie did her best to lessen Caleb's injured pride.

Caleb didn't seem really agitated until the other men arrived to check on them. They soon began ribbing the younger man about his missed shot. Maggie didn't want Caleb to get upset and did her best to deflect their comments away from him, towards herself.

"Gentlemen," she said, "I think I was at fault. My shot was ahead of Mr. Kennedy's, and it must have frightened his buck off just as he was about to shoot."

"So, Caleb," one of the men said with a laugh, "you not only missed the shot, but you were beaten to it!"

Caleb's blushing cheeks triggered something within Maggie and in a flash of temper, she said, "Let us be, gentlemen. We still have time to find a couple more deer. Also, I must point out that none of you have your hands full of game."

The three men stopped for a moment, but soon one of them piped up to offer a suggestion, "How about we make this interesting? We three will leave you to this field and we will start to head back towards the camp. We will meet back at the camp within an hour and the group returning with the most game wins."

Caleb was quick to jump in and accept on their behalf, "We will take your bet, only what is at stake?"

The three hesitated again, discussing the wager in hushed tones. Finally, the same man piped up, "We all know Captain Murray doesn't like us to gamble, so how about this? The team that returns with the most game gets to keep the hides of all the kills."

Maggie stepped in and added, "My, I mean our, buck counts towards our number."

"Sure," the man agreed before adding one more caveat, "but Caleb needs to make up for his miss and bring back a buck as well."

The three men laughed and confidently moved back into the deep woods before any further barbs could be exchanged.

Maggie and Caleb stood silent for a minute, waiting until the three were out of earshot. "We will get you that buck, Caleb," she said forcefully.

He didn't speak, but simply pointed at the tree line just to their right.

Maggie followed his finger and saw a large buck carefully checking the clearing while three doe and their late summer fawns waited in the cover of the brush. The hunters waited patiently for all the deer to come out into the open to begin grazing.

"It's your shot, Caleb," Maggie whispered. "I'll take one of the doe."

Caleb said nothing and shouldered his primed and loaded musket.

Maggie did the same and pointed it in the direction of the doe. She had no plans of hitting her mark, partly because it would leave some of the fawns without a mother over the harsh winter. Also, if she missed, it might let Caleb reclaim some of his bruised ego.

This time, Caleb tapped his foot to count down to their shot. They fired simultaneously once more. Before the smoke could clear, Caleb was up and running to check on how he did.

"I think I got him, I think I got him!" Caleb shouted.

Maggie smiled at this unabated display of excitement.

"Look at the size of him, Maggie!" Caleb smiled proudly. "He is a real beauty."

"He certainly is, Caleb, but we need to dress him and get him back to the camp. With all the noise we made, if there are any Delaware in the area they will be sure to come and check out what happened here."

"Right, sorry for my reaction; I just wanted to prove to those three that I was a good shot. Honestly, I'm less fearful of the Delaware than I am of the wildcats and bears that might catch the scent of this blood." Caleb said and heeded her advice.

The two proud hunters dragged their prizes back to the camp and received a hero's welcome. They were pleased to discover that their three opponents had arrived a few minutes ahead of them, carrying only a ratty-looking squirrel and a small weasel. Maggie held back a laugh when she heard Caleb tell the men that they were free to keep the skins of their meager harvest.

While Caleb and Maggie skinned their bucks, the rest of the men built up two large fire pits to roast the feast. The general atmosphere in the camp was one of good cheer, and it was infectious. When the flurry of activity settled down somewhat, Maggie rested near the fire to wait for Israel.

Chapter | **Nine**

Without explanation, Jacob ordered his men to follow him up the trail. Private Taylor looked like he was about to say something, but Jacob quelled him with a sharp look and said, "Don't, private; we will speak later. Hold your tongue for now and just move along."

Taylor backed down and remained quiet. The rest of the men looked confused and distraught about leaving their mates behind, but they followed Jacob as ordered.

Nightfall was rapidly approaching and a short way up the trail, Jacob could see their escorts. There were a dozen French marines, along with two Huron scouts frantically waving the Englishmen forward. When the prisoners finally reached the group, the two Huron were sent ahead and disappeared into the dark woods, while the French split into two smaller groups. Six men took the front and the other six took up the rear position. Jacob and his men were now surrounded, but at least they were not facing certain death at the hands of drunken savages.

The lack of light and the heavily wooded trail fatigued the already exhausted English captives, and they continued to noticeably struggle. If the French guards in the rear hadn't continued 'urging' them to keep moving, most of them would have just collapsed on the ground.

Thankfully, the trail was reasonably even and straight and the trek itself lasted less than an hour. Jacob was glad he had picked the healthiest of the men. Judging by the shape they were in by the time they passed the camp's pickets, many of the other men in that shack would have died before they had gotten this far.

The camp was situated at a large cleared meadow next to the river. It was bordered on two sides by the thick unforgiving wilderness they had just exited and on the other side by a large swampy area that looked like it stretched for miles.

The rest of the French company had arrived by boat much earlier and prepared several roaring fires and tents for the arriving men. They even had some food roasting over a couple of pits and the smoky aroma welcomed the scraggly men as they approached the center of the camp.

Jacob smiled at the thought of spending the evening indulging in food and a fire. He could see that the other men were also relieved at the turn of events. Their night was sure to be more peaceful than they had anticipated.

The fires lit the cold, dark night, and Jacob finally spotted Lapointe near the woods, speaking with some of the marines.

"Sergeant, I'm glad to see you finally made it," Lapointe called out in a friendly tone when he caught Jacob's eye. "I hope your men are not too exhausted to enjoy a good meal." The officer appeared far more relaxed than he had been back at the Delaware village.

Jacob felt strangely welcomed amid a camp of their enemies, and he tried to reassure his men that all was well. They stood huddled near him, not wishing to mix with the French.

Lapointe approached them and motioned towards the campfire, saying, "Gentlemen, please take a seat, we made room for all…please."

Jacob sat and the others soon took his lead. They saw one of the marines stirring the contents of a large pot, as a man dressed in civilian clothes chopped and added other ingredients. There were also several animals roasting on a spit over the fire. It was difficult to identify them, but they smelled delicious and it enticed the captives to relax somewhat.

The sights and smells thrilled the men's empty stomachs and they began to gladly anticipate the promise of a meal. With the exception of Jacob, who had left the comforts of his fort three or four days before, the prisoners had not eaten in well over a week.

Lured by the wonderful aromas emanating from the large pot, Jacob approached the cook and watched as he cut up some pale roots and something that looked like a carrot. He quickly tossed all the pieces into the boiling water and took the spoon from the marine. The cook stirred the boiling soup and seemed satisfied. When he stood back from the pot, he finally noticed Jacob watching his every move. He offered the prisoner a small wooden spoon to taste his concoction. "Monsieur, please," he insisted.

Jacob gladly accepted the offer and put a spoonful of the soup in his mouth. It was extremely hot and Jacob enjoyed feeling the warmth travel through his cold, tired body.

"Wonderful, monsieur," he said with a polite smile.

He waved the rest of his men over to try the soup. They all stumbled over each other to be the first to have a taste and the cook happily obliged their enthusiasm.

Lapointe strolled over and said, "Please gentlemen, grab some bowls and a nice loaf of bread for each of you."

As the Englishmen rushed to avail themselves of his offer, Lapointe smiled at the chef and said, "Philippe, it must be nice to finally be appreciated." The chef chuckled and walked away to check on the roasting meat.

Jacob made sure each of his men had food before he grabbed a bowl for himself. He looked at Lapointe and said, "Merci, sir; I cannot tell you how heavenly this tastes."

"Please eat your fill and get your strength back, gentlemen. When you are finished, the men have gathered some clothing for you to replace the sad rags you have been forced to wear." The men nodded their thanks to the French captain as they continued to savor the hot liquid.

"Sergeant, I am glad you like Philippe's cooking. My men have been eating the same for the last several months, and they are happy that your men are eating it all up first."

Jacob stood next to Lapointe as he ate his soup and between bites he asked the question that was most pressing on his mind, "Sir, what are your plans for us? I must confess; your treatment makes us feel nothing like prisoners and I don't want anything to jeopardize our good standing."

"Sergeant, there will be plenty of time later to discuss any concerns you may have. Judging from the conversation I had with the Delaware chief, I can assure you that you are far better off with us than you would have been in their village.

"If the weather holds and your men are able to keep up, you will join us at Fort Machault and enjoy the luxuries the fort will provide us. We should arrive after a full day's march or two. We will discuss your concerns and your future when we arrive." Lapointe smiled and dismissed himself.

Jacob watched the French officer seat himself at a small wooden table the men had set up for him to dine on. While he knew that he and his men were in safer hands with the French, the captain's ambiguous answers left him feeling somewhat uneasy. His main goal was to get these men stronger and then plan an escape, so they could find their way back to his fort.

After the men had their fill of the hearty soup, they gladly accepted the kind offer of some fresh clothing from their French counterparts. With their new clothes, the men now looked more French than English, but they were happy to rid themselves of the torn, smelly rags they had been wearing since their capture. Each of the men kept their old clothes, despite their condition, and rolled them up in a couple of old sacks they were provided.

They continued to indulge in all the food available. After a few hours, they settled in the two tents designated by the French for them to use for the night. Jacob remained by the fire until all his men were fast asleep.

He watched the rest of the French empty their plates and retire to their own tents. Jacob counted four sentries stationed around the perimeter of the forest line.

There were also several Huron scouts a few yards from the main camp. They had kept to themselves all evening, eating food they had gathered themselves. Two warriors were sent to guard the bateaux by the water, and the rest of them slept on the bare ground or sitting upright against trees.

Not wanting to disturb his men while they rested, Jacob tossed a couple more logs on the fire and decided to sleep under the stars despite the chill. He managed to sleep soundly for several hours.

Just before dawn, he was awakened by the sound of movement around the camp. Once he cleared his head and his eyes focused, he saw Lapointe near the trailhead, speaking with his pickets and several of the Huron scouts. Both the Huron and the French pickets were pointing into the blackness of the thick woods.

Jacob quietly rose to his feet and brushed the leaves from his clothes. He put a log onto the flickering embers of fire and walked towards Lapointe to see what was happening.

As soon as the French captain spotted him, he called "Sergeant, please get your men up and have them eat; we plan on leaving very shortly. Merci."

Jacob ignored the order and continued walking towards the Frenchmen and Huron scouts. By the time he reached them, six marines were walking into the dense woods holding lit torches, followed by two Huron.

"Sir, is there a problem?" Jacob asked Lapointe quietly.

"Nothing too serious, I would wager," he replied. "A number of the pickets thought they heard voices in the woods, but I expect it was probably all in their overfed imaginations."

"Ah," Jacob said with a nod. "Yes, these woods make all kinds of noises that can make a man tremble in his boots. With all the wild beasts roaming about and the way the forests echo for miles, who knows what they really heard?"

"I feel the same, but I am a tad concerned that the Delaware might have changed their minds regarding your release. The Indians in this area are not always trustworthy or honorable in their dealings," Lapointe confided as he and Jacob walked back towards the center of camp. "Now, please, get your men up and ready to leave by first light."

Jacob obliged the request the second time and moved to prepare his men for the next leg of their march. As he got closer to the tents, he could see that most of the men were already up and folding up their blankets.

Only Taylor was causing an issue. He refused to get up no matter how much the others pleaded with him. He would wake long enough to growl at the men and then fall back asleep.

Jacob had no patience for his antics; he walked right up and kicked Taylor in the ribs. The kick wasn't particularly hard, yet it was well placed.

Taylor immediately leaped to his feet and screamed, "What the hell? I was getting up for bloody sake!"

The others laughed at the sight of Taylor reeling in pain, but Jacob just stood nose to nose with the man. "Shut your mouth, private," he said, "or I will beat you until you do so. I should have left you behind with the Delaware."

Taylor backed down and grumbled under his breath. He clutched his ribs, milking the attack in front of the others.

Jacob took a deep breath to calm down before he addressed the men. "Gentlemen, the French have been unusually kind to us. They fed us, gave us shelter and have permitted us to move about the camp relatively freely. I don't want any man here to ruin our good fortune as it stands presently; now get ready to leave in short order."

The men nodded and went back to work. Taylor scoffed, but did as he was told.

The morning sky struggled to brighten through the heavy canopy of clouds. Jacob left his men to their work and took a moment to check the deep forest line himself. He was careful not to step too far into the woods or draw unnecessary attention to himself. The thought of the Delaware, especially Captain Jacobs, returning to take back their captives particularly scared him. He vowed to never again allow himself to be a Delaware prisoner.

Jacob returned to the men and asked Private Wilson, one of the youngest of the men, to check with the cook to see what he might be able to provide them for a quick breakfast.

Just as he finished speaking with Wilson, Jacob noticed Taylor walking over to the edge of the woods. Jacob shouted at him, "Taylor, what do you think you are doing? Do you want to get yourself shot?"

Taylor kept walking and called out over his shoulder, "A man's not allowed to relieve himself? Do the Frenchies expect me to hold on 'til tomorrow?"

"Make it quick, Taylor, and keep your eyes open. We don't know who is lurking about out there." Inwardly, Jacob hoped that if the Delaware were out there, they would take care of Taylor themselves and save him some grief.

As Taylor continued to walk into the first line of trees and stopped, a couple of French sentries gave him a quick glance then let him be. Jacob turned his attention back to finding some food for his men and waited to see if young Wilson had any luck with the cook. The other men had finished all their work and stood nearby.

"Sir, do you know what the French have planned for us?" one of the men asked quietly.

"All I know is we are heading to Fort Machault. Other than that, I am honestly not certain. I am made somewhat suspicious by how nice they have been, but I think we should just enjoy it for now."

Private Wilson returned with an armful of food, and Jacob said, "Good work, private! Looks like you had some luck!"

One of the men laid a cloth out on the ground and the private unloaded his arms. Just as they were about to dig into their quick meal, Taylor came rushing towards them. His face had gone completely pale and he was barely coherent as he muttered, "Lads, I just saw a bloody ghost! It looked like a devil man with his face all scarred and discolored. It looked like it just came out of the fires of hell."

Jacob could tell that this was no joke. The normally irritating private was genuinely shaken by whatever it was he had seen.

"Taylor, get ahold of yourself, man," Jacob ordered, handing the man a piece of dried meat. "What are you babbling about? Tell us exactly what you saw."

"Damn, sir, it was some ungodly thing," he said, breathing heavily. "It was dressed like an Englishman but wrapped in some dead beast's hide. It had no useable hands. He had bloody clubs for hands…bloody clubs. Its face was like it had been melted and the only hair on its head was a few withered strands that barely covered its mangled skull." He pointed frantically towards the woods then held his face in his hands.

"Did it say anything?" one of the men asked as they all strained to look into the woods.

"Aye, it did. It spoke English. Its voice was gravelly and almost impossible to understand. I think it asked what unit I was with, but before I could answer it just turned and ran off. It was a bloody ghost, I tell you…a ghost."

Jacob handed Taylor a piece of bread to go with the meat and asked one of the men to get the terrified man some water. "We should keep this between us lads," he said, looking at each of the men. "Taylor, we have all been through a lot and maybe your eyes were just playing tricks on you."

Jacob disliked Taylor with his entire soul, yet seeing him in such a state of fear made him feel sympathetic. He scanned the forest to see if he could see anything like the 'ghost' the private had described.

Nothing more was said about the incident. The men ate their food in silence and stood in a line waiting to move out.

The French once again divided their forces. The majority happily traveled by boat along the river, while the remaining dozen men had the unenviable duty of escorting Jacob and his men through the woods to the fort. Most of the Huron stayed with the land party, raising the ranks to around eighteen, depending on how many of them decided to make the entire trip. Four of the Huron had already made their way up the trail, scouting for any problems they might run into.

Lapointe made an effort to speak with Jacob and his men before he left with the bateaux. "Sergeant, please keep your men in good order. We shall be at the fort by nightfall if the weather holds. Safe travels to you all until we meet at Fort Machault."

Jacob gave the captain a half-hearted salute and turned to his men. Taylor still greatly concerned him and Jacob remained by the man's side as they headed out.

He attempted to remain focused on the trail ahead, but Taylor's frightened rambling played over and over in his mind. First the French sentries and Huron scouts had thought they had seen something, and then came Taylor's frightening episode. Jacob could feel his own reluctance increase the farther they walked into the woods.

The thick forest seemed unusually noisy. Every crack or snap made all the men overreact. Jacob noticed that even the Huron scouts appeared unusually apprehensive. The scouts hung back closer to the main body than they normally would.

The start of the trail was particularly windy with many blind curves and elbows. It slowed the progress of French as they were forced to send ahead some of the men to assist the reluctant Huron to check the trail. A couple of times they even pushed Jacob and his men to the front as human-shields against the threat of an ambush.

After a few miles, the trail got a bit wider and much straighter. Most of the men began to relax, but the Huron scouts were still visibly upset. Jacob watched them repeatedly talk with the French officers and gesture to the ridges along the trail. It appeared that they were nervous about an upper trail that ran parallel to the main trail. The French sent two of the marines ahead with the scouts to offer some reassurance.

Not much happened over the next several miles. They passed a number of spots that Jacob believed would have been ideal opportunities for an enemy to launch an ambush against them. The farther they traveled, the more their overall fear seemed to dissipate.

Soon the Huron scouts pulled back once again to speak with the French, and the leader of the unit stopped everyone for a rest. Jacob's men had remained completely silent and withdrawn since they entered the forest. As he watched the nervous gestures from the Huron, Jacob took a moment to speak with his men.

"Gentlemen, it appears the Huron are worried about something in the woods. I honestly have never seen them so outwardly afraid. Keep your eyes on the trail and the surrounding area. If you see anything out of the ordinary, please speak up. Don't be afraid to tell me, no matter how strange you think it is." Jacob looked directly at Taylor, but the man was still shaken and kept unnaturally silent.

"One last thing," he added. "If we are ambushed, get yourselves into the forest. Don't look back; just run as fast as your legs will take you. Do your best to keep together, but make sure you get into the woods. We will be sitting ducks on this open trail. Without weapons, our best plan is to keep on the move." Jacob looked around at each man and prayed that his words were sinking in.

The French signaled Jacob to get his men up and moving and he obliged their order. This time the Huron scouts remained with the main body; they were very jumpy and reacted to every sound that resonated through the forest.

Jacob stayed by Taylor but kept his eyes focused on the woods. Several times he thought he had seen someone or heard a noise his instincts told him was not that of any wild beast.

He kept this to himself so as not to alarm the men. They had their own fear and mounting fatigue to contend with.

Jacob wondered how far they were from the fort and was just about to ask one of their escorts when the French and Huron ahead of them suddenly stopped. They seemed to be in a heated discussion, and Jacob assumed the Huron's nerves had caused an issue once again.

As the French and their scouts argued in front of him, Jacob noticed some movement in the woods to his left. He could make out what he thought was a dark figure moving from one large oak tree to another. Just then, several more figures moved closer to their position, within the first line of trees.

Jacob wondered if his eyes were playing tricks on him, but one of his men whispered, "Did you see the shadows following us? They have been following us for the last few minutes."

Yet again, the French officer waved Jacob and his men forward. They made it only a few paces before the forest began to reverberate with hideous screams and taunts from their indiscernible attackers.

Everyone in the unit stopped instantly, despite orders from the officers to keep moving. The marines shouldered their muskets and pointed them blindly towards the dark woods to the left of the trail.

Most of the 'shadows' had moved closer to the trail, directly in front of where the French and the scouts stood nervously staring into the blackness of the surrounding woods. Seeing all the confusion, Jacob mouthed the order to his men to slowly move towards woods on the right side of the trail.

The men did as Jacob commanded and watched as the rear guard rushed past them to support the marines up ahead. Jacob reminded them to back away slowly so they didn't draw any unwanted attention from the French or the still unidentified attackers.

As he continued to monitor the surrounding woods, Jacob looked high above his head. He clearly saw a couple of men hidden amongst the high branches. He guessed that they were the best marksman among the ambushers. They most likely had the orders to take out the officers first to create panic amongst the ranks. Jacob was careful not to look up at the men for too long in case he accidentally alerted the French to their presence.

The shouts and screams had quieted, and Jacob could hear the attackers muttering to one another. He thought that he heard a few English words and felt immense relief but still remained guarded.

The noise level in the woods began to increase again, and one of the French officers ordered some of his men to form up and follow him into the woods to flush out any possible ambushers. As the Frenchmen charged blindly into the woods, a wall of bullets and smoke greeted them. It pushed them back and blew a swath of blood and bone onto the trail. Some of the reluctant men in the rear were spared the opening volley but found themselves being splattered by fragments of their fellow marines.

Just as the trail exploded in deafening noise and chaos, Jacob ordered his men to take cover within the first line of the woods on the opposite side of the trail from the attackers. They used massive tree trunks and fallen logs as cover.

Jacob looked up at the men in the trees and saw them taking aim towards the cluster of Frenchmen below. A moment later, the officers had fallen and the rest of the men tried desperately to reorganize. Another deadly volley sent a wave of musket balls whistling through the leaves and brush.

Foolishly, another group of marines charged headlong into the woods towards their invisible attackers. Jacob watched as the men in the trees systematically picked off the Huron scouts.

A third organized volley blasted from the tree line and then all the guns fell suddenly silent. As the smoke settled, Jacob counted only two marines and one Huron scout still living. All three men were badly injured; the Huron was trying unsuccessfully to move closer towards his fellow warriors, but his shattered left leg hindered him.

The attackers still had not shown themselves and Jacob kept his men well hidden and back towards the next layer of underbrush. He had seen the aftermath of battle before: the dead, the groans from the injured, the savagery of the victors and the blood. This ambush was particularly ruthless. The two marines who had miraculously survived clutched each other and pleaded for their lives.

Finally, the men who initiated the brutal attack exited their wooded fortress and worked their way onto the open trail. Their faces were smeared with mud and their disheveled clothes were equally dirty. Jacob wasn't certain if their attire was intentional, or more because they hadn't cleaned themselves in a while. Either way, it was an intimidating look that equally matched the fierce manner of their attack.

They were a motley-looking crew to say the least. Some carried war clubs, others hatchets and the rest a mixture of English long muskets, French-issued muskets and old hunting guns. They wore a dirty rainbow of colors, from the ragged red-coats of the British regulars to green colonial militia jackets to brain-tanned deer leather leggings and breech clouts. The men themselves were as varied as their clothes. There were dark skinned men, a few Mingo warriors, and pale skinned soldiers, all working together in a military-style attack.

Careful not to draw their attention until he knew their intentions, Jacob kept down and watched as more of the men came out from the cover of the woods. They were busy searching the dead for anything of value and keeping their eyes on the three injured men.

Suddenly, a voice shrieked from the woods, "Tie the Huron to a tree for now, but kill the rest of the French bastards. I want no survivors."

Jacob's first reaction was to dive farther back into the woods. He was not going to be mistaken for one of the French, and he motioned to his men to get down and stay down.

The two French marines' screams and pleas for mercy reached a fevered pitch, and Jacob was able to see the sheer horror on their faces. They were butchered where they lay, and the only mercy shown by the attackers was that of a quick death.

The crippled Huron would not be so fortunate.

Two of the men grabbed him under the arms and pushed his back hard against the first tree they picked out. A long length of thick hemp rope was then used to tie him tightly to the trunk. Unable to squirm, the warrior let out a hideous screech before one of the men jammed a piece of dirty cloth into his mouth, muffling all further outbursts.

With all the French dead, the attackers turned their attention towards Jacob and his men. Just as it appeared they were to meet with a similar fate, the same voice called out again from within the woods.

"Stop! They are English; bring them to me."

Jacob, despite hearing the order not to attack, instinctively took up a defensive position. He held a thick branch as a weapon. It would stand no chance against a barrage of bullets, but at least he would be able to cause pain for the first couple of men who ventured too close.

Noticing Jacob's defensive posture, the men lowered their muskets and took up a much friendlier manner. Jacob relaxed slightly, but when the men tried to approach him to take him to their commander, he resisted and held the branch even higher.

The men slowed their advance and seemed to wait for further direction from the voice in the woods. They were also distracted by the sight of their mates scalping the dead Huron and stripping clothes and equipment off the dead French.

Jacob remained on his guard as the men slowly dispersed to join the others in collecting souvenirs.

Finally, as he stepped out of the cover of the forest, Jacob and his men got their first, brief glimpse of the man they assumed was the leader of this gang of misfits, thieves and murderers.

The man approached the scene in a large, full length bear skin capote-style coat that used the beast's head as its hood. It still had its upper set of teeth menacingly hanging down into the man's hidden face. A heavy bear claw necklace hung around his neck and his features remained completely shrouded within the massive pelt.

Jacob guessed that the man was as tall as he, but it was difficult to tell by the sheer size of the well-worn black bear pelt. Standing to his full height to confront the man, Jacob watched as he slowly lowered the heavy hood from his head.

"You are surprised to see such a man?" The man shrieked in a low, almost inaudible, tone.

Jacob could offer no reply and just looked at the man facing him.

The tall, confident man stood directly in front of him, covered in the scars of a horrible fire or terrible torture at the hands of savages. What was left of his face was melted onto his nearly-bald skull, and the lack of a nose and ears made him appear demonic. He had no need for war paint or dirt to make him appear terrifying; the discolored reds and deep purple tones of his skin took care of that.

His lips were basically gone and only when he struggled to speak did Jacob notice any sign of them. His eyes were piercing, blackened and deeply set, giving Jacob the odd feeling they reached right into his soul.

He had a difficult time just looking directly at the man for more than an instant, but tried not to insult him.

"Bloody ugly bastard; don't you agree, sir?" The man said gruffly, trying to alleviate the discomfort with some humor. "I also must apologize for my voice. It does sound fierce, yet I confess it comes more from my burns than any attempt to terrify my enemies."

Jacob finally realized that he had not yet spoken a word to this man and did his best to hide his fear. He politely held out his hand to introduce himself, but recoiled when the man struggled to extend his arms past the end of his sleeves. Each arm ended at the wrist in a grossly molded stump of melted fingers.

"Alas," he said, pulling his arms back into his sleeves, "the fire took more than just my face. My hands have been taken from me as well."

Refocusing his thoughts, Jacob quickly made his introduction, saying, "Sir, we are British Colonial soldiers attached to Major Stevens' Virginia Ranging Company. I am Sergeant Sims and these men were captured on their way from Fort Cumberland to my fort north of Fort Duquesne. May we ask who you are and what are your intentions?"

Jacob and the others waited for a reply.

"No need to fear us, Mr. Sims," the man said. "We are all on the same side, but we must gather what we need and leave this place shortly. This area is teeming with savages, and I'll wager they'll run to inform their French allies as soon as they stumble upon this place. Although I have little to fear from the French, we have been tracking your escorts for miles and are honestly a bit tired."

The commander then turned to his men and in a voice only they could understand, said "Finish getting your trinkets, lads. Peters and Butler, please do your usual work."

He turned back to Jacob and his men and said in a deep, throaty tone, "Please excuse me, gentlemen, I must ready myself to depart and I suggest you do the same. Feel free to grab a musket or whatever strikes your fancy from our French friends over there. We do not tolerate stragglers, so please keep up."

Jacob looked at his men and ordered them to arm themselves and meet him at the far side of the trail. He then stood by and watched to find out what the 'usual work' was that two of the men had been assigned to do.

Peters and Butler were busy hacking down two small trees and then carving two sharpened ends with their hatchets. Once they had sharpened both ends to a point, they drove one of the ends into the ground.

One post now stood at each end of the battle area.

Jacob could not fathom why they had a need for the sharpened poles, but what they did next was more disturbing than he could have ever imagined.

One of the men rolled a good-sized boulder over to the first post, wedging it against the base. The other man dragged one of the half-naked French corpses over and propped it up against the boulder. With one fluid motion, the two experienced men lifted the body straight upwards and then drove it down onto the pole. The pole itself entered the man's back and came out the base of his neck. The body stopped as it hit the boulder and was grotesquely displayed to anyone traveling from the north.

Scalping the dead was one thing, but Jacob could not understand why anyone would want to degrade a corpse even further.

He then watched as the two men moved to the other end of the trail and untied the only survivor of the ambush. The Huron scout was forced up and with the strength from the two men, he was shoved up and down on the pole…still alive. The Huron was facing south to greet anyone coming from that end of the trail. He managed to let out one last desperate scream before his head drooped down.

Jacob prayed that he was dead and not forced to endure hours of unspeakable pain and a slow death.

"Bloody hell, sir," one of Jacob's men said anxiously. "I think we might have been better off tortured by the Delaware."

Jacob gave no reply, uncertain if he agreed or not.

The leader soon returned to check the two men's handiwork and noticed Jacob and a few of his man standing nearby gazing at the ominous display.

"I hope you have each grabbed yourself a musket or war club to defend yourselves," he struggled to say. "If we are ambushed, my men will not put themselves in harm's way just because you have no weapons."

Jacob refocused and checked to see if all his men had found something to defend themselves. They all seemed to have found something to their liking and he knew he must do the same. He quickly found a nice, clean musket and a nearly full cartridge box. He tied the box around his waist and searched for an axe or tomahawk.

Most of the bodies had been picked over, but just as the men were heading out, he noticed that the Huron scout dangling from the nearby post still had a beautiful neck knife and sheath hanging from his bloody neck. He only hesitated for a moment. Good knives were critical in the wilderness. A jammed musket, hand-to-hand fighting or just to slice a piece of meat made a knife an indispensable necessity to surviving on the frontier.

He took a look where the others were heading and made a mad dash over to the post. He stepped up on the boulder and quickly pulled the sheath over the dead scout's head. The lanyard caught momentarily on the post, but he yanked hard and it thankfully dislodged immediately. He quickly wiped off the blood that had splattered on it, put it around his neck and jumped off the boulder.

"Sims, do you want to stay and play with the dead, or are you coming with us?" the leader shouted as loud as his damaged throat would permit him. Reacting to his raspy voice, Jacob ran towards the path where most of the men had already disappeared.

Jacob was swift to catch up and followed right on the heels of the heavily scarred man. "You move pretty fast for someone in your shape," Jacob blurted out before he could catch himself.

The man stopped and laughed. "Sims," he said, shaking his head. "Why Sims?"

Jacob had stopped as well and stood silent and confused. He didn't understand the question or how he should answer.

"The last time we saw each other," the man continued, "you called yourself Murray... Jacob Murray, so... why Sims now?"

"How do you know me, sir?" Jacob asked, struggling with how he could ever forget meeting such a man. "Have we met before?"

"Damn it, Jacob; I'm Israel. I might be a little uglier than before, but I'm still your brother."

Jacob's mouth fell open, but he had no words to say.

"Keep moving and we can continue our reunion later," Israel said wryly before he continued along the uncut trail as swiftly as before.

It took Jacob several minutes to gather his thoughts and catch up to his brother.

Once the large party reached a distance of several miles from the scene of the ambush, they stopped to re-organize and rest.

Israel remained back aways from the main unit so he could speak privately with Jacob. One of the men attempted to ask him something, but he was immediately waved him away.

"Now, dear brother, we have much to talk about," Israel said as he rested on a lone tree stump.

"I thought you were dead. I...I even came back to find you, but..." Jacob struggled to explain.

"There's no need to justify what you did Jacob. I know that you did everything in your power to help me. One of my men was part of the militia that refused your offer to fight the French once you saw that they let their militia and savages murder the injured men." Israel's voice cracked several times as he did his best to reassure that he knew Jacob hadn't simply abandoned him.

Israel's reassurance did little to comfort Jacob. He was still so shocked by the unexpected revelation that his brother was alive, that he could not manage a coherent reply.

Israel had expected such a reaction and tried to console his brother. He changed the subject and said, "So, why Sims? You never did answer me."

"I deserted." Jacob said quietly. "I did it to find you, Israel. I have been running ever since." There was so much more to the story, but Jacob couldn't think of where he should start. Thoughts of Abby sprang to his mind for the first time in a year and he knew that he could never be the one to tell Israel about the last time he saw her.

A slight tear fell from Israel's eye just as he looked away, "I heard you did such a foolish thing for me. I feel torn between thanking you for such a gesture and wanting to smack you for being so…" "How did you get involved with these men?" Jacob asked, cutting Israel off abruptly. He was unsettled and certainly did not want to talk about his desertion.

"These men are all misfits, much like me. Do you really believe that with this face I could walk around some trading post and not notice the stares from others? I have seen mothers shield the eyes of their youngsters, but most people simply look away from me. What about my own family? Who would want to live with this?" Israel again looked away from his twin.

After an uncomfortable pause, Israel continued, "These men are my family now. See Paterson over there? He is judged by the color of his skin before people ever see his unwavering loyalty. His choice in life is to be some rich landowner's slave or be a free man with us. The two savages are the only people left from their village. How would they survive without us? These men would all fight and gladly die for one another, and that is what makes us family."

"You still have family, brother," Jacob said with a flash of anger in his voice. "What am I to you now? Our faces might differ now, but we are still brothers. No one can take that from us."

"Yes, dear brother," Israel said as gently as his gravelly voice would allow, "we are still brothers…just not the same as we once were."

Those words were reassuring yet at the same moment disturbing. Jacob sensed a distance between them that had never existed before. He instinctively knew that he might never be able to bridge the gap.

Israel excused himself before they could continue their conversation. "I should check on my men," he said, "I would like you to lead us to your fort."

Jacob watched him leave and spent a moment trying to catch his breath. Over the past couple days he had gone from being a prisoner of the Delaware, to a parolee of a French officer whose kindness deserved a better fate, and now he was in the company of the brother he thought he had lost over a year ago.

His head spun and all he wanted was to get back to the relative safety of the fort. He needed to check on Joshua and the rest of the men and try to make some sense of all that had just transpired.

Chapter | **Ten**

The camp was ready to greet the returning men. The festive atmosphere reminded Maggie of the homecoming celebrations each Indian village she had visited would offer to their returning warriors.

It was almost dark when the advanced scouts entered the main camp. They were in good spirits, especially once they saw the two large bucks roasting over the fire pits.

As more men began to trickle in, the camp was abuzz with the news that a group of colonial militia men had been rescued from the French patrol. Maggie anxiously awaited Israel's return and only lent half an ear to the stories of the short yet brutal battle.

Those who were already in the camp did not wait for the rest of the men to arrive before they began enjoying the feast. They carved hunks of meat off the animals as they hung over the fire, and sat to enjoy their well-deserved meal.

Maggie waited patiently for the rest of the men to arrive and kept herself busy by pouring cups of the freshly brewed beer made from roots, herbs and some liquid she had drawn from a nearby sap tree. She tried a taste of it, but found it too bitter and strong for her liking. The men gladly gulped it down and thanked her for the nice treat.

Actually, Maggie was well-schooled in making root-style beer since most of the English, French and Indians in the region preferred it and found it safer for their digestive systems than water straight from a river or lake. Even though the men said that they enjoyed the taste, she still wished that raspberries were still in season to sweeten it up some.

Most of the men had already gotten themselves fed and settled by the fire when Israel, still covered by his bear-skin coat, walked up the concealed pathway to the camp. Six ragged, dirty men walked ahead of Israel. They were dressed in what appeared to be a combination of French marines' uniforms and scraps of their own militia company's clothing. Their hair was matted and entangled with mud, and their faces were drawn and unnaturally pale. None of them spoke a word and looked more like walking corpses than men. They seemed reluctant at first to enter the busy camp, but they were greeted with cups of beer and plates of meat. They accepted the meal graciously and took seats by one of the roaring fires.

Maggie had been so engrossed in studying the colonial militia men that she had lost sight of Israel. Finally, she spotted him, still on the far side of the camp by the entrance and saw that he was deep in conversation with someone. She couldn't see who it was, as Israel blocked the person from view. Trying not to appear overly curious, she tried to change the angle of her head and body to see who was with him, but she still only saw her brother-in-law.

When the conversation ended, Israel walked fully into the camp with the last of the newly freed soldiers. The man was as tall as Israel, and his long, stringy hair and wild, untrimmed beard covered most of his face.

Maggie didn't want to be caught staring and she immediately looked away when she saw Israel motioning towards her with a jerk of his chin. Curiosity got the better of her and she looked back only to see that the bearded man had a wide grin on his face.

She knew that smile well and let out a scream that made all the men in the camp stop and look at her. Caring nothing for their curious gawks, Maggie tore across the camp towards the newcomer.

It was her Jacob.

He met her halfway and crushed her in his embrace. Her tears flowed freely, while Jacob himself was unable to hold back his own.

Israel simply patted each of them on the back as he walked past them towards the first, half-eaten deer carcass.

"Give them some privacy, you heathens," he barked, "and somebody get me a cup of that beer!" Israel looked back at the embraced couple and shook his head with a smile on his scarred face.

Maggie pulled back as Jacob softly wiped her tears from her face. "You look different," was all she could manage to say before her tears started again.

"Aye, Maggie," he replied, "a bit more weathered, but mostly the same." He was finally holding her in his arms and couldn't let go, despite the horde of curious men sitting a few feet away.

Israel took a seat and screeched at the two lovers, "Get yourselves some food; there will be plenty of time to enjoy each other later."

His statement drew laughs from the others, but Jacob and Maggie paid him no mind.

"We probably should get some food before the hungry buggers eat all of it," Jacob suggested, still not letting Maggie free of his hug.

"Maybe we should," she laughed. "I think the men have had enough of a show." She used the cloth she had around her neck to wipe off her face.

They walked hand-in-hand to the fire and sat beside Israel.

"Thank you, dear brother," Jacob said as he accepted a plate of food from one of the men, "I will never be able to repay you for this."

"I will think of something, Jacob, I promise you that much," Israel said, attempting to laugh, but his shattered throat only spat out a couple of grizzled gargles.

Jacob looked at Maggie and said, "Let me check on my men before I forget..."

"They are all being well looked after Jacob," Israel interrupted. "Pay them no mind and spend your time with Maggie. God knows, she deserves it after what you put her through."

Jacob was happy to hear Israel's brotherly teasing, and said, "We have all been through our own hell, dear brother, but you are right. Oh, and thank you so much for mentioning that Maggie was here."

"How could I spoil the nice show you two put on for all of us?" Israel said with another attempted laugh, which came out as a small screeching whistle.

Maggie sat as close to Jacob as she could manage and only left his side to help Israel eat or take a drink. The trio sat in friendly silence through most of the meal. There was so much to say that they didn't know where to begin, so they just enjoyed each other's company.

Caleb came by to check on everyone and said, "Sir, do you need anything else? If not, may I gather up your cups and plates?"

"Caleb, this is my husband, Jacob," Maggie introduced the two.

Jacob stood and shook the young man's hand, and Caleb said, "Nice to meet you, sir. Your wife has certainly brightened up our camp, and she is one good shot. One of the bucks the men are enjoying is her handiwork."

"Aye, lad, she is a better shot than most men I know," Jacob said as he took his seat. "It's a pleasure to meet you as well. Thank you for helping Israel to keep my wife safe."

"Would anyone like a cup of coffee or tea?" Caleb asked as he gathered the dishes they had finished using. "I must warn you, it is pretty strong and it might keep you up most of the night!"

"No thank you, Caleb," Maggie answered for them, "but go get yourself some and enjoy your evening."

Caleb smiled and quickly returned to the rest of the men. One whole deer had been consumed, and many of the men were still filling their plates with what was left of the second. Things in the camp were growing quieter as the men's stomachs grew full and the beer weakened their desire to do much of anything.

As darkness fell, Israel pointed to a canvas tent that had been set up in one of the more isolated corners of the camp. "I had the men set up a tent that we had borrowed from a French officer awhile back. I just thought you might want some private time together."

"Thank you, Israel, but I feel like talking more than sleeping; we all have so much to speak of." Maggie said, kissing Jacob on the cheek.

"I told you about my experience already, and I am sure that Jacob doesn't want to re-hash all the old pains we had at Fort Necessity," Israel said, doing his best to keep his voice from cracking as he looked at Jacob for confirmation.

"Then tell me when you first recognized each other," Maggie said with a smile.

"I had no idea who he was," Jacob said. "Neither of us looks like we once did."

"Well, I only look slightly different, brother," Israel joked, "but a good shave and cut would work wonders on you."

When neither of them reacted to his jibe, Israel let out another painful laugh and said, "You two need not to be afraid to say something that might hurt me. I am regrettably stuck with my exterior."

Silence fell over them for a few moments, as Jacob finally said, "I'm so sorry I couldn't do more for you, Israel. I deserted as soon as I could. I did find two badly burned men when I got back to the remains of the fort, but they were so damaged, I had no idea if one of them was you."

"You do not owe me an explanation, nor do you need to feel sorry for me. You did everything you could. How could you have cared for me, even if you knew it was me? You were a deserter and, we now know, our homes and families were gone." Israel did his best to articulate his feelings to his brother, despite struggling to get his words out.

Maggie changed the subject back again to keep the mood lighter. "Who recognized whom?" she asked.

"I had no idea he was one of the captives, but when I first saw him I had a sneaking suspicion it might be Jacob. Then he introduced himself as Sergeant Sims, and it cast me into some doubt. Of course, once we spoke, I knew that it was indeed him."

"Who is Sergeant Sims?" Maggie asked, turning to Jacob.

"It's a long story, my dear. Let me answer the question about Israel first. I have to be honest; I had no reason to think it was Israel. If he hadn't said something after the battle, I would still not know who he was. To say the least, I was overwhelmed with all kinds of emotions. My hands haven't stopped shaking since I got here."

"My face really does work well as a disguise," Israel said thoughtfully. "I know it even scares the hell out of the damn savages!"

"How did you get here?" Jacob asked Maggie.

"Israel and his men rescued me from the French as well. Before that, I was a captive of the Delaware and a kind French officer helped me escape from that horrible place."

Jacob kissed her forehead and said, "I should have never left you and the children."

"I think we would all turn back time if we could, Jacob," Israel said, "but alas, we are here now and need to deal with the present."

"So back to Sims," Maggie said.

Jacob chuckled at her persistence and said, "Without going into all the details, it became imperative for my safety that I reenlist with the militia. Obviously, I couldn't be recognized as a deserter, so I used a different name. Sims was an old friend of my father, and I just went with it."

As Jacob finished talking, a scout arrived in the camp to report and Caleb led him to Israel.

"Pardon the interruption, sir," the scout said, "but I have some news about Captain Jacobs and his raiding party."

Israel rose from his seat with a hand up from Jacob. "Mr. Turnbull, it is very good to see you again."

He turned to Maggie and said, "I'm sorry, but I would like to take Jacob with me to hear this report and I promise I will not keep him long."

Maggie waved them on and remained seated. She watched the three men walk towards a small tent that Israel used for such matters.

As they entered the tent, Israel said, trying to keep his voice from cracking, "Gentlemen, we will be far more comfortable in here. Turnbull, this is my brother Jacob. Mr. Turnbull is one of the many men we have out in the field."

Jacob shook Turnbull's hand and eagerly awaited his news.

When the formalities were completed, Israel asked, "So what is your news Turnbull?"

"The Delaware know of today's attack on the French unit," the young man responded. "I received word that Captain Jacobs and his warriors are out, as we speak, burning and murdering any English homesteads they can find. Many have escaped to the newly built fort near the mountain trail, so the savages are now launching an attack on the fort." Turnbull detailed.

"How are the men at the fort holding up?" Jacob interrupted. He feared that Joshua and his men would not be able to defend themselves against such an attack.

"From what I have heard, they are well fortified and have managed to keep the Delaware back." Turnbull explained.

Jacob was unable to hide his concern for his men and waited for Israel to speak.

"Have you spoken with the others?" Israel asked. "Do they want to send in a relief force to help the fort?"

"They have not said as much, sir, but I think they expect you to send your men to reinforce the fort."

"Thank you, lad," Israel said. "Go get yourself some food. I'll have a message for you to return with momentarily."

Turnbull nodded and went off in search of food.

Israel looked at Jacob and asked, "What are your thoughts? I know they are your people at the fort, and you know the area far better than I."

"I was going to suggest that you and your men over-winter at the fort anyway. If Captain Jacobs wants a fight, I think we should oblige him."

"No doubt, my men will be eager to fight the Delaware," Israel said. "We have all witnessed Captain Jacobs' work against the unprotected settlers."

"How soon can we leave?" Jacob asked, excited by the prospect of fighting the Delaware again, especially alongside his brother.

Israel paused a moment to clear his throat and asked, "What do we tell Maggie? The poor woman just found you again and we are leaving her to go off to fight."

"I fully expected her to come along with us," Jacob replied immediately. "We both know she can handle a musket better than most men."

"Shooting a buck is completely different than aiming at another human and pulling the trigger. I know she can shoot; I am just not as certain that she could shoot at the Delaware. What about your men? They are in no shape to walk, let alone fight." Israel pointed out.

Jacob understood what Israel was saying. He might have agreed with his brother if he hadn't just found her again. He felt like he would never be able to let her out of his sight again. If she came along, he would be able to protect her.

"I hope you see that I can't leave her behind, not now." Jacob tried not to show too much emotion. He knew Israel would try to convince him that he was using his heart instead of his head.

"I need to speak with a couple of the men to see how they feel about an attack, and I think you should do the same with your men. Then take some time to discuss your options with Maggie. She always could handle the tougher decisions better then you." Israel struggled to smile.

They left the tent and Israel called together his more senior men while Jacob walked over to check on his handful of men. He was pleased to see that they appeared to be doing relatively well. They had eaten their fill and indulged in a few cups of beer.

"Gentlemen, how are you all getting along?" Jacob asked just as he approached them.

The men were much more energetic than they had been when Jacob had met up with them a few days earlier. As usual, Private Taylor spoke up first, "I must say that it is nice to have some good food, and the beer is a good treat. We are all wondering what you have planned for us?"

Jacob had feared all along that Taylor might sway the men against their commander, and he watched them to see if it was so. "Are you the group's mouth now, Taylor? We are thinking of leaving to spend the winter at the fort. We should all be there right now anyway, if you hadn't gotten yourselves into trouble. I was asked to check on you men and see if you were up for the march and a fight if necessary."

Taylor answered immediately, "We are all still very tired and mending our injuries. Probably after a few more days of rest and food, we would be better able to judge the situation."

Jacob ignored Taylor and asked the others, "Do you all feel the same?"

None of the men said a word, simply allowing Taylor's words to speak for them. When Jacob finally glanced at Taylor, he was greeted with an all too familiar smirk.

"I will let you know of our plans once they have been decided," Jacob said with obvious disappointment in his voice. "Be warned, though, that you better choose the right side to hang your hats on. I will be departing with the others and if you lot think Taylor can navigate his way around this wilderness then so be it."

He left them to their own thoughts and sought out Israel. His brother stood by the entrance to the camp speaking to two scouts he was sending out to confirm the exact location of Captain Jacobs.

"How are your men?" Israel asked after dismissing the two scouts.

"They are well fed and appear to be getting their energy back. My only concern is that one of them, a Private Taylor, has cast his influence over them. That snake is trouble and he holds information on me that could get me hanged if the right people believe him."

"Well, brother," Israel said solemnly, "I care little for what he has on you, but father always told us about snakes. Chopping the head off is the surest way to kill one. Maybe it's time to kill this snake."

Jacob could hardly believe this man was the same Israel he once knew. He was far more decisive than he had ever been before, but he was also colder and more calculating. He had, of course, experienced horrors no man should be forced to face. Jacob just hoped that some of the less attractive changes to his personality would dissipate now that they were reunited.

"Point out the snake to me, brother," Israel said, looking towards Jacob's men.

Jacob's finger pointed directly at Taylor.

"He doesn't appear to be much," Israel said. "Do you think he is able to go out for a short scout with a couple of my men?"

"I think we can convince him, if he wants to or not." Jacob replied, understanding Israel's intentions.

"Mr. Jenkins, may I have a word?" Israel barked to one of his men, careful not to strain is throat. "Jacob, maybe you should go check on Maggie."

Jacob could tell that he had just been dismissed and walked slowly back to his wife. Before he could take a seat beside her, a loud commotion broke out where his men were sitting. Israel's Mr. Jenkins was using some physical persuasion to get Taylor to follow him to the camp entrance. A couple of the private's mates attempted to intercede, but were persuaded to stand down.

Jacob started to move towards the ruckus, but Israel appeared at his side and said, "Please sit with Maggie. Remember that this is my camp and I hate snakes."

Jacob sat and watched as Taylor walked out of the camp with two scouts. It was plain to everyone that Taylor was given no musket and carried no other weapons.

Maggie looked at Jacob for an explanation, but he remained silent. She looked at Israel, who said, "I apologize for the interruption. I just asked the men to check on a rumor that some Delaware scouts were spotted near our camp."

Jacob could feel his brother's eyes on him, so he attempted to redirect the conversation. He turned to Maggie and asked, "So, have you seen anything of that young man…I think his name was One-Ear? Joshua and I got separated from him. We followed a merchant's carriage towards Fort Duquesne and l assumed that One-Ear followed you to the north."

Maggie hesitated; she was not sure what was happening around the camp. After a moment, she answered, "We both made it to a large village on the lake above the fort at Niagara. The last time I saw him was when I was taken away by the Ottawa. They shot One-Ear as he tried to save me. I don't know if he is dead or has recovered from his wounds. I can only pray every day that he still lives. I would never have made it this far without him."

Jacob could see that Maggie was trying not to cry, and he tried to ease her pain. He rubbed her back and said, "Joshua is back at my fort. I owe him my life many times over as well. You will see him again soon."

Maggie's head shot up and she said, "We are leaving?"

Jacob looked at Israel and waited for him to tell her.

"My brother is right," Israel said reluctantly. "I always thought to move towards the fort for the winter, even before I knew it was Jacob's. I had hoped we could wait a little longer before we moved, though. Unfortunately, there have been reports that the Delaware have launched an attack against the fort. That certainly complicates our next move, but also makes it imperative that we move out soon."

Jacob could see that Maggie was confused by everything and was about to explain further when the camp erupted. A lone musket shot echoed from the woods just to the west of the camp. The men grabbed their muskets and started to form up to leave the camp.

Israel stood and screeched out to calm them, saying, "Let's not get too excited men. The scouts might have shot at a bear or maybe they did see some savages…either way, we must remain composed. I will send out a small group to check on the others."

Israel and Jacob stood together and waited for any other noises coming from the woods.

"No reason to get excited," Israel said quietly, sitting back down and urging Jacob to do the same. "I assume the snake has just been dealt with."

No other sound came. Less than half an hour later, Jenkins and the other scout returned. Taylor was not with them. Israel immediately went over to talk with them, but Jacob stayed by Maggie's side.

"What is going on Jacob?" Maggie asked.

"Nothing, dear," Jacob replied. "It's not for us to worry about now."

"You don't appear to be the least bit worried that one of your men went with them and hasn't returned," Maggie insisted. "A blind person could see that something bad has happened to him."

"This is Israel's camp, and I need to be careful not to overstep my authority…or question his," Jacob said firmly.

Maggie knew by Jacob's tone that she needed to leave this matter alone.

"What do you think of Israel?" Jacob asked bluntly.

Maggie was surprised by the question and said, "He does seem to be a very different man now, but he has been through a lot. I honestly feel sorry for him; I wish I could do something to ease his pain, both physically and emotionally."

"We all have been through things we would rather forget," Jacob said, "but he just is so cold now…so unfeeling."

Israel returned and said simply, "The snake is dead."

Jacob and Maggie sat in uncomfortable silence and Israel finally said, "It is far too late to depart or even think clearly to plan our next move." His voice was cracking from all the talking as he forced himself to continue, "We will meet early in the morning to discuss this. Please excuse me and have a good night."

As Israel turned to go, Jacob jumped up and said, "Before you retire for the night, may I have a quick word?"

Israel looked like he expected this and simply nodded towards a secluded spot a few yards away.

Jacob said, "The men will ask me about Taylor; what do you expect me to tell them?"

"You can tell them that the scouting party ran into some Delaware. After a brief exchange, your Taylor was taken captive. My boys did their best to retrieve him, but they were driven off when more savages suddenly appeared." Israel took a drink of water from his canteen to relief his voice and waited for some kind of reaction from his brother.

Jacob looked at his brother and thought to leave it at that, but he still needed to know the full account for himself. "I trust your judgment and your authority here, Israel," he said slowly. "I will tell the men your version, but I must know the truth of what happened."

Israel displayed little emotion and simply said, "If it will help you sleep tonight, then you should know that the snake was shot in the stomach by Jenkins and dragged to a tree where my boys tied him up. They were just following my orders. I told them to leave him somewhere for the wildcats or the Delaware to deal with."

"What if he screams or escapes?" Jacob asked.

"No real concern of that. They removed his tongue, and Jenkins was an old sea hand. I doubt any of us could get out of one of his knots."

Israel waited for any further questions, but Jacob had heard all that he required. He didn't approve of the brutality of his brother's methods, but he felt an immense relief at knowing Taylor would never be able to accuse him of Braddock's death.

"Please thank your men for me," Jacob said quietly. "I do appreciate your help with this matter."

"It's what brothers are for, is it not?" Israel callously retorted.

He abruptly excused himself, leaving Jacob standing alone. Still taken aback by his brother's matter-of-fact account of Taylor's death and his parting comment, Jacob walked back to Maggie.

He took her hand and pulled her to her feet. Silently, they walked toward their tent. A small pit to the left of the tent had been laid for a fire and Jacob had it lit in a matter of seconds. He dragged two stumps over to the fire and they sat for a few minutes while Jacob tended to the fire.

Maggie tucked her hand around his arm and asked quietly, "How was your conversation with Israel? Did you find out anything about poor Taylor?"

"First off," Jacob said as he stared at the flames, "Taylor was no one you need to feel sorry for. Israel did explain to me what took place, but I think you are better off not knowing much about it. Just be glad that this Taylor fellow is out of our lives. Trust me, as bad as that sounded, he could have caused us a great deal of problems down the road."

Maggie could see he was troubled by the entire situation and decided not to press him for more details. If this Taylor would have caused them trouble, she was glad he was gone. They had already had enough trouble to last them for life.

Jacob gathered a number of good sized logs and stacked them next to the fire pit so he could keep the fire going all night. "It feels like we might get some snow," he said. "My head is starting to ache; that was always a sign of some kind of bad weather."

"Come sit over here and let me rub your head," she said.

Jacob happily obliged and sat on the ground with his back against her legs in front of her stump.

"It feels like a lifetime since we had some time together," Jacob said as he enjoyed Maggie's slow massage of his temples.

"Have you heard anything of James or Becky?" Maggie suddenly asked. "I fear little Henry and Mary might not even remember much of us by now." She tried not to cry, but the thought of her children being raised by an Indian family was too much for her.

Jacob returned to the stump next to Maggie and put his arms around her. He had waited to talk about the children until she brought up the topic first. He rubbed her back and thought of how to proceed. It was not going to be a happy conversation.

"I have heard nothing of them," he admitted. "Tell me what happened to them after the Huron captured you."

Maggie took a shaky breath and started to rehash the painful memories of the day their homestead was raided. "Things happened so fast. You would have been so proud of James. He tried so hard to fight back, but he was so small. When they gathered us all up, they prevented us from having as much contact with any of the captive children as possible. One of the last times I saw them, I told them not to cry. James was taken north early on in our march. The girls and Henry were taken away at a small village. It was actually the same place I saw Abby for the last time. I pray she survived all of this…"

Jacob jumped in quickly and said, "Actually, I saw Abby at a small village a while back. I don't know if it was the same one. She honestly looked content and strangely happy, but I saw nothing of the girls or Henry."

"Did you tell her about Israel?" Maggie asked before he continued.

"No, at the time I thought he was dead. I didn't want to cause her more pain. No good would have come from me telling her that he was gone."

"Does Israel know that you saw her?"

"I have had no opportunity," he said defensively. "I had only just found out he was still alive when I saw you here. At any rate, I wonder if he should even be told. Like I said, she seemed happy, and he is so convinced that she would never want him again if she saw him."

"That is not really fair, Jacob," Maggie scolded him softly. "You shouldn't defend your silence because it is your opinion that they are better off."

"Aye, you are right as usual, dear. I think I missed your common sense more than anything, and I am certainly happy that you are here to keep me under control." His sarcasm was met with a sharp pinch and he let out a low chuckle.

They sat for a long time watching the fire until, as Jacob predicted, the night sky gave way to heavy, wet snow. The snow began sticking immediately to every surface in the camp and accumulated quickly.

The fire hissed with every flake that landed in it and Jacob suggested they retire to the relative comfort of the tent.

Maggie agreed and stepped through the open flap. She smiled when she saw two large deer skins covering two heavy blankets. Between the covers and the fire and Jacob's warmth next to her, she would certainly not freeze.

Before he joined Maggie inside, Jacob placed three more large pieces of wood on the fire to try to keep it going as long as possible. The snowfall had grown even more intense, and Jacob wondered how quickly they would realistically be able to depart for the fort.

Jacob opened the tent flaps carefully, trying not to let too much cold air in. "Bloody cold out there," he said as he fastened the flaps from the inside. "It looks like this will be a good storm."

He pulled back the thick hides and blankets to lie down and saw that Maggie had already fallen fast asleep. Without disturbing her, he lay down quietly and pulled the covers back over them. He closed his eyes, but it was a long time before his thoughts quieted and he was able to sleep.

Jacob awoke very early to clear the extra weight of the snow from the top of the tent. The storm ceased, but it had dropped over ten inches of heavy snow on the camp.

The only other poor soul up at this early hour was Israel. He crouched in front of his tent, trying to get a fire going.

"Need a little help with that?" Jacob shouted across the quiet camp as he managed to relight his own fire. "I hope this isn't a sign of what the whole winter will be like."

"Keep your bloody voice down, you old fool," Israel hissed. "Do you want to wake up the entire camp?"

Jacob walked over and immediately had Israel's fire pit going. He threw a couple handfuls of snow into a pot and set it near the flames to melt.

"Maybe a nice hot cup of tea will put you in a better mood," Jacob said. "Did you get much sleep last night?" He grabbed a small cache of herbs that were stuffed in his pocket and added them to the pot. He found a twig under the snow and used it to stir the tea.

"Sadly, I never sleep much anymore," Israel said. "My scars make it impossible to get comfortable. I usually find myself wandering around the camp or taking a midnight stroll in the woods. I can't honestly remember having a single good night's rest since Fort Necessity." He pushed several inches of snow off a tall boulder and leaned against it.

"Damn shame, brother. I guess it's not enough that you look like hell," Jacob joked, but got no reaction from Israel.

"Have you decided whether to move the whole camp to the fort?" Jacob tried in a more serious tone. It was evident that his brother was not in the mood for banter this morning.

"This damn snow certainly limits our options," Israel replied. "This is a great location for a camp during the rest of the year, but it is obviously very exposed to the snow. It was never my intent to stay here for the winter. Ordinarily, the Delaware would have moved into their southern winter villages by now, and I intended to move south as well.

"This Captain Jacobs is a strange bird though, and has not yet flown south for the winter. Of course, this could be last his ditch effort on their part as they leave their northern villages. Maybe it is just a reminder that they will be back soon to reclaim their land." Israel swallowed hard to clear the pain in his throat.

"I pray that is the case," Jacob said. "I worry that if the Delaware's plan is to remain in the north, we may not be able to reach the fort. They will certainly try their hardest to prohibit us from moving around the territory freely."

"The only reason I thought to leave any men here, as I suggested last night, was to protect Maggie and your men while they convalesced. Is your fort large enough to accommodate all of my men? You heard the scout say that many frontier families are also seeking shelter there."

"Well, we were expecting to house a hundred additional men at the fort this winter, but only five of them are left," Jacob said seriously. "We should have enough room for you. It might be a tight fit, but it will be livable."

Jacob paused then said quietly, "Israel, I need to return to my men regardless of what you choose to do, and I'm taking Maggie with me."

Israel nodded and said, "Well, the one good thing about this weather is that it makes the decision much easier."

Jacob poured two cups of tea and let them both sit until they cooled enough to drink comfortably. By this time, most of the men had risen to re-light the remaining fires and clear enough snow so they could get around the camp.

"I guess I should speak with the men to tell them to start getting ready to move out," Israel said. "On second thought, I will order most of them to start making snowshoes. I think they will be more important than anything."

Israel couldn't drink the hot brew and said, "Take this for Maggie; she probably would enjoy it more than I."

Jacob took up both cups and returned to his tent. Maggie was still sleeping, so he put one of the cups near the fire to keep it warm and sipped the steaming liquid from the other cup.

He sat by himself thinking about getting back to the fort and taking Maggie with him. He was looking forward to seeing Joshua, Tate and the rest of the men who had become more than just soldiers to him.

Taking a long sip, Jacob pushed some of the logs in the fire around with his foot and took a deep breath of the cold morning air. Maggie would soon be up and they would be leaving this place and make the snow covered trek to the fort that he missed so much.

Chapter | **Eleven**

The snow was causing a number of problems for the men. The high boulders that encircled the camp provided ample opportunities for the snow to drift, making it even deeper and more unwieldy. Jacob could tell that it would be hours before they would be able to move out.

Once he finished his tea, he stood up and stretched his tired muscles. Standing, looking around at the snow covered encampment, he heard Maggie stirring in their tent. He entered through the flap and gave her a quick kiss and the extra cup of tea. She was grateful for both and smiled.

Jacob briefly explained the plan to relocate to the fort then excused himself to organize his men. He left her with another quick kiss and a guilty smile. She didn't mind much; even the briefest of his kisses warmed her and she felt safe just knowing that he was nearby.

Maggie had enjoyed her extra hour of sleep, but she had work to do.

The early morning cold air made her cringe, as did the fresh snow that had engulfed the area. She tended the largest fire in the camp and made sure that there were ample amounts of hot herbal tea ready to warm the men as they fought to clear away the snow.

She thought over the plan to winter at the fort her husband had built. She cherished the thought of spending more time with Jacob and Israel and seeing Joshua again. The only things that could have made her happiness complete would have been the presence of the rest of their family and One-Ear.

Israel's men supported the idea of over-wintering at the fort. They were, as he had predicted, particularly excited by the prospect of engaging Captain Jacobs.

Approaching Jacob to talk over what they needed to do before they left for the fort, Israel asked, "How are the trails to the fort? We usually use the much smaller side paths or cut our own. I haven't used the main trails for a long time."

"Without snow, it is normally a quick run to the fort," Jacob replied. "I certainly hope that there were enough leaves left in the canopy to shield the trail from some of this snow, but I'm sure we will still run into quite a bit along the way."

"I think it would be prudent to send out a small scouting party to check the trail and see exactly what the Delaware are up to," Jacob added. "If I may be so bold, I think I would be the best man to lead it since I have good knowledge of the area."

"I'm glad you brought up the subject of leading," Israel's raspy voice cracked as he spoke. "The only question my men had was once we are at the fort, who is in command?"

Jacob was caught off guard by the question, as he had honestly not given the issue any thought. He worded his answer carefully so as not to insult his brother, "You can assure your men that I am the fort's commander, but you will still be their leader. I would never order them to do something without consulting with you beforehand. My only issue would be if your men do something that would undermine my authority in front of the men under my command. They must agree to be under the same rules as the militia and be subjected to the same punishment as the others. No matter who leads them, a thief will be flogged, as would a troublemaker. Do you find such conditions fair?"

"I can assure you," Israel said, "my men will be on their best behavior and will be available to hunt, scout and take turns in the regular garrison duty. They are all good men and are used to the discipline of an army-like company."

"As for sending you with the forward scouts," Israel said after a short pause, "I agree that you would be best suited for such a detail. You may pick among the best of my men to take with you." Israel offered.

"I think we will need to leave soon or be forced to wait until early tomorrow," Jacob said. "If we take your snowshoes with us, the trail should be fairly passable. Maggie will not be happy, but you will still be with her. That should give her some peace of mind."

Israel moved off to update his men while Jacob looked for Maggie. He prayed that additional snow would hold off and give them a window to move the whole party to the fort safely.

Maggie had left the fire to tidy up the tent. He found her straightening blankets and the image of domesticity made him homesick for their old life. He smiled and grabbed her in a tight embrace.

She gave a little squeal and said, "Are you trying to snap my back, Jacob?" She stepped back from his hug and ran her hands over her clothes to straighten out the wrinkles.

"You just looked so beautiful standing there; I couldn't help myself," Jacob smiled and fought through Maggie's futile attempt to stop him from hugging her again.

"Mr. Murray, you are pushing your luck," she laughed, enjoying the return of this playfulness she had missed over the last couple of years.

"I hate to spoil our fun," Jacob said seriously, "but I have to tell you that Israel wants me to lead a scouting party to check on the trail to the fort and clear out any Delaware."

"It makes sense," Maggie said. "You obviously know the area around your fort better than most men. Can't I come with you? I just got you back; I'll be damned if I'll lose you again."

Jacob had expected this and he said, "I would bring you along, but with Israel here, it is much safer to stay with him."

"What am I to do while you are off scouting?" Maggie asked. She hadn't intended to sound quite so irritated. She knew that her husband wanted her safe. She was just worried about letting him out of her sight now that they had been reunited.

"I am just glad that Israel has agreed to spend the winter with us at the fort," Jacob confided. He and his men seem a bit nervous about where his authority will lie since I am in command of the fort. He insisted that you remain back with the main body of men, Not only will you be safe, but it will show him that I respect his authority as well."

"Our short separation will be a small price to pay, Maggie," he added, stroking her cheek. "Imagine how entertaining this winter will be! The three of us will be able to spend time together in relative safety. Joshua will be there as well, and he will be so pleased to see you."

She said nothing, but grabbed him in a tight hug like he had given her. This time he was not so quick to release his grip. Eventually, she pulled back and kissed him.

The rest of the morning was a busy one at the camp. Maggie helped some of the men prepare the midday meal and make up small packs of food for the scouts to take with them. Jacob, under the guidance of his brother, took his time picking out his scouting party.

He was satisfied that he had fifteen of Israel's strongest woodsmen. He also allowed Private McGinn, the healthiest of the five remaining men from Fort Cumberland, to join the group. Caleb Kennedy was also among the party, and the two Mingo warriors would be used as forward scouts.

Jacob advised them to take the least amount of gear, but to make sure they had a full supply of powder. They would be moving very swiftly. There would be little time to rest and no time to wait for stragglers.

It was early afternoon when they finally departed the camp. Jacob kissed Maggie goodbye and saluted his brother before leading the men to the trail that would take them to the old Seneca hunting path. He looked back in time to see Maggie wipe her eyes and crawl back into their tent.

He felt a twinge of guilt, but knew she was safer with Israel than a scouting party out on a trail that might be full of Delaware warriors. As the group turned onto the larger trail, Jacob's focus was solely on the matter at hand.

The snow was heavy and thick, yet Jacob was impressed at how easily the men worked through it. The lead scouts had the hardest trek, although even they made good time. McGinn and young Caleb made up the rear guard. Thankfully, the shallow streams and some of the smaller river crossings were iced over enough that the men could run across and not worry about getting their feet soaked and frozen.

The trail was more than passable until they got to the higher elevations near the first of the mountain ridges. The trail became steeper and the snow deeper until the tired men were slowed to a near crawl. Jacob decided that they should stop and make camp before they lost the remaining light. If they set out early the next morning, they could make the fort by nightfall.

He sent two men forward to recall the Mingo scouts and look for a safe place to stop to eat and sleep.

The snow certainly complicated their search, but they found a secluded rocky ledge that was far enough off the trail that it could be easily defended if they were attacked. The rocks formed a cave that provided shelter for all of the men.

Jacob was always cautious this time of year. The snow combined with this many men tramping through it, made it almost impossible to hide their tracks. While most of the men busied themselves collecting firewood, Jacob sent several men up the trail to make as many tracks as they could to throw off anyone who might be following them. It was an old trick, one that anyone with a lick of experience in the woods would know, but he figured it was still worth trying.

Upon their return, a young man named Tims said, "Sir, we saw signs everywhere that the Delaware are very active in this area."

"Did you see them or just their tracks?" Jacob asked.

"We almost ran into a small party of them, but they didn't notice us. We thought it was smarter to let them be for now. I must say I am surprised that there are so many of them still here. Usually they have already left for their winter hunting villages in the Virginia territory."

"Aye, they must be thinking about staying at Kittanning for most of the winter to continue their raids on the settlements in the area. I fear this might be a long and bloody winter." Jacob thanked the men for their good work and reporting, and told them to find a spot to rest.

Jacob always enjoyed scouting with other experienced woodsmen. They knew what they were about. A fire had already been lit at the mouth of the cave, and Jacob expected they could all look forward to a reasonably comfortable night's sleep.

He knew it was a risk to have a fire this deep into Delaware-infested territory but the cold overnight weather and snow gave him little choice. Jacob did consult with the men and they all agreed that a fire, despite the inherent danger, was for the best.

There was no time to hunt for fresh game, and most animals were tucked away out of the snow anyway. Each man carried one of the cloth wrapped packets Maggie had packed for them, which included some salted meat, bread and a hunk of cheese to keep them content.

The snow provided them with a source of water more valuable than food. A couple of the men had brought along small cooking pots and spent some time filling them with snow and melting it into drinkable water.

Jacob was relatively happy with their progress to this point, although the night sky quickly gave way to a steady stream of snow that would make the morning's march even slower and more treacherous. He felt for the men who were assigned to picket duties during the worst of the storm, but it was essential. The last thing he wanted was to let their guard down and awaken to a Delaware raiding party.

Despite the cold, the men managed to sleep. The pickets made sure to put more wood on the fire at every shift change, which made the sleeping conditions much more bearable.

As the morning light struggled to free itself from the clouds and snow, the wind began to howl. The steady snow gave birth to a blizzard, and Jacob could only stand at the entrance of the cave and watch the snow pile up.

All visibility was diminished and the men sat helplessly with their heavy capotes wrapped around them, waiting for the weather to subside. The pile of firewood was very low and they made a concerted effort to conserve as much as they could.

Jacob was frustrated by his inability to send out a scouting party, but he took comfort in the fact that the Delaware were likely just as stranded as they were.

The two Mingo scouts attempted to move out late in the morning, but they were soon pushed back by the wall of snow. They told Jacob that while they had managed to reach the main trail, they had only gone a few paces before they became disoriented. They had barely managed to get back to the safety of the camp.

The storm remained strong for most of the day, slowing only long enough for a group of men to seek out some wet branches to feed the fire. Earlier in the day, the fire pit had been moved a bit further into the cave to keep it from being smothered by the snow. Unfortunately, the wind often whipped around the entrance and blew the smoke back into the cave, forcing the men to keep their heads covered to avoid choking and inhaling the smoke.

The storm ended abruptly as the sun began to set. Jacob made sure the men were comfortable for the night. He sent out pickets, but allowed them to remain close to the cave and the small fire.

Thankfully, the next morning dawned bright and clear. The sunshine was multiplied by the glint off the snow and the men were reenergized and ready to head out. They were visibly eager to escape the confines of the cave and Jacob found they had themselves organized without him having to issue orders.

The scouting party had hit the trail before Jacob could even ask them. McGinn and Caleb Kennedy took up the rear guard, and despite there being well over a foot of fresh snow, the men gladly trudged through the drifts as they worked their way to the main trail.

The tree canopy was still not completely bare, and it had provided a tiny buffer over the trail so that the snow was not as deep as it could have been. Despite the men's energy, it was difficult to keep a strong pace. Several of the men slid in the snow, which slowed them even more as the others stopped to assist them.

None of the men complained. They simply strapped on their snowshoes and pressed on. The new snow was much lighter than the earlier accumulation, which made it easier to walk through.

Word had come from the forward scouts that the trail became more passable up ahead, which made it appear that the previous day's blizzard had been an isolated storm. They also reported that they had not seen any fresh signs of the Delaware.

Jacob grew more excited the closer they came to the fort. He was eager to see if Joshua and the other men inside the fort were safe. Around midday, when they stopped for a break, a messenger came from behind them and brought the wonderfully unexpected news that the rest of Israel's camp was already on the trail.

The man explained that Israel was worried that the early winter weather might strand them at the camp, so he had ordered them out shortly after Jacob had departed. They had not gotten as far as Jacob on the first day and benefited by camping outside the reach of the blizzard, so they were able to trek for a few hours on the previous day as well. As a result, they were only trailing behind Jacob by a couple of hours.

It wasn't long before Jacob and his men could smell the fires within the fort's wall. The other scouts appeared to be as excited as he was, and they picked up their pace a bit. Jacob reminded the men to be on their guard; they did not want to walk into a Delaware ambush. He had not heard from the lead scouts in quite some time and this worried him.

He decided to send four men ahead to check on the scouts and report immediately back to him. Another man was sent back to McGinn and Caleb with the message to stay closer to the main unit. The rest of the men were told to march in single file to prevent a single bullet from hitting more than one of them from the side.

After an ample amount of time had passed without word from the group of men he'd sent after the Mingo scouts, Jacob grew concerned. As he deliberated on ways they might reach the fort without using the main trail, they came upon proof that the Delaware were nearby.

The two Mingo scouts had been tied to a couple of trees along the path and butchered. They had been scalped and their intestines were torn out and wrapped around them.

Once they were clear of the bodies, Jacob stopped the men to address them briefly. He knew most of the men had likely witnessed much worse over the past months, but any man would be affected by seeing his friends slaughtered and put on display.

"Lads," Jacob said quietly, "we need to keep our wits about us. We now know that the savages are around us. We might be forced to fight through them to reach the fort or just to survive. God only knows what they did with the other scouting party, so prepare your stomachs to meet up with more of what we just saw."

"Should we take them down and give them a Christian burial?" One of the men called out in hushed voice.

"Regrettably, there's no time for that, lad. We have to keep moving and get to the fort as soon as we can," Jacob replied as he turned to lead the men forward.

Soon they heard screams and war cries of the Delaware in the woods ahead of them. Jacob realized that they were very close to the fort and turned to address the men once more. "Lads, let's stop here for a bit to regroup and figure out what to do next. It looks like the Delaware are indeed attacking the fort, and we will have to fight through them to get to it."

He set up a few pickets around their location to keep on the alert while most of the men remained in a huddle, waiting for their next order. Jacob certainly did not want to risk any more of his men being killed by the Delaware, but he needed to know exactly what they were up against.

He asked for a volunteer to climb one of the many trees to get a view of the surrounding area. Young Caleb was the first to step forward. Before Jacob could say anything, the young man had already climbed nearly ten feet above them. Jacob motioned him to move a little higher but to be careful not to be seen by the Delaware.

When he had reached a level of about twenty feet above the ground, Caleb stopped and looked through the thick branches towards the fort. He spent several minutes observing the entire field and was soon down on the ground to report. "I could see the fort," he told Jacob. "It looks like they are under siege from about two hundred, maybe as many as three hundred Delaware. We are only about fifty paces from the rear of the main war party, although they are off to our left."

After pausing to think over what Caleb had just explained, Jacob asked for more details, "Is the fort surrounded or are the Delaware spread out?"

"What I saw of them, the main body is concentrated west, directly across from the main gate. I did see some warriors near the tree line in front of us. As for other places around the fort, I honestly couldn't see much more."

"How are the soldiers in the fort holding out?" Jacob asked.

"Again, I couldn't see everything, but it appeared that they are in good shape."

Jacob stood and looked towards the west as though he would be able to see the Delaware through the trees. After a moment he turned to Caleb and said, "Good work, lad."

Caleb nodded and remained nearby. Jacob called out for Williams, McGinn and Turner to approach him. They were three of the most experienced woodsmen in the group and Jacob valued their knowledge and opinions. He asked Caleb to repeat what he had seen for the benefit of this informal council.

Caleb took a deep breath and gave his summation, "Basically, the Delaware are just ahead to our west. The fort sits just beyond their main war party. The fort looks to be in good order, despite the large number of Delaware laying siege to them. From what I could see, the Delaware number between two to three hundred. The fort appears to have around fifty, but Sergeant Sims can confirm the garrison's number."

Jacob saw their faces turn grim and, after thanking Caleb, did his best to reassure them. "Gentlemen," he said quietly, "the lad explained what we are up against, and I just wanted to see what your thoughts were?"

McGinn was the first to offer his thoughts, saying, "Aye, the way I see it is we need to get to the fort and the bloody savages are in front of us. The only choice is to fight our way through and get ourselves into the open field outside the fort's gates. We all know that the Delaware will not pursue us into the open and would rather remain cowering in the woods."

Appreciating the much older Scotsman's straightforward manner, Jacob nodded his approval and said, "Thank you, sir, but fearing I might be complicating matters, we also have to consider that Israel and the rest of the men should be arriving shortly. We might want to think about waiting it out for re-enforcements?"

The others stood leaning on their muskets, mulling over what Jacob said.

Williams was the next man to step forward and speak, "Sir, I fear if we wait too long, the savages will find us and decide our fate for us. I for one would rather fight than wait."

Jacob liked Williams even without knowing much about him. He was a fair-sized man with broad shoulders and looked older than his actual age. Williams carried himself with confidence and Jacob had noticed how hard the young man had worked around Israel's camp.

Jacob knew he had to get the men moving and couldn't stall here much longer. He had a great deal of confidence in these men and knew that they would do their best to reach the fort. He worried, however, that with the large number of Delaware around the fort, his remaining fifteen men would be easily wiped out before they even set a firm foot out of the woods.

In the seconds that he deliberated, a loud series of musket shots rang through the nearby woods, making Jacob duck instinctively. The rest of the men followed suit and took cover behind trees and boulders as the fire continued.

Jacob stood behind a large tree and tried to search around the surrounding ocean of leafless tree limbs and thick cedars that provided the perfect cover for the attacking Delaware. Waiting to see if the musket fire was directed at them, some of the men began to stand up and look towards where they thought it was coming from.

"Keep your heads down, lads!" Jacob called out.

"Caleb, where are you lad?" he whispered towards a clump of tall, bushy cedars to his left.

Caleb immediately replied from just over Jacob's shoulder, "Sir, I'm up here."

Jacob looked above his head and saw that Caleb had worked his way into the high branches of a nearly-bare chestnut tree. "What do you see, lad?" he asked.

"It's hard to see with all the smoke," Caleb replied as he tumbled neatly back to the ground, "but I am sure the fort is being attacked again."

"Mr. Williams," Jacob said, "would you please take four of the men and make a little trip towards all the fuss?"

Williams was quick to get his small scouting party in order and they moved off the trail through the woods to the west.

There was a break in the musket fire as Jacob looked around at his remaining men. There were only nine left and he felt vulnerable and exposed. He hoped that additional information from Williams' party would help him decide where they should position themselves to be most effective.

He also privately prayed that Israel would be arriving soon with the main body of men, to at least give them more fire power.

Almost as quickly as they had disappeared into the darkness, Williams returned. He only had two men with him.

As they got closer and he got a good look at the men, however, Jacob's face broke into a grin and he said, "Joshua! Is that you, lad?"

The young man was pale and visibly worn, but an answering smile reached his face and he said, "Damn, sir! It is certainly good to see you. We all thought you were dead, along with the men from Fort Cumberland you went after."

As Joshua approached, Jacob reached out in a fatherly embrace and said, "Good to see you too, lad."

Joshua's body felt very frail. Jacob took him by the arm and helped him sit on a rock that was shielded by two large fallen trees.

"Thank you, Mr. Williams," Jacob said, turning back to his scout. "What did you see out there?"

"Just this young man running towards us, though I do fear that he was being pursued. If they shift their position, we might just be under attack by the entire Delaware nation, sir."

"Where are your other men?"

"Still up ahead, sir, awaiting my return."

Suddenly, the men in question appeared through the trees as they sprinted as quickly as they could through the snow towards Jacob. They veered a bit to the left and dived head-long into the brush. Behind them came two painted and screaming warriors.

Jacob's men were spread out through the trees in an even line almost thirty paces wide. They stood shielded by trees, awaiting Jacob's order to fire.

Jacob scanned the tree line to see if there were any additional savages, but it just seemed to be the pair of them. He signaled the burly McGinn to take down the Delaware without using his musket.

McGinn smiled and nodded. Just as the two unsuspecting warriors started to slow to look for tracks left by the four men they were chasing, McGinn led two men down the warriors' flank. Jacob prayed that they wouldn't make much noise and attract other savages.

McGinn was quick and efficient with his surprise attack. The two warriors were easily taken down and dispatched into the woods. McGinn walked back into view, holding a fresh, bloodied scalp he had taken from one of the savages.

Jacob was not happy about the scalping, but he was relieved that none of the men cheered his actions. They kept their muskets shouldered, anticipating more warriors might be coming.

Moments after McGinn and his men returned to their covered position, Jacob caught a glimpse of a much larger party of warriors running towards them.

Jacob shouldered his own musket and before he could give the order, one of the men fired and all hell broke loose. Screams and confusion echoed through the already bloodied trail as Jacob's men continued to open fire into the startled savages.

Through the lingering smoke, Jacob could see how accurate the first volley had been. The experienced woodsmen had decimated most of the warriors with their expert marksmanship, and a few of them had already charged into the open to fight the last of the surviving savages.

Following their lead, Jacob jumped over a fallen tree with his small hatchet raised, searching through the heavy white smoke for any Delaware not killed or injured. He was taken aback by the sight of the men's merciless attack. They went about butchering them in the same way he had seen them act against the French when he was rescued. He prevented them from further mutilation and scalping by ordering them to drag the bodies out of sight and get back behind cover.

"Gentlemen," he said, "I'm sure this is just the first of the savages headed our way; we'd better get our muskets loaded and expect another onslaught."

He watched the men reluctantly obey his order and return to their previous positions. Most of the men just concentrated on cleaning the blood off their knives and hatchets, not making eye contact with any of the others.

With the small break in the action, Jacob checked on Joshua. "What happened, lad?" he asked as he handed him a wooden canteen.

Joshua struggled to swallow the small drink of water then cleared his throat. "We had the fort in good order until the bloody savages decided to make our lives hell," Joshua explained. "Every time we sent out a scouting or hunting party, they never returned. Each morning we'd see some of their bodies tied to the trees near the forest line. Even Major Stevens was forced to return to the fort with his light horsemen not long after you had departed."

"Stevens is at the fort now?" Jacob interrupted.

Taking another drink, Joshua continued, "He was, but he had somehow contracted the pox. He died a few days back, along with a number of his men. It was sheer hell trying to confine the infected men to keep from spreading the pox through the entire fort."

Jacob could see the pain in Joshua's eyes and let him rest for a moment. He returned to check on his men and soon found Williams. The man barely acknowledged his approach and Jacob could sense tension emanating from him.

"Have you heard or seen any further movement?" Jacob asked.

Williams was slow to reply, but finally said, "Nothing yet…sir."

Choosing to ignore Williams and his moodiness, which he assumed was the result of preventing the men from taking prizes, Jacob simply said, "Let me know if you see anything."

He returned to Joshua and hoped that the fight was over for now, so he could spend more time finding out exactly what was happening within the fort.

"Feeling any better, lad?" Jacob asked as he sat beside him.

"A little better, sir," Joshua answered.

"So tell me everything about the fort and what were you doing outside its walls?"

"Not much to tell, sir. We have been at the mercy of the bloody Delaware since you left. Even the snow hasn't slowed them down much. I volunteered to locate a rumored relief party approaching from the west." Joshua stopped and took a deep breath.

Jacob didn't want to push him too hard, but he needed to know what exactly they were getting themselves into, "How many Delaware? Do you know where they are the weakest?"

Joshua sat up and rubbed his dirty hands through his long, stringy hair. "Their numbers change like the wind. Sometimes they have hundreds and some days only a few dozen, just sitting in the woods watching us. My guess is the weakest point in their attack is exactly how I made it through. The eastern bastion side is the area where they appear to have only a few warriors. If you want to get to the fort without fighting through the main body of the savages, I feel that spot would be the best."

Just as Joshua finished speaking, they heard some low shouts from some of the men. Jacob rose and put a hand on Joshua's shoulder, motioning him to stay down.

It had only been a few minutes since the last Delaware attack, but now it appeared that a large group was approaching from the south along the path. Jacob saw McGinn, Williams and his men ambush a large party of Delaware and it sounded like they were about to do the same as another group of warriors approached from the southern end of the path.

Jacob watched McGinn, Williams and Turner organizing the men and telling them to shoulder their muskets. He got their attention and forcefully told them to wait for his signal to fire.

Once again, Caleb quickly climbed a nearby tree to see what he could of the approaching war party. Jacob remained calm and took cover behind a dead tree that had wedged itself against a hemlock when it fell. He planned to wait until the very last moment to open fire. Even though their undisciplined savagery in the aftermath of their last skirmish upset him, Jacob had admired how well the men had fought against them. They were excellent marksmen, and he wished to take advantage of that to avoid much of the hand-to-hand killing.

Jacob continued to watch the path and glanced up to see if Caleb might have spotted something. He returned his gaze to the path just as the main party came into view. The men adjusted their muskets on their shoulders, but continued to wait on Jacob.

Just as Caleb began to slide out of the tree to report, Jacob realized that this was no Delaware war party. He ran out into the path ahead of the men and called out softly, "Hold your fire, lads! Hold your fire!"

It was the advance scouts from Israel's main company.

The men stepped on the trail to join Jacob in greeting their mates. Both parties were happy to see each other, and with the addition of Israel and his men, Jacob knew that getting to the fort would be far easier.

"Good to see you, boys," Jacob said with a smile. "Your timing could not have been better!"

It wasn't long before the main body of men arrived and congested the small path and surrounding wooded area. Israel arrived with Maggie by his side and was met by Jacob, who said, "It's good to see you, brother. I prayed you would arrive soon. We've already fought off one small attack, but we need to get in position in case of another one. I will leave that to you, Israel." The brothers embraced quickly and Israel left to organize his men.

Jacob turned to Maggie and gave her a big kiss. He pulled away and grinned. "Maggie, if you will just look behind that fallen tree," he said, pointing, "I have a nice surprise for you."

She raised her eyebrow but did as she was told. She immediately covered her mouth and her eyes brightened with excitement.

"Ma'am, thank you for not screaming and alerting the Delaware," Joshua said with a smile as he struggled to his feet. "They have already caused us enough trouble today."

Jacob had left Maggie to the business of catching up with her old friend while he went to speak with Israel. The first thing Maggie noticed was how poorly Joshua looked. The last time she had seen him, he was much larger and stronger. Now his whole appearance was drawn and ragged.

"What can I do to help, Joshua?" she asked pleasantly as she helped him to sit back down on the rock.

"Is One-Ear with you, Maggie?" Joshua asked as he leaned back against the tree.

Maggie had expected the question, but she didn't want to distress him until he was stronger. She ignored it for the moment and said, "Let me get you some water. Don't you worry; Jacob's brother is here now. We should be in the fort by nightfall, if not before."

Joshua was instantly revitalized at the thought and said, "Water would be good; if you have some bread or cheese to add, that would be nice as well."

"I will see what I can do," she smiled and stepped over the dead tree to find Jacob. Jacob saw her immediately and called out, "How is the boy?"

She waited until she had gotten closer before she said, "He is skinny and starved, but in good spirits. He is thirsty and asked for some food."

Israel piped up and looked to one of the men, saying, "Mr. Phelps, please be so kind as to get Maggie some water and food."

She smiled at Israel and followed Phelps, reaching out for Jacob's hand as she passed.

"She is a strong woman, Jacob," Israel said. "I honestly can't think of too many who could have survived what she has."

"She is strong," Jacob said finally, "but I would rather resume this conversation when we are inside the walls of the fort and not in the middle of woods teeming with angry savages."

Forcing what passed for a sly smile, Israel said, "What are we facing?"

"We need to speak with young Joshua to confirm the numbers, but I believe that with the arrival of your men, the garrison can turn the attack on the Delaware." Jacob added.

"I am honestly still not sure that this fort is the best place for us to be," Israel replied. "The winter is hard enough without adding the constant threat from the damn Indians. We will all be just packed in and miserable."

Jacob was shocked at Israel's continued waffling on this point, especially considering that they were less than hundred yards from the fort. It irritated him that Israel was passing judgment on a place he hadn't even seen yet.

"Well, I should speak with Joshua before blindly deciding such things if I were you," Jacob spat back.

The two men approached Joshua, who was obviously enjoying being mothered by Maggie. "Joshua," Jacob said as he helped Israel step over the fallen tree, "how are you feeling now, lad?"

Joshua didn't notice Israel right away and said, "I'm feeling much better, sir, especially now that your wife is here with us."

Jacob was about to introduce Israel when he noticed the change in Joshua's expression. Jacob attempted to lighten the mood and said, "Joshua, this is my twin brother, Israel. As you can see, I'm the better looking one."

Israel stepped forward and countered, "He might be better looking, but I was blessed with all the personality."

Everyone let out a short laugh and the tension broke.

"We need to get some further details about the fort and the Delaware," Jacob said.

"Yes, sir. As I mentioned earlier, the fort is in good shape for the winter. We did have some opportunities to build up our stores and the men are in relatively good spirits. The bloody savages have been pestering us since you left but they have not killed many of us within the fort's walls."

Israel immediately interjected, "Why did the fort feel it imperative to send you out into the woods full of savages?"

"We had lost a couple of small scouting parties, and every time we sent out a hunting party it either returned empty handed or was attacked. We did get word that there was a company of men west of us, and I volunteered to attempt to get a message to them."

Jacob looked at Israel and then cut back into the conversation, "How many men are inside the fort as we speak?"

"Between fifty to sixty, plus several families who were forced to take refuge with us after their farms were attacked. The Delaware have been scorching the frontier without mercy and with each passing day, our numbers seem to swell."

"Do you have enough supplies to feed all the people currently at the fort? If my men and I decide to stay through the winter, how will you feed the additional mouths?" Israel pressed, clearly against staying at the fort and leaving his men vulnerable to the Delaware, starvation or disease.

"I have no authority to tell you to stay or leave," Joshua said brusquely. "I only know this land well enough to tell you that we are one good storm away from being snowed in for the next several months.

"I would rather have the numbers with me until the Delaware decide to move to their winter hunting grounds. Once they are gone, we will be able to set our traps and send out daily hunting parties to keep everyone fed." Joshua did his best to maintain a modicum of respect in his tone, but he refused to hear any slight against the fort.

Jacob stepped in and ended the conversation by saying, "We should let the lad get some more rest. Israel and I can discuss this further between us." He smiled at Maggie and nodded to Joshua before directing Israel back to the path.

Just before they reached it, Jacob stopped and said, "One last detail, lad, have the French been seen with their Delaware allies?"

"About a week ago, a small unit of regulars and some of their militia, but I have seen nothing of them since. My guess is that they prefer to stay in one of their cozy forts and not venture out in this weather." Joshua grinned at the thought and his smile seemed very large on his thin face.

"Typical of the Frenchies, boy," Israel responded, "they like their savages to do all their dirty work."

Chapter | **Twelve**

Jacob knew Israel still had second thoughts about overwintering with him at the fort. He wasn't sure if his brother was worried about giving up some of his authority or freedom. Possibly it was that he was uncomfortable being around strangers and their reaction to his appearance. Despite that, reaching the fort safely was still his only objective. Between the two, it had been decided that the main body of men would make their way to the fort during the darkest part of the night.

As time dragged on from the late afternoon to evening, Jacob began to feel very optimistic about their success. Another snow storm threatened to blanket the area overnight, but the thick clouds that rolled in would mask the moon and help the men to remain hidden for the time being. A number of scouting parties had reported that most of the Delaware had pulled back and the fort was now being watched by no more than fifty warriors, most centered on the distant forest line.

Jacob was eager to get back to the fort and agreed immediately when his brother suggested he lead a scouting party to warn the fort of their imminent arrival. He collected many of the same men from his previous party, including Williams, McGinn, and Caleb. The other four surviving soldiers from Ft. Cumberland joined them as well.

Before he departed, he stopped to check on Maggie and Joshua. The younger man was on his feet and looking much better. "I'm heading out to tell the fort we are coming," Jacob explained then asked, "Joshua, who is in charge of the fort now?"

"The head engineer is in charge. If you let me come with you, I can get you in without much trouble," Joshua boldly suggested.

Jacob looked at Maggie to see how she felt about losing her patient. She shrugged and Jacob said, "If you think you are up to it, lad, the trip will be tough in the dark."

Joshua smiled and simply nodded.

"Get yourself ready; we will be off within a half-hour," Jacob ordered. "Israel wants everyone inside the fort before dawn."

Jacob took Maggie's hand and led her to the path. Israel's men were preparing themselves to move once Jacob's party reached the fort, and there was a noticeable air of excitement in the men.

"Do you feel he is in good enough shape to make the trip?" Jacob asked, nodding his head in the direction of Joshua.

"He should be fine," she said firmly as they continued to walk. "He will have to make the trip sooner or later. I feel better knowing he will be with you, although I only wish I could go with you too."

Jacob was taken aback by her last words. He hadn't thought about taking her along, but now he stopped and turned to face her. "You are more than welcome to come with me. We just need to let Israel know you will be leaving with my scouting party so he won't think he lost you."

Maggie's smile warmed him and she abruptly left to make sure she had all of her belongings packed for the short trip. Jacob turned to collect some supplies, but his feet carried him a few paces into the pitch black of the northern path.

He stood alone, not focusing on anything in particular. Suddenly, anguish engulfed his entire body. Thoughts of his children, James, Becky, Mary and young Henry, flowed through his mind as he tried to fight off a surge of tears. It had been months since he had allowed his emotions to surface so freely; he usually managed to keep his pain well hidden in the back of his mind.

Maybe it was the realization that with Maggie at his side, if something went wrong and they were killed, their children would be orphans. It might also have been the reality of having Maggie at his side that made the chances of re-uniting the rest of his family even better. Either way, he fought his hardest to keep from crying, but his emotions had been suppressed for such a long time.

He walked a bit deeper into the darkness to prevent anyone from seeing him. After a few minutes he managed to compose himself and returned to the edge of the path. Israel found him there and said, "Are you alright, brother?"

Jacob nodded and Israel said, "Time is not on our side; you will need to leave now, or we will be forced to camp here in the woods for the night."

"The men are ready, and we will leave immediately," Jacob said. "By the way, I have decided to take Maggie and young Joshua with me, if you have no objections."

"Actually, Maggie had mentioned that she might ask you if she could go with you," Israel replied. "I have no objection, as long as you keep your men safe and don't get yourself in any more trouble. As soon as you gain entrance to the fort, send a messenger to let me know when it is safe to follow." Israel replied.

With that, Israel left to organize the rest of men.

Everyone was eager to get moving. As Jacob's unit departed, many of the men received pats on the backs and stifled cheers from the remaining men.

Jacob led them into the murkiness of the deep forest, having already sent out four advanced scouts to clear the way or send back word of any problems ahead of them. The men moved slowly, careful not to lose their footing on a fallen branch or a half buried rock. Most of the men were experienced enough with the Delaware to know that they rarely attacked at night.

The skies looked threatening and only waited for Jacob and his group to travel about four paces before they opened. Heavy, wet snow accumulated quickly on their path and soaked them all mercilessly. None of the men had carried snowshoes with them, so those in the lead were forced to struggle a bit more with their footing. Thankfully, the men in the rear could just follow in their footsteps but the trail was still quite slick and treacherous.

Jacob felt the snow already reach up to his calf just as the pickets' torches on top of the walls of the fort became visible. If not for these torches and light of the fires within the fort, Jacob's men would have been lost in the amassing snow storm.

They finally reached the edge of the tree line and Jacob sent a few men forward to inform the fort of their imminent arrival. He slowly stepped into the clearing and took a moment to scan the gloomy tree line, it was a futile exercise. He turned to the men and said, "We need to be even more cautious now. The night certainly gives us enough cover to help us make it to the fort's outer works, but if the Delaware are watching, the openness of the field will be our undoing. This snow might just be a blessing to us after all."

Jacob decided to send the men across the clearing in small groups, which would be harder to target than one larger unit. He turned to Williams and pointed at four men standing next to him.

"Williams," he said, "you will find the outer earthen works directly ahead, maybe a hundred paces or so. Once you reach the wall, signal us with three hoot owl calls and then make sure you provide the next group with some cover.

"One more thing, the field is littered with tree stumps that might be covered by the snow. Make sure you avoid them, or the men might just snap an ankle or worse."

Williams moved his men out immediately and Jacob kept his eyes on them until they were swallowed by the snow and the darkness. He made sure that the rest of the men were prepared to cross the clearing the moment the signal came.

After a few long minutes, Jacob heard three long hoots. He called back and motioned young Caleb to take another small group across the field.

"Just keep your heads down and follow the path Williams' men just took," Jacob said, patting Caleb on the back. He wished the men Godspeed and watched as they dashed into the darkness.

Two more groups had moved across the field successfully and it was finally time for Jacob, Maggie, Joshua and the two rear guards to cross. Even though the other groups had made it without incident, the danger grew with every crossing. The Delaware warriors in the tree line had likely become aware of their presence. They could not rule out a nighttime attack just because it was out of character for them.

Jacob had sent back a man to tell Israel it was safe to move up the rest of the men. A good track to the fort had been trampled down in the snow by Jacob's party and should make it easy for Israel's column to follow.

"Joshua, how are you feeling, lad?" Jacob whispered keeping his eyes peeled on the earthen wall and the nice pathway in the snow that the previous groups had flattened down for them.

"Better, sir, and ready to get back into the fort," Joshua answered.

Jacob reached back to squeeze Maggie's hand then stepped into the night. Once he got his footing, he ordered everyone to run.

It was not a long distance, yet it still was an open field and the snow was still falling. It was made much easier by not having to deal with the deep snow. However, this run was even more nerve-racking than any gauntlet Jacob or Maggie were ever forced to endure.

Jacob was breathing heavily and kept his head down, expecting a hail of bullets from the forest edge with every step. He had tried to hold on to Maggie's hand, but she had fallen back with Joshua. He encouraged them to keep moving and follow his lead.

Maggie and Joshua were right on his heels. As soon as he reached the relative comfort of the shoulder-high pile of earth, Jacob turned to make sure the group made it over the wall ahead of him.

Safely within the first line of the fort's defenses, they were greeted by the men on picket duty pointing their shouldered muskets directly at them. Caleb and Williams, along with the rest of the men who had run ahead of them, had their hands in the air and were guarded by three other men from the fort.

Joshua stepped forward to greet the pickets, "Put your muskets down; can't you see who this is?"

The surprised pickets simply replied, "Sorry, Joshua, but we observed men running across the open field and sent word back to the fort to be ready for a possible attack. You are lucky they didn't open fire on you from the walls."

As they were explaining their actions, Jacob moved beside Joshua and the pickets just stared at him like he was a ghost.

"Here we were worried about the bloody savages shooting at us but instead our own men were a greater threat." Jacob said.

"Sir, we heard you were dead."

"Not yet, lads. As you can see, I am still alive so please let us pass and get into the fort. My men are freezing and need to enjoy the many fires inside." Jacob tried not to be too hard on the men just for doing their duty.

"Yes, sir, we will signal the fort that you are coming," one of the men respectfully said.

"Thank you. You can expect more of us to arrive soon, so please give them a friendlier greeting." Jacob smiled and patted a couple of them on the backs as he passed by them.

Joshua led the way through the works towards the high wooden gates of the main entrance. They were embraced by the light of the torches along the fort wall as they longed for the warmth of the campfires they could smell burning inside.

As they approached the entrance, Joshua called out to the two guards that had dutifully watched them work their way to the entrance. "Good evening, gentlemen," he said. "It is Joshua, with a small party of English militia. Please open the front gates to let us get out of this bloody weather."

The two men stared curiously at the small party for a moment before one of them left. As the remaining guard continued to look silently down on the wet, shivering party, Jacob lost his patience.

"Damn it, boy, let us in!" he screamed, not caring if the Delaware heard him. "I am your commander, Sergeant Sims. It is bloody cold and you might want to consider not testing my patience on this terrible night!"

Just then, John Tate appeared above him and said, "Is it truly you, sir? We assumed you were killed at the hands of Captain Jacobs and his heathens."

"Mr. Tate, I assure you I am certainly not dead. I would love to catch up with you, but I am cold and tired and would much prefer to talk about this by one of the fires inside."

"Joshua, how are you boy?" Tate called back.

"For bloody sake, Tate!" Jacob exploded. "Open the bloody gates! Were you not informed by the scouts we sent ahead of us that we were coming?"

"The gates are being opened as we speak, sir. As you know, they are very heavy. It takes a minute or two. This is the first time we had word that you were even out there." Tate disappeared from the wall and Jacob assumed he was climbing down to meet them.

Once the gates were finally opened, the group was ushered in and introductions were made quickly. As the rest of the party moved to the nearest fire, Jacob stood with Tate by the open doors. "I'm glad to see you are well, Mr. Tate; we have much to discuss. I do need to find out what happened to the men I sent earlier to let you know of our arrival."

"Sorry but we received no such word." Tate confided, motioning for more of the men to the walls.

"Then you don't know that we are just the advance scouting party of a larger company that is still waiting in the woods," Jacob replied, clearly concerned that the Delaware were planning to ambush Israel and his men.

Tate just shook his head.

"The Delaware are still out in the woods," Jacob continued. "They must have taken the messengers we sent to you. I fear they may have intentionally let us through so they could ambush the larger group instead."

"What can we do in this weather, sir?" Tate asked.

As he walked towards the fire, Jacob asked, "How many healthy men do we have left?"

"At last roll call, we had nearly fifty men in relatively good shape. We have been depleted by some illness, a couple desertions and, of course, the damn savages."

Jacob scanned the interior of the fort and saw Joshua. "Lad, where did my wife get to?" he called out.

Joshua was rubbing his hands together over one of the other fires and called back, "I took her to the officers' quarters to get some rest."

Jacob smiled and turned his attention back to Tate. "I must say, you have done a fine job on the fort; even in the short time I've been away, you've continued to make it more comfortable. It certainly gives the men a good spot to spend the winter."

"Thank you, sir. The men have been working hard despite all the other distractions. I am very pleased with their work as well." Tate proudly said.

Jacob gestured for Williams and Caleb to get the men in order. "Mr. Tate," he said, "I am certain my brother will be attempting to reach the fort shortly. If I'm right, the Delaware will be waiting for them. Please double the pickets and get all the remaining men onto the walls. I will take the men who came with me back to the earthen works. If my brother makes it through the forest, he will need us to provide his men with some cover fire. To the walls, sir, and keep the men alert for any movement."

Just as Jacob's men were exiting the massive gates, shots echoed from the forest line.

Running with Caleb and Williams, Jacob directed them to spread the men along the southeastern outer wall and look for any sign of the Delaware.

All that could be seen was the sparks blasting from muskets and the accumulating white clouds of smoke. Muffled voices and cries could barely be heard in the woods just opposite where Jacob had set up his men.

Looking back towards the fort, Jacob was happy to see the walls packed with men. They waited with weapons ready to rain fire down on any savages foolish enough to come near the fort. The Delaware were aware of the range of English muskets and rarely ventured close enough to risk being shot.

Earlier, the scouts had reported that there were only about fifty warriors left in the woods, but clearly, the rest had merely been waiting for this attack. The snow stopped and the clouds parted to allow the moonlight to illuminate the field. The break in the weather was both an aid and a hindrance as it would assist the Delaware in their attack and on the other hand, help Israel's men in moving more quickly across the open field.

Screams and shrieks from the waiting war party pummeled the ears of the men waiting in the outer works of the fort, and Jacob stood up on the highest of the walls to get some kind of picture of what was happening.

"Damn it, sir," Williams shouted over the din, "get down before you get yourself killed!"

Jacob's first instinct was to send the men into the woods to launch a counter-ambush on the unsuspecting Delaware, but he knew that such a rash act would never be successful.

Helpless, frustration gripped him, but he did his best to keep his emotions under control. He could not sacrifice the lives of all these men just to save his brother.

"Sir, what about torching the woods?" Joshua called out.

Jacob's head snapped towards the young man he had left behind in the fort. A smile crossed his face when he saw the two familiar faces of the men who had escorted Joshua to the outer wall.

"White! Sinclair! It is good to see you both well and alive!"

Jacob glanced once more to the woods and considered the merits of intentionally setting the woods ablaze. He jumped down from the wall to speak directly with Joshua. "That's a nice thought, lad, but wouldn't it be dangerous for Israel and his men?"

"Yes, but they are going to be ambushed either way. It might provide them with an opportunity to break the savages' line and get to the fort."

Jacob was still uneasy with the idea and remained silent, understanding he needed something to force the hand of the attacking Delaware.

"I have seen it done before, sir," Joshua continued. The Huron used it several times when they fought the Iroquois."

Jacob looked at the others for any input, but no one said a word.

"Sir, have you ever smoked out a hornet's nest?" Joshua tried to explain his unorthodox idea.

"Very well," Jacob said, "I know we can't just sit here and wait for something to happen. We can't warn Israel, so what do you need? If we wait too long, the wind might kick up and all hell will break loose."

"I just need some torches; if we plan this right, the fire and smoke will be at the backs of the Delaware. They will be left with no choice but to move forward or to their other flank to escape. We just need to distract them long enough to let Israel get his men out of the woods and into the fort."

"Am I the only person here that finds this foolish?" Williams stepped forward, finally having found his tongue. "The woods have been drenched with snow. How will you get the fire spread?"

Joshua smiled and continued, "Maybe I failed to explain the plan clearly. All we need is to start some small fires along the trail line. It is the smoke that will make this whole thing work. If we do it correctly, the Delaware should be in a panic and our men will have an avenue to get to the fort."

"This is foolhardy; we might just end up roasting our own boys to death!" Williams objected once more.

"Enough talk," Jacob ordered, irritated by the hold up and the continued musket fire in the woods. "If you have a better idea, Mr. Williams, please feel free to let us all know. In the meantime, Joshua, get the torches lit. The rest of you, grab some wood from the fort and start a fire here. We will each carry a torch to the woods and see if we can smoke the savages out."

Jacob was desperate to help his brother and thought that Joshua's idea might just work. He sent word to Mr. Tate of the plan and asked him to send twenty men to guard the earthen works while Jacob took his men into the woods.

With the Delaware concentrating their efforts on Israel's men, the trip across the open field was relatively easy. The noise from the trail intensified as the men quickly got a roaring fire started. They lit ten large torches and readied themselves to play out Joshua's unusual plan.

Joshua led the men down the snow-packed trail towards the forest line and immediately had the first of the fires lit and burning well. "If the fires get out of hand," he called out softly, "just pile snow on it. Remember, the more smoke the better."

Jacob stationed four men at the edge of the tree line to keep watch. He had no idea exactly where the Delaware were positioned, but he pushed the men forward, deeper into the woods than he initially wanted. Williams' concern about the wet forest actually worked in their favor. The damp tree bark let off swathes of smoke as the heat hit them.

The plan appeared to be having an effect as the shots began to slow and the wall of smoke consumed much of the nearby forest. Joshua had even brought along a few large trade blankets and had a few of the men flapping them against the fires to push the smoke towards the still unseen savages.

Jacob took ten of his men forward to see what was happening ahead of them. The smoke burned their eyes and throats, yet Jacob continued to push forward until their visibility was reduced to only a few paces.

The forest grew eerily still as they waited for the smoke to slowly dissipate. Jacob ordered his men to take cover and keep their muskets at the ready. He sent word back to Joshua to extinguish the fires while he evaluated what needed to be done next.

The silence was even more disturbing than the earlier musket fire. Just as Jacob was considering having his men fall back, he noticed some movement on the upper trail. The light was dim as clouds began to hide the moon and a smoky haze lingered in the air. Jacob ordered the men to stay low and wait for his signal to fire.

As he waited, the dim outline of three men slowly materialized. They came near Jacob, but he remained calm. At the risk of giving away their position, he decided to call out to the approaching men, "You there, stop and identify yourselves!"

There was no response, but Jacob could vaguely see that the figures were still moving very slowly towards their position.

"Last warning," Jacob called out, waiting for some kind of clue as to their identity.

There was still no response and Jacob signaled the men to be ready to fire. The stillness was interrupted only by the sound of a few men adjusting their muskets against their shoulders.

Just as Jacob prepared to open fire, the men staggered close enough that he was able to identify them as members of Israel's company.

"Put your muskets down, lads, and go lend them a hand," Jacob called out.

A raspy voice called out from behind the approaching men, "Who was the fool who thought starting a fire in the woods was a good idea?"

Jacob laughed with relief and said, "It was a good idea, Israel, and it appeared to have worked out well."

"Aye, brother," Israel said with a sarcastic chuckle, "it's always a good idea to set ablaze a man who has already lived through an inferno."

Jacob searched the path for Israel, but didn't see him until he realized that his own men were relieving Israel's tired and staggering men of the extra weight they had been dragging behind them. It was a rudimentary stretcher made out of branches and a coat, and bundled onto the contraption was a seriously injured Israel.

Several of Jacob's men had been sent up the path to search for any other survivors and privates White and Sinclair now helped the men across the meadow to the fort.

Jacob called out to Joshua to assist Israel into the fort and have Maggie look at him. The two men who had been dragging Israel stood nearby Jacob and he said, "Thank you, gentlemen, for risking your lives to care for my brother. What the hell happened?"

The two men simply removed their grimy hats from their heads and looked at the ground; their faces and clothing were covered in a black, sooty film from the smoke-filled forest.

Jacob waited them out, knowing that they were just having difficulty reliving their recent encounter and clearing their lungs of the smoke.

One of the men quietly replied, "Not sure, sir, everything just seemed to explode just as we came within view of the lights of the fort."

"Exploded is right," the other man said. "Your brother was speaking with a couple of men from the advanced guard he had sent out. Suddenly, the damn savages were everywhere. Israel was hit during the first round of musket fire. Once he was down, the rest of us just did our best to survive."

Jacob didn't want to linger in the woods any longer than necessary and when the rest of the men had exited the tree line, he motioned the other two to move towards the fort. "My men only have located fifteen survivors, is that all that managed to make it?"

"Yes sir," one of the men responded as he helped his mate negotiate around one of the many tree stumps. "The Delaware hit us hard. Most of us figured we were safe from an attack since the savages rarely look for a fight once the sun sets."

Jacob called out to the four men he had set up as pickets and said, "Keep your eyes on the trees, lads, and fall back to me. I think the Delaware had enough, and I pray they let us be for the night."

As he waited for the last of the men to climb up the earthen works, Jacob grabbed a handful of snow and wiped the black, smoky grime from his face. He climbed the earthen wall and stood atop it once more, staring into the deep shadows of the surrounding wilderness. He was tired and saddened by the loss of so many men, but he was relieved to finally be back at the fort.

He had family here now and he felt like he was home.

Chapter | **Thirteen**

Jacob made his way to the fort and was greeted by a flurry of activity.

Mr. Tate was still on the high wall with several of the men, watching for any signs of a potential Delaware counter-attack. Jacob offered a polite nod and continued past, searching the dimly-lit inner fort for any sign of Maggie, Joshua or Israel.

He could hear several of the men struggle to get the main gate closed and secured. Stopping, Jacob called up to Tate, "Mr. Tate, have the men watch for any possible survivors. Tell the pickets to do the same."

Tate waved his approval and Jacob then continued to look around the grounds for any signs of his brother.

Private White approached him and said, "Sir, I'm glad you made it back."

"Thank you, but have you seen where they took my brother?" Jacob replied as his eyes continued scanning the area.

"Joshua had him taken directly to your quarters, sir," White said, pointing to the small building that housed the officers.

"Of course; I'm sorry for being so short with you, private," Jacob said, offering his hand to White.

"Understandable, sir," White said, accepting his hand with a smile. "I take no offense."

Jacob rushed to his quarters and was greeted by the sight of Israel lying comfortably on a large bed. Maggie was rubbing a wet cloth over his forehead and Joshua was standing next to him.

"How is he doing?" Jacob whispered to Joshua, seeing that Israel had his eyes closed.

Maggie looked up and her face exhibited a sadness that Jacob had never seen before.

"I cleaned the wounds the best I could," she said, holding back tears, "but with the shape he is in, I am not sure if the lead balls went clear through him or if they shattered any bones."

Jacob studied his brother as Maggie continued to keep a wet cloth on his head. Finally he said, "What are his injuries? I see a lot of blood but I honestly can't see where he was hit."

Joshua tore his eyes from Israel and said, "His men told me he was hit in the right hip and his left thigh. I think Maggie is more worried by the fact he has not stayed awake for any period of time. He was awake when we saw him in the woods, but he's been unconscious since then. His men did their best to control the bleeding with a couple of well-placed neck cloths. I think their actions might have honestly saved his life…to this point."

Jacob didn't know what else to ask. He waited a few seconds and said, "Do you know if Mr. Tate sent for the doctor?"

"Stevens was supposed to send us a doctor, although I'm not sure if he was part of the company that got captured on the way here from Fort Cumberland. He might be coming in the spring. Honestly, even if there was a doctor somewhere in the territory, it is unlikely we could get him here through this weather."

"Would you be kind enough to ask Mr. Tate to report to me?" Jacob asked quietly.

When Joshua hesitated, Jacob decided that whispering for Israel's sake was a waste of time. "Joshua! Mr. Tate, now!" He demanded more firmly, opening the door for the young man.

Once the door closed, Jacob walked slowly over to Israel's bedside. He sat on the edge and heard a slight groan escape his brother's scarred lips. He placed his hand lovingly on Maggie's shoulder and offered a half smile. "How are you holding up, love?"

"I just wish we could enjoy one brief moment without someone we know or care for dying," Maggie said as her eyes filled with tears.

Jacob was unsure what to do. They had only been reunited for a short time, but they had not been able to spend any quality time together to enjoy each other's company. He reached over and held her, trying to get her to stop crying. Over the past number of months, he had amassed so much suppressed sadness that Maggie's deep sobs threatened to undo him.

They sat and cried into each other's arms.

They grieved for the loss of their children, of many good friends and Israel. They had only just found him and he appeared ready to leave them forever.

Their embrace was interrupted when Joshua swung open the door. Maggie quickly rubbed her eyes with an unused cloth, as did Jacob.

"Sir, I brought Mr. Tate as you requested," Joshua said as he held the door for the engineer.

A gust of cold air threatened to extinguish all the candles Maggie had set around the room. "Close the door before poor Israel catches a draft." She called out.

When his eyes were dry, Jacob approached the engineer and said, "John, thank you for your assistance through all of this."

Tate nodded and waited for Jacob to continue.

"We need a doctor for my brother, but I was informed that there is none to be found in the area."

"As you'll recall, Jacob," Tate began, "we did put in a request for a doctor to be sent before winter set in. We even constructed an office as part of this building. Unfortunately, one never arrived. Even when we had our episode with the pox, no doctor was available to us."

Tortured by the thought that his brother could live if there was a doctor present to care for him, Jacob pressed Tate for a solution. "You mean to tell me there is no person within the territory that has any kind of medical training, formal or not?"

"The closest we have is a gentleman that used to care for horses for a family back in the Virginia territory," Tate offered sheepishly. "His family settled just to the east of us a few months ago."

Jacob changed his focus to the earlier attack and said, "Mr. Tate, could you double the nightly guard? Once the sun rises, please send out a group of men to search the woods for any survivors of the ambush. I fear we were forced to leave some good men behind in the confusion and our rush to clear the area."

"What about the Delaware?" Tate asked.

"Damn the bloody Delaware," Jacob shouted, losing his temper. "If they want a fight, they better be ready for one. I will not have this fort held prisoner by a band of savages."

Maggie looked at him sharply, but he didn't offer an apology for his outburst.

Tate excused himself with a polite nod towards Maggie. "Good night, sir," he said quietly. "I will have the men on full alert."

Jacob remained standing, staring at the door that had closed behind the engineer. He was embarrassed by his loss of temper, particularly at the loyal Mr. Tate's expense. He hesitated, but decided he had to turn and face the others.

He was met by a very dark scowl from Maggie.

"Please excuse my poor behavior, Joshua," Jacob said, avoiding his wife's eyes. "I fear seeing my brother looking as he does has gotten me all flustered."

"There is no need to explain, sir," Joshua responded. "I will speak with Mr. Tate. I'm sure he will understand, given the circumstances. Losing one's brother is a difficult thing indeed."

Jacob lowered his head and stared at the ground.

"Sir…speaking of brothers." Joshua said softly. "Maggie…where is One-Ear? I have to know. He was as much my brother as Israel is yours."

Maggie inhaled sharply and Jacob's eyes met hers. They had known they would have to tell him, but neither had wanted to.

"Oh, Joshua," Maggie said and rushed to put her arms around him in a motherly embrace. "He saved my life several times as the French tried to take me to the fort at Niagara. We escaped them and managed to get to a tribe of his people. I even met his blood brother, who died in a battle in which they fought bravely. At an Indian village in the New York territory, Chief Pontiac of the Ottawa kidnapped me to be his wife. One-Ear…he…"

Her voice faltered and Jacob walked up to take her hand. He put his other hand around the back of Joshua's neck and watched the young man as he accepted Maggie's account of his friend and brother.

"It's alright, Maggie," Jacob said. "Take your time. Joshua has the right to know."

"One-Ear rushed to intercede on my behalf. Pontiac's men are very harsh. They act without regard for others; they are far more savages than any of the Indians in this territory. One of them shot him mid-stride. They dragged me away before I could even check on him.

"Joshua, I'm so sorry. I wanted nothing more than to be with him, to care for him. I don't know if he's alive, but I pray every day that he is. I pray that we will all be reunited someday."

Joshua nodded and hugged Maggie then Jacob. He left without a word and Maggie turned back towards the bed. She wiped her eyes and Jacob did the same.

Maggie said nothing and turned back to care for Israel. Jacob knew she was upset not only with their emotional conversation with Joshua, but by how he had treated John Tate. His behavior was inexcusable no matter the circumstances, and he would have to offer his sincerest regrets to his wife for his actions.

"Sorry you saw me lose my temper with Mr. Tate." Jacob said, breaking their emotional silence.

"No need to apologies to me. Poor Mr. Tate is the person who deserves your apology." Maggie scolded him.

"I will find him and speak with him first thing in the morning." Jacob offered.

Maggie said nothing and just continued to care for Israel.

They started out taking turns through the night caring for Israel while the other slept, but at some point they both fell asleep at the same time.

Jacob was jolted awake in his chair by a loud shout coming from the direction of the bed.

"How can a man get some food around this place? By God, I'm starved."

Jacob jumped up and tried to clear his head from a deep sleep as he rushed to Israel's side. His brother had pulled himself into a sitting position and stared at Jacob's disheveled appearance.

"What the hell? Israel, you're up. How long have you…?" Jacob struggled to make any sense.

He saw that Maggie was still fast asleep and before he could get to her, Israel said, "Let her be. She's earned the sleep."

"Damn good to see you awake, brother," Jacob said. "I really thought we lost you again." One of the men had thoughtfully dropped off a kettle of freshly brewed tea and Jacob poured two cups.

"I honestly felt I was done, but for some reason I am still here." Israel took a cautious drink but it was far too hot for his frail throat.

"How do you feel?" Jacob asked.

"Good, my body is sore and I am not certain if I can stand. Though considering what happened, I am fortunate to be alive. How are my men? Did we lose many of them?"

"I am still not clear what exactly happened last night, but I ordered a scouting party to leave at daybreak to search for survivors and answers," Jacob said, not sure how he would breach the topic of how many of Israel's men were killed.

"They hit us pretty hard and we were completely unprepared," his gravelly voice said softly. "Shame on me for not having the lads ready, but most of us felt the Delaware would never fight us at night. I really thought we had little reason to expect any problems."

Jacob excused himself to see about getting some breakfast for Israel and went outside into the frigid morning air. Stale smoke still hung over the fort and nearby scorched woods, and it immediately stung his nose.

The chill easily seeped through the light coat he had put on before he stepped outside. There was a fresh dusting of snow added to the previous inches they had fought through last night, and it made for a slippery walk.

Most of the men were either out scouting or splitting the endless supply of wood for the winter fires. Several men who had late night guard duty were tucked away in the warm barracks, trying to get some much earned rest.

He found one of the men with a plate of dried pork, a few small boiled eggs and a fire-burned piece of bread with nuts and berries and was pleasantly surprised to find that the tray was on its way to his quarters. With Israel's breakfast being delivered, Jacob continued his walk around the inside of the fort. He spotted Tate, still perched on the upper western wall, watching intently into the woods.

"John, how are you doing this fine, cold morning?" Jacob called up to the engineer who still remained staring off into the sea of snow and trees.

"Cold. Bloody cold, Jacob. You can see the damn fresh Delaware tracks all over the place, and I pray every morning that they let us be and just move south for the winter." Tate confided.

Jacob then called back and asked, "Were men sent out to search the woods for survivors, or to bury the dead?"

"As you ordered, I sent out twenty men just as the sun broke," Tate answered. "They have been out for the past hour or so, and I have heard nothing from them as of yet."

Jacob climbed the steep ladder that led him to the upper steps of the bastion and remained quiet as he too stood and observed the hundred or so fresh moccasin prints in the snow. Some of the tracks were far too close to the earthen works for Jacob's comfort.

"Sorry about my tone last night John, you deserved a much better reception." Jacob did his best to apologize for his actions.

"No need Jacob to say anything; we are all a bit on edge." Tate simply offered.

The two men returned their attention back towards the woods. The height of the corner bastion gave Jacob a nice panoramic view of the surrounding area. The mountains threw a high shadow over the open field, and from this vantage point, he could view the mass of trees that covered the land for as far as he could see.

He thought to himself that a man, newly arrived to this wilderness, would fit into one of two groups. Either he would be frightened all the way back to Philadelphia, or he would see the wild, untamed ocean of trees as an adventure and would dive right into it. Jacob was thankful he was the latter type. He took a deep breath of the fresh mountain air and exhaled a stream of warm, white air that soon disappeared over his head.

"John, if you would be so kind, please conduct a roll call and have some of the lads man the bastions," Jacob ordered politely. "I fear that the Delaware are up to something, and God knows we can't afford to lose any more of our men.

"Also, I never formally thanked you for the fine job you and your men did constructing this place. It will certainly be a good place to keep us protected from the long winter and the Delaware."

Tate nodded with a smile and climbed down the ladder to go organize the men. Just as he reached the snow-covered ground, Jacob shouted after him, "Have you seen Joshua?"

"He left an hour ago with the group that went out to search for survivors."

Jacob did his best to hide his concern for the small party that he had ordered out so early on this brisk morning. He scanned the forest once more and thought that it should not have taken them more than an hour in the light to get out to the site of the ambush and back to the fort.

It was only a few short minutes before Tate had most of the men standing at attention and manning the main walls of the fort. He made his way back to Jacob and said, "This is all the healthy men. I counted fifty-five, with eleven sick or injured. I let your brother's men take their leave for now since they had a pretty difficult journey last night."

"Thank you, John. I will leave you in charge while I go out and check on the missing party." Jacob offered a quick salute.

As Jacob returned to his quarters to check on Israel and to grab his gear for his short trip into the woods, snow began to fall once again. He opened the creaky wooden door and was greeted by the sight of Maggie sipping a cup of tea while Israel was sitting up in the bed recovering.

She appeared happy, even in these odd circumstances, and it reminded him again of their old life. The only things missing was the sight of the small children running around the room and James whittling on a block of wood with the knife Jacob had given him for his birthday.

"Close the damn door, Jacob!" Israel barked with a twisted smile. "Do you want to give me a fever as well?"

Jacob jumped from his reverie and did as he was told. With the door closed, he could feel the warmth of the large fire that crackled and spat tiny embers on the floor from the hearth.

Maggie moved towards the kettle and asked, "Do you have time for a cup?"

"No, Maggie, I have to go out and search for the whereabouts of a scouting party that was sent out over an hour ago."

"Do what you need to do, and we will have a cup later," Maggie replied, returning to her seat.

"I assume there are no real problems, brother, or have the savages hit us again?" Israel asked, propping himself up higher to a more comfortable position to talk.

Jacob didn't have any real details or answers, but he also didn't want them to be alarmed. "No great concern," he answered. "I just want to see for myself what happened to your men last night." Leaving it at that, Jacob quickly gathered his musket, a powder horn and his heavy blanket coat.

Just as he was ready to step back into the cold, Maggie called out, "Here is a nice knitted woolen hat I found in one of the dressers. It might keep you a bit warmer while you are out."

She tossed it to him and Jacob caught it and placed it over his long hair. "Thank you. I will be back soon."

Jacob rushed back out into the cold and snow. He ran as fast as he could towards the main entrance, but the snow was already accumulating and becoming a nuisance. Before the two guards began to pull open the heavy doors, one of them offered, "Sir, I have a good pair of snowshoes that I got from some Mingo in a trade. You might want them to help you move faster over the snow. It is getting especially deep in the fields, and I don't think you want to spend too much time in the open struggling to get into the woods."

"Thank you, lad; I would certainly appreciate the extra traction," Jacob replied.

The man had them leaning against a post by his small stool. He grabbed them and unstrapped the heavy leather tethers that held the user's feet in place.

Jacob took a second to strap them on and, although they were on the smaller side, they definitely helped him over the snow much more efficiently. Taking a few steps while the men struggled to open the snow blocked doors, he was off at a fast pace and had already reached the halfway point between the fort and tree line before he waved back and said, "Thanks again, lad! This is so much better!"

He noticed that Tate was still watching from the western bastion and called up to him, "Please leave the main gates open, just in case we need to make a run for it. Keep the lads on the ready, and if you see any Delaware in range, please be kind enough to kill them." Jacob smiled and waved again, then turned to dash across the thick snow.

When he reached the first line of trees, he quickly unstrapped his snow-shoes, tied them to his back and began to walk. The snow was far less accumulated on the trail because of the natural barrier from the trees, and he was also much more mobile without the wide, cumbersome snowshoes.

It was clear from the number of tracks that the party had moved south of where he was and he easily followed them for a good while. It was difficult to know how far they had traveled in the dark the previous night, but he didn't think it could have been very far. He had only just entered the woods, but was already growing concerned by the fact that he hadn't yet run into the scouting party.

He hadn't seen any signs that the Delaware were in the woods either, but he remained vigilant of the fact that they could be anywhere. He watched the path and kept his eyes on the nearby woods for any evidence of their presence.

As he pushed farther along the trail, the sunlight was obscured by the large number of bushy winter trees along the trail. Jacob slowed to get his bearings and scanned the upper trail for any sign of his men. Concerned that they may have also been ambushed by the Delaware, he decided to move off the path and work his way around the mass of trees. It was much harder as he struggled to take each step, but he felt much safer as he maneuvered through the snow.

Just as he was about to turn back towards the fort to get some reinforcements, he got a brief glimpse of some movement up ahead. Jacob strained to see through the intertwined branches and tree trunks, but he finally made out a few shadowy figures that he was sure were men from the search party.

He decided to press forward to get a better look. Finding a nice clear vantage point, Jacob was satisfied that it was his men and waited to hear any voices that might just confirm his thoughts. He was still too far off and became tired of his slow, cautious pace.

Jacob ran through the dense trees as quickly and silently as possible until he finally got close enough to hear that the voices were indeed those of English men. Satisfied he was safe to call out to them, Jacob was careful not to alarm them, "Lads, it is safe to approach?"

His voice immediately made the men react with shouldered muskets and calls to disperse into the woods.

"It's Sergeant Sims; stand down so I can come join you," Jacob said, trying his best to reassure the men it was safe.

One of the men returned his call, saying, "You can approach, but with your hands up and your weapon in clear view."

Jacob obliged their request and stepped out with his arms up.

He had only made it a few steps before two men were behind him with their muskets pressed against his back. The cold weather had made Jacob cover his head and most of his face with his hooded blanket coat, so the men still could not clearly identify him.

Losing his patience, Jacob called out again, "Lads, if I was the French or a Delaware warrior, do you think I would have called out to warn you that I was here?"

The only answer came from one of the men behind him as he pushed Jacob forward with the muzzle of his gun and barked, "Keep moving!"

Jacob wheeled around and finally faced his two assailants. He threw back his hood, pulled off his woolen cap and said, "I told you, it's me!"

The men were shocked and flustered. They did their best to explain their actions, and Jacob quieted them down. "Lads," he said, "you were just doing your duty. I can't fault you for that, but next time please listen before you decide to rough up your prisoner.

After their brief exchange, one of the men called out to the others, still waiting with their muskets aimed blindly towards them, "All is clear, we are escorting Sergeant Sims to you."

Still embarrassed by their actions, the two men spent the short trip back to the others, apologizing to their commanding officer.

When they reached the others, Jacob saw Joshua and said with a laugh, "Nice way to greet me, lad."

The surrounding area was covered with mounds of piled rocks and packed down snow. There was also an assortment of wet and used equipment scattered about. It was clear that this was where the main ambush had taken place. "Did you find any survivors?" Jacob asked while he watched the men clean up as much of the debris as they could. Most of the remaining gear was either unusable or frozen solid into the snow.

Joshua moved to Jacob's side, and they walked the perimeter of the area. "Not a soul," the young man answered. "Realistically, if any of the men were fortunate enough to survive the attack, the cold would have gotten them. A terribly slow way to die, I think I would rather have been butchered by the savages."

"How many did you find?" Jacob continued, seeing that there were more stacked mounds of stone as they walked along the path.

"I counted well over twenty-five dead just in this area alone," Joshua explained as he pointed to a large cluster of mounds directly in front of them. "We wanted to keep the animals away, but the ground is too frozen to dig suitable graves."

Still looking around the killing zone, Jacob could imagine how the men would have tried to fight, despite the darkness and the Delaware having the trees as cover. It would have been much like Braddock's disaster, only on a much smaller scale.

Seeing what was left of the carnage, Jacob was amazed how even a handful of the men had survived the previous night, including his brother. He dreaded having to speak with Israel once they returned to the fort.

"It appears there is not much more we can do here," Jacob said. "I have not seen any fresh evidence of the Delaware presence, but if they are still lurking about, I suggest we get back."

Joshua gathered the men for the return trek and Jacob sent four men ahead and two men to the rear. He had the remaining men spread out as much as the forest permitted. He was still concerned that if there were Delaware nearby, they just might decide to ambush them before they reached the field.

Jacob stayed by Joshua's side, keeping his eyes on the surrounding woods. "How are you holding up, lad?" he asked quietly.

Joshua kept his eyes on the trail, but answered without hesitation, "I am alright, sir. Burying these men was almost therapeutic, like I was burying a part of One-Ear as well. I still have hope that he is alive, though. I don't know if I would have been able to feel that way a week ago, but seeing your reunion with Israel has given me some hope. You knew your brother to be dead, yet he survived the catastrophe at Fort Necessity."

Jacob patted Joshua on the back and they moved on in silence for a few minutes.

"What do you think about everything you have seen recently, lad?" Jacob asked.

"It is strange, sir, the Delaware should have gone south a month ago. I fear if they don't leave shortly, we will be in for a long winter. They will harass every hunting party and destroy any trap lines they find. If that happens, they might just starve us out. No relief party will be able to help us until well into spring."

It was a grim picture indeed, but Jacob knew Joshua's assessment was correct. He ensured the men remained on high alert and kept his own eyes peeled for any signs that the Delaware were still around.

Thankfully, the trip back was uneventful, except for the knee-high snow. The men in front bore the brunt of the struggle as they were forced to march through the fresh snow to leave tracks for the men in the back. Jacob did lend the lead man his set of snowshoes to help him navigate the dangerously open field towards the fort.

A cheer could be heard from the walls of the fort as they finally returned. Most of the party opted to go directly back to their warm beds for some well-earned rest. Jacob appreciated their hard work and the effort they put forth ensuring their dead mates had a reasonable burial. Digging up the number of rocks and leaves they had required to cover all of those men had not been easy work. Jacob also understood that most of their fatigue would have come from the stress and emotions of seeing so many fellow soldiers killed at the hands of the enemy.

He offered a polite wave to Tate, who waved back but remained dutifully on the lookout for any signs of the Delaware. Jacob dismissed Joshua to the barracks and returned to his quarters to check on Israel.

He found Maggie sitting in the main room alone, staring into the fire, and walked to the bedroom to check on her patient. The bed was empty and he returned to her and asked, "Where is Israel?"

She stood to offer Jacob a hug and explained, "He is with the horse doctor. Apparently, Mr. Tate was good enough to risk sending a messenger last night to the man's home, and he arrived here shortly after you left. Some of the men moved Israel to the empty doctor's quarters."

"Good, how are you holding up?" Jacob asked, kissing her on the forehead as they walked to the small table near the fireplace.

"I am well," she said, retrieving a small plate. "Have some tea. One of the men was kind enough to bring us some cornbread and cheese."

Jacob obliged her and took a few slices of cheese and a large piece of bread. He ate and drank quickly and pushed back from the table, saying, "Sorry, Maggie, I need to see how the rest of the men are holding up and then go by to check on Israel."

Her expression spoke for her and he responded with another apology, "I'm sorry, love, but you know I have my duties. It is snowing and cold. You will be far more comfortable staying inside. We have a full load of wood to keep the fire burning, and I will be back as soon as I can."

Maggie was trying her best to be the good understanding wife, but the months they had been separated had given a boost to her inner strength. "What of your duties to me?" she snapped.

Jacob had been married long enough to know when not to answer such a question. He kissed her cheek, grabbed his coat and hat and stepped outside once again. He understood how she was feeling, but his concern for his brother and the safety of everyone at the fort outweighed his love life for the moment.

Most of the snow had been cleared from the center of the small parade grounds, and was pushed to the sides of the fort. The pile was nearly as tall as he was and would have to be removed to outside the walls soon. As he walked towards the barracks, Jacob noticed the British flag flapping high on the tall, wooden pole. He was glad he wasn't the poor bastard who had to get up in the early morning cold and raise it.

The parade grounds were smaller than most English-built fortifications, primarily because Jacob did not want to waste the space, but also because colonial militia didn't see the need for drilling the men senselessly like their more disciplined British counterparts. Besides, with the way the British army had abandoned the defenseless settlers, no colonial wanted to participate in anything that would remind them of the disasters of the past year.

Jacob reached the barracks and stepped inside. He was greeted by rows of uncomfortable-looking beds, each of which would be shared by two men, and a large fireplace that covered most of the far wall. Jacob saw a ladder leading to a man-sized hole in the ceiling and remembered that Tate had decided to build additional quarters above. He had also built-in several lockable muskets slots in the outer wall, just in case they were attacked. There were only a handful of men resting on their beds, and the noise of shuffling feet could be heard overhead.

"Have any of you lads seen Joshua?" Jacob called out, not expecting anyone to offer an answer.

Another difference between the British army and colonial militia was in how officers were treated. Even though Jacob was a low ranking officer, he was still an officer. In the strict British army, when an officer entered a room, all the men would be expected to rise and salute or be flogged for insubordination. In the militia, no one bothered. In battle, they might listen to the officers; but on their own time, they only took direction from themselves. Jacob didn't mind as long as they fulfilled their duties when asked and stood to fight when the enemy faced them.

As expected, none of the men bothered to reply, so Jacob decided to climb up the ladder to check out the upper barracks himself.

The ladder was particularly steep and Jacob wondered how anyone could climb this after a hard night of guard duty or a few pints of beer. Still hearing muffled noises from above, he pulled himself through the hole. He was greeted by a similar layout as below, but here there was a comfortable sitting area around the fireplace, and even a bookcase with a meager selection of old text books. The noises that he heard were made by only three men, Mr. Tate, Joshua and another man that Jacob didn't recognize. They sat in the only three chairs positioned by the fire.

"Sergeant Sims, I'm glad to see you, sir," Tate greeted him with a smile.

Joshua rose and said, "Sir, you may have my seat."

The other man, who looked to be much older than any man in the fort, just remained in his seat and said nothing.

"Sir, this is Mr. Shnarr," Tate said. "He lives in a German settlement a few miles from the other side of the ridge. He was just here visiting and looking to do some trading with us."

The man finally stood up and formally greeted Jacob, "Sir, my name is Franz Shnarr. I am the pastor at a very small settlement a few miles east of the Delaware village at Kittanning."

Jacob knew that the supplies they had in the fort had to last well into April and he had little interest in trading any of them with anyone. In a friendly tone, he said, "Mr. Shnarr, what are you looking for in particular?"

"Horses, Sergeant," the man said in a thick accent. "I have spoken to your Mr. Tate about trading for a couple of the horses that you have stabled here."

Jacob hadn't thought much of the German settlers that he had encountered in the past. He understood they normally kept to themselves and established settlements that they defended on their own. They did interact with the various tribes in the area, pushing them to convert to their religious ways and forego their own beliefs. He found them very cold and unfriendly, only bothering with other settlers if they needed something in particular. The only good he saw in them was their ability to handcraft a good musket. Jacob knew a few gunmakers around the territory and most were German.

"We have done some business with Mr. Shnarr in the past," Tate said. "He is a good, fair man."

"How is your village holding up through the Delaware raids?" Jacob asked, having no plan of trading anything with this man. He knew the fort stables had horses, he had smelled them when he first arrived. He assumed in addition to the horses that had first arrived months ago, Major Stevens' and his men's horses were also there. It would be foolish for him to trade away any potential food source. It would only be out of desperation that he would ask the men to eat horse meat, but he couldn't be sure at this point how harsh the winter might be. Trading away food at this time might prove to be fatal later.

"We have fared well, sir," Shnarr responded with a noticeable amount of arrogance. "The Delaware have no reason to kill us. They see us as their friends and little threat to them."

Before Jacob could reply, Tate interjected, "Sir, could I have a word with you please?"

Obliging Tate's request, Jacob followed Tate over to the back of the barracks.

"If I may, Jacob, Mr. Shnarr can be trusted. He has been to the fort on several occasions and has been more than honest in his trades. The horses are of little use to us, especially during the winter. They have to be fed and watered, and they create an awful smell around the place."

Jacob looked over Tate's shoulder towards the German and watched him sip on a tiny glass of sherry.

"My only concern, despite my particular dislike of Germans," Jacob explained, "is about being cautious with our trading so we do not give up a possible food supply. The winters are unforgiving in these parts and food

is food. Those horses might just save us all if we are forced to eat them."
He spoke just loud enough for Shnarr to hear his appraisal of the situation.

Tate looked shocked, but said nothing.

"You have never indulged in horse meat?" Jacob smirked. "Most of
these men have likely been forced to eat a horse or two…possibly even
their own. If it comes down to starving or eating your horse, most men of
any intelligence would enjoy the meal. Honestly, it would never be my first
choice, but cooked right, it does make an edible stew."

Again, Tate said nothing.

"Sir, I will speak further with this man," Jacob informed Tate loudly
enough for the trader to hear once again, "if he can give me his word that
if we trade him some horses, he will not turn around and trade them to the
bloody savages in the spring."

Jacob watched as Tate glanced over to where Shnarr remained sipping
on his drink.

"Permit me to ask the man, and then maybe we can see how to
proceed," Jacob offered and this time escorted Tate back to the fire.

Shnarr immediately rose and waited for the two.

Joshua remained seated on the hearth, saying little and making sure the
fire was well stoked.

Jacob approached the older man and said, "Sir, my only concern with
such a transaction, beyond my concerns over the winter months, is about
your plans for the animals. I have no interest in having our livestock fall
into the hands of our enemies."

Jacob could tell he had struck a nerve, but the man replied calmly. "In
trade, sir, once we have agreed on terms, the property changes hands and its
future is no longer the concern of the previous owner."

Jacob just looked at Tate, who offered nothing in reply.

Tired of holding his tongue and being diplomatic, Jacob lashed out
towards the unsuspecting trader, "Excuse my bluntness, but we will never
do business with anyone who trades with our enemies."

Jacob finished and watched Shnarr look at Tate, seemingly waiting for
him to intercede.

Politely dismissing himself, Jacob said one last thing just as his head disappeared down the ladder, "I must say, for a pastor, you sure seem to enjoy

a good drink. I would be wrong not to warn you that anyone who deals with our enemies is also an enemy. Good day, sir."

Leaving them to simmer on his last words, Jacob reached the last rung of the ladder when he noticed Joshua had begun climbing down.

Jacob opened the door a bit prematurely as he waited for Joshua and heard the grumbling from the men relaxing in their beds.

"If I may sir, you were a bit hard on our visitor," Joshua said as they walked through the snow.

Jacob laughed and said, "I might have been a bit blunt, but we need to protect our interests."

"I didn't disagree with you; I just meant you could have been a little nicer," Joshua added, joining in Jacob's laughter.

The two walked towards the door that led to what was meant to be the doctor's quarters. As they moved across the parade grounds, Jacob asked, "What is being built outside the main gates?"

"We were in the midst of building a trading post before the snow came. We have cut all the wooden planks and the pile of trees to the left of the foundation, will be used to eventually make the frames."

"I thought as much," Jacob replied. "Mr. Tate had mentioned he was going to build some outer buildings."

Pulling the door open to the small building, Jacob immediately saw Israel lying on a table with an older man standing over him.

"Shut the bloody door!" the man shouted without turning to see the newcomers. "Can't you see this poor man is in pain?"

"My apologies, we are just here to check on the patient," Jacob said, closing the door quickly.

Israel propped himself up quickly, exposing a couple of blankets soaked in blood and several bandages strewn across the floor. "Jacob, is that you?" he yelled. "Get over here and get this damn fool off of me!"

Both Jacob and Joshua stood frozen by the door, unsure what they should do. Jacob finally called out, "How is it going, brother? You sound much better."

"Enough chatter," the man said peevishly as he pushed Israel back down. "Can't you both see that I am doing some delicate work?"

A hollow clang rang out as the man tossed a small fragment into a tin bowl that sat by his feet.

Jacob moved closer to investigate. As soon as the man sensed him moving, he pointed a bloody finger to the other side of the table and barked, "If you want to lend a hand, boy, then get yourself over there."

"Jacob, get me out of here," Israel pleaded. "This damn fool is making things much worse."

"Shut him up and hold him down while I work on his hip. If he keeps moving, I just might have to close him up and leave the rest of this mess inside him. I'm Adams, by the way. Jack Adams and I prefer to work on horses. They tend to be far more cooperative."

Adams looked to be in his sixties, although the poor light in the small room could have been adding years to him. He was grey-haired and thin, and he certainly didn't look the part of a doctor, be it horse or human. He had a pair of spectacles balancing on the top of his head and Jacob prayed they were more for show than for sight. They did him little good on his head, and with the lack of proper light, Israel might be right to be concerned.

"Sergeant Jacob Sims," he said, not bothering to shake the man's hand since it was covered in blood, and he was too busy anyway. "I think you have heard that I am the patient's brother."

Jacob put his arm across Israel's chest and held him down while he stroked the top of his head with his other hand. He watched as Adams searched inside the larger incision he had made into Israel's injured hip. He worked quickly and bits of shrapnel clanged into the bowl in a constant rhythm.

"How does it look, Adams?" Jacob asked after a quarter of an hour.

"How does it look to you? Damn, boy, I normally work on horses not men. I think I pulled a dozen pieces of splintered lead plus a few fragments of bone out of him. I just hope that I find everything. If I can't get to it all, they will just grind against his bone until there is nothing to grind against. I finished cleaning out his thigh earlier but it was nothing like this mess." Adams stopped to wipe some beads of sweat away from his forehead.

Jacob looked at Israel, who had thankfully passed out about ten minutes ago from the pain, and saw a man who had already suffered more than any man should.

"I don't ask for perfection, Mr. Adams," Jacob said. "I just ask that you do what you can. Under these conditions, it would be a miracle to find every little piece."

A brief smile crossed Adams' face, but he soon returned to concentrating on Israel's hip.

The men remained silent for the next half hour. Jacob continued to hold Israel, who slipped in and out of consciousness. Joshua stood nearby, watching the doctor and ready to spring into action if there was anything that needed to be done or fetched. The only sound that punctuated the silence was the constant clang of the bowl each time the doctor found another piece of bloody bone or lead.

"There's not much more I can do for the poor bugger," Adams eventually pronounced. "If your lad would bring me the wood poker that I put in the fire earlier, I can seal this wound shut. We will have to watch him over the next several days to see how he does. I just hope he doesn't catch a fever."

Adams let out a deep sigh and tried to clean most of the blood off his stained hands in a bowl of discolored water that sat on the nearby dressing table.

Joshua was quick to bring the red hot poker to the doctor, who said, "Now, keep him still. He will jump when I touch his skin, but I need a few seconds to seal it."

Jacob and Joshua both put their weight across Israel's chest and the doctor touched the poker to the wound. Israel was still unconscious and aside from a slight jerk, he did not move. The skin sizzled for a moment and Jacob thought of the last time he had closed a wound in a similar fashion.

Joshua gave Jacob a quick glance, intuitively moving his shoulder after being reminded of his own backwoods surgery.

When Adams was satisfied that the wound was closed, he barked at Joshua, "Get me some water and a clean wrap for him, lad."

Adams took the jug of water from Joshua and slowly poured it over the swollen scar. When it was wet and cleaned, he grabbed a handful of what Jacob guessed was bear fat, and smothered the wound with it. Joshua handed him the bandage and it was quickly placed over the wound.

"I will dress the wound once he wakes, so right now we can relax and wait to see how he feels," Adams said, taking a well-deserved rest in a nearby chair.

"Thank you Mr. Adams," Jacob said, holding out his hand. "You did a fine job considering the situation."

"It's Jack, and I pray all this work helped your brother," the older man said as he shook Jacob's hand. "By the looks of him, he has seen enough pain already."

Jacob took a seat by the fire and said, "Do I hear a hint of Scotland in your voice, sir?"

"Aye, I was born in Glasgow and raised in the Highlands, but I was shipped here as a young man after all the problems with the English. My father was a rebel and fought at Culloden. He was forced to leave and start all over in this Godforsaken wilderness."

"My father was at Culloden. Please call me Jacob. I'm not one for titles."

"Good, I wasn't going to call you sergeant anyway! It sounds too much like the English army." Adams let out a long laugh.

While the two talked, Joshua offered them a glass of rum that he had found in one of the cabinets.

"Thank you, lad," Adams smiled. "I'm not much of a drinker, but after this mess it sure would calm my nerves some." Adams raised his glass to Israel and downed the contents in one gulp.

Joshua quickly refilled the glass and Jacob remained silent, letting the man enjoy the well-earned drink.

"Is this lad yours?" Adams asked as he took small sips this time.

"No, but he might as well be," Jacob said with a smile for Joshua. "He is a good friend and has saved my life on a number of occasions. I'm the only family he has after his were killed by the Huron."

Joshua smiled brightly at the praise.

"Bloody hell, boy," Adams said as he set down the glass and asked, "I'm sorry for your loss. How did you manage to survive the butchery?"

Joshua replied simply, "They took me captive and then adopted me into their tribe. I spent a few years with them until I escaped."

"Sorry, lad, I won't make you rehash old memories. Maybe later, under better circumstances, we can have a little chat about your experience."

While they spoke, Israel finally regained consciousness and struggled to get up. They rushed to his side and held him down, trying to prevent him from losing his bandages or reopening his wounds.

"Stay down and rest, Israel; you need to let yourself heal!" Jacob shouted as his brother continued to struggle.

"You should have been out for hours yet, lad," Adams explained as Jacob finally eased Israel back down. "You need to let the wounds heal some before you get on your feet."

"I'm fine; I just need to take a walk and get some fresh air," Israel said, but the others would have none of that.

After a few minutes of struggle, Israel was once again fast asleep.

"Jack, you have done enough for today," Jacob said as he walked the older gentleman to the door. "My wife can see to my brother's dressings. I assume you would like to get back to your home before dark. Thank you again. Your family is always welcome at the fort."

Grabbing his woolen hat and a large, bison wool coat, Adams replied, "Thank you, Jacob. It was very nice meeting you. Keep him down and make sure he gets some rest. I will check back on him in a few days to redress his wounds."

Jacob opened the door on what was quickly becoming a deceptively sunny day and said, "I will have four of our men escort you as far as the ridge, just in case there are any Delaware stragglers around. Safe travels, and thank you for your help."

Adams stepped out, turned to offer a slight wave and walked towards the main gates.

Jacob sent Joshua after him to organize the men to accompany Adams. "If you see Maggie, ask her to stop by here," Jacob called out just as Joshua made it to the far barracks.

Closing the door, Jacob pulled a seat closer to Israel and sat with his arms crossed. He too was soon fast asleep.

"Jacob, get up," Maggie said as she jostled his shoulder. "I thought you were watching your brother, not taking a nap."

He jumped out the chair immediately and said, "I was just resting my eyes. I was…"

"Jacob, calm down. It's just me. You have been out for almost six hours. I have been by several times to check on you both. I just thought you might be hungry." Maggie smiled and tried not to laugh at her guilty schoolboy of a husband.

"Sorry about that, Maggie. I really only thought to close my eyes for a second."

"So what did Mr. Adams say about Israel?" Maggie asked. "He does look somewhat better."

"I assume he has slept the entire time? He did try to get up before Mr. Adams left, but we kept him down until he fell back to sleep. He said that Israel needs to rest. I told Mr. Adams that you would be able to keep an eye on his dressings."

Maggie nodded and took a moment to check on the bandages. She peeked under them carefully and appeared to be impressed by the work.

"How does it look?" Israel spoke suddenly, making Maggie jump. "The bloody horse doctor is a madman!"

"Israel Murray, do you think that was funny scaring me half to death?" Maggie screamed before quickly calming herself down.

"How do you feel, brother?" Jacob asked through his laughter.

"Good, despite the pain. It will be nice to be able to walk around and get a good look at the place."

"You need more rest," Maggie said, "there will plenty of time to go for a walk later. Just sleep for now and I will make up some soup for you to try."

After a few weeks, Israel was up and walking by himself. His injury left him with a permanent limp, but his spirits seemed higher than they had been in some time. He became good friends with Mr. Adams and even spent a couple of nights at the man's cabin for dinner.

Thankfully, the Delaware had not shown themselves since the nighttime ambush on Israel and his men. Jacob maintained a strong picket around the fort at all times, but there were never any signs of savages present. He assumed they had either left for their usual winter villages in the Virginia territory, or they kept to the area around Kittanning. He figured that in either case, they were readying themselves to resume their raids once the snow melted and the rivers were clear of ice.

Jacob was careful not to allow the men let to their guards down. He made sure any hunting party or wood cutting detail was always accompanied by a group of heavily armed escorts.

The winter was like most of the previous that Jacob had experienced. Some nights were so bitterly cold that no amount of clothing, blankets or warm fires could keep it from seeping through to your insides. Thankfully, there were a number of days above freezing, providing the men with some much needed relief.

The men kept themselves busy cutting firewood, patrolling the nearby wilderness and checking the trap lines. With the exception of one severe cold snap when the men were forced to butcher two of the horses for meat; beaver, porcupine and opossum remained plentiful. Occasionally, a deer or wild cat would wander into the men's sights and offer some much needed variety.

Maggie did her best to cook a nice hot meal every few days to add some variety to their standard diet of smoked meat and cornbread. The men appreciated her efforts, but by mid-March, everyone was sick of soups and stews of every kind. They were ready for larger game, fresh berries and greens.

The men seemed to get along very well with only a few minor episodes, but Jacob was still happy to see the dusk hours shift. It was a sign that winter was beginning to fade, and the additional sunlight seemed to cheer the men and allow them to keep busier.

They had been isolated for several months with little word from the rest of the territory, but Jacob would soon send out a scouting party to the east. He planned to send men to aid in building forts, if they were still being planned.

In addition to longer daylight hours, the snow began to recede and the trees began to show tiny buds. Herds of deer, elk and some bison left tracks and signs of their presence as well, but there were more ominous signs of spring.

The Delaware had returned.

Chapter | **Fourteen**

By the end of April, all but the highest mountain elevations seemed to have thawed. Spring rains helped dispel the last of the snow leaving behind muddy trails and damp trees, but there was a tangible sense of refreshment about the forest and meadow. The men's spirits were noticeably higher and Jacob could see that most were ready to resume their duties to the frontier families surrounding the fort. A real bond had formed between many of the men and the families they protected.

Jacob began sending out multiple scouting parties each day. He wanted to show the settlers that they were not alone and the lurking Delaware that the militia was still present and active.

He heard that many of the settlers had begun calling the men by the nickname they had given themselves back at Fort Cumberland. The men were the 'Sentinels', and the fort had been dubbed 'The Pines'. Jacob had not considered a name for the fort before, but now he thought of calling it Fort Stevens to honor his commander and friend.

Mr. Tate kept his small group of engineers and craftsmen busy by completing several outer buildings, including the trading post that sat just outside the main gates. There were also several small storage buildings and a new horse shed. The horses that survived the winter were moved out of the fort not only to keep down their smell, but to control the ever-present hordes of flies and biting insects that plagued the men and visitors.

Both Jacob and Tate understood the importance of maintaining a strong trail system around the fort. So Tate also organized a detail to start clearing the nearby trails of any fallen trees or other debris that might had accumulated over the winter.

The mosquito population appeared larger and more aggressive already, and Jacob put it down to a wet spring and the nearby swampy countryside. He felt for the men on late picket duty; they were exposed to the bugs and unable to do much to discourage their bites. Some of them just yielded to their bothersome irritations while others smeared their exposed skin with anything from bear fat to mud. One poor private even covered himself in horse manure at the assurance of one of his mates that it would keep anything away. He soon learned that it was just a joke and had to live with the constant ribbing from the men for several weeks.

Reports of Delaware raids had begun in late April and only increased over the next several weeks. The rains had soaked the woods and led to a veritable explosion of vegetation and leaves when it paired up with the sunshine of early May. The wild regrowth provided effortless concealment for the Delaware. With every passing day, the forests grew greener and more dangerous for the scouts and settlers.

Uneasiness forced many frontier families to take refuge at the fort despite the tight quarters and lack of privacy. The men enjoyed having women around the fort for their company and their cooking. Maggie also enjoyed having female companions and their children nearby.

"Sir," Private White said as he approached Jacob one afternoon, "a scouting party has just returned from a short trip over the ridge. They found the Turner place burned out and no signs of the family."

"Did they search the area thoroughly?" Jacob asked as he climbed the ladder to the top of the wall. He waved White to follow him and said, "That makes the second report in as many days that the Delaware are taking captives as opposed to killing them."

They stood peering over the vast countryside for a moment before White answered. "They did check the entire plot and even went as far as the next homestead. That family had neither seen nor heard the attack."

"The Delaware must have had a particularly hard winter," Jacob said thoughtfully. "Maybe they lost some of their people to the fever or pox. If this is true, they must need to rebuild their numbers and are supplementing with captive settlers."

White just stood by, waiting for his orders.

Jacob's eyes were drawn to a pillar of black smoke just over the northern horizon. He pointed and said, "It appears they have hit us again. Please organize a search party to check out that area and check on the other farms to the north. Please get yourselves back here as soon as you can, especially if you run into any Delaware war parties."

White saluted and was soon down the ladder calling for volunteers. Jacob remained on the wall and let his eyes drift over the sea of trees.

Each morning, over the next several weeks, the fort was greeted with the harsh aroma of burning cabins and scorched land. Increasing patrols did not stop the merciless raids, and there was a limit to how many families could reasonably be housed at the fort.

Jacob had issued a shoot to kill order for any patrol or scouting party that ran across a Delaware raiding party. It was the same story each day, a hunting party or a group of scouts would arrive just after the raiders had gone. Each time, they were left with nothing but the sight of burning homes and slaughtered livestock.

Despite encouragement from some of the men, Jacob refused to offer a bounty for scalps. He feared the possibility of an escalation of the Delaware raids if he did so. He also felt that if he paid for scalps, it would make him no better than his enemies. Jacob simply wanted to protect the settlers and keep the Indians at bay.

The Delaware resumed killing the settlers during their raids. Jacob's men were infuriated and urged him to be more aggressive against the Indians. He understood that with any further killings, he would have to consider attacking the numerous Delaware villages that were within striking distance of the fort. He knew Kittanning was the largest village and home base to Captain Jacobs and his band of raiders, but it was far too large to attack alone.

Jacob's biggest concern about attacking the Delaware villages was that a full scale assault would leave the fort's defenses weakened. If he only left a small garrison to man the fort, it would make them vulnerable to a counter-attack. He certainly didn't want to fall into a trap that would make it easy for the Delaware to destroy the only permanent defense in the region.

While the raids continued, Israel had used the winter to recover from his injuries, and his mobility strengthened to the point where he started to lead some of his own men out to strike at the Delaware. Jacob received reports from some of his men who had been assigned to Israel's command that he was particularly brutal to any Indians they encountered. He even went so far as to personally offer bounties on scalps.

Israel's presence in the wilderness did appear to affect the Delaware. Their attacks lessened a bit, and news filtered its way back to Jacob about the exploits of the 'Forest Sentinels'.

Jacob was careful not to insult his brother, but asked him to report or send messengers to keep the fort informed of his progress against the Delaware. Israel did send the odd message back to appease his brother, but they were vague at best and didn't really give much to go on.

The attacks may have seemed to be subsiding, but Jacob knew that the Delaware would just start pulling back from the fort to attack the most remote and isolated settlers. This had been the one drawback to the idea of a chain of forts. They couldn't really stop or block the attacks; they could only reroute them.

Jacob had sent a small contingent of scouts east to Fort Shirley to check on the status of the chain of forts that had been planned by Washington. It had been two weeks already since they left and Jacob had expected them back by now. Young Caleb Kennedy numbered among them, and he knew that his wife shared a special bond with the young lad. He prayed that they were safe and mulled over the thought of sending another group to search for them.

With his brother keeping the Delaware in check, Jacob decided to take a small company out towards Fort Duquesne instead. Little had been heard or seen of the French and he wanted to find out for himself what they were up to.

With Israel and his men defending the surrounding woods, Jacob felt that the fort could spare enough men to make up a decent size scouting party. He chose Joshua, White, Sinclair and thirty militiamen and left John Tate in charge of the remaining garrison.

"It will feel good to be back in the woods," Jacob said to Joshua as they stood outside the gates waiting for the rest of the men to form up. "All this waiting around for word from the other forts and news of the Delaware was getting tiresome."

Just as they were ready to leave, Jacob noticed two men arriving from the eastern trail. He called out to them saying, "You there, what news do you have for us?"

"We are looking for Sergeant Sims," one of them called back.

"I am Sims," he said and waved them over. "Hurry yourselves, lads."

The men ran directly towards Jacob and offered a pleasant greeting before one of them said, "Sir, we have news from Colonel Armstrong and a sealed note from Philadelphia."

Jacob took the letter and placed it in his coat pocket and said, "I am not familiar with this Armstrong of whom you speak. What news has he for us?"

"The Colonel is the commander of the army to the east, including the fortifications from Fort Augusta to Fort George," the other messenger was quick to explain.

Jacob was unimpressed by these credentials and just looked at the men silently, waiting for them to relay the message from Armstrong.

"He wanted us to inform you he is organizing a couple of battalions of militia and volunteers to fight the Delaware and Shawnee. He also told us to tell you that the Pennsylvania government has put a seven hundred dollar bounty on the two Delaware leaders, the ones they call Captain Jacobs and Chief Shingas.

"What does Armstrong want from us? I have several families in this area to defend and only a hundred or so woodsmen and militia to do so."

"We were asked to see if you could send a scouting party north to get some information on the Delaware village they call Kittanning. There are rumors that both Shingas and Captain Jacobs reside there and use it as their headquarters. As for your own need, I fear that no additional men could possibly be sent to bolster your numbers. Most of the other forts are scarcely garrisoned at half strength."

Jacob looked over the messengers' shoulders and saw that his scouting party has assembled and White and Sinclair were walking towards him to report.

"Sir, the men are ready to leave at your command," White said and waited for Jacob to issue his orders.

"One moment lads, I just need to speak with these fellows, but we will be leaving shortly."

"So, gentlemen," Jacob said, returning his attention to the messengers. "What am I supposed to do? Does this Armstrong want me to change my plans and head north now?"

"We do have a note that the colonel wanted us to present to you, and I assume it clarifies the issues at hand for you, sir," one of the men said.

Jacob politely accepted this second letter and unfolded it, scanning the contents. While he read it he asked the pair, "What do you think of our little fort?"

"It looks very fine, sir," the quieter of the men said. "We have seen all five of the forts that sit west of the Susquehanna and this one is much larger and well situated. Captain Jacobs will certainly have his hands full if he thinks he can burn this down to the ground."

"Captain Jacobs has tried to attack us and we sent him running," Jacob said proudly. "We feel we have built up a good defensive position and the Delaware have given us enough attention that they must see us as a threat. We are honestly more concerned with what the French are up to and that is why we were just leaving to scout around Fort Duquesne."

"What name have you given the fort?" one of the men asked.

"Fort Stevens," Jacob offered as he folded up the note and placed it in his inner vest pocket. "I expect you are to return to Armstrong immediately to report on our progress?"

"Yes, sir. If it is alright, we would like to rest briefly before we get back on the trail. Is there anything you would like us to pass on to Colonel Armstrong?"

Jacob nodded and said, "By all means, please rest. Have some food and fill your horns. I will write a reply to his note."

The two men hurried to the front gate, walking past the curious glances of the waiting scouting party.

Jacob began to approach the scouting party before he remembered the other sealed note the messengers had presented to him. Retrieving it from his coat pocket, he used his knife to break the waxy seal.

As Jacob unfurled the note, he saw that it was signed by Washington himself. It was short and to the point, stating:

'This is to confirm the promotion of Sergeant Jacob Sims to the rank of Captain.'
Lieutenant Colonel George Washington, Commander of the Provincial Army of the Pennsylvania Territories.

Jacob closed up the note before he spoke with the men.

"Sir, what is the news?" Private White asked as he stepped forward. "Do you want me to send out an advanced guard, or do you want us to leave together?"

"I am sorry for the delay, gentlemen, but I need a few more moments," Jacob explained. "We just might be leaving for Kittanning instead of south-west now." He turned back towards the fort and motioned to Joshua to accompany him.

Jacob walked in deep thought until Joshua broke the silence, saying, "Sir, what is going on? The men are excited about getting out of their daily routines around the fort."

"Oh, I'm sorry, lad. I just have a few things on my mind. Our Washington has given me a promotion to captain. I'm not exactly sure if it means much, but it sounds nice."

"Congratulations, sir!" Joshua offered. "It's well-deserved, if I may say."

Jacob motioned Joshua to keep his voice down and said, "Thank you, lad, but please keep it between us for the moment. I need to tell Maggie before it gets all over camp."

As they passed through the main gate, Jacob asked the guards, "Have you seen the two messengers come through?"

"Yes, sir," one of the guards replied respectfully, "they headed for the far barracks."

Jacob thanked the man and continued walking. He looked at Joshua and said, "I have been ordered by some officer that I have never met, to head north to scout the Delaware. What are your thoughts about that?"

"I do worry about the French," Joshua said slowly, "but honestly, it is the Delaware that frighten me more. We both know the French are sitting back, keeping their hands clean, and letting the Delaware do their dirty work."

"Point taken, lad, I just wish Israel was around so we could coordinate with him." He held the door to the barracks open for Joshua to pass.

The two messengers sat alone by the fire, enjoying some bread and dried pork when Jacob approached. "Gentlemen," he began, "did you happen to come across a couple of my men either at Fort Shirley or on the trail to get here? They have been missing for close to two weeks now." Jacob stood before the fire and held his hands over the comforting heat.

"Can't say we have," one of the men replied. "The fort is always busy with traders and scouts coming and going, though."

"Did you boys get some supplies for your trip back?" Jacob asked as he walked over to a small desk and pulled out a sheet of parchment paper. He searched for something to scribble down a quick note and finally found a newly sharpened quill and dipped it into a small tin cup of ink.

The men thanked him and said that they had already been well taken care of. Jacob nodded and scratched a few lines in reply to Armstrong. He blew on the ink before creasing the paper and spotted a small wax seal on the desk. He sealed up the letter and scribbled 'Colonel Armstrong' across the front.

"Please give this to your colonel," Jacob said as he handed one of the men the envelope. "When you are ready to depart, I will have four of our men escort you as far as the creek that sits five miles to the east."

"Much obliged, sir, and we will pass your best to our Colonel Armstrong," the man said and they both saluted.

Jacob returned the salute and departed with Joshua. As they exited the barracks, they noticed Israel returning with some of his men.

"Israel, I am glad you are back," Jacob called out. His brother had been away for several days, but Jacob hoped he might be willing to lend him a hand in scouting the Delaware around Kittanning. As he watched Israel move, he noticed that his limp had become more pronounced.

When they closed the distance between them, Jacob asked, "What news do you have for us, Israel?"

"The Delaware are certainly out there and they appear to have moved further east. I spoke with a Dutch trader who told me that the Delaware and Shawnee have been concentrating their efforts on attacking the Susquehanna area to our east."

"Have you seen anything of the French?" Jacob asked. "I feel we know what the Delaware are up to, but the movements of the French remain a mystery."

"The same Dutchman told me that he had visited Fort Duquesne a few weeks back and noticed that the garrison was much stronger than he recalled from a visit before winter hit."

Jacob glanced at the men who still waited for him outside the gates and said, "I had planned to lead a scouting party to Fort Duquesne, but I just received an order from some new commander to scout around Kittanning. I am just about to head out with thirty men."

"If you wait a few minutes while I clean up and restock my supplies, I would like to join you," Israel responded.

"Are you certain you are able?" Jacob asked, honestly hoping that Israel would accompany him. "You just returned; surely, you need some rest?"

"My men will remain behind to rest and bolster the numbers here at the fort, but I am up for the trip."

Jacob looked around and asked, "Where are your men, Israel? I only saw you return with a handful."

"I left them in the woods to camp for the night. Most of them prefer living in the forests versus being confined to the fort. They are set to return in the morning and I will leave them orders to stay here until I come back." Israel answered as he walked to the blacksmith's shop.

"Be out front shortly," Jacob called after him. "I will be sending out an advanced party in a few minutes, so please don't make us wait."

He looked for Maggie and found her helping some of the women keep watch over the young children who remained inside the fort. He smiled at the sight of her surrounded by the cheerful chaos and said, "Maggie, do you have a moment?"

"They take me back to better times," Maggie said with a smile.

"I have been ordered to head north to scout one of the Delaware villages," he said, feeling an overwhelming guilt for leaving her once again. "I shouldn't be gone more than a few days or so." Jacob explained.

She could hear the remorse in his voice and rushed to assure him that she understood. "Jacob, you have no reason to feel guilty. We had a wonderful winter together. You have your responsibilities and my full support." She embraced him and gave him a kiss that elicited several giggles from the curious children.

Jacob stood with his arms wrapped around her and whispered, "Washington promoted me to captain."

Maggie smiled and gave him another kiss and firm hug.

When she let go, he kissed her forehead and said, "Keep well. I will be back soon."

He felt her gaze on him as he walked to the gate and he turned to offer a final wave. When he reached his men, he found them prepared to leave. It was already late afternoon and they were anxious to get on the trail before they lost much more of the available sunlight. Private White and Joshua stood looking into the far woods, but turned when they heard Jacob approach.

"Gentlemen, we will be heading north to the Delaware village at Kittanning instead of south to Fort Duquesne. Let's allow an advanced party to get a few minutes ahead of us before we depart."

The men's concern gave way to excitement and Private Sinclair immediately took five men with him and departed to the north. They would be using the old Kittanning Trail, a far more direct route, despite the fact it was heavily used by the Delaware. It would take them north then west towards the Allegheny River.

Israel joined them a few minutes later and Jacob quickly organized the men into smaller, more manageable groups. Private White took the rear guard, while Jacob and Israel each took a group of the remaining men.

"I don't expect I should have to say this, but I will anyway," Jacob said. "Keep your eyes open for any signs of the Delaware or the French and your muskets at the ready. Also, keep conversations to a minimum."

Joshua remained by Jacob's side until they had advanced well into the heart of the trail. Jacob then asked Joshua to take up a position behind him and keep close to the edge of the woods.

The trail was flat and well-used, clear of any roots and low-hanging trees. It was a main trail from the northern lake and west to the river and Jacob imagined it had been used by the Delaware and the Shawnee long before any French or Englishmen had arrived in the area.

By the time they reached the banks of the Allegheny River, the last of the sun had all but disappeared. Darkness made the trail risky to travel on without the aid of torches, which were out of the question.

Sinclair's scouts had discovered a good site just off the trail to spend the night. Jacob and Israel were both impressed by the encampment and thanked Sinclair for his good work.

They planned to leave at first light and most of the men settled down to sleep as soon as they arrived. Jacob set up additional pickets to those Sinclair had already positioned. He alerted each of them to Israel's tendency to spend some portion of the night wandering the woods.

Jacob propped himself up against a tree trunk and spent an uncomfortable night adjusting his position frequently. Thankfully, dawn came early. Jacob rose just as Israel was returning from his nightly walk.

"Anything out there to be worried about brother, or was all quiet?" Jacob asked when Israel had moved closer.

"Nothing that I could see or hear," Israel replied loudly enough to purposely wake the sleeping men, "but the town must be close. I could smell the fires and hear voices off in the distance."

The men ate a quick breakfast of dried meat and hard bread before Sinclair's advanced guard departed. Israel's followed them closely and Jacob ordered White's rear guard to stay within sight of the main party.

The day was clear and it was not very long before they reached the hill that overlooked the village and gave them a good view of the town below. Jacob was glad to see that pickets had already been positioned towards the river and the eastern side of the hill. He approached Israel and Sinclair and stood looking down on the sprawling village. He was flooded by the harsh memories of standing here with Captain Jacobs. It already seemed like a lifetime ago.

"How are things, gentlemen?" Jacob asked quietly. "Have you seen much movement?"

"Not much, sir," Sinclair replied. "It looks like only some women and children around."

Without a word, Israel began working his way down the hill and got far closer to the village than Jacob was comfortable with before he stopped. He took cover behind a large maple tree and watched the village below. Jacob and Sinclair watched his progress and were relieved that he stopped prior to reaching the main trail entrance to the village.

White and Joshua approached them and began to discuss what they saw before them. Joshua had a piece of parchment and a stick of charcoal and was busily scribbling notes and a rough map.

During the short time he had gotten to study the village and before Lapointe took him away, Jacob had been struck by how strangely unorganized the layout of the village had seemed to be. This higher position showed that there really was no pattern; just a tangled mass of buildings and paths between them.

He quickly began noting details for Joshua to mark down. "Did you count thirty wood-framed houses with flat bark roofs, lad? They surround a thirty foot long house, but there doesn't seem to be any particular order. Crude huts by the river are probably mainly for storage. There is a large cornfield on both sides of the river…"

"As well as another, smaller village," Israel added as he returned from his jaunt down the hill. "You can't see it past the trees from up here. I also noticed a couple of French bateaux docked on the shore by the cornfield. I'm not sure if we can get any closer without giving away our position."

"I was just about to mention the other village," Jacob said peevishly. "Remember, I was a captive here not all that long ago."

"If you know so much about this place, why did we travel all this way?" Israel said, matching his tone.

"Point taken brother, I was a prisoner here, so there was not much time to stop and study the village building by building. I'm just saying that I got a good look at that second village from the banks of the Allegheny when I was here last."

"It looks nothing like the main town," Israel said. "It looks like crudely-built huts. Do you think it is used for visitors?"

"I think it is actually where they keep some of the white captives that they've adopted into the tribe," Jacob responded. "Look, you can see them working in the fields surrounding the town."

Sure enough, while the village seemed relatively empty, except for some Delaware women and children, the fields were full of additional women and a few children. Jacob counted roughly fifty. They were dressed in Indian clothes and most of them had skin darkened by the sun. Upon closer inspection, the men on the hill could see that they were white captives, working the fields in preparation for the early spring planting.

Israel's anger flared and he was barely able to keep his voice down as it cracked when he said, "We should attack the village while they are at their weakest and free these captives. If we burn it to the ground the savages will know how all the white settlers they have butchered felt."

Jacob had contemplated such action himself, but decided it would be foolhardy. Not only were there only thirty of them, but he was here on orders to scout for information for a future attack.

Jacob did his best to calm his brother and said, "God knows, I would strike at this village in an instant, Israel, but not without knowing all of the details. We cannot see the village on the other side of the river and you yourself said that there are French bateaux docked there. I won't leave us open to a flanking attack with so few men."

Jacob could tell that his brother was struggling to hold his tongue. He was thankful that Israel wasn't with his own men because there would have been no way to restrain him.

Israel walked away and Jacob looked around at the other men. He sensed that if he had ordered it, most of the other men would have gladly charged down the hill to attack and slaughter the inhabitants.

He looked at the maze-like village and thought of how easily a group of soldiers could become overwhelmed by villagers who knew their way around, even if they were mostly women and children. Besides, what if the buildings were full of warriors, resting up for another attack on the frontier? They could walk into a battle outnumbered and outgunned. Jacob could never take such a chance with his men. No matter what Israel thought of his decision, they would have to wait for a better opportunity to strike.

When he finished mulling over his thoughts, Jacob said, "Gentlemen, let's get ready to depart. It is still early; if we push hard, we can get back to the fort after nightfall."

"If we walked down the hill or use the cornfield for cover, we could also have this entire town burned to the ground by nightfall," Israel scoffed, but his remark fell on deaf ears.

Private Sinclair once again took the advanced guard and White positioned himself at the rear. This time, Jacob took the lead group and Israel followed reluctantly, refusing to look at or speak with his brother.

The group made good time. The fresh breeze and sunshine lightened the men's steps and they pushed on without stopping to rest. They were only a few miles from the fort when the sky began to darken.

"Do you smell that, sir?" Joshua asked quietly as they neared the fort, taking Jacob by surprise.

Jacob had noticed the smell of burning wood for a mile or two, but thought that it must have been blown to them from a nearby cabin chimney. Before he had the chance to answer, Private Sinclair approached running back down the trail towards them, shouting and gesturing wildly.

"This doesn't look promising," Jacob muttered to himself before calling out, "Form up, men; it looks like there's some trouble ahead!"

As Sinclair got closer, Jacob was finally able to understand that he was shouting, "The fort is under attack! The fort is under attack!"

Jacob let Sinclair reach him and listened as the panicked man reported through gasping breaths, "Sir, the bloody Delaware are attacking the fort. From what I saw, they have made it over the outer earthen works and set the trading post, horse shed and other outer buildings on fire."

"Private, how many are there?" Jacob grabbed Sinclair's arm, trying to calm him down.

Without warning, Israel rushed past with his group of men and headed towards the action.

"There was too much smoke and fire to tell, sir," Sinclair answered Jacob, "but there are no warriors in the woods, so they must have launched an all-out attack."

Jacob was concerned for everyone at the fort, but especially for Maggie's safety and screamed, "Forward gentlemen, at double time!"

The men reached the edge of the tree line quickly and saw that all was as Sinclair had so dutifully described.

Jacob noticed that Israel had been joined by some of his own men that must have still been camping out in the woods. He was concerned that

Israel would do something foolish and expose them all to a counter-attack, but he noticed that his brother was in a good position to reach the works with a short run across the field.

Nightfall had consumed the fort, but the light emanating from the torches around the upper walls of the fort and the ones that were being tossed against the fort's outer walls, provided sufficient light for the men to see what exactly was happening. Fifty painted and screaming Delaware warriors were attempting to set the outer wall of the fort on fire. The men on the bastions did their best to force the Delaware back but the smoke made it difficult.

"Sir, what do you want us to do?" Private White called out.

Jacob knew that if he just charged blindly into the open field without a clear objective, the warriors would turn their attention to them and wipe them out. He and Israel were spaced far enough apart to set up on both of the Delaware flanks.

"Lads, we need to get to the outer earthen works," Jacob shouted. "If we can reach them and use them as cover, we can rake the rear of the Delaware ranks and possibly force them to retreat."

Giving a quick wave to his men, Jacob led them across the field, dodging the numerous tree stumps that littered the ground as they went. He was the first to reach the tall pile of earth and the others soon reached the soft earthen wall, wet from the spring thaw, to await their orders.

Catching his breath, Jacob prayed that Israel's men had also reached the works. He called out to his men, "Climb to the top of the works and at my command, fire into the damn savages. Keep up a steady fire after that and we will see if they decide to turn on us."

Jacob led the way and could just see Israel's men farther down the work doing the same.

When all the men were in place, Jacob took a last look at Israel. He saw his brother nod and screamed, "FIRE!"

The initial volley decimated the rear of the attacking Delaware. Taken completely off guard, the force of the musket fire pushed the warriors forward and exposed them to additional fire from the top of the fort's walls.

The men reloaded quickly and sent another murderous blast into the confused and trapped Delaware. Jacob could see Israel ordering his men to fix their bayonets or take up their weapons of choice to attack.

With a terrible screech that echoed around the field amid all the confusion, Israel led his men into the remaining Delaware warriors.

Their sudden movements made Jacob's own men follow despite his shouts to pull them back.

The fort's main gates had been opened and the remainder of Israel's men ran out of the protective walls and straight into the midst of the savage attack. The Delaware were sent into utter panic accompanied by bloody screams and yelps.

Some of the Delaware managed to run into the nearby woods and Jacob ordered several of his men to form up in front of the gates to prevent any of the fleeing warriors from trying to take cover inside the fort. He scanned the interior of the fort for some sign of Maggie and then noticed her at the top of the wall with a musket in her hand.

"I'm glad to see you're well," he yelled at her after she fired her weapon. She just smiled and calmly began reloading. She looked so at home in all the action, Jacob just shook his head.

When the last able-bodied warrior had retreated or been cut down and the smoke began to clear, Jacob got a clear view of the damaged inflicted on both their enemy and the fort.

With torches provided by some of the men inside the fort, Israel and his men were searching the dead bodies that were all over the field adjacent to the burnt out trading post. A few of the militiamen were nursing small wounds while the rest rounded up the few Delaware who had survived the onslaught but were too injured to escape.

Israel's men were methodically scalping the dead and displaying the bloody prizes on a large woolen trade blanket they had spread on the ground.

Jacob was furious.

He was vehemently against the taking of scalps and swore to himself that he would speak with Israel about it when the danger had ended.

Some of the garrisoned men showed an interest in joining in on the mutilation, but Jacob headed them off by ordering White and Sinclair to ready the men in case the Delaware launched a second attack.

A couple of the men had taken three wounded Delaware warriors as prisoners and Jacob said, "Throw them into the old stables inside the fort and keep your muskets on them until I have some time to speak with them."

By the time Israel and his men had completed their butchery Jacob was speaking with John Tate next to the smoldering remains of the trading post, trying to figure out if any damage had been done to the fort itself. Jacob was in mid-sentence when Israel approached and said, "Can I have a word with you, Jacob?"

Jacob ignored Israel, but was visibly upset by his brother's rudeness. "Mr. Tate," he continued, "Please get a building party organized as soon as possible and check that all the fires are out and won't do any further damage."

Tate walked away to fulfill his orders and Jacob finally turned to his brother.

"Now Israel, what do you need from me? Your men appear to have little concern that the Delaware might attack us again tonight. Do you think the Delaware are just going to sit idly by, watching from the woods as you and your boys scalp and mutilate their brothers?" Jacob tried his best to keep his temper in check but found it increasingly difficult in talking to his brother.

Israel briefly hesitated before responding in mocking tones, "Do you have an issue with me or my men? With your vast knowledge of the Delaware, I would expect you to know that they would do the same to our dead and probably far worse. You have obviously softened a touch, dear brother. Have you forgotten we are at war with these savages?"

"Whether I agree with you or not, this is not the time or place to discuss it," Jacob said. "If you would be so kind, brother, please exercise control over your men and take them into the woods to check on the Delaware."

The two brothers stood almost nose-to-nose, until they seemed to realize their disagreement was on display. They each stepped back and Jacob glanced up at Maggie who looked at him with a brief frown on her face.

"I'm sorry, Israel," Jacob said. "The excitement of the battle has gotten me all heated up. Please have your men search the area and find what is left of the savages and send me a report of their findings. If we are lucky, maybe they ran all the way back to Kittanning."

Israel mockingly saluted his brother and called his men to get into the woods. He watched as Israel's men's torch lights danced through the woods. This was the second time the Delaware had broken with the tradition of not attacking after dark and Jacob refused to let them reorganize without being pursued.

He stood alone scanning the dead and wondering how his life had gotten so messy. He looked up at Maggie again and this time she smiled. He wished he could take her away and return to their old life.

"Sir, I counted the dead and have the numbers if you need them," Joshua's quiet voice startled him out of his thoughts.

"Yes…thank you, lad. What do you have for me?"

"There are twelve dead Delaware with three captured. We had three men killed in the fort and five men injured to varying degrees. One man, John Temple, is severely hurt with what appears to be a scalping gone badly." Joshua finished speaking and handed Jacob a small piece of paper with the numbers scribbled down.

"Thank you, lad," Jacob said quietly. He was still in a daze from the battle and the aftermath. "Please organize a detail to give our dead a reasonable Christian burial."

Jacob watched Joshua leave before a couple of musket shots rang from the forest line. They sounded like they came from a distance away, but he still ran to the earthen works to have the men prepare for a possible attack.

They waited a couple of long minutes and still nothing happened. After discussing the situation with White and Sinclair, it was decided that they should pull the men back into the fort. The confines of the fort offered safety and the top of the bastion presented a much better view of the field and surrounding wilderness.

Staying with the rear guard, Jacob made sure all the men were in the fort before the main gates were slammed shut and locked into place with a large piece of cut timber.

A small detail placed torches all around the earthen works and towards the pathway to the fort's massive doors. It was to keep the area lit, as well as to assist Israel and his men with bright markers to guide them back.

Jacob had called Joshua and the small burial crew back before they had time to get any of the men into the ground. It was less than ideal to leave them unburied overnight, but it was necessary. He would send a larger detail out the next morning to clear the field and bury the dead.

Exhausted and wanting nothing more than to retire to his quarters to rest, Jacob remembered that there was still the matter of the three Delaware warriors waiting for him in the old stable. He motioned for Joshua to walk with him and they soon found the prisoners tied to three posts.

They were an impressive sight though they were no older than teenagers. Each was heavily painted and tattooed and wore an air of dignity and pride despite being captors of their enemy.

"Joshua, can you speak their language?" Jacob asked. "I just want to get some information from them so I can go get some sleep."

Joshua did his best to converse with them and appeared to get some information.

"They want to know what you are going to do with them," Joshua said. "They want to die like warriors and asked to be tortured and burned."

"I want to know about their leader, Captain Jacobs, and what he is planning." Jacob ignored their request for a warrior's death.

Joshua spoke with them once again and, after a short conversation, reported to Jacob what they had said to him. "They have little to say, but they did say that their chief has sworn to burn every English fort to the ground."

Jacob could see this was a fruitless endeavor. He turned towards the door and said, "We certainly won't kill them tonight, lad. Maybe we can trade them for some white captives. Have a couple men keep their eyes on them tonight and get some sleep. We have a lot of work ahead of us in the morning. God willing, the Delaware will give us a break for a few days."

More than three long hours had passed since Israel and his men ventured out into the woods to search for the rest of their attackers. Aside from the two musket shots heard shortly after they departed, the woods had remained silent.

Jacob's attempts to rest lasted no more than an hour before he returned to the western wall. He eyed the tree line, straining to see any movement in the dim sea of trees and bushes. He prayed that he had not sent Israel into another ambush.

Eventually, his fatigue and the chilly night air drove him back to his quarters in search of a mug of hot tea.

"Stay in bed Maggie, no reason for both of us to lose sleep." Jacob said, but no sooner did he enter his quarters than the call of 'men in the field' rang out.

Maggie smiled again and said, "I hope Israel made it back."

"I do too. I should be back soon."

He rushed across the parade grounds, up the ladder and onto the bastion. He could see a long line of lit torches stringing along the field's outer border. One of the guards started to call out to the approaching men until Jacob silenced him and said, "Keep your voice down, man. How do we know if they are our men or the Delaware trying to deceive us?"

The upper walls were now packed with curious men, watching the slow approach of the unidentified torch carriers.

Jacob waited until the first of the men came within the first line of earthen works and called out, "Stop and identify yourselves. The order is to shoot anyone if they refuse to reply and stand down."

He knew something was wrong with all of this. After a rough count of the torches, Jacob could see that there were far more than the number of men Israel had taken with him.

No reply came and the men within the fort simply watched as the line of torches congregated in a group just short of the works.

Jacob called over to Joshua and Private White who had both joined the others, "Make sure the men are ready for another fight. Send twenty or so down to the main gates just in case. I want all other available men on the walls immediately.

Doing his best to remain patient and not over react, Jacob called out one last warning, "Identify yourselves or you will give us no other option but to fire on you."

A few tense seconds passed before a raspy voice called back, "Is this how you welcome all of your guests? It is Israel, returning to give you my report as ordered."

Jacob recognized the same level of sarcasm in Israel's voice as when he left and immediately requested that the main gates be opened. He climbed down the ladder to greet his brother, but ordered the men to remain on guard for anything that appeared out of place. The gates were swung open and Jacob stood under the massive timber that supported the heavy frame of the door.

The party was approaching very slowly across the distance from the works to the gate and Jacob got an uneasy feeling in the pit of his stomach. He could clearly see his brother but nothing of his men. Most of the torches remained a few paces back and the way they moved made Jacob suspect something was not right.

Jacob was unsure what to do, but trying not to cause a panic, he calmly took a couple of steps forward and called out to Israel, "How was your scouting trip, dear brother?"

Israel stopped within fifty paces of the gate and looked like he was trying to signal something with his face.

Before Jacob could call out again, he heard a short blast shatter the darkness. The spark from the pan shot into the air as Israel fell face down on the ground.

Jacob finally saw Captain Jacobs in perfect detail, holding a smoking pistol as he stood over his crumpled brother.

There was no time to close the large heavy gates before the hordes of Delaware rushed towards them, and Jacob screamed, "Fire, lads! Kill the bloody bastards!"

The deafening war cries from the charging warriors drowned out the first volley that rained down on them from the fort's upper reaches. Jacob shouldered his musket and blew an apple sized hole in the face of a Delaware warrior three paces in front of him. The dead warrior stumbled past him and slammed into the base of the wall.

Before he could get his musket reloaded, he was joined by the group of twenty men he had sent down to the gate. Joshua and White stood by him as they unleashed another deadly volley into the main body of charging warriors.

The bravery of the relentless Delaware was soundly matched by the accurate volleys that Jacob and his men threw at them. Their own bravery pushed the attackers back.

As quickly as the surprise attack happened, it was over.

The Delaware had retired to the confines of the woods and, after another couple ill-directed volleys fell well short of the forest line, Jacob signaled the men to stop and save their powder.

Leaning on his musket, his face blackened by its repeated use, Jacob was close to tears as Joshua approached. "Sir," he said, "should I send some men to search the field for Israel and any possible survivors?"

Jacob's hands were shaking and his voice cracked as he replied, "Please…if you can lad…do what you can…but watch for the bloody savages. They might be waiting to attack us again. Kill any of them you find still alive."

The men were spent. Emotions were running high and even Joshua seemed to struggle to muster enough energy to search the darkness. After less than fifteen minutes, Jacob called out, "That is enough, lads. We can search the field once the sun provides us enough light to do it properly."

Once the men returned, Jacob walked out into the darkness alone.

"Sir, shall I come with you?" Joshua called out.

"No need, lad; just watch for the bloody savages and give me a moment." Jacob walked blindly out to where he thought he had last seen Israel. He used what little light shone down from the fort walls.

All the torches set out earlier had burnt out or were extinguished by the Delaware.

Stumbling around the dead, Jacob finally found his brother.

Israel was face down with a massive hole in his back. At such a close range the blast from the pistol had mercifully killed him in an instant, sparing him much pain.

Overcome by the attacks and the emotional trauma of witnessing his brother's death for the second time, Jacob fell to his knees and gently stroked Israel's head. His eyes filled with tears, but he was far too angry to openly cry. Slowly placing his brother's head back on the soft ground, Jacob offered a silent prayer. He contemplated dragging the body back into the fort, but he thought better of it. He certainly did not want Maggie to see his brother this way.

Jacob decided to leave his brother where he had fallen until the burial detail could go to work at dawn. He removed his outer coat and placed it over most of Israel's body.

As he rose, he felt numb and called to Joshua, "Bring the three Delaware to me."

Joshua pleaded, "Sir, do not let the actions of the Delaware make you do something you might regret."

"Get them," Jacob ordered in a tone Joshua had never heard from him before.

Joshua pulled one of the prisoners by the arm and four other men helped escort the others. Jacob was waiting just outside the main gate.

He looked in the eyes of the young warrior, but saw no fear there. He almost reconsidered his intentions, but the image of Israel being shot in the back brought on a surge of anger.

Before Joshua could react, Jacob pulled out his scalping knife and sliced across the first warrior's throat. The Delaware dropped instantly, blood flowing across Jacob's leggings and moccasins.

The other two were shoved forward, awaiting a similar fate.

Jacob's powder blackened face showed lines of clean flesh where his tears had begun flowing freely. He jerked the two warriors around so their backs were facing him, and he lifted his knife. With two swift moves, he ran his knife over the thick leather ropes that tied their arms.

The warriors stood still, looking at their dead mate and uncertain what they were to do next.

Jacob took a step back and yelled, "Run, you bloody heathens. Run."

They glanced at each other as if they didn't understand, but when they saw Jacob shoulder his musket, they ran.

Jacob coolly fired. The shot echoed through the open field and struck the faster of the two in the back. He bounced along the ground a few paces, nearly tripping the surviving warrior.

The man froze and watched as Jacob calmly reloaded his musket. The young warrior seemed unwilling or unable to move and Jacob shouldered his musket and squeezed the trigger without hesitation.

White smoke blinded his sight for a minute, but he knew it had been a clear hit. He stepped forward into the darkness, ignoring the calls from Joshua to get back.

Walking as far as the first Delaware, Jacob could hear the short whimpers coming from the second savage. He was only a few paces away and Jacob followed his gasps for air and soon stood directly over the dying warrior.

Jacob knew that Captain Jacobs and his warriors were still out in the nearby woods watching his every move. "I will kill every one of your warriors and leave you for last so you can watch their deaths!" Jacob screamed into the darkness and plunged his knife onto the chest of the defenseless Delaware.

The woods remained silent and Jacob screamed again, "I will come to your village and kill you, Captain Jacobs! I will feed your remains to the dogs."

The woods erupted with the cries and howls of the Delaware, but their screams were blocked by the shouts of the men at the fort urging Jacob to fall back.

Joshua and a handful of men had finally made their way to Jacob and found him defiantly standing on the highest part of the earthen works.

"Sir, please get back to the fort," Joshua pleaded and reached to pull Jacob back. "The Delaware might just flood back onto the field and kill us all."

As though he was waking from a trance, Jacob realized his foolishness and climbed down. He didn't want to have any more of his men killed, and he followed them back to the fort. A few musket shots rang out from the woods but soon stopped once the men reached the gates.

Jacob looked around and saw dazed looks on the faces of all the men. He looked up at the wall and said, "They will not bother us again tonight, so get some sleep and be ready for tomorrow."

Maggie was the first to greet Jacob upon his return into the fort. He tried not to break down, but it was nearly impossible. Joshua and John Tate saw to the gates while White and Sinclair organized the night watch. Maggie nodded her thanks to them as she guided Jacob to their quarters.

As soon as the door closed, Jacob began to cry. His brother was dead, for certain this time, and Jacob had been unable to save him for the second time. Whatever respect or honor he may have held for the Delaware or their leader had died with Israel on the small clearing in front of the fort.

Wiping his teary eyes, he vowed to Maggie, "The Delaware will pay for this. I will never again treat them like an admired foe, but as the savage heathens they truly are."

Chapter | **Fifteen**

The morning sun broke over the mountain with a dazzling brilliance that seemed to pierce Jacob's weary eyelids. He awoke to the sounds of Maggie preparing tea by the fire and tried to process the events of the previous day.

He knew that he would need to organize a detail to go out and bury the dead, but he could barely find the strength to leave his bed. Eventually, Maggie coaxed him from the covers with a steaming mug and an understanding smile. She rubbed his back as he drank and they quietly talked about all that had taken place.

About an hour later, just as a clear-headed Jacob finished dressing, a light knock was heard at the door. He opened the door and found Joshua standing on the threshold.

"Good morning, Joshua. How are the men holding up?" Jacob stepped into the bright morning sun and shaded his eyes.

"As well as expected, sir. They each had the opportunity to get some sleep, but we managed to keep a strong post through the night."

"Very good," Jacob said, straining his neck to see who was manning the upper western wall.

"Sir, I also have the report from the field," Joshua said.

Jacob looked at him in surprise and said, "You already had the field cleared?"

"Yes, sir. The men were out early and removed the dead from the field."

Taking his hat off and rubbing his hand over his hair and face, Jacob asked, "Did you find Israel?"

"We did, sir," Joshua said without elaborating.

Jacob was overwhelmed by deep sadness and embarrassment for losing his temper the previous night. He did his best to suppress the emotions and asked, "What else did you find?"

"We found ten dead Delaware, but none injured. I assume they were carried back to wherever the savages decided to make camp. There was no sign of Captain Jacobs, but we did locate two dead French marines."

Jacob drew in a long, steady breath, "So the French have finally come out of their winter dens and joined forces with their damned allies."

Joshua made no response apart from a nod.

Jacob was not surprised that the French had reappeared. He had been expecting it, but he turned the focus back to his brother. "Tell me, lad," he said quietly, "what did you do with his…Israel's body?"

"Your coat was still with him, so we laid him out under it next to the rest of the graves. I thought you and Miss Maggie might want to pay your last respects to him before he was buried."

"Thank you, lad," Jacob said as he wiped away the tears that had fallen down his cheeks. "You are like a son to me, and I have so much that I owe you."

"You do not owe me a thing, sir," Joshua said with a sad smile and handed Jacob a clean cloth to wipe his face. "You and Maggie are like family to me as well. I must warn you about Israel, though, sir. The brush wolves and vermin did some work on him last night. He was in an awful state when we found him."

Joshua dismissed himself to give Jacob a moment to recover. Jacob stood alone watching the men go about their daily duties. He could feel curious stares and the whispers from the men and some of the settler families who had taken refuge in the fort. He felt remorse for his actions—not for killing the Delaware, but for displaying his anger in such a manner in front of the men.

He stood helplessly for a moment then he felt a hand on his shoulder and a light kiss on the back of his head. Jumping slightly at the unexpected touch, he turned into Maggie's embrace. Without speaking, they turned and walked slowly towards the gates.

As per the fort's usual routine of the day, the gates were open and guarded. The guards on duty respectfully saluted the pair as they exited into the meadow.

The sun was bright, but the air was stale. The initial smell made Maggie reach for her nose and this was greeted by a slight laugh from Jacob. "For a woman who has slaughtered a pig and skinned a deer, I am surprised by your reaction to this."

"I have done so, but this smell is much worse because I know it is the smell of human death," Maggie said as they did their best to skirt around the area where the most blood still marred the grasses.

Neither said much else as Jacob guided her towards the northern wall of the fort. The base of the wall was lined with small markers on the graves of over forty men and women who had perished since the fort had been built. Some had died from Delaware attacks and others from the pox or fever.

They slowly approached the lone body that remained unburied. Israel's face and most of his upper body were still covered by Jacob's green coat, but his legs and lower torso were exposed. Jacob remembered what Joshua had said and could tell even from a distance that his brother had been mutilated by some of the animals that frequent the area.

As they got closer, Maggie pulled back on his arm and said, "I can't, Jacob. I have witnessed so much death since we have been separated. Most of the dead were strangers or people I had just met, but this is family. I don't think I can…"

Jacob knew exactly how she felt and admired the strength she had shown through all of the terrible events she had faced over the past years. "I understand, Maggie. I must say my goodbyes, though. He was a good brother and he would do the same for me." He slipped out of her grip and walked up to Israel. He knelt on one knee and pulled back the green coat.

Jacob could have identified Israel by his height and some of the visible burn scars that remained, but his body was in worse shape than the previous night. The wild beasts had done their best to hide his identity.

His brother was no longer in pain and the realization made a brief peace wash over him. He had spent all of his tears the night before, so he draped the coat back over Israel's face and prayed for him.

The burial detail had already dug a grave deep enough to keep the animals from returning. Jacob dragged Israel's stiffened body into the pit. A small wooden shovel sat upright in a mound of dirt and he began shoving the soft dirt onto the body below. He continued until the entire mound was gone and the hole was completely covered.

Jacob slowly moved over to a pile of rocks that the men had gathered to cover the dirt on the graves. He loaded his arms with rocks and meticulously placed them on the freshly turned dirt. After several more trips, he managed to completely cover the grave. He finally placed one large rock at the head of the grave.

Dirty and sweating from the task, Jacob returned to Maggie's side.

She took his hand and said, "I would have thought you might ask a priest to say some words before he was buried."

"No need," Jacob replied. "We both know Israel had no real use for religion and such. He would have appreciated the simplicity of all of this."

Maggie wiped the tears and sweat off Jacob's face with a small cloth she had in her apron. "I think I made it worse," she said through her own tears.

"No bother," Jacob said with a small smile. "I will just tie my hair back and dunk my face in one of the horse troughs."

While the two remained standing near the grave site, several men from the fort came over to pay their respects. Two survivors from Israel's ranks hammered a small wooden cross next to the large stone and hung one of Israel's favorite old woolen hats from it.

The parade of men continued for most of the morning. Each man respectfully offered a hand to Jacob and a polite kiss to Maggie's cheek for their loss.

When the pair finally worked their way back to the fort, Jacob spotted young Caleb Kennedy just inside the front gates.

"Maggie," Jacob said after his wife had finished greeting the young man, "why don't you relax back at our quarters and I will be there shortly?" She nodded and walked away.

Jacob was anxious to find out what Caleb had learned on his scouting trip and what had caused them such a long delay. Most of the men that accompanied him on the scout were milling around the parade grounds trying to get caught up with all the news around the fort.

"I assumed you had been either killed or taken captive by the Delaware, Caleb," Jacob said as he extended his hand to the young man.

"Honestly, it did look that way a few times," Caleb replied. "Poor Mr. Warriner was not as lucky as I, and was killed in one of our many skirmishes with the savages."

"Have you and your men had any food or drink?"

"I had a few bites, sir, but I honestly wished to make my report first."

"Very well, lad, I have news for you as well," Jacob said as he gestured for Caleb to sit by one of the main fires. "I just pray yours is better than mine."

When they were settled, Jacob said, "So, boy, tell me the news from the east."

"Well, sir, the Delaware appear to be working their way around the forts, focusing their attacks on all the more isolated farms and settlements. The word is that Captain Jacobs' warriors have threatened to burn down all the forts in the territory. The day I left, there was word around that the Delaware had attacked a small garrison at Fort Granville and murdered most of the soldiers. A few unfortunate men were taken captive, but I wasn't sure if that was fact or rumor."

Caleb took a moment to scan the fort, "I also learned that Colonel Armstrong's brother was the fort's commander and was assumed dead. To say the least, Armstrong was pretty upset with the news and was in the midst of gathering a few hundred volunteers to launch an attack on the Delaware."

Jacob listened quietly and sat in silence for a moment before he said, "If Armstrong leaves the line of forts defended with only a handful of men, the Delaware will just simply work around Armstrong and hit each fort before anyone can stop him."

Caleb just gazed into the fire and made no response.

"Get yourself some food and rest, Caleb. We will talk again later."

As Jacob stood to go, Caleb looked up and asked, "What was your news, sir? It appears you have had your share of fights with the Delaware."

"We certainly have, lad. I think you should get some rest and I will speak with you in a bit."

"Sir, where can I find Captain Murray?" Caleb asked as Jacob started to walk away. "I would like to let him know I have made it back."

Without bothering to turn around, Jacob simply replied, "No need, lad, Israel was murdered by Captain Jacobs and his raiders last night."

Jacob turned in time to see a look of horror cross Caleb's face and wished he had not been so blunt. "I'm sorry, lad. I just buried him a few moments ago and am still in disbelief of what happened. He was shot in the back before we could do anything. I know you were close and I am so sorry for the way I told you."

Caleb just stood with a blank look on his face and finally murmured, "Where are the others?"

"Get yourself some food and rest first, boy" Jacob said, unwilling to add the death of most of his comrades to Caleb's misery. "We will talk about all of this later. Now get some rest and thank you very much for your hard work. I'm glad to see you back safe."

He watched Caleb slowly walk towards the barracks to make sure the boy found his way. A few of the men who had accompanied him on the scout were waiting by the door. Jacob assumed they had just heard the news as well.

Jacob reached his quarters and hoped Maggie was still inside. He desperately needed an escape, if only for a few brief moments.

She was sitting by the fire cleaning her musket when he entered.

"I just spoke with young Caleb," he said when she smiled up at him. "I fear the rest of this year will be a long, bloody one. The damn English abandoned us to protect themselves and we are paying for their cowardice with the blood of families who just want to lead a peaceful life."

Maggie stood up and leaned her musket against the fireplace and greeted her husband with a deep hug. She didn't know what to say and just let him bury his head in her shoulder.

After a few minutes he said, "I'll boil some water and we can have a nice cup of tea."

Maggie nodded and resumed her seat.

"What next?" she asked as she watched him place the heavy cast iron pot over the fire.

"Not sure, but it does appear that some of the folks at the other forts to the east want to seek some form of vengeance on the Delaware," Jacob explained. "I just hope they leave us out of it all."

As he waited for the water to boil, Jacob propped his arm against the massive stone fireplace and asked, "Did I mention that Washington sent me a letter promoting me to captain?"

Maggie looked at him with a glint of mischief in her eye and said, "Tell me, Captain Sims, have you seen my husband Private Murray anywhere?"

Jacob chuckled and said, "I told you, if I had remained Jacob Murray I would have been hanged for desertion a long time ago, and you would be a widow. Washington would have issued my death warrant if he knew the truth."

"My husband, the deserter," Maggie said with a smirk. "How do you manage to get yourself into such scrapes?"

"You know I did it for Israel after the disaster at the Great Meadows. When Joshua and I decided to join up with Braddock's men, I needed a different name."

"So you deserted just to re-enlist," Maggie said with a shake of her head. "Sounds like a lot of trouble just to stay in some army that has since left us alone to fight off the savages."

Jacob grinned at her playfulness and scooped two mugs of boiling water out of the pot. He added a handful of dried herbs and waited for their tea to steep.

Maggie unfolded a small silk cloth and divided up a couple of pieces of hard cheese and some dried pork. Jacob grabbed what was left of a loaf of corn bread and sliced it into several pieces.

"Heaven," Jacob teased.

"Sadly, at one time we would have thought so," Maggie replied as a small tear ran down her face.

They ate and drank in silence, but peace had settled over them once more. When they finished, Maggie began to clean up when a loud knock sounded at the door.

"Sir, may I enter?" Joshua respectfully called out before entering.

"Come in, lad, we were just finishing our meal." Jacob replied. He was not particularly ready to resume his duties, but it couldn't be helped.

Flushed from a sprint across the parade grounds, Joshua tried to catch his breath as he spoke, "Sorry for the intrusion, but we have some visitors that you might want to speak with."

"No need to apologize, Joshua, you are always welcome here," Maggie said.

"Thank you, Ma'am," he said as he touched his hat and walked inside.

"What is the news, lad?" Jacob asked gruffly, annoyed that his time with Maggie had ended.

"I was out with a few of the men scouting the eastern forest and we ran right into the advanced guard of Colonel Armstrong's company. We escorted them to the fort and he is outside waiting to speak with you."

Jacob moved slowly as he looked for his coat and straightened his clothes. "I wouldn't want to appear unkempt before the colonel, would I?" he asked with feigned innocence.

"The two messengers just gave us word a few days earlier; they certainly didn't give us a lot of time to prepare," Jacob muttered under his breath.

Maggie smiled and said, "Joshua, please keep him out of trouble."

Joshua smirked and followed Jacob outside.

Most of the fort's garrison was gathered up on the bastions looking down on the large company stationed outside.

Jacob saw that an older gentleman and several other officers had entered the main gate and stood looking around at the inside of the fort's well-built walls.

"Captain Sims I presume," the man said as Jacob approached him. "I am Colonel John Armstrong. This is a very nice fort you have built for yourself."

"Thank you, sir," Jacob said politely. "I accept your compliments on behalf of Mr. Tate and his engineers. They did an outstanding job on her construction."

Jacob noticed that Armstrong's clothing was actually a tailored suit that had been fashioned into a military style uniform. He was well groomed and Jacob's first thought was that this was a man with very little experience fighting in the wilderness. He was probably far better suited for the stuffy halls of the provincial legislature or some Philadelphia courthouse. The need for a politician had passed and Jacob feared that any assault against Captain Jacobs proposed by Armstrong would be futile.

"I am surprised that you arrived so soon, sir," Jacob said, trying hard not to sound defensive. "We just received word of your efforts a few days ago."

The small contingent of officers lined up just behind Armstrong as he offered his hand to Jacob and said, "Good to finally meet you, Sims. Your reputation has reached as far as Philadelphia."

"I hope it is all good, sir," Jacob laughed as he returned the handshake.

"Of course," Armstrong replied and turned to introduce his officers. "These are captains Potter, Steel and Mercer from Fort Shirley, and Captain Ward from Fort George."

Jacob nodded and said, "Gentlemen, it's nice to have you this far west. To what do I owe such an honor?"

The colonel smiled and said, "I like that you don't waste time, Sims. If you would be so kind as to give me a tour of your outer earthen works for a moment, I need to speak with you privately." He motioned the others to wait and walked with Jacob towards the main gates.

"I heard you have been attacked by the damn Delaware," Armstrong began.

"Yes, sir, they hit us last night and killed my brother."

"I too lost a brother at the hands of the savages. Have you heard about the siege on Fort Granville? The Delaware butchered the entire garrison, taking only a couple captives. My brother was the fort's commander." Armstrong spoke without sadness, but his voice was steely.

As they worked their way along the southern stretch of the earthen works, the colonel stopped and looked into the woods, where the trees were thick and the tangled brush had grown as high as a man's head.

After a moment, he continued, "I want Captain Jacobs and that bloody Shingas to pay for their actions. God knows I want to avenge my brother's death, but more importantly, we need to rid this land of all the savages and their French protectors."

Jacob felt the hatred in his voice and began to rethink his initial impression of the man.

"What do you need from us, sir?" Jacob asked, still unsure why he had asked for this private meeting.

Armstrong walked a little farther from the fort towards the woods and said, "I would like to leave some of my provincial troops here while I organize additional volunteers at Fort Shirley. I plan on attacking the Delaware at their main village at Kittanning. Your fort practically sits right on the old Kittanning Trail. If we use this place as a point to gather all our forces, the attack will be far better organized. I also need you to scout the village and give me some details of the layout and surrounding terrain."

Jacob bristled at Armstrong's assumed command of the fort, but he was a superior officer and it was a military fort. The thought of having the chance to strike back at the Delaware with some force smoothed his ruffled feathers and he began to look forward to their victory.

When Jacob didn't respond, Armstrong began speaking again. "I hear you are part of Stevens' Ranging Company. I have never had the pleasure working with rangers, but I am sure you will prove to be useful."

Ignoring the slight against him and his men, Jacob calmly replied, "Well, sir, as I'm sure you're aware, Major Stevens died from the pox last winter. I'm not certain what we should call ourselves now, but we have already scouted the village, sir. I will have one of the men draw up a detailed map of the area. I have personal experience with this trail as I've traveled it many times. It will be nice to take the fight to the Delaware for a change."

"I had never met Stevens, but it is always a shame to lose a good officer," Armstrong said without evidence of sympathy in his voice. "A map would be very helpful indeed. What are your thoughts about the place?"

"The main village appears to be just a number of unorganized bark homes with a large longhouse meeting place in the center. It is situated between two facing hills with the river on one side. The hill on southern side of the village provides a great vantage point to view the place and possibly launch an attack. The town itself is very maze-like and there is another smaller village directly across the river from it."

As Jacob spoke, he sensed that the colonel was not paying him any heed. Instead, he seemed fixated on the nearby forest.

When Armstrong spoke, he was unfailingly upbeat despite all that Jacob had described. "The plan is to leave Fort Shirley at the month's end. I will amass enough men to lead a sufficient attack and bring them here to reorganize before the assault. I feel you will be a valuable piece to all of this, Sims."

The two men resumed their walk and Jacob asked, "What of the French? Have you heard anything about their intentions?"

"I have no fear of the bloody French," Armstrong scoffed. "They have shown us all that they prefer is to let the savages to do their dirty work. I will leave seventy-five men with you and I've heard that I will be able to collect another two hundred or so by the end of August."

They walked near enough to the tree line for the colonel to snag a massive leaf from an over-hanging branch. "This is damn beautiful country, Sims, and I plan on making it better once the bloody heathens are killed off."

Jacob's mind was clouded with the excitement of making Captain Jacobs suffer as he had suffered with Israel's murder. After a few moments he said, "The last time we scouted the village, we only saw women and children and a large group of white captives. That means the warriors were probably out raiding. If we leave only a small garrison at each fort, what will stop them from avoiding us and attacking each of the under-manned forts?"

"If we attack the village and it is filled only with their women and children," Armstrong responded with a sneer, "we will kill them and leave the Delaware a warning. We will not just sit idly by while they attack our homesteads."

His own attitude towards the warriors had certainly undergone a transformation the previous night, but the thought of killing women and children as an offensive tactic did not sit well with Jacob. He made no response.

"The bloody savages have killed their share of our women and children, so we will respond in kind," Armstrong added, walking ahead of Jacob.

They returned to the fort in what was for Jacob an uncomfortable silence. They passed the new company of provincial troops that was already starting to organize their encampment between the earthen works and the fort's western wall.

Jacob let Armstrong walk into the fort to find his officers while he took a solitary walk to gather his thoughts and check on the pickets he had placed around the four corners of the field. He returned just as Armstrong and his officers were ready to depart for Fort Shirley.

Armstrong noticed his return and immediately called out to him, "Captain Sims, we are just about to leave, but I just need to go over a couple additional details."

Jacob nodded and walked directly to where the other officers waited patiently. "I'm sorry I made you wait, sir," he said. "I was just making sure the pickets were all in order."

"Fine, Sims, but we must get on the trail shortly. I just want to clarify that the men left behind are under your watch, but you should speak with Corporal Butler. Also, I need you to organize a local militia to add to our numbers. Since I am not including the men you already have under your command now, I expect another fifty good men added to the ranks."

Jacob made no reply, but simply gave him a half salute. He was relieved when Armstrong and his officers were on their way, and decided to look for this Butler character to introduce himself.

He walked through the gates and looked at the growing field of white tents set in a circular design with a large fire pit in the middle. A lone, informally dressed man sat on one of the many tree stumps, cleaning his musket. Jacob assumed he was on duty, but the man didn't once look up as he approached him and said, "Soldier, where can I find Corporal Butler?"

Without glancing up, the young man asked, "Who wants to know?"

Jacob sensed that this group was left here because they were the problem unit. "Get on your feet, boy," he snarled, "or I will have you tied to a tree for the Delaware to deal with."

The man said nothing, but stood up. It was clear that he was expecting to stand eye to eye with the man that was disturbing him, but his eyes met Jacob's chest instead.

He looked up at Jacob's face and stammered, "Sir…excuse me, um…Sir, Butler should be by the fire pit in the center of the camp…sir."

"Sit your sorry bottom down, boy!" Jacob ordered as he walked past. "Next time, show me and my men some respect."

He didn't look back, but made his way through the first line of tents. He was welcomed with glares and whispers until he finally found his way to the center of the camp.

He was met with a large roaring fire and a handful of men standing around it. "Gentlemen, do any of you know where I can find Corporal Butler?" Jacob asked.

The only man who bothered to reply stepped from behind the fire and asked, "Who wants to know?"

Tired of these men already, Jacob looked around the camp to see what he was going to be dealing with. Although the tents were in some order, the men were far from orderly. Jacob was used to militia volunteers being dressed in various styles of clothing, yet these men were particularly poorly attired. Some only wore Indian-style breechcloths; others had different combinations of used British uniform coats and waistcoats. They were dirty and the odor that waffled through the air made a skunk's musk rival the best of Maggie's rose water.

"I'm Captain Sims, and your Colonel Armstrong put you sorry lot under my command," Jacob shouted back, having earlier spent all his patience on the guard.

"I am Butler; what do you want?" the man replied in the same tone as before. Butler was short, thin and would never frighten a sane man. His nose was far too large for his face, and it was hard not to stare at it. Jacob guessed that if they stood side by side, Butler would only reach his armpits. The very sight of him made it difficult not to laugh out loud. If he were cleaned up and dressed better, he'd look more like a school teacher than a soldier ready to fight the Delaware.

Jacob knew the men were testing his authority, so he decided to give them something to think about. "Butler, where did you get the wood for this fire?" he asked. "I assume your men cut down a couple of trees."

Attempting to show up Jacob, Butler smiled and said, "No, sir, we grabbed a load from the wood pile near that burnt out building."

Jacob stepped forward, lowering his head until he was level with Butler's face. "So you stole the wood? That wood is for the fort, not for you or your men."

Butler remained defiant and calmly explained, "I will have some of the men go into the woods and cut down a few trees. We will replace what we took and no one will know the difference." He obviously thought their conversation was over, because he took a seat on a tree stump.

"Butler, back on your feet," Jacob ordered and waited for him to get up.

He ignored the request and remained on the stump, rubbing his hands and putting them near the fire.

"Stealing is a very serious offense in any army, even in an army of no-good volunteers." Jacob could see he had finally gotten the attention of Butler and several other men as they began to congregate around the fire.

Butler stood and looked confused. His tone was far less defiant when he said, "Sir, we did not steal your wood. We merely borrowed some. We have full intentions of replacing every piece we used."

Seeing he had all the men's attention now, Jacob stepped closer and glanced at the fort. A large crowd was still gathered on the high bastions and he called out, "Mr. Tate, please have some of the men come out to the camp, and please prepare the flogging post."

Butler's men saw Tate wave his approval and, within moments, fifteen heavily-armed rangers stood behind Jacob awaiting his orders.

"Sir, please…we meant no disrespect," Butler pleaded, all signs of defiance banished.

Jacob had no intentions of backing down, but he also had no intentions of putting any of the men under the lash. This was not the strict British army, and the colonial militia was not nearly as disciplined. However, militiamen would fight to the last man, and that was hard to say about the abused British regulars.

"Corporal Butler, please give me the offending thieves and we will deal with them. If you refuse, you will be put in the stockade and stay there until Armstrong returns." Jacob motioned his men to shoulder their muskets.

That act made some of the provincials do the same, so it became a standoff with close to forty muskets pointed at one another. Everyone waited tensely for someone to take the first shot.

The sight of Jacob and fifteen muskets pointing at him, made Butler back down and advise his men to stand down as well. "Save your powder for the Delaware," he said. "Captain, please have your men do the same, then maybe we can talk like civilized men?"

Jacob knew he had won the day, but he wanted to have more fun with this Butler character and teach him a good lesson. In a grave tone he said, "Butler, you must realize that we have gone too far with this. If I don't make an example of someone, then either you or your men will think that if you break our laws, I will just turn away and ignore them."

Clearly at a loss for words, Butler stumbled to save some face, "I will take responsibility for the men's actions. You can throw me in your stockade."

"That is all well and good, Butler, but what shall I do with the whipping post I just had my men construct? If I back down, how can I be a leader to these men?"

A brief silence settled over the camp until Tate called down from the upper wall of the fort, "Sir, we have the post up and ready for your orders. Mills, the blacksmith, has volunteered his services in issuing the lashes."

Butler was in a full panic, as were a number of his men. "Now, sir," he said, "please…you can't."

Butler's pathetic objections were met with a deaf ear as Jacob said, "You heard Mr. Tate; he has the post and the smithy waiting for some action."

"Can I have a private conversation with you, man-to-man?" Butler asked breathlessly.

"Private White," Jacob said, "have the men disperse this sorry lot and wait for my return." He turned and smirked at White as he led Butler away.

White immediately shouted, "Get your sorry behinds back into your tents, boys, or I will decide who else should meet the whip's end."

Jacob allowed the much more polite and gracious Butler to lead him to his spacious tent. He remained at the entrance and waited for Butler to speak first.

"A glass of rum, sir?" he asked nervously.

Jacob made no response, so he continued uncomfortably, "I must first offer an apology for my rudeness. I am a big enough man to admit that I was wrong."

Covering his barely repressed laughter, Jacob continued to stare at Butler as the man continued to nervously babble.

"Sir, your point is made. I will not do anything like this again. I just want to somehow start over?" Butler pleaded.

Jacob slowly replied, "All I need from you is the men who stole our wood," and began to walk away.

Butler jumped up and grabbed Jacob's arm, saying, "Damn it, man, we are on the same side!"

Jacob quickly pulled Butler's hand and twisted it back over the shocked man's shoulder. Putting all his strength on the middle of Butler's back, Jacob pushed him into the tent and forced his face down onto the small table where the silver flask of rum sat. The rum fell to the ground and emptied onto the dirt. Butler let out a brief moan, and Jacob figured it was due more to the sight of the rum soaking into the ground than any pain that had been inflicted.

Jacob put his mouth close to Butler's ear and spoke in a soft voice, "Now, Mr. Butler, from this point forward you will call me 'Captain' and nothing else. If I see or hear any of your men causing problems around the fort, you will be held accountable. The flogging post will remain up in the parade grounds as a reminder to you and your men that I have no patience for any issues that might arise from this camp."

Butler struggled to reply but Jacob gave him no opportunity, "I will leave you to organize a scouting party to head north and follow the main trail to the Delaware village; it's about a day's march from here, probably two for your sorry lot. You will also send out two more work crews to cut down trees and replace the wood you 'borrowed' and supply your own camp with wood."

Jacob finally released his grip and slowly took all his weight off of Butler's back. He let him up and said, "Do not cause any problems with the Delaware. I just need you to scout the area and bring back a report of what is happening around the village."

Leaving Butler to nurse his wounded pride and his sore back, Jacob departed and walked back to the fort with Private White who had stood near the opening of the tent.

"I assume the men gave you no problems?" Jacob asked.

"They talk a good fight, but they had no stomach for it," White said with a laugh. "I pray they will change their minds if the Delaware come calling again."

Just before they reached the main gates, Private White asked, "Sir, did you have any intentions of putting one of them under the lash?"

"Never crossed my mind, White," Jacob laughed and patted White on the back. "I don't believe in the punishment, but it does make a great threat!"

White walked into the fort and just shook his head.

Jacob made his way up the ladder to find Mr. Tate in his usual perch. He shook the engineer's hand and said, "Thank you for your assistance, John. The men got the point and the post makes for a good reminder to all of them."

"No need to thank me, Jacob. I gathered you were just trying to make a point."

Jacob remained on the wall long enough to see Butler and half of the men depart towards the Kittanning Trail. He watched as two other groups

made their way into the forest. The sound of falling trees and men chopping wood echoed through the fort for several hours; each loud thud made
Jacob smile.

It had been almost a week since Butler and his men left to scout around
the village of Kittanning. Jacob thought to send out a search party to find
them, but if something was happening with the Delaware, weakening his
garrison would leave the fort exposed to an attack.

Jacob spent most of his days standing on the western bastion, watching for any sign of the returning party. The thought of pulling the rest of
Butler's camp into the fort's walls had crossed his mind, but he quickly
decided against it. He wagered that the sight of so many tents would make
the Delaware think twice about raiding such a well-manned fort.

During the same time, Jacob had received several messages from
Armstrong that the rest of his army of volunteers would be arriving within
the next week. Jacob had found very few volunteers for the militia; most of
the nearby settlers decided to stay and defend their own homes. He could
hardly blame them. He had reminded them that their families would be
welcomed at the fort, but many settlers questioned how safe the fort would
be if most of the men were out attacking Kittanning.

The next morning was a particularly foggy one when Butler and his
men made their way into the camp. Before their advance scout had even
reached the fort, Jacob stood waiting in front of Butler's tent.

"Where the hell were you, Butler? I have not heard a word from you or
your men for a week."

"Sir, we lost track of time. For two days, we walked in circles trying to
find the damn village. This bloody wilderness is just a big maze of trees and
swamps. I'm not sure what was worse, the bloody Delaware or the packs
of mosquitoes that ate at us for the entire trip." Butler scratched at his face
covered in bites.

The man was clearly fatigued and showed signs of a rough trip, so Jacob
lightened his tone as he continued, "Next time, send a man back for help.
We thought you ran into the Delaware and got yourselves killed."

"Damn near did, sir," Butler explained, searching through his belongings for something. "We even ran into the French near the river."

"Tell me more about the French," Jacob asked with his interest fully peaked now. "Where did you see them and how many were there?"

"It was a few miles from the main village. There were four large boats, packed with men. I guess they were heading towards that Kittanning place." Butler explained still searching as he spoke.

"Damn it man, what are you looking for?" Jacob finally asked the distracted Butler.

"I need a shot of rum sir…to calm my nerves." He explained and finally found a small jug that he immediately uncorked.

Jacob could see that Butler was in no condition to offer much more and dismissed him to his tent, adding, "I expect a full, detailed report before dusk, Butler. For now, get some rest and make sure your men do the same."

Looking back, Jacob watched Butler take a long drink directly from the jug and fall into his small chair. He smiled to himself as he walked through the rows of tents that were now pleasantly quiet with resting and tired men.

He hoped now that Butler and his sorry lot understood how challenging this wilderness could be. This scouting trip they experienced would probably turn out to be a far more effective deterrent than any threat of lashes ever could.

Jacob continued to spend time each day on the wall, overlooking the wilderness. His second conversation with Butler upon his return several weeks ago had yielded few additional details.

The weather had been uncomfortably hot for several months and the biting insects were becoming a problem with the men. One of the only parts of Armstrong's plans Jacob was happy with was the timing. By late August, early September, the hot days of summer would likely give way to much cooler air and provide the men some relief from the hordes of mosquitoes and sand flies.

He sent small groups of scouts out every few days into the bug-infested woods, but nothing was reported back aside from the usual signs of some minor Delaware activity. The French were on the move, but they were sticking close to the river.

One afternoon, Jacob stared off into the distance, hoping that somehow he might be able to see signs of what the French and their savage allies might be planning. He was so lost in his thoughts that he failed to hear the arrival of the advanced column of Armstrong's provincial militia and volunteers approaching from the east. If not for Joshua's polite call from the front gates, he would have kept staring off into the endless wilderness.

"Excuse me, sir," Joshua said. "There is a Captain Mercer here who would like to speak with you."

Shaking himself back to the present, Jacob immediately rushed down the ladder to greet the new arrivals. He quickly noted that Mercer was one of the officers that had visited a month earlier with Colonel Armstrong. "Captain, it is good to see you again," Jacob welcomed the man graciously.

Mercer was well-dressed and Jacob guessed him to be in his thirties. Despite the fact he carried himself like a military man, this young officer had no more experience than Jacob had.

"Sims, it's good to see you as well," Mercer replied, offering a firm handshake. "How did you get along with our Corporal Butler and his group of vagrants and thieves?"

Jacob paused to choose his words and said, "Fine, once I set the limits of his authority. Frankly, he did a reasonable job scouting for us, despite getting himself lost in the woods."

Mercer laughed and changed topics. "I was sent ahead by our commander to make sure your fort is ready to receive the approaching companies."

Jacob watched Mercer scan the outer walls of the fort and it was difficult to know what he was thinking.

"When do you expect the arrival of the rest of the men?" Jacob interrupted Mercer's visual inspection.

"They are a half-day behind us and should be here by dawn tomorrow," Mercer replied, stepping through the gates to take another good look around. "It does appear you have prepared well. How many men do you have under your command?"

Jacob laughed to himself and wondered exactly what he had done to prepare for their arrival. He followed Mercer inside and replied,

"I have seventy two rangers and militia, along with seventy five of Butler's contingent."

"How many of the men around these parts volunteered for the militia?"

Annoyed by so many questions, Jacob simply replied, "Not many, most of them have decided to stay behind and defend their families. What is Armstrong bringing with him?

"The colonel has five companies to add to your two. Frankly they are not at full strength, but I think we were going to supplement the companies with some of your men." Mercer spoke with an authority that was meant to show Jacob he was friends with Armstrong.

"Captain," Jacob said coolly, "it appears that you and the colonel believe you have assumed command of my fort and my men. Let me set the record straight and tell you here and now that my men are under my command and I will decide where and when we fight."

Mercer was clearly taken aback by Jacob's blunt question of authority and a ferocious scowl clouded his face as he said, "I see you and Butler have the same attitude towards authority within a military operation."

Jacob cut him off before he could utter another word and said, "No disrespect, captain, but what experience do you have fighting in this part of the territory?"

Once again Mercer showed his disdain for Jacob and scoffed, "And you, sir, what of your own military experience?"

Jacob just smiled and knew he had this arrogant, spoiled man right in his sights. "Next time you have tea with your dear Washington, ask him about the Great Meadows and Braddock. I have also spent time in the stockades in Fort Duquesne and have been a captive of the same Captain Jacobs you both seek to kill. In fact, I was held prisoner in the same village your commander hopes to defeat, but at the time it was inhabited by more than just women and children."

Jacob waited for Mercer to offer up his own credentials or defend his friend, but the officer remained silent. Jacob turned the conversation back to the matter at hand, "Once the rest of you arrive, what is the plan for continuing on towards Kittanning?"

Mercer acted as though the previous conversation had never happened and simply offered, "That is up to the colonel. I assume he will tell us what he expects from us."

Jacob had nothing further to say. Conversing with this man was a futile effort. He waited for Mercer to add anything else relevant to the conversation, but was relieved when he touched his hat instead and excused himself.

Jacob looked around for Joshua and saw him speaking with the blacksmith's assistant. He called to him as he walked closer, but it took him a few moments to get the young man's attention over the noise of the smithy's hammer on a red hot horseshoe.

"Lad, I need you to gather up a small escort to head east and find the rest of Armstrong's army. I was told they were a half day's march from here, so if you leave promptly, you should be able to lead them here just as the sun rises."

"Yes, sir," Joshua responded. "Do you have a message for Colonel Armstrong?"

"No, I just want to make sure they get here in one piece. They have a grand plan, after all, to finally rid this territory of the Delaware. You know, if we're really lucky, they might even let us tag along." Jacob hadn't meant to be so sarcastic or even bother Joshua with the details of his conversation with Mercer, but he found it difficult to hide his frustration.

Joshua looked at him with some surprise and plenty of curiosity, and Jacob quickly added, "Sorry lad, please don't mind me; just do as I requested and get the colonel here safely."

Joshua nodded and departed to organize his escort party. Jacob stood thinking for a moment and decided to check with Butler to collect any details from his scouts that he may not have heard yet.

He spotted privates White and Sinclair entering the parade grounds and approached them as they rested their muskets by the small fire.

"Gentlemen, what word do you have for me?" he asked.

He hadn't expected much from them, knowing that if they had any real news to report, they would have come straight to him. Therefore, White took him by surprise by launching into a tirade of his own. "What is with the men at that bloody camp out front? Have any of them spent any time outside in the woods at all? They are all bloody daft. They couldn't shoot into the forest and hit a tree."

"I have nothing much to say about them," Jacob said, keeping his amusement to himself. "I just pray that if we do end up in the fight with the

Delaware, they stay in the rear." The other two nodded and Jacob walked away to let them enjoy the fire.

Jacob decided not to bother with Butler, leaving Armstrong to deal with him. Instead, he did a quick inspection of the barracks and visited with a couple of the families who had decided to remain at the fort.

After an uneventful night, Jacob rose before the sun. Unable to sleep and worried that his pacing might disturb Maggie, he spent most of the early morning on the eastern facing bastion, waiting to hear any noise that would signal the arrival of the rest of the army.

He walked around the upper walls, casually speaking with the poor guards stuck on the late night picket duty. Jacob observed the large grouping of tents that now littered the field between the wall and the works. The fires that gave the camp some light flickered for most of the night, replenished by the men on guard duty.

Jacob was happy that Captain Mercer had spent the night with Butler, but he anticipated a heated discussion with Armstrong and the other officers about the role he was expected to play in all of this.

The sun had moved and produced enough light that the torches on the walls were extinguished, and the men scheduled for morning guard duty slowly made their way out of the comforts of their barracks. The sun also gave Jacob a much clearer view of the forest facing the eastern wall.

The first signs of the army started to appear in the far field and soon Jacob saw Joshua offering up a hearty wave just as he guided a company of men through the first line of tree stumps.

The men looked like the typical colonial provincial militia; they were clothed in various informal uniforms or attire they would have worn working their own fields. They marched in good order, but no match for the heavily drilled British regulars that Jacob had seen many times. Jacob looked them over from his distant vantage point and was relatively impressed with how they carried themselves. How they would fight once the Delaware unleashed their deafening war cries and their mates start to fall around them was another issue. He knew it was a test for the best of men and these men would soon be put in situations that most would never wish on their worst enemy.

Armstrong finally came into view, sitting on a nicely groomed horse as he slowly maneuvered his way through the stumps. He never bothered to look up, so he never noticed Jacob watching his every move. The open field was now a sea of men, tents and military equipment. The murmuring voices below converged into a constant hum that was impossible to clear from one's head.

Following the main group of men were four pack horses and two large, wooden carts filled with what looked like blankets. In the rear was a baggage wagon that Jacob assumed carried Armstrong's and his officers' personal belongings.

Jacob worked his way down to the gates and fully expected Armstrong to bring his horse into the fort's stable. Instead, he saw that the colonel dismount and let his animal feed on some grass, opting to visit with Captain Mercer. Jacob anticipated that Mercer would give a full report of their encounter.

He waited for Armstrong to inform him of his orders and what was expected of him on the expedition. He assumed he would be cast into a secondary role and most of his men would be used as a reserve company. Jacob knew that if that was the case, he would decline and face some form of discipline. He absolutely refused to leave his fort vulnerable to an attack for some secondary role in Armstrong's master plan.

In an attempt to keep busy until Armstrong decided to meet with him, Jacob found Joshua waiting outside the gates. Jacob smiled and asked, "How was the march?"

From the look on Joshua's face, Jacob could see that he was not impressed with the men who had just taken over the field. "I'm not sure about all of this, sir," he responded. "The commander appears to be grossly inexperienced and has no knowledge of this area. He refused to set up a vanguard and cared little if the men remained in any particular order. His indifference scares me. He was far more concerned with his horse or that his officers were taken care of."

Jacob shook his head and looked out at the hordes of men milling about the field. He imagined that the ever-present Delaware scouts would most likely send back word to Captain Jacobs that this disorganized army could be easily overwhelmed.

"Sadly, lad, I have the same fears. If we are expected to go with them, our only hope is we will be used as a scouting unit and keep ourselves away from this lot. We are no better off than when we were with Braddock himself."

The two men stood and watched all the confusion and noise from the newcomers. Jacob soon noticed Armstrong, along with Mercer and a few of the other officers, making their way towards the fort.

"Joshua, would you be kind enough to collect privates White and Sinclair and Mr. Tate and have them meet me at my quarters shortly?"

With an understanding nod, Joshua left Jacob standing alone as the officers approached him.

"Captain Sims, good to see you well," Armstrong said as he motioned to one of the soldiers to take his horse into the stables. "What news do you have for us? Do the Delaware know we are coming?"

"Good to see you as well, sir," Jacob said politely. "It appears you have brought a small army with you."

Armstrong stood near Jacob and looked over the field, boasting, "The men are ready and if I was a Delaware warrior, I would throw down my weapons and beg us all for mercy."

The other officers laughed and nodded in agreement.

Jacob didn't react, but their over-confidence proved to him that these men had no idea what they were about to face.

"As for the Delaware, sir," Jacob continued, "I would wager they have been following you the entire trip. I would even guess they knew you were coming here even before you did." He knew that such a statement would do little to keep him on Armstrong's good side, but he had to force these fools to understand what they were going to be facing.

Armstrong and Mercer both reacted in shock, and Mercer exclaimed, "The bloody savages have probably already deserted their village and taken refuge with the French at Fort Duquesne."

"Sims," Armstrong continued arrogantly, "it is to our advantage that the Delaware have seen what they will have to fight. I too feel they will most likely run well before we reach the hill above their town."

Jacob knew better than to continue to challenge these men and attempted to change the mood, "Sir, as you requested we made a map of the layout of the main village. The only concern I have is what might lie on the other side of the Allegheny. It seems to be where the Delaware keep most of their white captives, and I have heard reports that it is home to their other leader Shingas." Jacob knelt and stretched the map on the ground, using four rocks to hold down the large piece of parchment.

"I have my sights on the main village," Armstrong said in a bored tone. "I have no real reason to be concerned with some small camp that sits on the other side of the damn river. Besides, this Shingas fellow was badly injured a few months back; he might even be dead by this time."

Jacob ignored the colonel's misguided self-confidence and claims and said, "The last time I personally scouted around Kittanning, there were a couple of large French bateaux beached on the bank by the corn field on the opposite shore from the main village. If the Delaware have support from the French, we just might run into more problems than we have anticipated."

Armstrong pushed the rocks aside and grabbed the map for a closer look. "Despite Captain Sims' clear opinion that we have no chance to take this place," he said, "let me point out this good sized hill that sits above the village. There also appears no rhyme or reason to the layout of their village and that should give them some difficulties in defending their homes."

Armstrong pointed to the map, and the other officers gathered around to get a better look. Jacob stood by knowing full well that it mattered little what he thought or what ideas he could contribute. These men would do what they wanted, according to their own beliefs of the situation. He also knew that a leader blinded by revenge cared nothing for details. Armstrong wanted the Delaware to pay for his brother's death at all costs, no matter how many of his men were sacrificed.

Jacob could tell that most of these officers would trust Armstrong even if he asked them to blindly charge an entrenched company of French regulars. If their leader told them to do it, they would do it with no questions asked.

It had been the same misguided confidence that cost the British at Fort Necessity and on the shores of the Monongahela. Jacob privately wondered when these fools would finally learn that the Delaware would not run and their French allies' tactics were far superior to their European-style of wilderness fighting.

Unable to hold his tongue, Jacob pointed out, "Gentlemen, I marched with Braddock. He too felt the savages would not put up much of a fight. You know what happened to him, and that was in the middle of the wilderness, where there were no homes, women and children to defend."

"Braddock was a fool," Armstrong snapped. "Look what happened to the British…where the hell are they now?" He looked to his officers for their agreement and, as expected, they all sneered at Jacob's observations before returning their attention to the map.

Praying that he could just leave these men to plan their own deaths, Jacob said, "Sir, I need to organize my men and await your orders. Should I assume we will be leaving at first light tomorrow?"

Barely acknowledging Jacob's question, Armstrong replied, "Do what you need to do, Sims. I will fill you in with all the details in good time."

Jacob immediately left the officers and happily went directly to his quarters. He thought of how nice it would be to speak with men that had some common sense. The men Joshua had gathered would know very well what would transpire if they joined in with this band of raw volunteers.

He stepped through the door into the cozy confines of the room, and was greeted by the sight of Joshua, Tate, Sinclair and White sitting around the table enjoying a freshly brewed kettle of tea and some sliced bread compliments of his Maggie.

"God, gentlemen, I hope I am not distracting you lot from all this fine service," Jacob smirked and went over to kiss Maggie on the cheek.

Private White boldly replied, "Your fine wife has taken excellent care of us, despite our sad appearance."

"They have all been perfect gentlemen and I am glad to bring some pleasure to their miserable lives," Maggie laughed, patting Joshua gently on his head.

"Well, back to reality, lads," Jacob said as he took a seat next to Joshua and accepted a cup of tea. "We need to talk about this proposed raid on Kittanning. My fear is that this Armstrong character will lead these poor souls to their deaths."

While the men discussed their plans, Maggie sat in a chair right by the fire and did some needle work on one of Jacob's shirts.

"Do we know what this Armstrong wants from us and the fort?" Tate asked.

"Not entirely sure, but he appears to have a plan that includes us in some way. I fear he will want to take most of our men, leaving the fort dangerously under-manned. If the Delaware get word of this, they might go around us and strike the fort while we're left with an empty village."

"Have we spoken to the settlers around the fort and told them of the plan to attack Kittanning?" Joshua questioned.

"Most of them felt staying on their land was better, despite the fear that the Delaware might launch further raids to avenge the attack." Jacob replied.

The men all took a couple sips of their tea and waited for Jacob to suggest what they might do.

A hard knock on the door broke their silence. Maggie opened the door and welcomed Armstrong, Mercer and another officer that Jacob remembered was named Potter.

"Ma'am, may we speak with Captain Sims?" Armstrong asked politely as he removed his hat.

Briefly hesitating, still not used to the name Sims, Maggie graciously let them in and answered, "Jacob is over there."

Jacob had already gotten up and was near the door to greet the men, saying, "Gentlemen, please come in. I was just discussing our circumstances with my men."

"So you are trying to convince them this is a foolhardy scheme?" Armstrong calmly retorted.

Letting the slight against him slip, Jacob offered his seat to Armstrong and waited for him to continue the conversation.

Getting down to business and unraveling the map that he had tucked into his coat pocket, Armstrong pointed to his two captains to hold the corners flat. "Gentlemen," he said, "the plan is to attack the village from the hill, as well as using the cover of the cornfield near the river. If we all play our part, I feel that overtaking the surprised Delaware will be relatively easy. The only problem might be if they use the number of houses and huts as cover. Our boys will have to fight them at a slight disadvantage and it will possibly take a bit more time."

Armstrong stopped momentarily, expecting someone to speak up but was met with silence. He quickly continued, "What I would like your lads to do, Sims, is to do your ranging thing and clear the trail of any 'issues' that might arise. You will wait for us at the designated hill and, if you feel up to it, join in on the attack."

Jacob could hear the sarcasm in Armstrong's voice but refused to be bullied into saying something he might soon regret. "How many men will be left behind to garrison the fort?" he asked.

"I feel ten, maybe twelve bodies will be sufficient to man such a fort," Armstrong responded haughtily. "I think you can leave Mr. Tate and his carpenters behind to guard the place."

Jacob could see that Tate was about to speak out, but a slight touch on his arm kept him silent.

"I trust Mr. Tate's good sense and leadership," Jacob said, "and his men are outstanding engineers and craftsmen. However, asking them to take up arms to defend the fort without the assistance of additional militiamen or rangers is far too much to expect of them."

"With their skills and familiarity with the fort, who better to guard it while you are away?" Armstrong mocked, clearly trying to rile Jacob.

Not wanting to waste his breath, Jacob accepted his role and simply offered, "I will have my men ready and equipped to leave at dawn. We should be at the hill before nightfall."

He assumed the uncomfortable meeting was at an end, but he saw Armstrong giving significant glances to his two captains and wondered what was yet to come. "Captain Sims," Armstrong said, "you are to leave immediately. Please get your men in order and be on the trail within half an hour."

Jacob caught Mercer smirking like a little boy who had just tattled on his mate. Jacob could tell that the inexperienced captain had his hands all over this, but ignored him so as to refuse him the satisfaction of knowing he had gotten under Jacob's skin.

Armstrong appeared to have nothing further to add and stood up, tipping his hat to Maggie and walked to the door. Before he had a chance to reach for the latch, the dumbfounded Jacob said, "Sir, it is nearly midday. You want us to scout part of the trail at night? When should we expect your main force to arrive?"

"You fellows should be able to travel these trails blindfolded, at least that was what I've been led to believe. I was under the impression your backwoodsmen scouted any time of the day or night." Armstrong stepped out the door with his two officers trailing right behind him.

He poked his head back into the room and said, "One more thing, Sims, Butler and his men have been reassigned to Captain Mercer's company, and so you will be commanding only your own company of rangers."

Jacob just stood by the table and could not think of anything to say. He could tell that his men were just as shocked at Armstrong's audacity as he was.

Jacob looked at Maggie and wondered how he could ever make this up to her.

Chapter | **Sixteen**

After several moments of silence, Jacob looked around the room and said, "We might as well call this fool 'Braddock'. It does go to show that not all idiots are confined to the British army."

The men laughed and all appeared to agree with Jacob's frustration.

Private White was finally the first to offer his opinion, "We would better serve the settlers and the territory if we just remained at the fort and let Armstrong and his boys get themselves killed.

No one else offered their thoughts, so Jacob simply ordered, "Private you are so right but we all heard the plan; Sinclair and White, please get the men prepared to leave. Joshua, please check on our supplies and equipment."

Tate watched as the others left and waited until the door shut behind them, "Jacob, you can't expect my men to garrison this fort with any hope of fighting off the Delaware if they attack us."

Taking a deep breath, Jacob explained, "If we use the available men that are here with their families and I keep a few of the 'sick and injured' behind, I think you should have up to thirty men to keep the fort in order."

"Do you honestly feel thirty men, half of them carpenters and laborers, could possibly fight off all the Delaware in the territory?" Tate countered, openly concerned.

"I have little options John," Jacob said. "If I disobey the order, Armstrong will just remove me from my command and assign one of his men to lead the scout. Either way, you will be in the same position. At least my way I can give you some additional bodies and, if by chance the fort is attacked, you should be able to hold them off until we return."

Tate nodded but could not hide his frustration and left without saying another word.

"What are your thoughts?" Jacob asked Maggie once they were finally alone.

Maggie took a seat at the table and said, "This Armstrong character is going to get most of his poor boys killed. My only fear is that you might die with them."

Jacob sat beside her and put his arm around her. He knew she was only holding back tears for his sake. "No bloody fool or the Delaware are going to take me away from you," he said in a soothing voice. "I'll be damned if I lose you again after all we've been through."

When she didn't respond, he played to her strength, "Maggie, just make sure the families are getting along and help Mr. Tate to keep the fort going until I return."

"If you return…" Maggie said as her tears finally broke through.

Realizing he could not say or do anything to make this better, Jacob pulled Maggie out of her chair and hugged her. Fighting off his own tears, he whispered, "Have faith in me. I will come back and then take you away from all of this…I promise."

The two exchanged kisses and Maggie made sure Jacob had a sack full of food and supplies before he reluctantly departed.

She stood in the open door while Jacob waved and left to find Joshua.

Jacob didn't bother to speak with Armstrong or any of his officers before he left with fifty-five men. Joshua, White and Sinclair were among the scouting party, but Jacob decided to leave young Caleb Kennedy among the twenty-two men he managed to assign to John Tate. The men were a mixture of Tate's own unit with some of the soldiers who were recovering from injuries or illness. The garrison's number grew with the arrival of several families who had reconsidered the offer of protection from potential raids.

Still fearing a counter-attack from the Delaware, Jacob thought of taking Maggie with him, but he realized a single female traveling through the woods with three hundred men might cause some uncomfortable situations. It would have been nice to have her company and she was probably a better shot than most of Armstrong's men anyway. Jacob knew she would be useful in caring for the families that had taken refuge at the fort, and hopefully she was much safer behind its walls.

Despite his own foul mood and his lack of confidence in Armstrong's leadership capabilities, Jacob left along with the advanced guard of ten men. As usual, Private Sinclair was with the lead guard and Private White had taken up the rear about a half mile from the main unit.

They had all traveled the old Kittanning trail many times over the months. It was an easy, well-used path that would take them directly to the village. After a short march north along the Allegheny ridge line, it would veer west towards the river. Leaving so late in the day was not the best of circumstances, yet Jacob and his men had traveled this trail so many times they could, as Armstrong so aptly stated, scout it 'blindfolded.'

Jacob made his way back to Joshua and the main company after walking a few miles with Sinclair. For the most part, the men appeared to be upbeat. Jacob guessed probably from the change in routine and getting out of the monotony of the daily garrison duties. The summer had been long and hot, with periods of very wet weather thrown in. They were eager to escape the muddy meadow and direct sun at the fort for the opportunity of a long trek and the chance to fight. They all knew colder weather was on its way. Once it hit, they would be stuck in the fort most days, only taking short scouts when the weather co-operated or permitted them to.

It was very unlike Jacob to let his mind wander while on the trail. He was usually on his guard at all times, but he was concerned for Maggie and plagued by worries that the fort might be attacked during his absence.

"Sir…are you alright?" Joshua asked softly. "You seem a bit troubled."

"Sorry, lad, I'm just worried about leaving the fort so short of experienced men."

"Miss Maggie will be just fine," Joshua soothed, "I have seen her fight. If the Delaware do attack the fort, they better pray to every one of their gods and spirits that she doesn't shoot them all by herself."

Jacob laughed quietly. He knew Joshua was right, but leaving her this time was more difficult than it had ever been on any of the other scouting trips.

After two hours on the march, a Captain Hamilton of one of the provincial units surprisingly rode up beside Jacob. "How does it go, Captain Sims?" he asked.

"No signs of any trouble yet," Jacob said warily, "but I am certain we have been watched this entire trip." He glanced up at the officer sent by Armstrong to check on him and thought he appeared not only amiable, but an experienced wilderness fighter.

"The colonel just wanted me to relay the message that all the companies will depart well before dawn and will meet up with you near the village," Hamilton said.

"That is good to know," Jacob replied, watching carefully to avoid being stepped on by the large mare who was having trouble on the tight quarters of the trail. "If I push my men, we should reach the hill and have our camp set up a few hours after nightfall."

"I am about to head back," Hamilton said as he pulled the reins and turned the horse around to face Jacob. "Do you have anything to pass on to the colonel?"

"No, just remind him not to dawdle, and to try to keep up with us," Jacob smiled, knowing the message would not be passed on.

Hamilton tipped his hat and with a quick jab to the mare's ribs, he galloped back towards the fort.

"You really don't like Armstrong much," Joshua observed.

"It's not that I don't like him, I just think he is in over his head and has little experience fighting the Delaware. He looks at them as just simple savages, not a real threat. He is about to learn that they are proud warriors who will defend their homes to the death. I fear Armstrong will lead us all to our deaths if he remains blinded by revenge."

The men moved at a much slower pace once the heat of the unusually warm late August afternoon sun beat down on them. Jacob had sent back word to White to watch for stragglers and keep the men moving forward. Despite their sluggish pace, Jacob's men made it within five miles of the village just before nightfall.

Private Sinclair had pulled his advanced guard back to wait for further instructions from Jacob, who stopped the main unit and sent word back to White to set up a rear picket. Two of White's men were also sent back down the trail to see where exactly Armstrong and his troops were. Sinclair was then sent on a scouting detail with five men to see what was happening at the village.

Jacob decided to move off the main trail to give the men some time to rest. He knew of a small clearing that sat just to the west of them. It was easily defendable and a perfect place to rest and could be used as a camp if they decided to stay for the night.

Jacob worked his way to the small clearing and was greeted by Joshua who had already set up pickets to protect the rest area.

"I see you have the men organized," Jacob said as he sat at the base of a large maple tree. It felt good to get off his feet and to get under some shade. Even with the sun sinking behind the trees, he felt its heat on his tired and dusty body.

Joshua sat beside Jacob and offered him a wooden canteen. Jacob tipped the canteen back and gulped a large mouthful before he realized it was rum. Choking from the initial shock, Jacob forced the rum down and said, "You could have warned me that it was rum; I thought you had offered me a nice drink of water!"

"Sorry, sir," Joshua said with a laugh. "I should have told you."

"No harm, lad; I just wasn't ready for such a taste." Jacob wiped his mouth with the back of his hand and passed the canteen back to Joshua.

Jacob was relieved that there had been no signs of the Delaware around, despite the fact that he found their absence rather strange. The trail was a main Indian land route to the east, and with the harvest of late summer crops, he had expected to run into traders and small bands of Delaware or Shawnee.

After resting for a bit, Jacob walked among the men, checking on them and reminding them to keep a watch out for signs of the enemy. Waiting on word from Sinclair, he decided to remain where they were for now and send out a couple scouting parties to check for any Delaware activity deeper in the woods.

Reports of Armstrong's movements came in from White's rear guard and Jacob was surprised that the main army was already organized and had moved out ahead of schedule. It was moving more slowly than Jacob's party though, owing to the sheer size of the group.

It wasn't long after he had sent out the scouting parties that Sinclair sent back word that the trail was clear the rest of the way to the village if Jacob wanted to move forward with the men. Sinclair's messenger also reported that the village had around a hundred warriors, but they displayed no signs that they anticipated an attack.

Jacob understood the men would most likely not sleep much. Some of them would be excited about the attack while others would be scared and spend the night in prayer. Some like Jacob would be doing a bit of both. He decided to move the men forward to take up position by the hill so that they would not have to make the five mile march in the morning.

He sent another messenger back to Armstrong with two messages. The first was informing him that he was moving his men to the hill and the second was that he would leave White's rear guard in place to assist the main body of men along the trail towards his location.

The men quickly gathered their belongings and were ready to move out. The reports from the small scouting parties had both been positive; neither had seen anything of the Delaware. Jacob organized the men into smaller groups of five, spreading them out in a line just in case they walked into an ambush. Before they moved out, he reminded them to keep their muskets at the ready and their talking to a minimum.

Jacob walked next to Joshua and they spent the better part of a mile swatting at their ever present foe.

"I was hoping these bloody bugs would have been good enough to spare us," Jacob grunted under his breath, "but the evening has done nothing to cool us down. They are making us pay for being out here so late. I just pray the men can deal with the relentless buggers."

Joshua made no reply and busied himself with keeping the mosquitoes from biting his exposed flesh.

A large number of camp fires were still burning in the Delaware village, and the light from them had been visible for the last several miles of the trek. After greeting Sinclair, Jacob requested that they walk up the hill together to survey the village, which was greatly illuminated by the flames.

"As I had the messenger explain to you," Sinclair began when they reached the top, "the villagers have been quiet and most seem to be sleeping outside near the fires. I guess the bugs don't choose sides; they bite everybody!"

The village was visible in great detail as Jacob looked down from his position. He could see the cornfield and several boats beached on both shores of the river. He strained to see any signs that the French were present, but if they were, they must have been sleeping indoors. Jacob suspected that many of the warriors might've been sleeping outside because the French choose to sleep inside, not because of the mosquito-repelling flames.

Unable to have their own fire as it would give away their position, Jacob's men dined on dried pork and hard bread. They had little relief from the mosquitoes and just lay in the grass to rest until Armstrong's men arrived.

About an hour after nightfall, Private White and his men strolled into the camp. They looked particularly exhausted and immediately collapsed onto any patches of grass that weren't already occupied. Before White joined them, he reported to Jacob.

"All is well, sir," White said. "The men behind us have stopped for the night about fifteen miles back. The colonel sent you this message." He handed Jacob a small piece of paper.

"Good work, White. Get yourself some rest."

White was more than happy to oblige Jacob. He staggered over to an open spot, tied his neck cloth over his face, and lay on the ground with his blanket draped over his tired body.

Jacob opened the note and struggled to read it in the moonlight:

'Have your men take up position on the far north side hill across from where you are presently. I need you to stop any savages from escaping through the woods once I launch the attack. If you please, have your men in position before first light. I will send a messenger to inform you when the attack will begin.'
Colonel John Armstrong

Jacob rolled up the paper and tucked it in his sleeve. He was frustrated by Armstrong's arrogance in having them travel so far to be placed basically in reserve. Jacob sat at the top of the hill for a long time, watching the village.

He had only managed to get a couple hours of rest and was up well before the sun. He immediately called on White, Sinclair and Joshua to meet with him by the trail.

Fighting not to show his anger at the insult of not participating in the main raid, Jacob briefly explained what was expected from them and dismissed them to help wake the men and organize the move to their next position.

Jacob stood at the top of the hill and observed the village. The fires had burned steadily, but he noticed no movement and most of the warriors remained asleep. He had decided to move the men around the northeastern side to avoid the river. The small village that sat on the other side of the river was still a concern, but for the moment it was Armstrong's problem.

Sinclair moved ahead with his advanced guard and Jacob set a good pace for the rest of the men to get them around the outer reaches of the village. By the time the sun peeked over the horizon, Jacob and his men were perched on the far hill with a nice view of the village and the hill that Armstrong had chosen to launch his attack.

By the time Armstrong and the main companies of his men strolled up near the outskirts of the village, it was well past midday. The colonel was forced to delay his attack as it took most of the afternoon and well into the night for the entire army to arrive and get organized.

Armstrong had sent over a couple messages to Jacob but they went ignored. Jacob didn't want anything to do with this already disorganized ambush and decided to stay with his men. He feared that the element of surprise was surely lost while Armstrong stood around wasting an entire day before launching his attack.

The late summer heat was oppressive, and most of the villagers appeared not to bother doing much at all. They either just remained in their homes or lying around the fire pits.

Waiting with his men, Jacob just let them rest and prepare themselves for the expected early morning attack. They were still unable to have a camp fire of their own, but the men relished the rare opportunity to rest and do nothing at all.

As the next morning dawned and the sun grew brighter, Jacob could see that Armstrong and most of his men were working their way through one of the large cornfields by the river. From his vantage point on the northern hill, Jacob could see the smaller village across the river in clearer detail. He feared that Armstrong's movement would be noticed by those villagers. If they alerted the main village, any surprise would be lost and the raid would be an all-out battle.

Jacob immediately sent a group of his rangers west to the river to observe what they could see of the smaller village and report back to him.

Without warning, Armstrong's men were set upon by musket fire from warriors in both villages. Their movement through the cornfield had apparently startled some of the village dogs whose frantic barks had alerted the Delaware.

Armstrong had two companies remaining on the hill. As the Delaware poured into the cornfield, the colonel signaled the men to move down into the first row of houses.

Standing above the village, Jacob watched as some of the warriors took refuge inside the houses and began to fire at the approaching troops. The action below had already turned into a mass of confusion with several small skirmishes breaking out all at once.

The Delaware warriors who had rushed into the field were driven back by the sheer number of charging militiamen and forced into the maze of houses and huts. Musket fire still came from the other side of the river but had little effect on the unorganized troops.

The smoke from the relentless musket fire on both sides began to accumulate above the village. As the scene below became obscured from Jacob's view, his scouts finally returned.

"Sir," one of the men reported, "there are only a handful of warriors on the far side of the river. It appears that most of the women and children spent the night over there. We also saw several white captives. They appear to have huddled up in a couple of the larger homes when the ambush began."

Jacob didn't want to stand idly by while the battle played out. With the news of the white captives and the much smaller force sitting across the river, he ordered Sinclair to take thirty men and clear the village of what warriors were there.

While Jacob waited for a report from Sinclair, he continued to watch the action below through breaks in the smoke. Captain Mercer and his company were taking on serious return fire from several of the houses. One well-aimed shot struck Mercer's arm, shattering it so that it hung uselessly against his side. Meanwhile, Butler and most of his men had already retreated to the heights of the hills, severely weakening the disoriented assault.

Jacob noted that Armstrong had ordered his men to torch the houses, specifically targeting the longhouse in the center of the town. Despite being riddled with constant musket fire from the nearby houses, several men converged on the large structure. Once they had sufficiently lit the dry bark that covered the entire structure, the longhouse easily went up in flames and a billowing cloud of thick black smoke choked the sky.

The screams from the few women and children left inside easily muffled the war cries that had filled the air since the attack had commenced.

Jacob instructed Joshua to remain with a small party on the hill to watch for any retreating Delaware, and moved with twenty of his men down the hill to the edge of town. Close up, the scene was even more chaotic. Dead bodies, both English and Delaware littered the small alleyways amid the confusion of screams, gunshots and out-of-control fires.

Trying desperately to locate Armstrong to see if he could reinforce the men, Jacob found that the colonel had been dragged off into the trampled cornfield with a musket ball in his shoulder. He was still shouting orders and attempting to rally his men as Jacob ran to his side.

"Sir, what can I do?" he asked. "Mercer is injured and most of the men are fighting against small pockets of resistance."

"If we give them one last push, I think we can win the day," Armstrong insisted as he continued to struggle to see what was happening.

A constant stream of men ran back and forth to report how the raid was progressing.

"Let me take my men into the town and see what we can do to rally the men," Jacob suggested, seeing one house in particular already surrounded by several dead and injured men who had attempted to flush out the defiant Delaware inside.

"Do what you can, Sims; just get that bloody Captain Jacobs," Armstrong pleaded and dropped his head.

Jacob ran directly towards the house and found Captain Hamilton trying his best to return the fire that had forced most of the troops back behind a couple of nearby smaller homes.

"How are you, sir?" Hamilton shouted over the musket fire, reloading his musket and aiming it at the bark-covered house. "We sure got ourselves into a bloody mess."

"I'm going to take my men around behind and try to burn the devils out," Jacob said and dashed off without waiting for any discussion.

A few sporadic shots wildly hit near his feet and those of his hard charging men, but went mostly ignored. Reaching an abandoned hut that supplied some cover for a couple of the men, Jacob signaled for the others to stay behind two other buildings that were used to store corn.

Jacob knelt beside a fellow ranger named Waters and eyed the back of the house he was targeting.

"We need to act quickly," Jacob said. "Waters, get a torch and some fire and I will run over to burn the damn place to the ground."

Waters did as he was told, dodging several musket balls along the way. He returned with a large tree branch wrapped with a piece of old cloth; it was already lit and burning wildly.

"Bloody hell, boy," Jacob chuckled, "I didn't expect you to bring an entire tree with you!"

He checked his surroundings once more and said, "Now, give me some cover fire and I will do my best to get this damn house burning. Watch for anyone running like hell to get out; they should make for some easy targets." He grabbed the heavy, awkward torch in his left hand and readied himself.

Before Jacob could react, Waters grabbed the torch from his hand and made a mad dash across to a house that sat directly in front of the intended target.

Once Jacob recovered from his surprise, he shouted after the young ranger, "Run, lad, and keep your head down."

The musket fire intensified as some of Armstrong's men and several of the rangers did their best to give Waters the time he needed to set the dry, bark that covered the house, ablaze. He had managed to run across the small laneway between the houses and sat with his back pressed to the house and the torch held high. He paused for a moment as he tried to catch his breath.

Jacob shouted at him, "Light the bloody place and get yourself back here!"

Just as he attempted to ignite a loose piece of bark near one of the windows, a volley of musket fire erupted and knocked him down. The torch fell to the ground and rolled a few feet from his hand. It remained lit, but the house did not.

Waters was dead.

Jacob watched the scene in desperation then instinctively left the cover of the storage shed and screamed like his charging Scottish ancestors did at Culloden. The wild, unabated cry would have frightened even the mighty Ottawa. The unexpected shriek made the men and the musket fire stop for a moment.

Seeing Jacob courageously run full out across the open area between the houses, the rest of the men opened up a wall of fire that kept most of the return fire at bay.

With a single swooping motion, Jacob picked up the torch and drove its fiery end into the bark. Sparks flew in every direction; almost upon impact, as the side of the house caught fire. Several days of hot, dry weather had turned the building into parched tinder and the flames spread rapidly.

Jacob grabbed the stiff arm of Private Waters and dragged the dead man back to the safety of the storage shed.

The house was quickly engulfed in a mass of fire and the first of its residents, a middle-aged woman, ran out and was cut down immediately by the waiting militia. Right on her heels was an unusually tall young man who skillfully discharged his musket as he ran. He met the same fate and fell just a few paces short of the dead woman.

The last resident exited and Jacob could have sworn it was Captain Jacobs. The small man stood in the flaming door frame, firing his musket off before throwing the smoking weapon to the ground. Just before he attempted to fire his drawn pistol, Jacob shouldered his musket and shot towards him.

Several other men had shot at the same time and Jacob was unsure if it was his musket ball that struck and killed the defiant Delaware. The savage fell a few feet from the doorway, firing no more.

The house was now completely engulfed in flames and spewed flames and sparks several feet into the air. A mild wind helped spread the wild sparks and soon most of the surrounding homes were burning out of control.

Convinced it was Captain Jacobs, Jacob yelled to the other men to continue setting fire to the rest of the buildings while he went back to report to Armstrong.

The entire village was in utter chaos.

Jacob broke into to sprint just as a thunderous explosion rocked the entire village. He turned back in time to witness Captain Jacobs' home as it blew apart, spouting bark and splintered wood in every direction. The explosion pushed pieces high into the sky and as far as the cornfield and river.

The unfortunate militia and Delaware that fought within the exposed area were blasted by shards of wood that flew like grapeshot from a cannon. Several men instantly fell to the ground, groaning and crying in pain from being struck with debris. Others nearby were knocked off their feet and remained on the ground until the entire town stopped shaking.

The air was congested with a massive cloud of dirt and powder that blocked out most of the horrific scene. The fighting ceased for a moment and only the crackling of the flames could be heard. Then several sporadic musket shots broke the unnatural silence.

Jacob had taken cover behind a small house. Once most of the dust settled, he screamed as loud as he could over the din, "Be careful, lads, some of the homes are obviously storing their extra powder. Torch what you can, but make sure you stay clear once you light them."

He found that Armstrong had been moved and was now propped up against one of the only homes not riddled with musket ball holes or set ablaze. When the colonel saw Jacob, he yelled, "Good show, Sims! I think that was the damn murderer we were looking for, but what the hell was that explosion?"

Jacob knelt beside him and said, "Aye, sir, I think it was Captain Jacobs, unless the heathen has a twin. I think the bugger was storing some powder in his house, so I warned the men to take heed and be careful the rest of the way."

Armstrong was in noticeable pain from his shoulder wound, but he pulled himself up as straight as he could and said, "Well done, Sims. You did me a great service and I owe you a debt of gratitude."

Taken aback by this unexpected show of appreciation, Jacob simply replied, "We can congratulate one another after we are done here. For now, I need to rally the men and get them back into some semblance of order. I saw Mercer falling back to the hill. I hope he is setting up a defensive guard to cover our escape."

"Escape? I should say not!" Armstrong countered, returning to his usual confident self. "This is a great victory and we should hold the field until the last savage is dead."

Jacob could see that the remaining Delaware warriors were either retreating into the woods or fighting to the death in the few houses still left standing.

"It was a poor choice of words sir." Jacob said quickly. "I meant to say that I should get the men organized for when we leave the field victoriously."

He had forgotten momentarily that this was less about attacking the Delaware and more about avenging Armstrong's dead brother. Even severely injured, the colonel's ego blurred his judgment. Such a situation could still lead to a number of unnecessary deaths, and Jacob was cautious not to waste time arguing.

Jacob wanted to get back to his men and check on Joshua who had been left to hold the far hill. He was also worried about the men that he ordered to clear out the warriors in the small camp across the river.

Once again leaving Armstrong in the hands of two provincials, Jacob suggested to them, "You should move him to the hill. I saw Mercer and some of his men there; it should be much safer for him."

The men did as he suggested and eased Armstrong to his feet and walked him towards the hill. Jacob called out to four other provincial militiamen standing nearby and ordered them to aid their comrades and provide cover for their commander against any possible attack.

Satisfied that Armstrong was cared for, Jacob weaved his way through the maze of burning houses. He could still hear the sporadic sound of musket fire coming out of several of the houses that sat near the cornfield. Once he made it to the other side of the village, he could see that Joshua was still guarding the escape route over the hill.

Jacob had lost track of time during the battle. As he made his way up the hill, he studied the morning sun and knew by its position in the sky that the fight had raged on for almost four hours.

"Good to see you, sir!" Joshua said with a smile as he offered a hand to pull Jacob up over a small ridge. "We watched your fine display down there."

"It's madness down there and I fear we still have more work to do," Jacob said breathlessly. "Have you men seen much action?"

"We did have a small band of warriors with a few women and children try to work their way around us, but we gave them a good volley from our muskets and they ran back down towards the cornstalks."

Jacob took a moment to look at the hectic action below and could see that the surviving warriors had managed to set up a good line of defense. They were in or around the last few houses and used the cornfield as their flank. The men near their location, a mixture of provincials and his own rangers, did their best to overrun them, but the Delaware were in a good place to fight them off.

"Have you heard from Sinclair?" Jacob asked. "He should have returned from the camp on the other side of the river by now I'd have thought."

Before anyone could offer an answer, Jacob pointed towards the opposite hill, "Look at the fool Mercer and his men. They have already abandoned the carts and pack horses. He looks like he is ready to leave for the fort. Damn, if he only re-formed his men, they could charge down the hill and take the Delaware from behind. He only needs to send a couple men down to the cornfield and set it on fire, and the Delaware's only escape route would be cut off. They would have to surrender or die fighting."

Frustrated at the sight, Jacob turned to see Sinclair and the remains of his group slowly making their way up the other side of the hill. They were far fewer in number and several were injured.

"Sinclair, we are up here," Jacob called down and motioned to some of the others to lend a hand with the injured.

Sinclair made his way straight to Jacob and Joshua to report what had happened to his men.

"Sir, it is good to see you well," Sinclair said through gasps for breath. "Sorry to keep you waiting, but we ran into some trouble by the river."

"Not to worry, we all had our hands full this morning. What did you run into?"

"The bloody French," Sinclair said. "Almost two dozen of their best marines. They came out of a couple of the bark houses and unleashed a horrible wall of bullets that hit us pretty hard. The men fought like devils and we returned fire the best we could. We kept a steady fire on them and managed somehow to keep them back."

Jacob let Sinclair continue. Time was not on their side, but he was a good scout and would get to all of Jacob's questions without his having to ask them.

"We held them back as long as we could, but some damn Delaware and a bunch of Shawnee joined in and that really put us in some trouble. We did see some of the white captives and some did try to get to us until the French forced us to take cover in the woods."

"The French," Joshua piped up, "I'm surprised to see them getting involved in all of this."

"The bloody French are protecting their interests," Jacob snapped. "They care as little for the Delaware as we do."

He turned to watch the fires consume most of the buildings of the once impressive village of Kittanning. Small pockets of resistance in the homes left unscathed continued to keep the provincials busy.

By this time, Jacob was far more concerned by the presence of the French across the river than a few warriors below.

"Lads," he shouted, "we still need to cut off their retreat, but I think we should also do our best to free as many of the white captives as we can."

Without waiting to go over details, Jacob left a handful of men to keep their position on the hill while he led the rest down towards the other village. Running at full speed along a small creek that fed into the river, Jacob looked behind him several times to make sure his men were keeping up. Sinclair had mentioned a good place to ford the river, so he headed directly towards that point.

Carried by his much longer legs and his superior stride, Jacob found himself well ahead of the others. He dodged and jumped over the myriad of rocks and exposed roots that made him slow his pace enough not to accidently snap an ankle or split his head open on a rock.

Sinclair had failed to mention that many of the structures that made up the smaller village lined the shore right at the point where the river would be easiest to ford. As Jacob waited for the men to catch up to him, he was almost struck in the head by a musket ball that whistled past him and splintered the bark of a nearby tree.

He fell to the ground to take cover and screamed out, "Get yourselves down, lads, and fire at will!"

Sinclair and Joshua were the first to take cover by a massive old tree that sat almost at the river's edge. An incessant musket fire kept them pinned down until it slowed into more sporadic, less accurate fire.

Jacob signaled with his hand to some of his men to work their way farther down the river to find a safer crossing. As he awaited their return, he managed to get a better look from behind a cluster of tall reeds. He was able to see that the French had positioned a dozen of their marines along with a number of Shawnee warriors in the smaller outpost that protected the nearby village from be overtaken from the land side.

It wasn't much, only a few small huts and a few fallen trees placed around a large fire pit. Jacob guessed it was mainly used to warn the village of an impending attack. He still wasn't sure the importance of the small village that sat directly across from Kittanning but it still offered enough of a threat that he warned his men to be careful of a possible relief party from the village that would add to their numbers and possibly give the French the advantage.

Having superior numbers did him little good since the French had a far better position. As it stood now, they could just wait it out for his men to either make a foolish charge across the open ford or simply retreat and accept defeat.

Jacob had no intentions of leaving, or of losing to the French again, despite the relative insignificance of this possible little skirmish. He finally spotted some movement on the other side of the river. His small party of men had indeed found a safer place to cross and had taken up a position to outflank the unsuspecting French.

The new plan was to try to draw the French and their Shawnee allies out into the open. Jacob hoped that if he could show that he was contemplating launching a frontal attack, the French might take the bait and move towards the river. It meant that he would have to expose some of his men to French fire, but only for the few seconds it would take to get the marines to leave their secured positions.

A brief signal from his men on the other bank let him know he had to force the issue with the French and he did. With an ear-piercing scream, Jacob stood up and gave up his covered position behind the reeds. Most of the others did the same and the surprised French who formed up quickly to rain a poorly directed volley into the trees over the rangers' heads. Most of the musket balls either fell short, hitting the sandy banks, or went high and cut down a few branches. Jacob's men were either pelted with harmless sand or small splintered branches, but both were preferable to being hit with a musket ball.

On his order, Jacob shouted over the confusion and called on the waiting men to return fire. The result was a deadly blast that struck into the French lines simultaneously from their flank and the far side of the river. Most of the Shawnee retreated south away from the outpost, while the French valiantly attempted to re-organize and return fire. Their lone officer was struck dead shortly thereafter, and the remaining marines retreated into the woods.

The small flanking party worked its way into the outpost. A couple of the men stopped to check on the dead and wounded French marines, driving their knives into the few wounded men that struggled to fight back.

"Check the huts for any survivors and wait for us to cross," Jacob yelled, already hip deep in the cold, fast moving river. "Form up a couple men to the south, just in case the Shawnee have already warned the French back at the village."

Jacob reminded the men fording the river behind him to keep their muskets and powder dry. The water nearly reached his chest before it began to shallow out near the other embankment.

The men were greeted by a few cheers, and Jacob gave a hand to several of the men, including Joshua, to help them out of the freezing water. Jacob was numb from the short trip through the river and rubbed his arms and legs to keep the circulation moving.

Several of the men stood near a hut waiting for their captain. One of the men called out, "Sir, this should make you happy."

The hut was nothing more than corn stalks, river reeds and thin branches woven together. Cautiously stepping into the dark and dirty enclosure, Jacob heard soft whimpers. He could barely make out the silhouettes of several figures huddled in the far corner.

Not completely certain if they were French, Indians or English, Jacob called to them, "You are safe now, please…"

Something moved and startled Jacob who stepped back defensively for a moment. He then moved forward and held out his hand into the darkness. A small, thin hand reached his and Jacob gently pulled it forward.

A young, white boy came out, covering his eyes from the light of the midday sun and grabbed onto Jacob's chest. Not sure what to do, Jacob returned the boy's hug and was pleased to see four more people come out. There were two young women, each holding onto a toddler.

Once the young boy recovered his sight, he asked Jacob and the other men, "Are you British soldiers?"

Smiling, Jacob replied, "No boy, we are Virginia Rangers."

The young boy, Jacob guessed, was no older than six or seven. Most of his blonde hair had been removed except for a small scalp lock. He was frail and weak, struggling to walk but did his best. Jacob helped him outside and sat him down near an old tree.

"When was the last time you ate, boy?" Jacob asked, searching his pockets for some food, the other men did the same and handed what they had to the liberated captives.

Joshua stood by Jacob, knowing how these people felt finally being freed from their savage captors.

He whispered to Jacob, "Sir, we should keep moving. The noise from the muskets or their fleeing mates would have alerted the other French and I suspect they might just come to check it out."

"Yes, Joshua, you are right. We must get these folks back across the river and to the hill. They should be relatively safe there until the rest of us return. I want you to take them back and make sure they are all safe." He still held the hand of the young boy who had refused to let Jacob out of his sight.

"Now, go with Joshua," Jacob said as he handed the boy over. "He will take you and the others to a safer place. We can talk later; I promise."

Resisting at first, the boy cried out, "Don't leave me! Give me a musket and I will help you fight the French!"

Seeing the fight in the boy's teary eyes almost convinced Jacob to say yes, but he could not afford being slowed down. "I need you to help protect the women," he explained. "You and Joshua need to get them to safety. If you want, grab yourself a musket from one of the dead French."

Jacob smiled but knew if he waited much longer, they might be overwhelmed by the French and Shawnee whom he fully expected would be headed their way.

Turning his attention to the French, Jacob took his men into the darkness of the woods. They moved as quickly as the untamed tangle of trees and bushes permitted them. As they moved south, Jacob split his small force into three units. He kept one in the rear to guard against a flank attack and to provide cover if they were ambushed.

If the French decided to use the river and canoe down to the outpost, they could arrive in minutes. Jacob warned the men again to be vigilant and keep ready for any possible action.

Surprised by the lack of any resistance, Jacob moved with one unit of his men into position just on the outskirts of the main village that had caused the provincial militia so many problems. He waited for the other unit to move around to the far side to cut off any attempt to retreat farther into the woods. Now the only route left to the French was the river. If they chose to take it, Jacob and his men would have free shots at the fleeing men.

The camp was eerily still. Jacob waited briefly before he decided that it might just be abandoned. He motioned to the other unit to cover them as he stepped out from the woods and into the perimeter of the assembly of huts and small, bark covered houses.

Jacob took a moment to look across the river at the smoldering homes of the once impressive village. By now, most of Armstrong's men had abandoned their efforts and were either back on the trail to the fort or reorganizing on the other side of the hill to the east.

The effectiveness of the ambush was striking and Jacob knew that the Delaware had just lost one of their key bases to launch their raids on the frontier settlers.

By shape of this village, it was clear that the French and their Indian allies had left quickly. There were still a couple of small fires, and one still had a half-full pot of stew simmering over it. Going hut by hut, the men soon determined that the French had left and most likely taken the missing bateaux back towards Fort Duquesne.

Jacob walked down by the river and could not find any canoes or bateaux left. He did notice that there were several deep indentations in the muddy banks that appeared to be drag marks from the men pulling the vessels into the water. He also noted that on the opposite bank, no canoes remained and must have been used to escape from the ambush. That led him to wonder how many of the warriors actually died, or had they just taken to the river once they realized the battle was lost?

They set the small cluster of buildings ablaze before they departed, leaving them unusable for the French, Delaware or the Shawnee in the future. Satisfied that a threat no longer remained, Jacob ordered the men back to the other side of the river to aid in taking the rest of Kittanning.

Jacob knew he had to get his men moving if they were to join the main force before Armstrong ordered the men back to the fort. He preferred to move with the larger force because many of the French, Delaware and Shawnee had managed to escape from both villages and could conceivably launch a counter-attack. Even though the French had left with the boats and could easily reach Fort Duquesne after a good day of hard paddling, they might still choose to cause issues for the army on its trek back to Fort Stevens.

Just as they were set to leave, one of the men shouted that there was some movement in the nearby woods. Jacob ordered some of the men to find out what all the noise was and to flush out anything that was causing the problems. A few musket shots rang out and he decided to see for himself what all the fuss was about.

Just as he reached the woods, two of his men had found the culprit. It was a young Delaware boy, no older than ten. He was kicking and trying to scream although his mouth was covered by one of the men.

"This little bugger almost shot me," the men explained.

Jacob tried not to laugh at the funny sight of two good-sized men struggling to keep a mere boy under control. "What have we here?" he asked as he calmly strolled up to the young boy.

The lad had no hair except for a long, braided scalp lock on the crown of his head. His upper body, including his face, was completely blackened with soot which made him appear rather threatening. He was thin, probably from the lack of food, yet was a good size and showed signs of being quite tall once he finished growing. Jacob imagined he might be as tall, if not taller, than he was.

The boy wore an old deer hide that looked like someone just cut a neck hole in it and put it over his head. He also wore a nicely made pair of brain-tanned leggings that were attached to a blue, Indian-style breech-clout. His skin was tanned from being exposed to the summer sun, yet he was still recognizably English at such close range. Seeing this child dressed in savage clothes brought a wave of anger and resentment at the thought of his own children's ordeals, assuming any of them had survived.

Leaning down to speak to the boy, Jacob asked, "Do you have a name?"

He initially said nothing but just defiantly looked directly at Jacob.

Jacob motioned to one of his men to hand him his canteen of water and before the boy could react, Jacob dumped the entire canteen of cold water over the boys head.

While all the men laughed, Jacob scrubbed the boys' face with his hand to remove most of the black markings.

The young Delaware boy kicked and screamed as much as he could but the two rangers held a good grip on his arms and Jacob simply stepped back.

"Now you look better. So again do you have a name" Jacob asked again.

"The Delaware call me White Wolf, but my real name is James," he proudly answered. "My mother and father are both dead and I have no idea where my brother and sisters are."

The name 'James' hit Jacob hard. Yet, with the French and their Indian allies so close, he did not want to press the poor boy for more information. There would time for that later.

An odd sensation hit him. Could this be his James, or was he just hoping it was? He did his best to keep his head clear. He knew that if he didn't get his men back, all this would mean nothing.

He told the two men, "Hold the boy and if he screams or tries to escape, give him a good beating. We need to get across the river and don't need him slowing us down."

"It will be my pleasure to teach the heathen some manners," one of the men replied, looking at James, but the boy looked away and glared at the destruction across the river. "The boy has shot at me, bit my hand and tried to kick me already, so he is due for a beating."

"Give him a good dunking in the river and get rid of the rest of that mess on him." Jacob added.

"It will be my pleasure, sir." One of the rangers replied and pulled the boy towards the river crossing.

Jacob moved quickly, keeping his men on alert and still maintaining a rear guard. They retraced their steps back through the woods to the site of their previous crossing and immediately waded through the cold water.

As they walked back up the hill where they had been stationed during the entire battle, they were greeted by the pickets Joshua and Sinclair had positioned. Having no time to talk, Jacob found Joshua in tears.

"What happened, lad?" Jacob asked. "Where is the young boy?"

"The brave boy was swept away when we were crossing the river," Joshua explained, fighting back more tears. "One second I had his tiny hand in mine then the next I felt nothing."

"No time for this, lad; we can talk about it later," Jacob said brusquely. He was far more worried about getting to the trail and was oblivious at how callous he sounded.

Joshua said nothing more, but followed Jacob who ordered everyone to cut down the hill through Kittanning to reach the trail back to the fort.

The only living beings left in the town were some of the wild dogs that had begun feasting on the dead bodies. Jacob led the way through the devastated remains of the once proud village. They ran into a number of dead provincial troops; many were scattered around Captain Jacobs' destroyed home, while another large grouping lay dispersed by the longhouse.

Jacob led his men through the burned-out cornfield where smoking stalks of corn still stood here and there. It was difficult to avoid stepping on the dead militia and Delaware, but he encouraged his men to keep moving and only paused to wait for the two women to make it through. A couple of Jacob's men had taken the toddlers from them, allowing the women to move much faster. Young James did his best to keep up and with all his paint removed he started to look much more like an English boy.

Jacob even got a hint of a smile from the boy as he ran past with Joshua right on his heels.

When the group crested the hill, they were greeted by hundreds of abandoned blankets, carts and equipment. Armstrong's troops had already beaten a retreat so hasty that they had failed to even set up a rear guard.

There were so many blankets left behind, Jacob was told that the men dubbed the hill, 'Blanket Hill' and gladly gathered what they could carry for the long trek back to the fort.

It was well into the afternoon, and Jacob had to decide what they should do next. He assumed that Armstrong would take his men back to the fort, but he couldn't be sure of that. He did consider sending out a small scouting party to find the retreating army, yet he could see that the men had been weakened by the day's events.

"Joshua, please organize the men and give me some numbers and send Private White to me if you see him," he said. "We might have to camp here tonight and just head back to our fort before dawn, but I want to see how the men are holding up before I make my decision."

Joshua nodded and walked away, and Jacob looked for the boy called James. He found him with his two escorts on one of the blankets, which the boy had spread out on the grass.

"So, boy, what do you think?" Jacob asked, unsure of what to say.

One of the men kicked the boy, "Answer the captain or I'll thrash you good."

"No need, lads, go get yourself some rest and I will take care of him," Jacob ordered.

"Careful, sir, he's a handful to say the least." the ranger replied as the two walked away.

Jacob was aching to determine if this was his son, but he was unsure how best to go about finding out. His heart told him that it was so, but his mind struggled with doubts. Aside from his height, the boy really did not resemble the innocent English boy that Jacob had left behind with Maggie and his siblings nearly three years ago. Also, James had already told him that his parents were dead, so he did not want to play with the boy's already shattered emotions.

They fell into silence until James suddenly asked, "What is your name, sir?"

The question wasn't surprising. If this was James, he was not the only one who looked drastically altered. Jacob wore a uniform now, albeit a dirty and somewhat tattered one after the events of the day. His hair was long and wild and his beard was longer than he had ever worn prior to leaving home, even during the coldest of winters.

"My name is…Jacob; I'm with Stevens' Rangers," Jacob barely managed to get the words out.

"Good to meet you, sir, and thank you," James said and offered his small, dirty hand.

Jacob gladly accepted the hand, but was inwardly disappointed. His heart had beaten wildly for a moment, thinking that the boy had perhaps recognized him as well. He rubbed his face and ran his hand through his dirt-covered hair.

They resumed their silent observation of the debris left behind by Armstrong's army.

"Sir," James said quietly with his eyes downcast, "I need to ask you something, but I don't want you to think I'm strange for asking."

Jacob held his breath and waited.

"By chance, are you Jacob Murray?"

Without a word, Jacob pulled James to his lap and held him.

Reluctant at first, James accepted the display of affection as Jacob wiped away the tears that threatened to pour down his face. Finally, he found his voice and said, "I can't believe it, James…I can't believe I found you."

He was hit with a myriad of emotions: guilt, happiness, love for his son and hatred towards the people who had ripped his family apart. Each sensation washed over him as he held James as closely as he could.

They had so much to talk about, but Jacob knew this was not the place for it. He thought of how Maggie would react, but he dared not mention to James that his mother was only a few miles away. He didn't want the boy to be too overwhelmed with everything.

"James," he said after a few minutes, "we have so much to talk about, but right now I need you to be strong until we get back to the fort. I don't want anything to happen to you again, so please stay with me unless I say otherwise. Don't cause any trouble, and listen to me."

James nodded his acceptance but remained surprisingly stoic, not shedding a tear or displaying the slightest smile as he said, "Yes, father, I will."

Being called father was such a simple thing, and even with James' lack of emotion, Jacob found it difficult not to get up and scream out in sheer excitement. He kept James by his side and his eyes on the trail, hoping that nothing was waiting for him once they decided to depart east. He sent Sinclair out with a small group to watch for any signs of the French who might possibly return by the river.

Before they could continue their emotional reunion, Joshua reported back with his findings.

"Sir, I counted seventeen dead Delaware plus five dead French marines. We had thirty-two dead Provincials, along with ten of our own." Joshua slightly hesitated.

"What is it boy?" Jacob asked at Joshua's uncharacteristic tentativeness. "Is it how I reacted to the young lad's drowning? I'm sorry for that, and I hope you understand that I needed to get the men moving."

Clearing his throat, Joshua explained, "Private White was found amongst the dead and I asked a few of the men to give him a decent burial before the wild beasts mutilated him."

It was obvious that Joshua was particularly saddened by the loss of the well-liked Private White, and Jacob did his best to console him, "Damn. Poor White; he was a good man, a damn good lad."

Jacob hid his grief. The loss of Private White, with whom he had experienced so much, was difficult. Even after witnessing so much death already, when it struck so close, it became overwhelming. Jacob never knew how to react to news like this. Even when his own father died, he never really cried and kept his feelings buried.

His reunion with James did help to lessen the pain, but he was sure once they returned to the safety of the fort, he would mourn the untimely death of his good friend and reliable soldier.

"We also found an injured Delaware warrior," Joshua continued, "who told one of the men that a large number of warriors and several French regulars left yesterday, heading towards the east. The Delaware said they were to launch raids on any English fort they could find. I took a moment to get the men organized and waiting for you to address them."

"Bring the Delaware to me, so I can get more details out of him," Jacob ordered. His initial fear seemed to be coming true, that the Delaware would indeed launch attacks on the undermanned forts to the east.

"Sorry, sir," Joshua replied quietly, "but the savage is dead. Once he gave up all that information, the men killed him."

Jacob had a hard time hiding his anger at this lack of discipline in his men. The consequences of their actions were dire. He did his best not to think of the tiny garrison back at Fort Stevens, but the image of Maggie firing, loading and firing again from the western bastion as they desperately fought for their lives was a hard image to clear from his head.

"We must get back to the fort to reinforce them, but what are your thoughts, lad? Do the men look in any condition to travel? We can spend the night here, but honestly, we must consider that the dead bodies will attract all kinds of animals, including swarms of flies. If we stay, we will have to keep a couple fires going all night to keep the bugs away. I hate to do that; we both know those who escaped this attack will not let it go without some kind of retaliation."

James had walked up to where his father was and piped up before Joshua could offer a reply, "Sir, I know of a good, safe place just off the main trail. It sits about five miles from here and has a number of huts and basic shelters for the men. The Delaware use it for the hunting parties they send east. It isn't much, but it offers better shelter and is far enough away from this place that the smell should be lost in the woods."

"How far did you say, boy?" Jacob asked. He liked the idea of moving to a more secured place. Truthfully, his only concern was for his men, he didn't want to force them to march towards the fort only to be too fatigued to assist the garrison.

"Just about five miles clear of here," James said, confidently pointing into a vast cluster of trees. "It is pretty easy to get to and only a handful of the Delaware know it exists. They took me out on a number of hunting trips and we always used it. I ran away a few times and slept there during the night; it is far more hospitable then this place."

Joshua nodded in agreement and said, "Sir, the men are tired and in need of some rest. If we push them, they might not be worth anything once we get to the fort. If we can get some sleep and reorganize, we can get to the fort well before nightfall tomorrow. We have to remember that

Armstrong and his men are already heading back. They will be close to the fort by this time tomorrow to offer any relief the garrison might need."

Jacob had not considered Armstrong's men, but he realized that if the fort was under attack, Armstrong could offer a far better relief force then his own men. He turned to James and asked, "If I send you ahead with Joshua and a few men, could you find this place?"

James leveled a glance at Jacob that seemed to ask if he'd lost his mind and retorted, "I wouldn't have suggested it otherwise."

A broad smile covered Jacob's face. He had forgotten James' confidence and how eager he had always been to prove himself as a seasoned woodsman, despite his age.

"Thank you, boy," Jacob said as he knelt on the grass in front of him. "Keep close to Joshua and do what he tells you. He will report back and let me know if we will use this place."

"I'll get some men together and we will be on the trail in minutes," Joshua said. "The boy will be well cared for, sir."

As Joshua left to gather a small scouting party of twelve of the best conditioned men, Jacob looked at James. "Good work, son," he said, "but keep safe and do what Joshua tells you."

James nodded in agreement and waited for Joshua to return.

Jacob thought to tell Joshua that James was his son but time and opportunity was not at hand. He knew he could tell him later and make his introductions once they got settled at James' camp.

Feeling his own fatigue from all that had transpired back at Kittanning and the other isolated village, Jacob led the rest of the men, plus the two women and children, down the trail. They soon met two men Joshua had stationed to bring them the rest of the way.

Jacob was impressed with the so-called small hunting camp that James had described. Expecting some poorly built, rotting huts and a couple hastily thrown together piles of branches to be used as shelters, he found the camp well-constructed and nicely laid out.

He was happy to find James and Joshua sitting on a carved out tree trunk that sat right by a large, well-used fire pit. They both had huge smiles on their faces, waiting to hear all the accolades that Jacob would throw at them.

Seeing their confident smirks, Jacob was not so quick to offer his appreciation and said seriously, "I assume this is the camp for the pickets?"

Joshua rolled his eyes, but James looked particularly disappointed with his father's reaction. Jacob smiled and said, "You did well, boy."

"Joshua," Jacob continued, "can you make sure we have all the pickets set? I don't want any of them to get lazy and feel we are safe from a retaliatory attack."

Joshua immediately got up and went to check on the men, leaving Jacob with James.

Taking up Joshua's vacant seat, Jacob put his arm around James' shoulder and said, "Thanks for telling us about this place, son. The men should get a good night's rest and be ready to head out early for the fort."

Jacob was still waiting for the right time to tell James that his mother was waiting at the fort. He could not help but imagine the look on her face when she realized that he had found James. In the meantime, Jacob just wanted to enjoy a good rest and have some time alone with his son.

"So, how long were you with the Delaware?" Jacob asked while he kicked at the fire, moving around the hot embers before he dropped another piece of wood on it.

"After the Huron raided our home, they broke us all up and took me and Thomas north. We were on the water for hours but soon stopped at a small village that sat on the banks of a small creek. They took Thomas away almost immediately and I never saw him again."

James spoke slowly and Jacob could see that recalling this horrifying experience was upsetting for him. "I'm sorry, son," he said. "I don't want you to get all worked up. We can talk about all of this when we reach the fort."

James kept his head down, doing his best to avoid showing his father his tears. "No, I'm sorry," he said and cleared his throat. "I haven't had to think about it for a while. Have you heard from mother or anyone else in the family?"

"I have been searching since I found out you all were taken, but there are miles of suffocating wilderness and I think I covered only a tiny bit of it so far." He decided not to tell James about Maggie. If the fort was in danger of attack, he could not be certain of her safety and didn't want to get the boy's hopes up. He had already experienced far too much for a boy his age.

James didn't say much after that and just stared into the fire.

Jacob found the musket that James had used to defend himself from the two men who had so much difficulty capturing him. He looked it over and picked up a fairly sharp stone, which he started to dig into the barrel just short of the wooden stock.

When he had managed to make a dent the whole way around the hard barrel he said, "It's not loaded, is it, boy?"

"I just cleaned it; it should be like new," James proudly answered, "What are you doing?"

"Just trying to cut the barrel down to make it easier for you to handle," Jacob explained as he held the barrel over the fire. "If I can heat it up enough, I should just be able to snap it off where I scored it with the stone."

After a few minutes of constantly rotating the barrel over the fire, during which he was careful not to burn the wooden stock, Jacob said, "Get me my water jug."

James brought back the wooden canteen and Jacob handed the musket to him, saying, "Now, just turn it slowly as I pour water over it."

Doing as he was told, James turned his head as the water hit the barrel and a cloud of steam spewed all over them.

"Keep turning it," Jacob said. "We are almost done." When he had emptied the entire contents of his canteen over the barrel, he picked up the same stone and struck exactly where he had weakened the metal. After two strikes, the long piece of the barrel fell to the ground.

"How does it feel?" Jacob asked as he watched James move the musket around, pretending to shoot it. He was reminded of the young boy he had left behind. James would always run around the farm with a stick, pretending to shoot at birds, cows or anything else that crossed his path.

"I like it, but will it still shoot?" James asked, rubbing his hand over the warm end of the barrel.

"Give it another good cleaning and let it cool down overnight and you can probably give it a try," Jacob said. He sat back and enjoyed watching his son handle the musket like he had been shooting it for years.

A few hunting parties had been sent out shortly after the camp was organized. They had all been gone for more than an hour and Jacob started to get concerned. He didn't want to send out more men in case the French or Delaware were waiting to ambush them, but he did increase the pickets and ordered all the men to keep their muskets by their sides.

Sinclair finally made it to the camp with his tiny scouting party, and reported directly to Jacob. "Sir, I took the men up the river several miles and hiked back almost to the remains of Kittanning. We never saw any French or the retreating Delaware, but we found signs of them. Some of the men spotted several footprints in the banks of the river and proof that they had dragged four or five boats to shore."

Jacob's mind was awhirl, but he forced himself to listen patiently.

"I fear it was a large party that set ashore," Sinclair continued. "We lost the trail and continued through the woods until we found your guards on the trail.

"I feared as much," Jacob said, "yet we have heard nothing from them. I have two hunting parties that have been out for over an hour. Frankly, I think they might have gotten themselves into some trouble." Jacob looked out towards the main trail, straining to see through the mass of trees.

Joshua had approached while Sinclair was giving his report and confirmed that word had not come in from any of the pickets about the missing parties.

"Damn, lads," Jacob said. "We certainly didn't need this. We will need to send out a larger patrol to search for them, especially before we lose the sun."

"Let me take out some men, sir," Sinclair immediately spoke up.

Appreciating his enthusiasm, Jacob quickly replied, "You and your men have done enough and deserve to get some rest. I will take out ten men to scour the area."

Jacob decided to take Joshua with him and nine of the more experienced trackers. He spoke with James before he departed, saying, "James, I will be back before nightfall. Please help Mr. Sinclair and do whatever he needs from you. Please also check on the women and make sure they are well looked after."

Jacob didn't want to be out in the woods any longer than was necessary, so he sent Joshua and four men ahead along the Kittanning trail. Jacob stayed near the trail, using a narrow, side path that almost followed the main trail step-for-step. After about a mile, the two parties converged and stood on a small landing that sat just to the side of the trail.

"It is like they just disappeared," Joshua said.

"Aye, they didn't leave a single clue for us to follow," Jacob replied. "If we don't head back soon, we will not have much light to guide us. Let's retrace our steps; maybe we will get lucky."

While they walked back, Jacob said without warning to Joshua, "That young boy we found back at the village…is my son, James."

"I figured as much and the boy told me when we were setting up the camp." Joshua admitted.

"I can't believe I have found Maggie and now James. It's a bloody miracle." Jacob added.

"If you don't mind me saying, the boy is pretty confused by everything, so go easy on him for a while." Joshua suggested, as they continued to walk.

The return trip was thankfully uneventful, but Jacob could tell some-thing was wrong before they even reached the camp. Private Sinclair was pacing by the entrance to the small trail.

When Sinclair caught sight of Jacob, he ran down the slight slope of the trail calling out, "Sir…sir, we have word of the hunting parties."

Barely able to understand him, Jacob instinctively motioned to him to keep his voice down. They both knew how a man's voice could carry for miles through the woods.

They met halfway and Jacob waited for Sinclair to catch his breath. "What is it, lad? You have made enough noise to scare most of the beasts away for miles."

"Two men from the…hunting…parties, made it back shortly after you had left…they were ambushed by the French just southeast of here," Sinclair spoke through panting breaths.

"Show me the men, lad, and save your breath," Jacob said, directing Joshua to take the others into the camp.

The camp was in a panic, and Jacob followed Sinclair directly to the two recovering men.

"This is Turner and Bullen, sir," Sinclair said. "They were part of one of the hunting parties. Gentlemen, please tell the captain what happened."

Jacob waited a moment for the two men to look up at him. They were both pretty disheveled and had some minor cuts and bruises. Turner attempted to get up, but Jacob gently touched his shoulder to keep him down.

"What happened, lads?" Jacob asked quietly, allowing for their shaken nerves to clear. "I need details on numbers and strength."

He stood over them waiting for a reply, but when none came he spoke more forcefully, "Gentlemen, I need you to tell me what happened to you and the others."

"Sir, we were tracking a large buck just on the edge of a small swampy area when all hell broke…excuse me, sir, when we were attacked from all sides by the savages and the French," Bullen replied.

Turner added, "We walked right into their ambush and barely made it out with our lives. We ran for almost five miles, chased by a number of savages until we lost them in a cluster of thickets. We hid for an hour before they left us and I assume they went back to the swamp."

"How many were there?" Jacob repeated.

The two men looked at each other and Bullen spoke first, "My guess would be twenty Shawnee or Delaware and just as many French regulars."

"It was hard to count them, sir, once they opened fire on us," Turner said. "They killed most of the men after two volleys and rushed the field to kill the rest of us." Turner added.

"Damn…if they are between us and Armstrong, we will have hell to pay," Jacob said and looked at Sinclair and Joshua, who had arrived to listen. "I just hope Armstrong gets to the fort as fast as he can."

"Thank you, lads," Jacob said, turning to the men. "Get yourselves something to eat and some rest."

Jacob walked back to the fire where James was sitting close to the flames to keep the annoying gnats from buzzing around his head.

"Sinclair, get the men together for a short talk," Jacob said and sat down with James.

"Did you see many French around the town before we attacked?" Jacob asked.

"The Delaware kept most of the young children and the women in the smaller village once most of the warriors returned," James recalled. "I did see two large boats full of French soldiers arrive a while ago, but they left well before you came."

"They were good to me, Father," James added when Jacob remained silent. "They taught me many skills like hunting with a bow, tracking a wild cat right to its den and what plants you can eat or not."

Jacob shot back, "I taught you those things as well, or did you forget all that? The bloody Delaware would just as easily sell you if they could get something useful for you."

"They adopted me into their village, clothed me, fed me and made sure I was safe," James replied defensively. "You should appreciate that they treated me so well."

"Why did the savages put you in that pitiful hut and abandon you then? They just left you behind like an old, useless hide."

"They are not savages, Father. They only killed the old or sick captives because they would take food from the rest of us. They treated me like one of their own and I could never call them savages."

In an effort to end the conversation and drive his point home, Jacob said, "They killed your uncle and possibly your brother and sisters. Then there's your mother. They took her and would have killed her if she hadn't escaped."

"What do you know of mother?" James asked as he jumped to his feet.

"She is at the fort," he said quietly. "I wanted it to be a surprise."

James went silent and Jacob left him to his thoughts. There were far more critical issues to be dealt with. Sinclair had gathered most of the men near the fire.

Jacob could plainly see that his men were in no shape to take the fight to the French. The best they could do was to spend some time setting up a defensive position around the camp.

"Gentlemen," he addressed them, "we have all just been through a difficult raid, but we are not done with our duties yet. We have received reports of French around the area and must do our best to fortify the camp. We are all tired, but if we work together, the task will be much easier. Please drag, cut or carry whatever you can to build up some protection for us to get through the night. We will leave for the fort before dawn. I know I don't need to explain but we must also put out any fires so we don't give up our position."

The men worked hard and did what they could before they lost the last shreds of light. As soon as the fires were out, the bugs returned with a vengeance. Jacob knew the men earned a better fate. Being overrun by the French was not an option, so any inconvenience would have to be dealt with.

The pickets were doubled and he kept a couple men down near the main trail to monitor any movement. Understanding he would not get much sleep, Jacob made sure that James rested and ordered Joshua to do the same.

Dawn could not come fast enough…

Nodding off briefly a couple times through the night, Jacob was up well before the sun shot beams of light through the forest's canopy. He was joined by James and Joshua in enjoying a cold cup of bitter root tea while they waited for the men to wake.

"Did you get much sleep, sir?" Joshua asked, blowing into his hands.

"I got what I could, but I would be lying if I told you that I didn't feel uneasy all night," Jacob admitted while he sipped his drink.

It didn't take long for all the men to get themselves up and ready to leave. The pickets and the men stationed by the trail reported that the night had been thankfully quiet.

Private Sinclair joined Jacob and asked, "Sir, would you like me to take out an advanced guard? If we head out now, we should certainly make it to the fort by nightfall."

"Yes please, and make sure you keep the lads moving and on full alert. I still have a funny feeling in my gut that the French are lurking about. We certainly do not want to make it easy for them."

Sinclair nodded and collected a dozen men on his way to the trail. Jacob did not want Sinclair to get too far ahead and asked Joshua to get the men ready to leave.

"What do you want me to do?" James asked eagerly, drawing a broad smile from Jacob.

"First, go check on the women and ask them to prepare to leave. Then keep by me, and make sure your musket is primed and ready." He patted James on the back as he hurried off.

The men appeared relatively happy to be back on the main trail, walking single file in groups of five. Jacob had five men take up the rear guard and two men on each side as vanguards. The women and two toddlers were positioned in the middle of the company, safely covered on all sides by the men.

They kept a strong pace, making no stops along the way. They ate as they moved. Occasionally, a man would leave the trail to relieve himself, but he would get back in line quickly.

Jacob kept an eye on the women in case they tired, but they kept pace and required very little assistance. James made sure the women and the two toddlers had raw berries, some roots and nuts to keep them from tiring out.

They saw no signs that the French or their Delaware allies were around, but Jacob grew somewhat concerned that he had not received word from Sinclair yet. After almost ten miles of marching along the relatively easy terrain of the well-used trail, Jacob spotted one of the men from Sinclair's advanced guard running towards the main body of men.

Jacob got the men to form up in a defensive position just in case something was wrong, and walked ahead to greet the man.

The man stopped short of Jacob, offering an informal salute and reported, "Sir, Mr. Sinclair sent me to warn you that we have found the remains of some of Armstrong's company. It looks like they were ambushed just around a slight bend and were easily overwhelmed by a much larger force of French and Delaware."

"Do you know how long ago?" Jacob asked, motioning to his men to stay ready and spread themselves into the nearby woods.

"Hard to tell, sir, but the wolves and coyotes had their way with the dead. My guess would be sometime in the late afternoon yesterday."

"Damn it…damn it," was all Jacob could manage as he glared up the trail.

"Sir, should I get myself back to Mr. Sinclair?" the man asked uncertainly.

"One minute, lad. Did you get the number of dead?"

"Again, sir, the animals did some terrible work on the poor buggers, but I would say between ten and twelve dead. There were no French or Delaware to be found, so they either took their dead or had none."

"Thank you, lad," Jacob said. "Get yourself back before the boys get too far ahead of you. Please tell Mr. Sinclair that I appreciated his report and make sure the men keep moving…no breaks or permitting any of the men to lag behind."

Before Jacob could continue, the messenger was sprinting back up the trail and was soon out of sight.

Jacob called on one of the men to pass the word that they would be running into the remains of an ambush. They would pass straight by as there was no time to dawdle. Another man was sent back to inform Joshua what was happening and to keep the men moving forward.

The odor of the decaying corpses met them long before they actually found the bodies. Within a few miles, Jacob and the men encountered the terrible scene of butchered bodies. Most of the men kept their eyes forward and avoided looking at the bodies that the advanced guards had thought-fully moved to the edges of the trail. The women covered the toddlers' eyes and their own sight was screened by several men on either side.

The combination of the horrid smell and the packs of flies made it difficult to walk past without some of the men reaching for their noses.

"Keep moving lads," Jacob called back. "We can pray for these poor boys once we get inside the fort." He held the back of James' neck to keep him from looking at the mangled bodies.

Anger towards their enemies made the men move with renewed vigor. They were driven to get to the fort as quickly as possible.

They turned off the old Kittanning trail onto a side trail that would cut south along the ridge of the mountain. Jacob knew that they would soon be close enough to smell the welcoming parade grounds fires at the fort.

"What is that smell?" James asked as he sniffed the air. "It is like my old village after your men attacked it."

"I smell it as well, lad," Jacob replied. The scent of burning wood was far too strong to be that of several camp fires. The sun was low in the sky, but it became quite dark as a thick, murky cloud formed overhead.

They moved cautiously. Within a few miles, shouts could be heard ahead of them on the trail. "Sir, get your men forward as fast as you can!" they shouted.

Jacob remained cautious in case they were false calls from the French, waiting to ambush them.

Several of the men from the advanced guard suddenly came into view. They were running, waving their arms shouting even louder, "Sir, please get your men forward...the fort is under attack!"

Jacob reacted immediately and ordered his men to advance as fast as their tired legs would carry them. He grabbed James' hand and pulled the much shorter boy along the trail, ignoring his pleas to slow down.

The hazy, black cloud hung even lower and was joined by wind-blown, red-hot embers. The sounds of musket fire and the all too familiar wild war cries of the Delaware assaulted their ears.

Just shy of the edge of the tree line, Jacob let go of James' arm and shouted, "Find the women and stay with them, son. Run if you see the French or the savages."

"Father, let me help...don't leave me..." James pleaded, but he was met with deaf ears.

Jacob never hesitated, and just kept running towards the musket fire and the source of the pungent, eye-watering air.

Chapter | **Seventeen**

The fort was under siege and the thick smoke suffocated the woods surrounding the outer earthen works as the men got closer.

Spotting Private Sinclair a few paces ahead of him, Jacob dodged a couple low-hanging wild grape vines and stopped next to him.

"Oh my God," he murmured as he finally got his first glimpse of the sickening ruins of the once mighty fort.

Most of the outer walls were ablaze and had been easily breached by the attackers. Jacob could barely manage to make out the desperate silhouettes of the handful of the surviving defenders being led away, linked together by a thick hemp trump line.

"Where the hell is Armstrong and his bloody men?" Jacob shouted above the din.

Neither Sinclair nor any of the other men who had reached the meadow could offer a logical explanation. They just stood frozen and watched the horrific scene play out as several of their friends and members of the poor families who had come there for protection were led away as captives. Many more had been killed and lay butchered around the grounds.

The men stood rooted to the ground, left powerless at being unable to assist the overrun garrison. Jacob understood that he would just be foolishly asking his men to rush forward to their own certain deaths if he ordered them to defend what was left of their home. His influence and authority could make them, but his heart could not bear seeing them wasted on a senseless endeavor.

Jacob asked Sinclair if he had any thoughts or suggestions. The private remained lost for words for a few moments before answering, "Sir, if we attack, the French will just set their savages upon us and kill us all. God knows, we would fight to the death but..."

Jacob stopped his loyal private, "I know, lad, but my wife is in there. I lost her once and I'll be damned if I will lose her again!"

He fought off tears and watched the flames climb higher. "Keep the men back," he shouted. "I won't ask them to come with me, but I can't just sit back and watch all of this. I am going over to the fort. When it is safe, I will signal the rest of you to join me." Before the men could react, Jacob sprinted into the meadow and began weaving around the stumps.

He had no idea of what he was going to do once he reached the earthen works, or if he was spotted by the French or the dozen or so Delaware warriors who remained behind to scavenge. Jacob prayed the smoke and darkening sky would provide enough cover to shroud his movement across the open field.

Diving head-first into the dirt, hardened by the lack of rain over the past few days, Jacob jammed his left wrist into the ground. Pain shot up his arm and his grotesquely twisted wrist started to swell immediately. He feared it was broken, but it mattered little at the moment. He was tormented by an intense rage and felt that nothing could stop him from rescuing his Maggie.

He pulled the sweat-stained cloth from his neck and tied it around his wrist to try to splint it. The pain surged through his entire body and even after he tightened the cloth the best he could around his wrist, it did little to reduce the throbbing. Ignoring the discomfort, Jacob propped himself up and took a quick look at what sat in front of him.

Struggling to think straight and fight off the thrashing pain that by now made his wrist practically useless, Jacob dropped his musket and pulled out his favorite long-knife that was always strapped to his left calf.

Leaning against the earthen works, Jacob was just about to scramble up to the top of the mound of dirt just as a lone figure plowed feet first into the dirt beside him.

"What the hell are you doing, lad?" Jacob whispered to the young man who quickly recovered and pulled himself to an upright position.

It was Joshua, panting and struggling to get himself together.

"What's the plan, sir?" Joshua asked, ignoring Jacob's question. He climbed up to the top of the mound to take a brief look around.

They both realized the siege was for the most part over and the unfortunate survivors who hadn't been taken captive would now be dragged out and killed.

"I don't know," Jacob said, desperately wanting to charge over the embankment and kill as many of the attackers as he could.

Joshua looked over the edge again and slid back down, saying, "There are too many of them for us to do much. If we do something foolish they would just kill the captives and then wipe us out. What good would that do for Maggie?"

Jacob knew he was right and they just stayed down until they were certain the last of the French had moved on. He thought of sending a couple messengers to warn the eastern forts, but his disgust with Armstrong and the fact he must have bypassed the fort to get home faster, made him curse the bastard.

He could see the other men waiting in the woods and once they were sure that the enemy had left the field, Jacob waved them to join him. The few Delaware staying behind were far too consumed by finding themselves some souvenirs of the attack to notice Jacob's men accumulating on the other side of the works.

Jacob got himself up and over the earthen works. By this time most of the men were with him, including James, and they slowly walked towards the smoldering frame of the main gate.

The stench of wood and blood soaked the air, mercilessly burning at their noses.

Jacob made sure that James remained by his side and sent Sinclair, Joshua and a handful of men forward to inspect the destroyed fort and take care of the last of the Delaware stragglers.

He ordered a party of twenty men to form a defensive line just outside the destroyed main gates. It wasn't out of the question that the French might return, but mainly he didn't want any of the Delaware still inside the fort to escape.

Jacob stood eyeing the scorched wall timbers that still maintained their footing. He was frozen, unable to drag himself across the fallen debris for fear of what he would find within the fort.

"Kill any of the bloody savage you find, but please leave me one to 'speak to'." Jacob called out, caring little if the Delaware now trapped inside, heard him. "I need to know what the French are up to and where they might be taking the survivors."

"Did you see mother?" James asked. "I could see that the Delaware had taken some captives, but they were too far away for me to identify any of them."

Without answering, Jacob started to move forward but stopped again when he heard musket fire within the fort.

"Lads, stay in formation and watch for any Delaware running out of the gates," Jacob reminded them and gripped his knife with his good hand.

Just as the men shouldered their muskets, ten Delaware warriors ran out between the once impressive gates, kicking up embers as they rushed through.

"Fire, lads, and reload as fast as you can!" Jacob screamed.

Several more musket shots rang out from inside the fort as Jacob's men kept pouring deadly volleys into the surprised Delaware. The escaping warriors were unable to react in time to defend themselves since most of them were bogged down with extra gear they managed to pilfer from inside the fort.

Jacob and his men fired with a vengeful intensity at the stunned Delaware. Most were struck down and were immediately pounced on by Jacob's men.

One warrior was spared, but was forced to watch the men kill his fellow warriors before he was forcefully dragged back into the fort. Jacob followed and watched the men tie him up against the curiously unscathed flag pole that still flew the fort's blackened and charred flag. The warrior remained equally defiant and sat straight, proudly observing the men as they searched through the rubble for any survivors.

He just stood and watched the men murder any warriors who had survived their wounds.

"Move, boy, you can't just stand there," Jacob shouted to James.

Jacob waited a couple of seconds before running back out of the fort and grabbing his son by the arm. "James, you need to get into the fort in case any savages return."

James boldly pulled back his arm and screamed, "You call the Delaware savages?"

His words were directed at the scene of Jacob's men mutilating the remains of the warriors they had shot. They pulled on the warriors' scalp-locks and, with brutal accuracy, hacked off the small strand of hair that stood for so much to the proud warriors.

Some of the men stopped and looked towards James but nothing more was said. Jacob did not want a repeat of their earlier discussion and forcibly dragged James into the fort.

Jacob almost emptied his stomach as he took in what was left of the fort's interior. Most of the once solid walls were barely standing. The support stakes seemed to have dissolved into ashes.

Almost immediately, he was summoned towards the remains of the blacksmith's shop.

"Sir, please come over here; it's Mr. Tate," Joshua called.

Rushing over and managing to avoid the smoldering debris that covered most of the parade grounds, Jacob left James to his thoughts.

Stopping just short of where Joshua and Sinclair were kneeling beside the badly injured body of John Tate, Jacob once again fought off the violent tugging feeling he had in his throat.

"Bloody hell, John, what happened?" he choked out.

Tate asked Joshua for another drink from his canteen, then with some assistance he propped himself up on his elbows. "They just came out of the woods liked possessed demons, screaming and throwing fire torches over the walls," Tate said before a coughing fit took over. After a moment, he continued to speak, "We fought the heathens off, but we just didn't have the manpower to keep them at bay."

Jacob got on his knees and poured some water into the blackened lips of his valued friend.

Closing his eyes before he attempted to continue, Tate suddenly jerked and once again forced himself up, "Jacob!" he shouted, "You must get the powder out of here. Get the bloody powder out of here before it blows us all to hell!"

Jacob had forgotten that Tate had built the powder magazine underground near the center of the parade grounds, almost directly under the flagpole. The kegs were encased in a solid stone, cocoon-like frame. Jacob had been vehemently against the original idea of placing the powder underground, but he eventually relented and gave Tate his blessing. One of the main reasons Tate had for this was an instance like this. If the magazine had been above ground during an assault like this, the entire fort would have been blasted apart much earlier.

Heeding his warning, Jacob immediately ordered the men to form up a line to get the powder outside the fort's wall. The risk of spoiling the powder far outweighed the possibility of being blown up inside the still burning fort.

At the same time, he sent a small detachment to attempt to put out what fires they could. They rushed over to the well and began drawing water to put on the more out of control flames. The air thickened with additional smoke as the water hit the flames.

Jacob adjusted the neck cloth he had wrapped around his wrist and pulled it as tightly as he could. He managed to brace his pained joint enough to give him some use of his hand.

While the men were busy fighting the fires, Jacob ran and smashed the lock off the sturdy, re-enforced oak door of the underground pit. He pulled the door aside and immediately tossed the first of the kegs to the waiting line of men. Ignoring the shooting pain that hit his wrist as soon as the weight of the keg hit his arms, Jacob pushed through the discomfort.

No one spoke as they systematically passed on the kegs and readied themselves for the next one.

Thankfully, the men's quick action got the thirty or so full wooden kegs out of the fort and stacked thirty paces away by the earthen works. Several of the men worked on a temporary structure to house the powder and keep it relatively safe from the elements and any wind-blown ashes.

Jacob returned to check on Mr. Tate, who by this time was sitting up comfortably and talking with Joshua.

"God bless you, John," Jacob said as he knelt once more by his friend. "We would have been killed if you hadn't reminded us about the powder."

Tate just nodded.

"How many did they kill?" Jacob asked bluntly, trying to get as much information as he could before Tate tired out.

"We did our best. My men defended the best they could, but there were too many of them to hold back. Your Maggie fought like a fiend, as did the few settlers that were left behind."

Doing his best not to appear that he only cared about his Maggie, Jacob waited for Tate to continue instead of overwhelming him with questions. "The French commander did give us a chance to surrender, but I feared their Delaware allies had no desire to follow any terms that we might have agreed to. Once the main walls were breeched, they just let the damn savages do what they wanted to our women and the few survivors."

"How did you happen to survive?" Private Sinclair interrupted.

"It certainly wasn't my intention to survive while my men were dying," Tate said in a tone that showed he was insulted by the question. "I was knocked down by the collapse of the western bastion and buried. I suspect they were unaware I was here. I managed to get out from under all of this and could only watch as they departed and dragged off the last of the captives. When your men entered the fort, the few Delaware who stayed behind to pillage through the remains of the dead ran away and left me here."

Jacob did his best to lighten the tension and said, "Private, please get the men to search through the debris for any other possible survivors. We will have to stay the night here, so ask them to remove any bodies they come across."

Joshua went to assist Sinclair, leaving Jacob alone to continue with Tate. By this time, some of the men had already begun the solemn task of carrying the dead bodies out of the fort and placing them near the recently moved powder.

"I'm thankful you are still alive, John, no matter how it happened," Jacob said. "I must ask you, though, if you know what might have happened to Maggie."

Tate straightened himself up, clearly struggling to get comfortable again; his left leg had been shattered by the collapsed wall. As he waited for Tate to answer, Jacob checked his arms and other leg for any obvious injuries. Finding nothing, he assumed that it might be his ribs as well or some other internal injury that added to his pain. Sadly there was little he could do to ease his pain except to give him more water and keep him upright.

"The last time I saw her," Tate spoke finally, "she was with the other women and their children, bravely fighting off the advances from the Delaware warriors. If she's still here, she would be over by what is left of the officers' quarters. If she is not there, then you must assume she is now a prized captive of the savages."

Not waiting to excuse himself, Jacob called over one of the men to watch Tate and ran to what remained of his quarters. It was still burning, but he cared little for that. He kicked hot embers aside and used his bare hand to toss the many collapsed wooden planks into the parade grounds.

Noticing James still standing alone where he had left him, Jacob called over to him, "James, lend me a hand; your mother was last seen here."

They found no evidence that anyone had been trapped under the debris. Jacob had James help him lift the heavy front door, which had fallen off its hinges.

Despite their feverish attempts, they found nothing. Not even a lone shoe or a discarded piece of clothing…nothing.

Jacob fell to his knees, surrounded by what was left of his beloved second home. Unable to fight off his tears, he put his head in his hands and cried. James put his small arms around him and did the same.

Why had he left her behind again? She had pleaded to go with him, but he felt she would be far safer behind the secured, heavy wooden walls of the fort.

Tired, sickened by the sight of all of this and blinded by thoughts of revenge, Jacob got up. He cleared his face of his tears, found a musket and went out to the powder kegs. James stayed silently by his side, afraid to ask what he was planning.

Jacob pulled out a full keg and smashed the butt of his musket against its lid, shattering wood in every direction. He dipped his powder horn into the keg and forced as much black powder into it as he could. He found a spare horn and filled it as well.

Afraid what his father was about to do, James blurted out, "What are we doing, Father? Can I help?"

Jacob was too angry to speak and just handed James a small sack. He pointed to him to fill it up with powder while he made sure he had both horns full.

By this time, most of the men were drained, both emotionally and physically. Joshua had noticed that Jacob was heading into the woods.

"Sir, what do you need from us?" Joshua called out, just before Jacob disappeared into the darkness.

Jacob stopped, not bothering to turn around, and with James in hand, yelled back, "I'm going after her, lad."

Jacob finally turned to see that most of the men were standing by Joshua, awaiting their orders. "Has anyone spoken with the Delaware yet?" Jacob asked.

"None of us are that fluent with their language," Joshua answered. "I could try again but their tongue is slightly different from the Huron."

Jacob just stood and looked towards the sad remains of the fort.

"I can speak with him." James spoke softly. "He is called Black Heart, and I have spent some time with his three boys."

"Bloody hell, boy," Jacob said as he put an arm around his son, "I forgot that you might be able to speak Delaware. Bring the savage to us and James will get him to talk."

The Delaware warrior was being pulled by a rope that the men had secured around his neck. His hands were tied behind his back, making it particularly difficult for him to maintain his balance.

Jacob could see that James was nervous. He stepped back when the warrior was brought in front of him.

"Don't be scared, boy; he can't hurt you now," Jacob reassured James and took the rope that secured the warrior's neck. He jerked the rope and forced the warrior to his knees so that he was face-to-face with James.

"Now, ask him what they did with the captives and where they were planning to take them," Jacob prompted James.

James quickly exchanged a brief conversation with the warrior and translated for his father, "He said he doesn't know because they left while he remained to clear the fort."

Jacob pulled hard on the rope and forced the warrior's face into his own, screaming, "Tell him we will kill him right now and cut his body into little pieces. His parts will be thrown in every direction to be feasted on by the wildcats."

James paused momentarily and then relayed the message.

Again Jacob let them talk.

"He said he still doesn't know and cares very little about what you will do with him," James translated.

"We should just kill the bugger now and save our breath," one of the men shouted from the crowd.

This suggestion was met with a chorus of shouts and claps, and the Delaware finally showed some fear.

Jacob decided to offer him one last chance to tell him where the French had taken the captives, and James dutifully asked the warrior again.

James was clearly as shaken by the yells of the men as the warrior was.

This time, the Delaware's answer was much longer and he spoke to James for almost two uninterrupted minutes. Jacob's patience wore thin and he demanded James to tell him what the warrior was saying.

"He said they most likely will take the captives north while the French and a few of his brothers continue on towards the English forts west of the Susquehanna. He honestly doesn't know, but he mentioned that he thinks they might be heading to the fort near the great falls. That might just depend on the weather and Mother Earth's plan."

Jacob appeared to be somewhat satisfied with the Delaware's story and handed the rope off to one of the men.

"What should we do with him, sir?" the man asked innocently.

"Do what you want with him; he is no good to me now," Jacob said as he pulled James behind him and headed back to the ruins of the fort.

"Just remember what he did to all these innocent settlers and our friends." Jacob shouted back as he continued to the fort.

Jacob prevented James from looking back at what the men might do to the warrior, "No need for you to see this boy, keep your eyes forward."

"He is a good man and he should be treated with honor." James shot back, trying to jerk his head around to see what was happening.

Jacob suddenly stopped and looked directly at James, "You speak of honor boy, where is the honor in killing innocent people?"

James said nothing and was obviously shaken by his father's outburst.

Joshua and Sinclair left the men and caught up to Jacob, waiting for their orders.

Before they even reached the fort's entrance, the Delaware let out a horrid screech that even gave Jacob pause. Ignoring the screams and cheers of his men, Jacob continued on to check on Mr. Tate and was happy to see him alert and still sitting upright.

"Greetings, John," Jacob said, doing his best to ignore the madness going on outside, "you are looking a bit better."

"I am much better now that some of the men gave me some rum they found near the officers' quarters. What are all the men screaming and cheering about?" Tate asked.

Jacob thought to ignore the question as he didn't know how Tate would feel about letting the men impart their own form of justice on the defense-less Delaware warrior, but he respectfully answered, "The men are having a little fun with our Delaware captive."

"I hope they kill the heathen nice and slow," Tate said. "He should endure the pain felt by all of the people that were murdered here."

Jacob said nothing more about the events outside and politely asked Tate about his thoughts on what the Delaware had said. "The savage told us he figured that they would be taking the captives north to the great falls, depending on the weather. What are your thoughts?"

Tate thought about it for a few moments and replied, "Good chance, but I'm not certain they'll make it before the snow flies. They will probably have to over-winter somewhere north of here."

Taking a deep breath and repositioning his back. Tate continued, "I assume your raid went well and they now have no village to return to?"

"I appreciate your thoughts," Jacob said. "We did destroy their town, but at the cost of our fort…and my wife. We should let you get some rest. James, stay with Mr. Tate until I am done with the men."

"One more thing, John," Jacob said as he began to walk away. "Did you see anything of Armstrong or his men after we left for our raid?"

"Not a soul, sir," Tate answered solemnly. "I heard nothing of the raid until now."

Jacob left James with Tate and continued on with Joshua and Sinclair. They stopped by the fallen gates and Jacob said, "I cannot expect the men to follow me into the north-country to find Maggie, especially at this time of year. Most of them have homes and families of their own to tend to."

Almost before he finished his sentence, Joshua said, "You know I will be with you."

Sinclair added, "Sir, I have no family and the small plot of land I have can wait awhile longer."

"I will only ask for volunteers and leave it at that," Jacob said and walked into the open field where the men were finishing up with their Delaware captive. Not wanting to see what they had done, Jacob called them to order and told them to stand at attention while he spoke.

"Gentlemen, most of you heard from the Delaware that he feels the captives have been taken north. That is where I will be heading. I am asking for volunteers to go along, we all have nothing left to keep us here and we can't be expected to remain here over the winter. I am simply asking as a husband, a friend and a fellow settler. No man will be thought of any differently, but if your obligations permit you to volunteer, please tell Joshua and Sinclair of your intentions. You will all be expected to return in the spring to rebuild and continue on with our orders. For those who can come, we will be leaving before the sun rises tomorrow."

Joshua left Sinclair to wait for the men's thoughts to speak in private with Jacob "Respectfully sir, but are you not asking the men to desert?"

Jacob replied to Joshua's direct question. "Not at all, I hold some authority and can justify my actions to any military court in this land. I simply appealed to them, not as their captain, but as a friend and husband."

"I fear some of them might consider it desertion," Joshua replied.

Jacob looked towards the men speaking amongst themselves and offered, "We have nothing left here that could be remotely considered a military operation. My responsibility is to fight the French and their allies and that is what I am proposing."

Jacob understood what Joshua was implying. The men knew this was about Maggie and no matter how he justified it in his head, it was only about her.

Joshua simply nodded and returned to the men.

Torn about what he should do and how this might look, Jacob had just made it to Tate's side when Joshua came running in to tell him what the men decided.

"To a man, they all said they would help!" he said excitedly. "A few needed to check on their homes, but will catch up as soon as possible. None of the men even hesitated, sir. They want to punish the Delaware for what they have done to this place."

Jacob did not know what to say.

Tate spoke up, "If you give me a couple of pieces of splints and tie my leg up, I'll be with you as well, captain."

Jacob appreciated his offer but said, "No disrespect, John, but I'm going to have a couple of the men get you to a safe bed where you can rest for a few months. One of the boys leaving for home can take you and get you healed up."

Jacob turned to Joshua and said, "Lad, please get the men to organize some pickets and secure the walls. We certainly don't want any more surprises tonight."

Jacob was still overwhelmed by his men's response to his call for volunteers. If it had just been for himself, Jacob would have been content to journey on alone or with Joshua as before, but James needed his mother and Jacob would do anything to make that happen.

Ordinarily, Jacob would not put his son in the danger he would be in by heading north, but this was no ordinary situation. He had left his wife behind to keep her safe, and the results had been disastrous.

He watched the men go about their duties and spoke his thoughts aloud to Sinclair and Tate, "We need to beat them overland to the Allegheny River. If at all possible, we must cut them off before they reach the big lake that will take them north to the falls."

Jacob was facing the collapsed northern wall of the fort and looked up into the star-filled night sky. He remained silent for a few minutes and said to no one in particular, "I only pray the weather holds for us so we can navigate the mountain gaps before the first of the heavy snows hit."

James had made his way beside his father and slowly reached out for his hand. Jacob felt him and grasped onto it, staring out into the black, cold wilderness he said, "I promise you boy that I will travel to the end of this land to find her and will die doing so if I have to."

A lone tear trickled down Jacob's cheek as he hugged James and said once more, "I promise you."

Timeline of
Important Events in
Forest Sentinels

1755 July 9   The Battle of Monongahela begins as the two forces collide in a small valley. Braddock's army is routed by a smaller French force a short distance from the shores of the Monongahela River. Braddock is wounded and leaves Washington in charge of the retreat.

1755 July 13   Braddock dies, ironically only a short distance from Fort Necessity. He is buried on the trail.

1755 July 17   The shattered remains of the army arrive at Fort Cumberland.

1755 Sept.–Dec.   A series of forts and blockhouses are constructed to protect the undefended settlers in the Pennsylvania territory.

1756 May 17   Britain and France formally declare war.

1756 August 30   Colonel John Armstrong and his militia depart Fort Shirley for Kittanning.

1756 September 3   Armstrong's main force meets at Fort Stevens to organize and move on towards Kittanning.

1756 September 7   The main force arrives outside Kittanning.

1756 September 8   Armstrong's raid begins at dawn.

1756 September 12   Most of the main force arrives back to Fort Lyttleton, bypassing Fort Stevens.

1756 October 5   Armstrong is presented a silver medal from the Pennsylvania Assembly. He is now known as the 'Hero of Kittanning'.

Author's **Historical Note**

The 'Forest Sentinels' covers a very tumultuous period in our history. After Braddock's disastrous campaign against Fort Duquesne in 1755, the defeated British army retreated back towards the much safer confines of Philadelphia and Maryland. In doing so, they completely abandoned the Pennsylvania frontier and left hundreds of honest, hardworking settlers unprotected and vulnerable to the French-backed Delaware raiding parties.

Left with little means to protect themselves, the settlers formed militia units and ranging companies to patrol the vast wilderness. The Pennsylvania Provincial Government did attempt to deter the raids by providing funds to build a series of fortifications, but that did little to thwart the vicious attacks by the Delaware.

'Forest Sentinels' tells the story of the courageous men and women who formed informal militia units, ranging companies and civilian armies to fight off the raiding parties bent on removing them from the frontier. Jacob's encounter with Captain Jacobs, nicknamed by the English military, gave him firsthand experience of the Delaware leader's hatred of 'white' settlers.

In the story, I used the more modern-day term Kittanning to describe the village, although the historically proper name used at the time was Ki' tan' in or "Great River". It was one of the main Delaware villages in the

Pennsylvania territory of the 1750s. Although there was a population of Shawnee people who resided at the site as well, it was traditionally known as a Delaware site. After Armstrong burned it to the ground, it appears the Delaware never rebuilt or inhabited the land again.

Armstrong was not a military man, nor were his officers, yet he greatly benefited from his actions at Kittanning. Even though he did successfully destroy the large Delaware village, it seems apparent that he exaggerated the number of villagers dead or captured and the relative success of the overall mission.

He was called a hero, but his tactics and implementation of his plan was lacking. The murder of Captain Jacobs and his family was one element that 'won' him such a misguided title. The raid had little or no influence on the war's ultimate outcome, and sadly it did little to stop further raids on settlers' homes.

I think Armstrong greatly benefited from timing more than anything else. The settlers hungered for some form of victory over the Delaware, and any small victory would have been better than what the British had given them over the past two years.

As for the forts, both those financed by the Provincial Quaker Government and by private citizens, they did initially provide some safe-havens for the settlers and a more military front for the militia. In the end, the raids continued and the raiders simply bypassed the forts. Much of the frontier remained undefended despite the efforts of men like Jacob and Israel.

Jacob appeared to have seen right through Armstrong's leadership quali-ties, seeing the man for the poorly organized and inexperienced military mind he was. Like many men of that time, money and political gains were at the forefront. Jacob had no time for such foolishness, and only wanted to protect the settler families that needed it.

Fort Stevens was a fictional fort, but there were many private fortifica-tions built throughout the frontier. Each might have consisted of a block-house, a fence around a clump of homes or something on a larger scale. Most of the forts financed by the government were well east of where Jacob positioned his, but it wasn't out of the realm of possibility for some brave souls to build such fortifications deep in French-held territory.

One only has to look at the garrison numbers at either a French or British fort during that time, especially over the long winter months, to see that Fort Stevens would have remained safe from the French. Most forts only had enough men to patrol a small radius. Harsh winters also weakened remote outposts and the men left behind to guard them. Food supplies would have been at a minimum, and most time would have been spent cutting wood or being on picket duty. The French ultimately had to pull back their troops towards Quebec because their lack of men and the remoteness of their wilderness forts became too difficult to maintain a healthy garrison.

In 'Forest Sentinels', Maggie once again showed her strength and deter-mination in her fight to stay alive, she truly represents the lesser publicized female influence in early America. If not for the women left behind to defend the homesteads while their husbands and sons were off fighting, the frontier would have been void of any families.

The real threat of being killed or taken captive was part of their daily life, and their stories deserve to be expanded upon and appreciated further. Maggie is my little contribution to that cause. It made sense to me that frontier women needed to be able to handle a musket and trap lines or face starvation while their husbands were away. I think it is one of the 'common sense' issues that seem to be lacking when it comes to historians and writers of this period.

The year 1756 was certainly a pivotal year in the French and Indian War. Frontier defenses rested on brave settlers who managed to hold off the French and their allies while the battered and bruised British army reorganized their strategy for defending America.

Please look for additional novels in Jacob and Maggie's story as they fight to reunite and find what they always wanted…a place to call home.

Acknowledgments

I must continue to express my gratitude to all the living historians, artisans, authors, artists and re-enactors who share my passion and love for this mostly forgotten time period.

Robert Griffing, David Wright, Doug Hall, Kyle Carroll, the amazing cover artist Todd Price, plus several other great artists have continued to inspire me with their work and dedication. I have had the pleasure meeting many of them, and their kindness and friendship made me even more appreciative of their hard work and commitment to keep this time period alive.

Once again, thanks to the great people at Lord Nelson's Gallery in Gettysburg, PA for supporting my books. Mr. George Lower, who took a chance and carried my first novel, is now a friend and part of my family. Madison and Kennedy always look forward to his hugs and smiles whenever they walk into the gallery. To be a part of History Meets the Arts every June is a highlight both personally and professionally. Thanks to George, Philippe and Marsha who welcomed me and my family into theirs!

Again, I must thank Frank and Lally House for extending an invitation to the CLA Show in Lexington, KY. The kindness of the folks at Lord Nelson's gave me an opportunity to sign books and meet many great people who encouraged me and offered kind words about my writing. Being part of Lord Nelson's booth at the show also afforded us more time to spend with George, Marsha and her husband Bob.

To my friends Roger and Stacy Moore, Jeremy Moore, artist Andrew Knez, Jr., Tim L. Jarvis and many more people who took time to talk with me over a number of summer events and inspired me to continue on with my journey…Thanks!

Once more, I want to clarify that any depictions of First Nations People in my stories are strictly fictional. It was simply a snapshot in time. They truly were the empire that lost the most and have been unfairly treated, both then and today. I am proud of my First Nation's heritage and my grandfather Thomas Power.

Jacob and Maggie will continue to endure their own journey in the wilds of the frontier as their story continues. A special thanks to all the readers who have taken the time to phone, send emails or support me at the number of book signings I do throughout the year; your feedback and kind words have provided me with the fuel to keep writing and honestly enjoying what I do.

Cheers and good tidings to all!

References and
Recommendations

I would be remiss if I forgot to direct interested readers to further materials on the French and Indian War. These are a few of my favorite books and other great resources to consider.

Books:

- Bud Hannings, *The French and Indian War-A Complete Chronology*. McFarland & Company Inc., 2011. Great reference for the war, and is particularly interesting for those who need a more in depth source.

- Fred Anderson. *Crucible of War*. New York. Vintage Books, 2001. The best and most extensive account of the war. Simply a must read for anyone interested in this time period.

- Michael L. Pitzer, *Native Reenacting Made Easy*, Axehead Publishing, 2009. Another great source book for information about the Eastern Woodland Warrior.

- *The Art of Robert Griffing*, by George Irwin. New York. East/West Visions. 2000. The follow up, *The Narrative Art of Robert Griffing*, by Tim Todish. Gibsonia, Pennsylvania. Paramount Press Inc. 2007. Once again for their amazing artwork and for putting faces and emotions to a time long forgotten.

- Matt Wulff, *Ranger-North American Frontier Soldier*, Heritage Books. Matt has a series of books on ranging companies of the early frontier. They are well written and an invaluable source for anyone wanting to learn more about the men who guarded the wilderness.

Other **Sources:**

- *Muzzleloader* magazine, by Historical Enterprises. Editor in Chief, Jason Gatliff. An amazing bi-monthly publication that keeps this period alive.

- Lord Nelson's Gallery, est. 1990 in Gettysburg, PA. A great place to view and purchase artwork depicting this war. As well as, powder horns, knives, quillwork, etc.

- DVDs on the war include the Paladin Communications great series, *Young George Washington, The Complete Saga, The War That Made America*. PBS Home Video, 2005. Narrated and hosted by Graham Greene.

- Douglas "Muggs" Jones has produced a great series of DVDs from the School of the Longhunter Series. Entertaining, informative and well worth purchasing. For more information check www.douglaswjonesjr.com.

- Please also pick up a copy of my good friend Tim L. Jarvis' soon to be released book, *Shadow In The Forest, Woodland Warriors of the Mississippi Valley*. Please look for it at your local book store or at www.warriorstrail.com.

- Look for Author and Historian Brady J. Crytzer's newest book, *Guyasuta and the Fall of Indian America* (Scheduled for release in April 2013). Also by Mr. Crytzer, *Major Washington's Pittsburgh and the Mission to Fort Le Boeuf* (2011) and *Fort Pitt: A Frontier History* (2012)

Websites:

www.nightowlstudio.net

www.lordnelsons.com

www.kylecarrollart.com

www.paramountpress.com

www.doughallart.com

www.friesenpress.com

www.smoke-fire.com

www.andrewknezjr.com

I am also a proud member of the CLA (www.longrifles.com) and the NMLRA (www.nmlra.org).

I also have to mention two gentlemen I have the privilege of calling friends and happen to own some of their work, Ken Bueche of Calumet Trade Goods at www.CalumetTradegoods.com and premier woodcarver Bruce Meurer at www.brucewoodpecker.tripod.com

Historical **Sites and Events:**

History Meets the Arts, Gettysburg, PA in June. Great artwork, great atmosphere and great people. Please check www.lordnelsons.com for details.

It's a good idea to plan a visit to historic sites when re-enactments are scheduled. Try Fort Fredrick, MD in late April, Fort Niagara in July and Fort Necessity anytime in the summer for their great atmosphere and historical accuracy. Fort Ligonier is another special place, and the staff is second to none!

The town of Kittanning in Pennsylvania is a nice place to visit on your way to Pittsburgh. Although the site of the Delaware village is marked only by a plaque, it is still nice to visualize what it might have looked like in the 18th century.

In Canada, make sure you visit the Fortress at Louisbourg and Quebec City. Visiting either place is like going back in time.

Visit a First Nations event in your area. It is one of the best cultural events to attend, and they deserve our support. If you visit a historical site during a re-enactment, you will see firsthand how critical the natives were to both sides and how much they truly lost during and after the French and Indian War.

Another reason to attend an event is Suzanne Larner. Suzanne does an amazing first person characterization of the true story of 'Mad Anne Bailey'. Captivating, informative and touching, it is a presentation that is a must see and gives you a real picture of the struggles a frontier family faced in the 18th century. Much like what Maggie Murray and her family experienced in all three novels. Please check Suzanne's blog at http://madannebailey. blogspot.com/ for schedule of events and more information.

A few more great places to visit that my family and I try to make every year include Fort Frederick's 18th Century Market Fair in Maryland. For details and dates, check www.friendsoffortfrederick.com. Old Fort Niagara's F&I War Reenacting Weekend in early July is an amazing event (www.oldfortniagara.com). Fort Pitt Museum in Pittsburgh is a great place to learn about the early years of The French and Indian War.

This is only a snapshot of what is available to the reader interested in expanding his or her knowledge of this great period. Please support our historical sites by purchasing a membership or planning a visit. Make your own list and remember to read, visit, watch, and enjoy. You will be amazed at what you will learn and what they didn't teach you in school.

If you see me at an event doing a book signing or just enjoying the sites, please take a moment to introduce yourself and say hello.

Author | **S. Thomas Bailey**

About the Author

S. Thomas Bailey is a multi-award-winning author and independent researcher of early North American life. He is a raw historian at heart and a writer by choice.

Bailey's own sense of history is enriched by a Mi'kmaq grandfather and a family tree that can be traced back to the young surveyor James Cook, who began his career mapping out the St. Lawrence River system during the French and Indian War.

He resides in a quiet hamlet north of Toronto, Ontario with his wonderfully supportive wife and two amazing children. His family spends each spring and summer visiting French and Indian War sites, attending re-enactments and living history events, and spreading the word about this wonderful period in North American history.

Bailey looks forward to continuing Jacob and Maggie's story. Watch for additional novels in *The Gauntlet Runner* Series, coming soon.

Follow, contact or connect with S. Thomas Bailey for updates and events:
www.thegauntletrunner1754.com
thegauntletrunner1754@yahoo.com
or 'like' on www.Facebook/TheGauntletRunner

CPSIA information can be obtained at www.ICGtesting.com
Printed in the USA
LVOW07s2119020714

392722LV00002B/307/P